THE
PRANK

THE
PRANK

L.V. MATTHEWS

WELBECK

Published in 2021 by Welbeck Fiction Limited,
part of Welbeck Publishing Group
20 Mortimer Street London W1T 3JW

Cover design by Black Sheep
Cover photograph © Michelle Livingston / Arcangel Images

Copyright © L.V. Matthews, 2021

A CIP catalogue record for this book is available from the
British Library

Paperback ISBN: 978-1-78739-522-0
E-book ISBN: 978-1-787-39-523-7

Printed and bound by CPI Group (UK) Ltd., Croydon, CR0 4YY

10 9 8 7 6 5 4 3 2 1

To my family, who always believed I could do it.

PROLOGUE

In the sixteenth century, the word prank referred to a 'wicked deed', though its modern definition is much lighter: a practical joke or an act of mischief.

We watch pranks on TV and online and we laugh at these innocent people being tricked. We enjoy their embarrassment and confusion and then we switch off and forget about them. We think of these pranks as harmless because that's how they've been sold to us, and most of them are, but human nature is progressive and we are always going to want to push the boundaries. Over the years, crueller set-ups are written and the line between what we call comedy and what we might call out as vicious has become blurry. We see people getting hurt: their physical discomfort is plain on the outside and perhaps on the inside it burns just as brightly. Perhaps the word prank has never strayed too far from its original roots as something cruel and humiliating.

Be kind, we all remind each other, but who is capable of being kind all of the time? There's a darker side to being a human and if we can't create ways to satisfy this part of ourselves, we will let others do it for us. But how far do we go in upsetting one person so that another is entertained? And who decides what is fair when it comes to comedy? Do we keep pushing further and further until a prank misses its mark entirely?

What if a prank that skirted dangerously close to merciless was played on you? How far would you have to be pushed to take revenge for the prank that had been called "harmless"?

ONE

There was a study that reported a 4 per cent tip increase when a waitress touches a male customer, so now Wendy touches all of hers – a finger on an arm, a hand to a shoulder.

'And if that touch is going to make a difference anywhere, it's here, right?' she says as she sails past me with oysters on a silver dish of ice.

She's right. The Cello restaurant is situated in Bloomsbury and rivals Claridge's, Le Gavroche, The Ledbury, and it attracts the wealthy. Tonight the dining room is fully booked and there's a background hum of conversation, the shrill of cutlery on porcelain. We have some of our regulars in tonight: the colonel who plays solitaire in the back corner, the media couple who are married but not to each other and the Turkish poet with an elegant scroll of a birthmark on his neck. The new customers marvel at the restaurant's decor; an elderly woman wants to know where we got the huge red china fox who glowers out over the bar at all the hunting portraits that gallop across the walls. I have a serious businessman on a corner table who spills brandy over a document and, as I dry it under the service-desk hot lights, we all bend our heads to read it and see at the bottom of the page that there's a sum of over one billion dollars.

'Holy cow!' Wendy says. 'Forget touching, you've got to *straddle* that guy!'

But she knows I won't, because I don't touch people. I read them instead: all the raised eyebrows, all the different smiles a face can own and nonchalant shrugs between spouses and lovers, friends and families. I see them laugh, see them argue and I see them cry – though, in those moments, I turn away because I don't like witnessing something breaking apart when I can't catch the pieces.

This is a good night for me for clients. Later, not that they'll ever know it, I'll sit at my kitchen table and draw them. I'll put them in my portfolio along with all the others, too many to count now because I've been at the restaurant for years, and wonder about them for a few days. It's easy to think about someone else's exciting or glamorous life when my life is far from either. I am the blank canvas in my own portfolio.

David sidles up to me. He's the restaurant manager, French, like the restaurant cuisine, mid-thirties with a hawkish nose. Tonight he's impeccably dressed in a pale blue suit and tan brogues. I draw him regularly, enjoy the angles of his body and the cut of his jaw.

'The tree,' he says. 'Does it lean?'

David worries about our tree constantly. It's a ten-foot-tall Norwegian pine covered in thousands of lights and silver bells and hand-blown glass baubles, and if it came down it would most likely set fire to the entire dining room.

It's Friday 11th December and there are trees up through-out the city. Shopping centres have had their Christmas displays up for months, the supermarkets have been stocked with food for longer and the roads are all lit with Christmas cheer. There's a house down my street with a tree in the window that reminds me of the ones we had when I was little. Tall with sprawling spindly branches decorated with multicoloured lights and school craft angels. It's a real family tree and I like to look at it as I go by because I owe it to the ghosts of Christmas past.

'I think it's OK,' I say.

He twists his mouth. He's worried about a tiny dog in one of the women's handbags which is looking up mischievously at the tree.

'That dog won't pull it down, David,' I note.

'You think not?' he says. 'Our family had a cat that brought down the tallest tree I had ever seen.'

'Did you own a leopard?' I ask.

He smiles and then looks to the door. 'Ah, table twelve has come in,' he says. 'Can you tell Wendy? Twelve is hers tonight.'

I look over and see a couple enter the dining room. She looks to be in her mid-forties, sun-kissed by winter sun, with bronzed, high cheekbones and wearing a copper fur hat over champagne-blonde hair. He is perhaps a decade older and is tall and broad, with thick, dark, clipped hair, wearing a tailored overcoat. He has a dimple in his cheek as he smiles out at the room. The staff all smile back at him and the diners who notice them avert their eyes but are smiling too. I wonder what is it about some people that makes them so magnetic that they can bewitch an entire restaurant of people. They must be famous – I never recognise anyone who comes in.

'Who are they?' I ask.

But David has crossed the restaurant to greet them. I walk to the kitchen because that will be where I find Wendy, with her rear end perched on the polished steel and twirling a finger around her hair as she talks to the commis chef, who is married with two kids. As soon as I open the doors, the noise of the kitchen hits my ears, but in the middle of the commotion there is Wendy, who skits from the worktop but then grins when she sees it's me.

'All right, babe?' she says.

'Table twelve is in,' I reply.

'Oh my God! Jim and Lucinda!' she exclaims. 'Yes? Is it them?'

'Who are they?' I ask.

But she's not listening; she's checking her hair in the small mirror by the wall and then she's off out of the kitchen. I follow and watch with her as David leads the couple to our golden table: the front and centre of the dining room, where they can be seen by as many people in the restaurant as possible.

'Are they famous?' I ask.

David takes their coats and they sit at the same time – Lucinda in a silky olive-green dress, throat and hands bejewelled with diamonds, and Jim in a black jacket, smart grey shirt and navy jeans.

Wendy tuts. 'Lucinda Kit used to be a model but she's more famous now because she married Jim Valente.'

Jim Valente. The name electrocutes my body, stomach – punches me and then ricochets off me.

'Jim – Jim . . . ?' I whisper. I look above my head, as if the name is some winged creature. 'What did you say?' I ask.

'Jim Valente,' she says. 'If you're a screenwriter or an actor, then he's the person to know. Oh wow, he's hot for an old guy. You think he's hot?'

My mouth is dry and I stumble. 'I . . . I don't know.'

Wendy looks at me. 'You OK?'

'I'm fine,' I say.

But I'm not fine. I recognise that name somehow, feel *worried* by that name, but I don't know why.

The night is busy and I find no time to quiz Wendy further on Lucinda Kit and Jim Valente or get to my phone to look them up. Instead I watch them. He sits straight-backed, his movements deft like brushstrokes as he smooths his hair, picks up his wine glass. Lucinda's movements are the opposite: considered and almost sensual. Her stockinged legs slip this way and that like butter, crossing and uncrossing under the table. They rarely break eye contact with one another and smile with all their perfect white teeth.

'If you've got it, flaunt it,' Wendy says as we pass each other across the dining room.

They eat red mullet with cuttlefish ink sauce, beef with shallot and tarragon, cheeses for dessert, and throughout service, Wendy wears a face reserved especially for the rich, all eyelashes and dimples. Pavel the sommelier, who never smiles, looks bashful whenever he's called to their table, and even no-nonsense David flicks his eyes over at them more than he would with other diners. The people on other tables sneak glances across the room and throw out smiles in the hope of having them returned, and all the while Jim and Lucinda play to the gallery.

On the dot of ten-thirty, Jim Valente raises his hand.

'They've probably got some sort of event,' Wendy says as she rings up their bill. 'A party to go to. Drinks on a rooftop terrace. Some amazing actor coming round to their house.'

'How do I know his name?' I ask her, but she whizzes away again.

I watch as she puts the embossed Cello black folder on the corner of the table and Jim takes a tan leather wallet from the inside of his jacket and puts his card on top of it, doesn't even open the folder to check the amount. I go to clear a table which is a few over from theirs so that I can keep looking at him to jog my memory, which fizzes with his name but spits out no answers, and then they stand together, their coats are brought and they sweep out of the restaurant.

The moment the doors have closed behind them, the remaining diners and all the staff erupt into conversation, but I leave to go to the kitchen, walk to the back freezer doors and put my head against the cold metal because I feel sick.

'David, who is Jim Valente?' I say.

It's nearing midnight and everyone except us, the kitchen porter and the cleaners, has gone home. We sit at one of the tables and I polish cutlery and David goes through the rota. I usually like this time alone with him because he never asks me questions about myself and we can be companionably silent, but tonight I'm on edge. I haven't stopped thinking about Jim Valente and I want to go home and find out how I might know his name.

'He is top tier,' David replies.

Top tier are the elite, the exclusive.

'He owns a production company called Cyclops,' he says. 'They make huge series.'

Cyclops. This doesn't jog my memory any further.

'My favourite, *Aircraft*, is one of theirs. You know it, *oui*? It is about the double agent who is a pilot and nobody knows he is carrying information between America and Russia?'

'No,' I say.

He smiles. 'You know *All the Long Days*? About a 1980s rock band on the road?'

'I lived in France for seven years,' I explain. 'I don't think I know those shows.'

He laughs. 'I am French also, Eleanor! A native! But I have seen them. OK, but you know *Pranksters*, *oui*? That is why people are talking tonight in the restaurant—'

David is interrupted by the restaurant phone ringing and we look at each other in surprise because it never rings at this time. He gets up to answer it at the bar and I continue with the silverware, rubbing the cloth up and down the stem of the last spoon so I can see myself reflected back in it: red hair, freckles all over my face and a scar on my forehead from when I fell on the glass of a fish tank when I was two.

'I need to run an errand,' David says, returning to me after a couple of minutes.

I look up at him.

'That was Jim Valente on the phone,' he explains. 'He has left his credit card here and I have found it behind the bar. Pavel must have forgotten to tell me.'

I stand up abruptly and bump the tabletop. The tray of silverware rattles. 'I'll go,' I say.

'You will do this for me?'

'Yes,' I reply quickly. 'I mean, if you want me to? You probably need to finish things and I'm done here.'

'That would be most kind, *merci*,' he says.

He holds out a thick cream envelope with 'The Cello' embossed on the front and I step to meet him and take it, tilt my head to read 'Mr J. Valente' written delicately across it.

'Get your things and I will flag a taxi for you,' he says.

I nod. 'Where is it that I'm going?'

'Wilton Crescent, Belgravia,' he says. 'The door number is on the back of the envelope, you see?'

I turn the letter and nod. 'OK.'

'Put it through the letter box, d'accord? And not a word to Wendy about where they live,' he says. 'That girl has pound signs in her eyes. She would camp out there with a banner, would she not? She would be perfect for it, actually.'

I frown. 'Perfect for what?'

'There has been a press announcement that Jim is looking for a new host for his programme, *Pranksters*,' he explains. 'It is why everyone was talking about it in the restaurant. The programme was their biggest asset, and they are making a new series after taking a year's break. It is silly humour. It is dark humour. Addictive, horrible, brilliant.'

'Does that mean you like it or you don't?' I ask.

He thinks awhile and then shrugs. 'I am shades of black and white, like everyone,' he says. 'I think that is why the show does so well. It taps into something, *oui*? The inner bad part of you that likes to laugh at another's misfortune.'

In the taxi, I use the first opportunity I've had all night to get out my phone. I open a web browser, enter Jim's name and am immediately flooded with hits. I click on a link to a professional profile.

Jim Anthony Valente – born 12 June 1962 – is an English-born media CEO. He started his career in the banking industry before becoming a senior editor for Our Times publishing company in 1989. He went on to become CFO at Our Times in 1995, where he held the position for eight years, simultaneously buying three small publishing magazines abroad, and then took the position as CEO. In 2001, he bought up fledgling production company Cyclops, originally RSM Media, where he has been CEO for twenty years and seen profits solidly and continuously rise.

Jim Valente married wife Lucinda Kit, fifteen years his junior, in 2006. Lucinda Kit was previously a cat-walk model, starting her career in native Norway, and is now fashion column writer for the *Sunday Times* magazine and guest editor for *Vogue*. Jim and Lucinda have one son, Benjamin Valente, born 2011, who attends Bradbury's Boarding School.

Jim Valente fronts four charities: an orphanage project in Vietnam, Water Aid in Senegal, the UK Independent Young Screenwriters Association and Save the Bears.

There's nothing here that taps into the anxious feeling I have around his name and yet this innocuous information doesn't soothe me, either. I'm hoping that in seeing him again, I might figure out our connection.

'Here, mate,' says the cab driver.

I look up from the phone's blue screen. 'Thanks, I'll only be a minute.'

Belgravia is one of the richest areas in London. I get out of the taxi and look up at the colossal houses in the crescent – pretty Georgian sandstone, towering up five floors with a basement underneath. Their house has white-framed windows with wooden shutters and a heavy black door on which hangs a huge Christmas wreath in silver and gold with red berries and holly. It's the most extravagant I've ever seen.

I notice the car outside the front door – a racing-green Aston Martin DB5 with the licence plate *5 JV* – and think that it must be Jim's. I remember Dad telling me that the fewer letters there were on a registration, the more costly the plate. I wonder if the 5 means they have five cars. I reach out to lightly touch it and the sleek, shark-like body is so cold that I snatch my hand back.

I walk across black and white chequerboard porch tiles to the door, which is framed with white pillars. Neatly trimmed tall shrubs in pots stand on either side. I pause before posting the envelope to glimpse through a huge window to the right of the door and see straight into a vast kitchen, which stretches from the front to the back of the house. Copper pans hang down above an oak-topped, white-cabinet island. There's a pristine chrome double oven, an elaborate-looking coffee machine and a cake mixer. At the far end of the room is a ten-seat farmhouse-style table with a bowl of fruit on it, all red apples, red grapes and pomegranates, and a vase of seasonal red poinsettias.

I put the envelope through the gold letter box and am turning to walk back to the cab when the door opens. I look back in surprise to see Jim Valente standing there with the envelope in his hand. His grey shirt is unbuttoned to his chest and, at close proximity, I can smell his cologne – sandalwood. He smiles at me before sweeping his gaze over my body, and I feel immediately self-conscious under the intensity of his eyes, which are so, so blue, like cold gemstones.

'What's your name, then?' he says softly.

I don't want to answer him; I want to get away as quickly as possible, but before I can turn around, a small dog shoots out from behind his legs and jumps up, barking excitedly.

'Gertie!' Jim exclaims. She runs to reach me on the chequered porch, but he grabs her collar, which I can't even see through the fluff of her honey-coloured fur. 'Come back in! No – this way, come on!'

He hauls her back inside and I see a tall, stocky woman rushing up behind.

'Sylvie,' he says. 'Take the dog, will you?'

I use the opportunity to leave, but as I turn to go he reaches out to me and holds my arm. I gasp at his grip, an involuntary sharp intake because I don't like people touching me, but if he notices, he doesn't comment. Or let go.

'You haven't told me your name,' he says.

The woman takes the dog while Jim and I stand locked together by his hand on my arm. He smiles at me again and I feel blinded by its radiation.

'Eleanor,' I reply.

'Are you lonely, Eleanor?' he asks. 'Like the song?'

I open and close my mouth, fish-like, unable to respond.

He laughs. 'Won't you let me offer you a drink for the effort, Eleanor? A bourbon?'

No way. All I want to do is shake him off. 'I should go,' I say, and I take a small step backwards so his hand falls from my coat.

He gives me an amused-looking smile. 'Goodbye,' he says. 'Perhaps I'll see you again.'

He shuts the door and I exhale. The fearful feeling I had earlier seems to have tripled, and as I walk back the few metres to the cab, my mind is transporting me back in time. There's a memory of someone saying his name and I was young and scared out of my wits, somewhere unbearably cold.

I don't ever want to see him again.

TWO

I have every other Saturday off work. It's our busiest day at the restaurant and the highest-earning tip day, but I've never wanted to jeopardise my time with my sister Lissy and Uncle Charlie. I get on the train out of London and, with each passing mile, I begin to loosen the threads of last night's bad feeling, which lingered overnight like something soured.

'You're here!' Lissy flings open the door to me. 'Why didn't you call me to pick you up?'

'It's fine, I got the bus,' I say.

It's a few miles from Winchester station to Charlie's tiny village and I like sitting on the bus as the buildings give way to the trees and hedgerows beyond the city. But, more than that, I like turning up at Charlie's front door and surprising my sister.

She's wearing a vermilion jumper over blue jeans and a black three-quarter-sleeve coat. Her hair is a voluminous blonde lion's mane because she hasn't brushed it, but she doesn't need to because she's even more beautiful like this – a wildling in the winter. Lissy is one of those people who moves and talks with speed and thinks like a rocket, bright and sparkling and leaving the rest of us in her stardust. I treat her how I've always treated her, like the little girl who used to take all her bears on holiday in her rucksack, the girl who insisted on wearing pink ballet cardigans for the first six years of her life.

14

Sometimes I want to squeeze her so tight that all her candy-cuteness is expelled into the air and I can catch the sugary snowflakes on my tongue. But my sister is nineteen now, and apparently 'cute is for losers'.

She's at Southampton studying English, but we meet up most weekends – mostly at Uncle Charlie's so he can see us both, but sometimes Lissy comes to London because she loves going to claustrophobic bars and insists I dance with her. She can make me do anything. We go shopping and I buy her nice clothes that I'd never choose to wear myself but which she shines in, and in the evenings we watch Netflix and *The X Factor* and eat pizza.

'You want tea or something stronger?' she says.

I shut the door behind me. 'Stronger? It's eleven in the morning.'

'So which is it?' she asks seriously.

'Tea,' I say, but maybe I should have something stronger. 'Is Charlie here?'

'He's on his pilgrimage to town,' she replies. 'Back any minute.'

Uncle Charlie visits his local town once a week under duress because he loathes social interaction.

'How's uni?' I ask.

Lissy puts the kettle on the hob, dipping her head so as not to bump it on the low ceiling. Charlie's cottage is sixteenth century, beamed and with uneven planked floors. It's littered with papers and books and countless plants in every room.

'It's good,' she says. 'I'm writing sad, lonely poetry.'

'Oh,' I say. 'Sounds . . . great?'

'It is,' she replies. 'It's inspired by Charlie.'

I smile. I can, and have, always relied on Lissy to make me feel better. Safe. Was that how I felt last night? Unsafe because of a name?

'Charlie's making noises about clearing the garage again,' Lissy comments.

I shrug. 'He threatens it every year.'

'But we're selling Pudding Cottage now, aren't we?' Lissy says.

'Hmmm,' I say.

It's bittersweet to be selling Pudding Cottage, Charlie and Dad's old family house in Norfolk. We rent it most of the year and it earns us good money, but Charlie has had enough of the responsibility and wants to free up the cash. I wanted to argue to keep Pudding Cottage, but how could I when I've not been there since I was eleven? Charlie is right to sell it. I wonder if he might feel better if he sells it? Will I?

'So we have to clear out Charlie's garage because all the crap from Pudding Cottage has to go somewhere,' Lissy explains.

'It's not crap,' I counter. 'It's all Dad's stuff.'

'It's Dad's crap,' Lissy says. She gets the milk from the fridge. 'All his writing stuff, his books. He never threw anything out. Zero. And we've never gone through it. And Charlie's garage is *already* full of Dad's crap from London.'

'Dad's "crap", as you call it, was his life.' I feel defensive on his behalf.

'Yeah, all right,' she says. She pours in milk, hands me my tea. 'You're definitely coming back here for Christmas, right?'

I nod. She's asking because for the last few years I've volunteered at a local food bank in London. She thought I was amazing helping all those people but really I was saving myself by being away from the day. But she wouldn't forgive a third Christmas away from her and nor would my uncle. As much as Charlie hates socialising, family is different and Lissy and I are valued on a par with his beloved plants.

'It's thirteen sleeps!' Lissy smiles. 'Got my present yet? You better not be sponsoring me a rhino.'

'It's not a rhino,' I reply.

'Good,' she says with a nod.

'It's a mountain gorilla,' I say.

She looks at me and I smile and then she laughs. She hops up on to the kitchen countertop, swings her legs over it. She starts to tell me about the screenplay she's writing and a new song she's working on and shows me some of her sad poetry. Her changes in conversation are like arrows through the air that I can't catch, but I'm happy to be shot by them. She's my life, my heartbeat.

The front door yawns open and in steps Uncle Charlie, with Polo, his big black Great Dane, in tow.

'All right, girl?' Charlie says to me gruffly.

He shakes off his coat. Whatever the weather, he dresses for his weekly shop in his old mud-stained mackintosh, a scowl and an eccentric hat. Today it's some sort of contraption made of faux fur and black velvet and feathers and it drips with rain.

'Hi, Charlie,' I say, and lean to kiss his cheek. It's rough and smells of earth and it makes me feel safe, this smell. He's always kept Lissy and me safe, even when he's not known the right things to say, or when he's not said anything at all.

Polo makes straight for me, tongue out for a slobbery kiss, and I bat his nose away.

'No thanks, dog brain,' I say, stroking his ears between my fingers.

Charlie looks at me. 'All OK?'

'Yeah,' I reply. 'All OK.'

'OK' isn't really how I feel and we all know it. It's Christmas soon and Christmas is hard for us.

'What's that on your head, Charlie?' Lissy says, looking at Charlie's hat. 'Did something die?'

'Elizabeth, didn't your parents teach you that if you haven't got anything nice to say, not to say anything at all?' Charlie remarks, and he removes his hat and shakes out shaggy grey windswept hair.

'No?' Lissy grins.

'Well, they should have done,' he says.

'I've lived with you since I was six,' she retorts. 'Why didn't you teach me?'

He rolls his eyes. 'Sassy mare.'

She grins and pours a cup of tea without a prompt. He chain-drinks, always from the same cup, which he's had for a decade – a chipped blue one with rings of tea stains on the inside.

He takes it and looks at me. 'Cello OK?'

Both my uncle and Lissy have long since given up asking me when I'm taking the next step in finding myself any sort of career in London. Working at The Cello was supposed to be a stepping stone, but it's become my life. Sometimes I show Lissy the portraits I draw when she comes to visit me and she looks at me with a sad smile on her face. She thinks I can be more than what I am, but I can't be.

'Yeah,' I say. 'It's . . . Charlie, do you know a man called Jim Valente?'

The air is sliced by the sound of Charlie's teacup hitting the floor and shattering into a hundred pieces. Polo jumps and starts barking.

'Shit,' Lissy says and throws a tea towel to the floor to soak up the tea that is bleeding out into the wood.

I grab Polo's collar so he doesn't walk over the shards.

'Charlie!' I exclaim. 'You OK?'

But Charlie is mute, staring at me. There's an emotion in his face that I can't read and I hold the dog's collar out to Lissy.

'Put him in the living room, will you, Liss?' I say.

She obeys me silently and takes Polo out.

'What's the matter?' I ask when she's shut the door. 'Do you know him?'

'I don't want anything to do with that man in my house,' he answers, and now I see that the emotion was pure hot fury.

'How do you know him?' I press. 'How do *I* know him?'

'I *don't* know him,' Charlie says definitely. 'But he . . . Don't you go digging all that up, Eleanor, you hear me? It's all buried with your dad now.'

I blink. 'Dad? What do you mean, Charlie? What's Jim Valente got to do with Dad?'

But Charlie isn't talking to me any more, rather he's muttering to himself and then he opens the kitchen back door and slams it shut behind him, leaving me tight-chested with confusion. Yesterday, I had never heard of Jim Valente and now my uncle says his name alongside Dad's. My head sings with white noise and I lean to steady myself on the kitchen counter.

'He loved that cup!' Lissy says, walking back from the living room. She bends down to clear up the pieces of china on the floor. 'I'll buy him a new one for Christmas. But, hey look, I *think* you were kidding, but I don't want a mountain gorilla, El,' she adds. 'OK?'

But I'm not listening because I've looked out of the window to see Charlie now inside his car, banging the door shut and starting the engine. Alarmed, I open the back door and jog over to him but he's already driving towards the road.

'Charlie!' I shout. 'Where are you going?'

He winds down his window and yells out, 'I'll be back late, OK? Don't wait up!'

It's late – one in the morning – and Uncle Charlie still isn't home. I lie in bed and listen to the rain clicking on the pane above me. Charlie's reaction to Jim Valente and having mentioned Dad has thrown me into a state of internal panic. I've sent him several messages and called him and I know he's read them but all he's sent back is a message saying he's gone to a friend's and that everything is OK.

I don't feel OK. For the last few hours, I've been on my phone writing my dad's name and Jim Valente into Google and trying to work out how they could be connected. I wondered if perhaps Jim commissioned one of my dad's children's books for a TV production, and typed in all of his eight titles, but the search engine drew a blank at connecting them. I thought they could have known the same people – agents, publishers – but all the names I could remember led nowhere.

I blink into the darkness of the room.

The bed is made up with mismatching bedlinen, the cream walls are peeling and the curtains are tatty because Charlie doesn't repaint or wash things like curtains. The only things loved in this room are the plants and the pictures from years ago – sun-faded moments of a carefree life. There is a picture of us all at Bude beach in Cornwall with nets in our hands beside a rock pool, looking for crabs. Lissy is two and has got her fingers tangled in the netting and is howling. I'm seven and unashamedly gawky, squinting at the camera. Dad has a straw hat on his head, bending down to tend Lissy's fingers. Mum is in the background, looking away. She always looked away from us. I think Charlie put this photo up here for me so I'd feel like this would always be my room but, in truth, it only serves as a painful reminder that Mum and Dad are both gone.

I hear a noise below the floorboards and, after a minute, footsteps ascend the stairs. Charlie is back and I'm suddenly caught between wanting to confront him right now because I'm angry that he left us without explanation and wanting to stay here in my bed because whatever explanation for his disappearance can't be good, can it? I hear him run the water in the bathroom, do his teeth and then he closes his bedroom door.

Five minutes pass where I'm paralysed by my own indecision before I make up my mind and slide my legs out from under the duvet, throw on my dressing gown and pad down the corridor past Lissy's room and then to Charlie's. Over the sound of the rain outside, I can hear canned laughter and see blue light flicker at the bottom of his door and I feel angry that he's come home after walking out on me to watch comedy TV.

My knuckles are inches from the wood to knock when my ears register another sound from within the room, muffled but unmistakable sobbing, which sends shock bolting through my body. Charlie is never angry and he *never* cries. I've only ever once seen him cry – at my dad's funeral. The memory of that day sears in front of my eyes, and I drop my hand to my side because I suddenly remember where I've heard that name before, Jim Valente.

The church smelt of damp clay and was cold, so cold that it seemed to seep from the stone up with graveyard fingers. I had only a thin cardigan over a cotton dress and my hands had turned blue. I remember thinking that it was like someone had traced the veins with felt-tip pen. Throughout the service, Lissy fidgeted on one side of me, pulling at her hair and spinning it around in her fingers, and Charlie sat on the other side, eyes staring straight ahead and still like stone. Helen, an aged great-aunt on Mum's side, sat next to him in a woollen black dress that was too big for her and she gnawed at the inside of her cheeks like a hamster. It made a thick ticking sound, like she was sucking sweets, and I wanted to tell her to stop but I couldn't. I couldn't find words any more, for anything or anyone.

I recall that the people behind me spoke the congregational parts after the vicar and their breath misted ghost-like past my face. The organist played with her shoulders slumped and wearing a black cape so that she looked a bit like a bat. I remember only the sound of those hymns, like rolling tidal waves through the church, but not the words. I didn't sing. I hardly breathed. Dad's literary agent gave the eulogy. I didn't understand most of the words but thought Dad would have liked it because he enjoyed long words, but everything about that hour was eerie and wrong. It all felt too grey and ordinary for Dad. He would have wanted colour at his funeral; he would have wanted a fanfare and hats. But that wouldn't have been appropriate for what had happened to him, so grey was the colour because grey was the mood.

I sat there, knowing that in the days after the funeral I would curl up in my bedroom with the door locked because after that day, when everyone went home to shed their black suits and dresses and get on with life, it was going to be the real lonely time. Those other people would have their dark day at the graveside, but my family's dark days were about to get going. Again. I was eleven, Lissy was six, and we were orphans. It was a word associated with stories and not something that happened to real people, but here we were. It had happened to us.

I remember glancing at Charlie as the service neared the end, but he still stared ahead with tears on his cheeks, crumpling a service sheet in his hands like it was some sort of joyless accordion. Only twenty-four hours earlier, he had pledged to look after Lissy and me and would take us to France with him, and although he'd never had children of his own and would never know how to tie our hair or talk about girlhood issues with us, I was overwhelmingly thankful for him. I remember looking at him to tell him this, but he spoke before I did, his eyes on the coffin and his voice quiet but loaded with anger.

'Jim Valente,' he said, his voice quaking. 'He's to blame for this.'

The memory stops short and I can hear my breath shallow and ragged in my ears. What is Jim Valente to blame for? My dad's death? Is that what Charlie meant? But how could Jim Valente be to blame for Dad dying when the person I blame is myself?

THREE

My dad killed himself. These are words that I rarely allow myself to say, even in my own head, because when I do, it's like they form into some dark mass inside my lungs and it hurts to breathe. Dad had forever been plagued with depression and was plunged further into it by Mum's death, but what sent him spiralling out of control was what happened to Christopher Barrows.

It was a bright day in November and I'd convinced Dad to take me to the park opposite our London house to play football with me while Lissy was at a play date. He didn't want to go because he was tired and he gave me every excuse not to leave the house. He told me that he had booked us tickets to see a film and that upset me because I knew that he would doubtless fall asleep as soon as the cinema darkened. I knew that life tired him out, I had lived enough cycles of depression with him, but that day I selfishly wanted him to engage with me. I said there would be enough time for football, too, and after a while he ran out of excuses. Delighted, I dragged him out of the door and to the park where, reluctantly, he kicked the ball about with me. We finished after thirty minutes, red-cheeked with cold, and waited at the lights to cross back to our street.

'You know how tired I get,' he said. 'I'm not like regular dads, you know.'

'I know,' I said, looking up at him. 'You're better.'

He smiled, but I knew it was only for my benefit because it was so fleeting and he did look exhausted. I bit my lip and worried that he wouldn't now take us out to the cinema. He slumped against the traffic light pole and I held the football.

'You could fall asleep in the cinema, Dad?' I suggested, and that was OK by me because I could eat his popcorn.

'Don't even think about eating my popcorn if I do,' he said, and I beamed at him because he knew me so well.

Two others joined us, a woman and her little girl, who wore a cute red coat and held a white teddy. Dad asked its name, when suddenly there was a loud yell behind us. All four of us turned to see a man dressed as a clown chasing a man in a lion costume thirty metres in front of him through the park. They both bungled big, slippered footsteps towards us and hee-hawed at the top of their voices.

'Jokers,' the woman said, but she was smiling. Then her daughter tugged on her arm because she couldn't do up her jacket. The woman bent down to help and I saw that the zipper was stuck.

There was another high-pitched call and I looked back at the lion and the clown, a grin spreading on my face.

'They're coming over here, Dad,' I said. 'They look so funny!'

But he wasn't smiling. He looked angry and put his hand on my shoulder. It felt heavy, which was unlike him, and the weight of it gave me a sense of unease. I looked to the traffic lights, at the cars passing fast through, and back to the lion, now rapidly approaching the road.

'Dad?' I said, because danger was dawning in my head.

The clown flip-flopped precariously with every step, shouting now, and the lion's head jiggled until it had twisted to the left and the fake macabre eyes were at a right angle to the all-in-one, fake-furred body.

'Dad, I don't think he can see out of the eyeholes,' I said, looking up at him, but he merely shook his head.

'Ignore them. It's a prank.'

His words confused me. I turned back to see the lion only metres from us with its head now totally askew and ploughing straight on past us. I thought that at that moment Dad would reach out to drag him back by the material of his costume, but he didn't. Instead, he leaned on the traffic light pole again, looking even more worn out than before, and folded his arms as the lion zipped past him within inches and fell forward into the road. A car skidded. I can't remember seeing the hit, but I can recall a thud and my own voice in my ears.

'Dad!' I cried.

The woman looked from her daughter's zip and she screamed, but still my dad smiled down at me. I remember feeling turned upside down by this because I was scared, yet he was weirdly smiling.

'It's OK, Eleanor,' he said. 'You wait.'

But after a few seconds, he looked to the scene before us like it was something new, and his smile died on his lips. The little girl was turned away from the road by her mother, but she pulled round to see.

'The lion, Mummy!' she said. 'What happened to the lion?'

The clown was running fast now, had kicked off his huge red shoes and ran barefoot into the road, shrieking. Other people were shouting and running into the road with him and cars were stopping and I stared up at Dad again and watched as his face seemed to melt in on itself. Then he started running too, and left me at the lights. I could see the feet of the man in the lion costume on the road and he wasn't moving, wasn't making a sound. I saw my dad join three others who were bent over the lion.

'Can you hear me?' a woman pleaded.

'Should we move him?' a man asked.

'Is this real?' my dad said.

The driver of the car that had smashed into him toppled out from the vehicle, fainting. Someone caught him on the way down.

'Can someone call an ambulance?' another man shouted.

'On their way,' another woman said.

I held on to the metal pole of the traffic lights. It was freezing to my fingertips, a quick burn, but I held it like I was at sea. I couldn't help but stare at the scene before me like it was happening somewhere else, to someone else. On a screen.

The mother of the little girl reached for me, gathered me into her embrace along with her daughter.

'Don't look,' she whispered to me. 'We'll go to that cafe. I'll tell your dad, OK? Stay here one moment and take my girl's hand, OK?'

She put her daughter's hand into mine and the little girl stared up at me with wide eyes. Her teddy was on the floor and my football had rolled somewhere. I didn't know I'd dropped it. I picked up her teddy for her as the woman came back.

'Come with me,' she said. 'Your dad will come in a second.'

She ordered us each a lemonade and a cookie and I nibbled at it anxiously, trying not to look at the reflection in the open glass door of the blue ambulance lights.

27

Dad came to the cafe after a long forty minutes, but the man who walked through the door didn't look like him. He wore the same face and the same clothes but he was changed. An invisible pair of hands had forced his shoulders down and his cheeks into jowls. He collapsed into the booth next to me.

'His name was Christopher Barrows,' he said. 'He was a groom on his stag do.'

The woman inhaled sharply, mirrored my own at the use of 'was'.

'Is he . . .' She paused, eyes flicking to her daughter and to me. 'Is he OK?'

'No,' my dad said. 'No.'

'Oh God,' she said and she leaned across to my dad. 'Are you all right?'

He nodded, but then started to cry.

The woman bought him a cup of tea and sat awkwardly with us for five minutes, before taking her daughter and leaving us.

Dad let his tea go cold and wept into my shoulder.

'I couldn't save your mother from dying,' he said. 'But I could have saved that boy! I *should* have saved him!'

A stone-like weight settled on my chest.

'I'm sorry, Dad,' I whispered. 'We shouldn't have gone to play. I tired you out and you couldn't reach him.'

He didn't answer me and his silence was confirmation of my guilt. *I* was partly to blame for what happened to Christopher Barrows and subsequently I had played a part in my dad's death, too. I had prioritised myself and playing football over his health and it had unrolled in the worst possible way.

I never played football again. I never played any sports and I stopped going out with my friends. I sat with my back to the future and closed all its doors because I didn't deserve happiness when I'd caused so much pain.

I wake early from a fitful sleep and come down to the kitchen and a note that Charlie has scrawled and propped on the table. It says he's gone to deliver some plants, but he's left no clue as to where he's gone or how long he might be and I know instantly that this vagueness is deliberate; that he doesn't want to have a conversation with me about Jim Valente and this makes me feel desperately alone in my confusion.

The rain is still singing against the glass panes and my brain hurts with trying to work out what to do. I have a shift at the restaurant, but do I wait here to speak to Charlie again? Would he tell me what he knows about Jim Valente, if anything? If he does know something, why has he kept it to himself all these years? What does Lissy know? I wish, not for the first time, of course, that Dad was here so I could ask him what to do.

I go back upstairs and open my sister's bedroom door. She's still asleep and I want to wake her and talk about Jim, about Dad, but instead I close her door again and go to pack my things and then I leave for the train station.

I don't start my shift until midday, but I want to go for a run beforehand and clear my head, because the journey back to London has only muddied my brain further. I feel that how I've spent the last fourteen years, hidden inside myself with the shame and guilt of that day in the park, hangs on finding out what the connection between Jim and my dad could be.

Like drawing, running is an easy cure when life gets noisy or stressful. I put on black Lycra, as familiar to me as a second skin, tie my laces and put in my earphones. I pass through the concrete streets of Maida Vale, down Edgware Road, weave around the scattering of people at Speakers' Corner and through Hyde Park towards the Serpentine. I could stop here, breathe in its freshness and loop back around, but I push on, to Knightsbridge, past busy shoppers and imported fast cars, until I reach residential streets, where I slow to a jog and realise where I've taken myself.

I'm standing right in front of Jim Valente and Lucinda Kit's door in Wilton Crescent. There's a high buzz in my ears and a sickness that isn't brought on from my run and it makes my body flush hot and cold.

I move away from their door and cross the street, where I steady myself against the iron railings of the private gardens. Then I have an idea. All Dad's belongings that we haven't yet gone through are in the old house in Norfolk. I need to go back to Pudding Cottage and into the loft, where everything that is left of Dad is kept.

FOUR

Yesterday during the lunch shift I told Wendy and David that I was feeling bad, and so this morning they believe my lie easily when I text and tell them I'm unwell and I won't make it in.

It takes two trains and a cab ride to get from central London to Pudding Cottage, and for most of the journey I'm galvanised by the prospect of finding something out about Dad and Jim Valente's connection. But as the taxi driver turns around and begins to drive away down the narrow lane out of sight, it takes all my courage not to run after him and jump back in the car. I haven't been back here for fourteen years and, yes, everything of Dad's is here, but, for me, so is his ghost.

The house stands neat and square with a low thatch brow, backing on to farmland. It used to belong to Dad and Charlie's parents, but when they died, Charlie was in Italy landscaping and Dad was happy in London living a writer's bohemian lifestyle. They decided to rent it most of the year, but in the summer months we would have it to ourselves. We used to sit on the back steps and eat peaches from the farm shop and watch the tractors harvesting. We'd play in the stream back down the lane, while Dad spent hours working in his room. It was an isolated, idyllic little chocolate box, but right now I'm staring at it and wanting to vomit, because all the good memories made here are overshadowed by the bad one that was hot-branded into my eyes.

I begin the walk down the pathway to the door. I have a key for the cottage, have carried it on my keychain for ever, and although it's a literal sharp reminder of Dad every day, actually using it now means facing far more of him than I have in years. I put my key into the lock, turn it and push the door open with caution. I haven't told the agent I'm coming and know from looking at the availability online that there are people renting this week, but I can't wait the five days until Friday for changeover.

'Hello?' I call. 'Is anyone here?'

In case anyone is here, I've come with the pretence of looking at the meters but, to my relief, I'm met with silence. I shut the door behind me and turn to the living room. The familiarity of it hits me in the face. I shouldn't hesitate; I should go straight to the loft and get on with what I need to do, but instead I pause and take it in.

The cottage smells of wicker and wood polish. It's always smelt the same. My eyes sweep the room. There's the plush grey sofa next to the hissing radiator where Lissy and I used to lie and watch films. There's the painting of the boat on the wall, blues and purples and oranges that I used to stare at when Lissy was trying to read stories to me before she could read. There's the little white and blue sailboat on the mantelpiece.

I can hear the tick of the clock on the wall and I don't like that the clock is here, that the artwork is here, all these things which are the same here, when everything outside of this place has completely changed. I shiver. The kitchen is behind me and the door is shut and I'm thankful. I don't ever want to go back into that room.

I notice that a dining-room chair has a jumper thrown over it and there's a pair of tortoiseshell reading glasses on the table and they remind me that I shouldn't be here. What would happen if whoever is renting the cottage found me in here? What would I say?

The soft wood of the banisters curves up at the back of the room to the two bedrooms above, and as I walk up the stairs, I feel the notch on the top spindle that I made with a knife once when I was angry at Dad for saying he'd take us out for fish and chips and then forgetting the time. I take in the scene from the window on the landing, see that the fields are ploughed over now. I can see the neighbouring farm on the horizon, the curling woodsmoke from the chimney. I have no need to go into the bedroom that Dad slept in when he was here, but I see the door ajar and I reach out for the latch, which creaks as it's always done. The sound of it makes my heart ache. Dad used to read us stories here.

'Words are worlds,' he once said to me when we were reading *The Lion, the Witch and the Wardrobe*. Lissy was already asleep, her hot body coiled into the small of my back. I remember Dad smiling down at me before he tucked me in and went to work some more on his book. I crept out of my bed and over to the wardrobe in his room and I sat in it, waiting to feel the breath of icy air on my skin, hoping to be plucked out of this world and into the snow. He came back hours later and found me asleep in there.

I pull the door closed and take the white chair out of the bathroom and climb on top of it to open the loft hatch. At once, I'm hit by the rich smell of the Norfolk rush thatch, of old cardboard and mothballs. The warmth of the cottage doesn't reach the loft and I button my coat before I pull down the steel ladder and climb it.

I'm met with crookedly stacked boxes, a mirror propped up against one of the rafters, a broken fan light and a painting upside down. It's one of mine – a stripy cat on a barn roof, which I barely remember doing. It's the boxes I want to look at because these are things that Charlie hurriedly packed away when Dad died. He did most of his writing and work here and all his correspondence with his agents and publishers should be inside. Perhaps there'll be something I can link back to Jim Valente.

I crouch by the first box and rip its weakened Sellotape. It's a box of his writing clothes and I'm slapped with nostalgia as I pick them out. Dad's white shirt covered with ink and biro stains, some parts even covered with text when he couldn't find his notepad to scrawl on.

'You know, Dalton Trumbo wrote in the bath at night,' he said once. 'With a parrot. Should I get a parrot?'

The second box is his music CD collection: film soundtracks, Bob Dylan and Jimi Hendrix, which he would blast out when he was writing. Last thing at night, though, he would type in silence. I can still hear the sound of his typing on that clicky ancient IBM keyboard, the sound of it was both my midnight lullaby and my alarm clock at dawn.

The next box is filled with papers and books and travel journals, his A4 notepad with a Harley-Davidson Shovelhead Chopper on its cover. There are his 6B pencils and his red markers that he used to strike whole paragraphs with, some random pages of notes with illegible scribbles. I pick up files and flick through his agency and publisher contracts and his royalty statements. Here's a scrapbook of all his achievements that I

34

made him one year for his birthday: his awards, the reviews, the praise of all his books. I didn't keep the criticisms because I knew he took criticism badly; he had a picture of one reviewer on his pinboard and he'd occasionally throw darts at his face.

The box is almost empty, with only a few miserable pages left, stapled together, upside down, and I nearly leave them, but I lift the pages out, turn them over. The first is a typed letter from my father and it's addressed to Jim Valente. I gasp and the sound is noisy in my ears.

Mr Jim Valente,

Once again I implore you to reconsider the airing of the episode. I may have consented, I may have signed, but I cannot let this be aired. I write this not as a businessman because I am not one. I understand there will be costs involved in removing this content. But I am writing it as one man asking another. I cannot have my girls see this.

Regards, Stephen Greene

I frown, turn the letter over. The second page is another letter; this one is on thick white paper with a circular logo of a silver eye against a black background in the top right-hand corner.

Mr Greene,

Regarding your latest letter dated 20 October 2006.

As my communications manager has already informed you thrice, we will not withdraw this piece of content for Episode 32, 'Lost Child'. Production and marketing costs have already been allocated and spent against it. As well you know and have indeed referred to, we have your signature for this content to be used. If you continue to write about this matter, I will contact my solicitor. I entrust you do not wish to settle this in court, because it will be costly. For you.

Jim Valente, CEO Cyclops Productions, London.

I sit back on my heels and feel hot now, even though the loft is arctic.

I read the letters again, more slowly, trying to make sense of what they mean, before I hear the sound of something small, animal-like, flitting in the thatch. I need to leave before whoever it is who is renting Pudding Cottage returns. I shove everything except the letters back into the box, close up the loft and escape the house.

FIVE

I walk a mile to the nearest village and find a table in the local cafe where we used to come as kids. I don't recognise anyone here now and no one recognises me, but that's a good thing. If I knew anyone here, they'd tilt their heads to one side, give me a look of pity, ask me about my dad, and I can't talk about him.

I manage to order an iced bun and a tea and then I sit at the furthest table from the counter and I take the letters from my pocket, smooth them out and reread them. Dad's words are clearly desperate, Jim's appear uncaring. Their correspondence doesn't make sense to me, but there's one thing that's standing out, that might piece it all together: Episode 32.

I take my phone from my bag and type 'Episode 32, Lost Child' into the search, along with my father's name and Jim Valente. A link to a YouTube clip appears.

Episode 32 – *Pranksters*: 'Lost Child'. First aired March 13 2007.

Pranksters? I inhale sharply. Dad was already dead when it aired and Lissy and I were in France with Charlie. Who has seen this footage? Has Charlie? Everything inside me is screaming at me not to watch whatever this is, but I put my earphones into the socket and click on the link. Straight away, I see my dad on the screen.

The viewpoint camera is perched on top of a lamp post or perhaps a tree, focused on an area no bigger than ten metres across. I recognise the location. It's near where we used to live in London, outside the little bank of shops on Norwood Road, opposite the park.

Dad steps out of the coffee shop and he's carrying a paper bag that I know will have Chelsea buns inside it. After Mum died, Charlie used to come over every Saturday and watch Lissy and me, while Dad went to try to write for the morning. I watch him fish around in his jacket and take out his sunglasses because it's sunny and my heart aches for him so hard, it's a physical pain in my chest. This is an ordinary weekend morning. Except that a little girl comes into view and walks up to my dad.

'Excuse me,' she says. 'Can you help me?'

Dad looks down at her. She's around eight, with blonde curls, and sweet-looking.

'Are you all right?' he asks.

'I've lost my mum,' she says.

Dad kneels down immediately and removes his sunglasses. 'Where did you last see her, sweetheart?'

'She went to the park to buy ice cream,' the little girl says. 'She said to stay here and wait.'

'How long ago?' asks my dad.

The little girl bites her lip. 'She's been gone a long time.'

'Have you got a phone?' Dad asks. 'Can we call someone?'

'Daddy is in the shop down the road,' she says and points out of camera shot.

'Let's go and find him,' Dad says. He pockets his glasses and reaches out his hand to her.

But the girl stares across the road, to the park. 'I want to find Mum,' she says. 'This is where she comes.'

My dad looks confused. 'It's probably safer to find your dad first,' he suggests. 'This is a busy road here.'

'No, look!' the girl cries. 'There she is!'

Dad looks across the road and sees a woman in a long white dress. Her hair is red and hangs loose behind her back, and she's barefoot.

The little girl waves in delight.

'Your girl lost you,' Dad tries to call to the woman, but she just waits at the roadside opposite, smiling.

The girl takes my dad's hand. 'Hurry!' she says. 'Let's go to her.'

'OK, but the cars are coming past now,' he replies. 'We have to wait.'

'There's no time,' she says and pulls at him. 'She'll leave.'

'No,' he says. 'Look, the lights are up there, we'll go to them.' He calls out to the girl's mother, 'We'll go to the crossing, OK?'

Hand in hand, my dad and the girl walk the fifteen yards to the traffic lights and wait for the cars to slow. Two long lorries pause and obscure the woman for a moment, and when they pass, she is gone.

'Where is she?' the little girl asks.

'I don't know,' Dad replies. He looks up and down the opposite pavement, and to the park.

'She always leaves,' the girl says. 'We need to get her.'

The cars stop and the little girl goes to cross.

'Wait,' Dad says, and holds her back. 'If we can't see her, perhaps we should get your dad?' He turns. 'Which shop was he in?'

But no sooner has he asked than a man runs up towards him, red with anger.

'What the hell are you doing with my girl?'

'Are you her father? She was lost,' my dad explains. 'She wanted to find . . .' He pauses. 'Oh,' he says. 'She's there.'

The woman has appeared and is behind her husband. She smiles at Dad.

'Mum,' says the little girl.

'Freya, no,' the man warns and he draws her towards him.

'The man said he'd help me find Mum,' Freya says, pointing at Dad.

'Are you trying to be funny?' the man asks my dad.

Dad blinks. 'I'm sorry?'

'Dad, Mum is there,' Freya says. 'Behind you.'

The father drops down to her. 'No, Freya. Come on, we've talked about this.'

My dad looks utterly confused, looks at the woman, who then bends to Freya, kisses her cheek and starts to walk away.

'Excuse me?' my dad calls. 'Where are you going?'

'Who the hell are you?' the man says, gripping his daughter protectively.

'Your wife . . .' my dad begins, but stops when the man's face falls into horror.

'Were you going to take her?' he demands. 'My Freya?'

'Take her? To her mother, yes. She has red hair,' my dad says. 'Your wife? That's her, isn't it? Over there? Walking around the corner?'

The man looks furious.

'He said he'd help me, Daddy,' the little girl says. 'Take me to Mummy.'

'I'm going to report you,' the man hisses at my dad.

'Report me?' my dad says. 'What do you mean?'

'What's going on here?'

A policeman has arrived in uniform, but he wears the most incredibly long clown-like red patent shoes. It takes him an age to flop towards them and the little girl smiles, but Dad doesn't. It's as if he doesn't see the shoes, he's so wrapped inside this moment, in the girl and the woman in white.

'This creep tried to take my girl,' the man says to the policeman. 'Talked rubbish about my wife who's dead.'

My dad's face drops. 'Dead?'

'Freya's mother is dead. She died in the hospital across the park. Freya told you, right? What sort of a sick and twisted shit are you?'

'I don't understand,' Dad says.

'He said I could find my mummy in the park,' comments the girl to the policeman. 'Because I never said goodbye to her.'

'You tried to take this girl, sir?' the policeman asks.

My dad shakes his head and then stops. 'No! Yes. I mean, we saw her mother—'

'Her mother is dead! What did I just say?' the father yells.

The policeman studies my dad, who stands wringing his hands.

'But I saw her,' Dad says. 'Red hair. Just like . . . just like my wife, too.'

The policeman gets out fluffy pink cuffs. 'I'll have to take you down to the station and file a report,' he says to my dad, and then he shrugs. 'You know, for seeing ghosts. And also attempted kidnapping.'

41

He grins, but Dad licks his lips, doesn't register any sort of humour behind what's happening.

'I didn't try to take her!' he says. 'I saw her, the child's mother!'

He looks at the father, who is beginning to smile along with the policeman.

'Come with me, sir,' the policeman says, and he takes my dad's arm, leads him to the edge of the pavement, points upwards towards the camera. 'Look up there.'

My dad looks up but cannot see. Tears begin to stream down his face. 'I saw the woman, her mother!' he says.

'Sir, look. You've been pranked!' the policeman explains.

'Pranked!' shout the father and the little girl.

And, as if burst from shells, these new shiny people all clap Dad on the back, laugh as streamers go off and a foghorn blares. The traffic stops, people applaud from their cars, laughing, in on the joke, but Dad stands in the middle of this bizarre fanfare looking like a lost child. He shakes his head. He doesn't understand. 'Is she dead?'

'Who?' the girl asks. She's smiling at him and he looks like he's wondering why.

'Your mother,' Dad replies.

The girl laughs at him. 'No!'

The woman in white suddenly appears beside my dad and he looks at her, terrified.

'That was a good one,' she comments.

'She's there!' my dad says. 'Can anyone see her?'

'What are you talking about, mate?' the policeman laughs. 'Look! The camera!'

'That was one of the best reactions I've seen!' A woman in her mid-twenties has burst in front of the camera with a microphone. She's wearing a crimson jumpsuit and black heels. 'Jemima Mataya sees it all, baby!'

'Would you sign this?' A woman in a headset has walked up to Dad with a clipboard. She holds out a pen.

Dad turns to her. 'For the police?'

The young woman called Jemima Mataya laughs. 'Good one,' she says. 'Great reaction. Cruel as fuck, right?' She faces the camera, winks into it. 'That's *Pranksters* for you.'

I watch as Dad take the pen, signs the piece of paper on the clipboard. He looks utterly bewildered. The credits roll and then the screen goes blank.

I sit on the train and stare out of the window at the blur of countryside. I'm crying, have been crying for hours, but can't seem to stop.

Because of *Pranksters*, my dad hadn't helped Christopher Barrows. His natural instinct to help someone had been exploited only a few weeks before and so he had stopped himself from pulling Christopher back from the road. He'd watched as a young man had run into traffic and folded his arms across his chest and looked around for the cameras and for whoever it was who would assume the role of 'idiot'.

I'd always thought that I was to blame for Dad not reaching out to grab Christopher, because he could have done, *should* have done, but now that's turned on its head. Now it makes sense that Dad smiled down at me, that he *told* me it was a prank. He held back because he didn't want to be the idiot again. But it was no prank and Christopher Barrows was no made-up character. He had died and Dad had blamed himself for it and had sunk into a depressive episode so deep that he saw no other choice but to end his own life.

43

I couldn't save your mother from dying, but I could have saved that boy.

My heart feels like it's been shattered for a second time. Why didn't I know about this when I was eleven? Why didn't he tell me what he thought he'd done? Did he think I wouldn't have understood? I would have done! I would have buried my face in his shoulder and kissed his nose and told him that he was a good man, a hero to me after all we'd been through with Mum. I would have showered him with all the things that Lissy and I loved about him. But it's too late now.

I don't return to my flat straight away. Instead, I stand on the pavement opposite Jim's house in Belgravia with my coat hood up. My body burns with fury. All I can think is that I want this man and his company to pay, somehow, for what happened to Dad and the false guilt I've lived with all these years.

SIX

'You're coming tonight, yeah?' Wendy asks.

It's four in the afternoon and she's putting on lipstick in the luxury powder-room mirror after our lunch shift and I'm lending her my mascara because she forgot hers.

'Our party night starts now!' she says. 'Sucks to be on late shift tonight!'

It's 17 December and the night of our Christmas party. It's been three days since I was at Pudding Cottage. I called in sick, legitimately, for two days and watched Episode 32 over and over until I could repeat the words back to myself and I couldn't cry any more.

'I'm not going to come,' I reply.

'What? Come on, El! I think that new guy wants to ask you out! What's his name? You know, the one that looks like he should be a footballer.'

'Kobi?' I ask.

'Yeah,' she says. Her lips gleam scarlet and she fishes inside her bag and takes out candy-cane earrings, fixes them to her ears.

'I'm busy tonight,' I reply.

She releases her dark hair from the confines of its bun and then holds out her hand for my mascara and I give it to her. 'Tell me,' she says.

'Well,' I say. 'Nothing exciting. I've got to do a few things online.'

She pauses with the mascara and looks at me in the mirror. 'Are you online dating?' Her face is splitting ear to ear in a grin.

'No,' I reply. 'Just some Christmas shopping.'

She screws the top on the mascara bottle and gives it back to me. 'You should meet a few people. You're going to become a whatsit. You know, a spinster.'

'Maybe next time,' I say.

'Kobi will be sad.'

'Do you think he's nice?' I ask.

'Oh God, yes,' she says.

'Then he won't be sad for long, will he?' I say.

She laughs, bouffing her hair at the roots.

'Wendy?' I say.

'Babe?'

'Tell me about Jim Valente and *Pranksters*.'

She arches an eyebrow, smiling. 'Why the interest? Are you thinking of applying to be host? God, I'll kill for that job.'

'You want to be an actor?'

She snorts. 'You think I worked seven years at The Cello because I wanted to serve rich people all day? The *Pranksters* host isn't an actor, though. The host is a brand.' She picks up her phone from the sideboard beneath the mirror. 'The company Cyclops is remaking the series.'

'David told me,' I say. 'Why is it such a big deal?'

'Here,' she says, tapping on her screen. 'You recognise her?'

On her phone is the face of the porcelain-skinned woman who was wearing the red jumpsuit and who winked at the camera while Dad stood gaping like a fish out of water. She's a decade older but has the same rosebud lips, luminescent bedroom eyes and shock of ash-blonde hair in a choppy pixie cut.

My fingers curl into fists. 'I do recognise her,' I say.

'Jemima Mataya. She was the host of *Pranksters* for years. She built the brand.'

'What happened to her?'

'She died a year ago,' she says. 'And they stopped making the series out of respect to her. That's probably why you recognise her if you haven't watched the show. It was in all the papers. Overdose.'

'Her job? You would really want that?' I ask.

'Fame and fortune?' she replies. 'Sure. Who wouldn't?'

'Doesn't fame come at a price?' I say.

'Hers did,' Wendy answers. 'But I don't do drugs.' She pouts into the mirror. 'They make me sneeze.'

I come back from the shift to find a man standing at my flat door, who shows me a badge. 'Good timing,' he says cheerfully but rearranges his smile when I don't return it. 'Your upstairs neighbour let me in. Can I read your electricity meter?'

I nod silently and unlock my door and he comes through with me. I don't like people in my space and it feels uncomfortable having him following so close behind me. His smell is cloying; cigarettes and sweat plume into my flat. I show him the meter and then I go to the bathroom and I stand and wait for him to finish because I don't want to offer him tea or talk to him, don't want to feel bad that I haven't tidied up from breakfast or that my laptop is out or that my dressing gown is draped over the sofa arm.

'Hello?' he calls after a minute. 'I'm . . . I'm done?'

I come out of the bathroom and open the door for him. 'Thanks.'

'OK,' he says and I close the door behind him, relieved to be alone again. Perhaps Jim was right. I am like the song, Eleanor Rigby. All the lonely people.

I sit at my kitchen table and open my laptop. The revelations of the last few days have lodged themselves in the form of an acute headache, but here I sit, with my laptop open in front of me, and I stare at pictures of Jim Valente. My eyes are drawn to one of him at some sort of event dinner, sitting at a table full of cut glass and dressed in a suit: cream jacket with blue shirt open at the collar. He's smiling at the camera and looks handsome.

I read up on Cyclops and its intimidating stable of writers, actors, producers and directors. Jim clearly pours money into it. I load the Cyclops company profiles and I stare at all the faces that work there, the freelancers, the permanent staff. There are black and white and smiling headshots, each with their own blurb: their likes and dislikes, hobbies and achievements. Universities, awards, travelling adventures, professional accolades. All the things I don't have and will never have, but could I have had them?

I scan the company's social media accounts. They're full of self-praise, upcoming events, smiling faces at parties. Famous actors, producers, directors litter the pages in their world of bright golden lights and soft filters. It's a well-oiled machine. How would I exploit Jim and this company as they did my dad?

I open a new page, type 'Pranks' in my search bar, because it seems fitting that I would do the same to Jim, and I click to websites with creative pranks to play on your friends and family. They're funny, harmless, and that's not what I want. I don't really know what it is I want, only that I want to feel like I'm doing something *bad*, even if it is just a cathartic exercise.

I delete the word 'prank' in my search engine and instead I type in 'revenge'. At once, a plethora of specialist pages load and I read their blurbs, click on a few. Reams of conversations and threads offer ways to expose an enemy, how to get even with back-stabbing friends, tyrant bosses, cheating lovers. There is an abundance of suggested payback techniques, ranging from darkly comical to outright psychotic.

Smear dog shit on all her door handles.

Sedate him and then drown him in the bath.

I read comments, lead myself down tangential threads. One website leads to another and I'm a twisted Alice in Wonderland, tumbling deeper inside murky tunnels. I grab a pen and pad, jot down the websites that intrigue me, scare me.

Should I use my sister as bait for my husband?

How do you make explosives?

More than once, I lift my fingers from the keyboard, think that this isn't me and I shouldn't be on these sites. I should be doing anything but pouring salt on to old wounds and delving into a black world I might be sucked into, but these people who are posting are fascinating and their lives, their energy, their charisma, albeit dark, is addictive. I didn't know people could be like this. Do I want to be like this?

I read through some of the threads and articles about how to avoid getting caught online and keeping yourself anonymous.

Everyone needs a VPN. Download a VPN client and your IP address can be routed to somewhere random. Brazil, Norway. If you want to do it properly, get a VPN that bounces from several global sites.

I sit back and rub my eyes. I can't feel my feet any more. Hours have passed and the heating has been off the entire time, but I don't move to get more clothes. Instead, I open a new web page that I've found through a labyrinth I didn't know I was in. It's called Anon and its background is black with white writing and there is a picture of a smiling man in a suit. A caption next to it reads, *Hate the corporate big guys? Wipe the fucking smile off their faces. Let us show you how.*

I click back to the web page with Jim's face on his Cyclops profile page, think about wiping the smile off his face and then I shut my computer just as the door buzzer sounds.

SEVEN

I open the front door to Charlie.

'Er?' I say.

'I know,' he says gruffly, and steps through the door.

'But you never leave the village?' I remark.

'I know,' he says again.

I follow him down the corridor to the door of my flat and we walk through to the kitchen together. My heart has started to thud. My uncle is as familiar to me as Lissy, but in all the years I've been in London he's never come to the city to see me. He looks like a stranger in my flat in his dirty mackintosh and flat cap.

'Are you OK?' I ask.

'I didn't want to do this over the phone,' he says. 'Over the weekend, you surprised me and I said . . . I said something about the fella you had talked about. Jim Valente.'

He sits down at the table and I glance at my laptop, overwhelmingly thankful I closed the lid, because what would Charlie say if he saw Jim's face on the browser?

'I want you to forget I said anything about him, OK?' he says.

'Why did you get upset?'

He waves my question away like a gnat above his head. 'Oh, they . . . they had some past dealings. But the link between him and your dad is tenuous at best. I didn't want you leaping to any . . . false conclusions.'

We meet eyes and his are imploring. He wants to bury this, just as we've buried everything for so many years. Is it because he thinks he's protecting me?

'It was your father's depression that killed him,' he says. 'It got the better of him.'

No, I think. That's not wholly true. But I nod. 'It's OK, Charlie,' I reply.

'And so I don't want you to worry about what I said,' he presses. 'I was only . . . There's no point. OK? And you've come too far forwards to go backwards, all right?'

'Yeah,' I say flatly.

But I haven't gone forwards, I think. I've lived my life from one day to the next with no vision of what's in front of me and it's only now, now when I've found out the truth, that I *can* go forward. I need to make up to myself for all the years I've lost and it's got to start by hurting that man. I jerk slightly at the thought that is so foreign to my passive character. Is that what I want? To hurt him? *Am* I passive or is that who I made myself become after years of guilt and self-blame?

'Remember what it was like,' Charlie says. 'You don't want to go back there, Eleanor.'

I know what he's talking about and I nod slowly because I don't want to go back there, either. After the funeral, I sank into someplace very dark and wouldn't talk to anyone, cried and was sick on repeat. I barely slept, and when I did, I woke up sweating and panicked. I sat in my room and watched reams of family video, went through every photo of Dad and wept over them. I wrote him letters and I trawled my memories of him and polished them in my mind.

After a few weeks, I lost sense of time, I began to refuse food, and after a few days of that, Charlie got desperate and bust open the bedroom door to deposit me, fully clothed, into a bath. He sat outside the door and he didn't say anything, but I could hear him breathing. He knew I could hear him and wanted that to be a comfort to me, but it was a reminder that the world was still turning, and so I submerged myself and blinked up through the water and wondered what it would feel like to die. I couldn't, though, because I had Lissy to look after, who was as lost as I was and terrified of the mess I was in.

I clawed myself back for her, but that hopelessness always threatened to overwhelm me. It's why I live alone, why I'm thought of as an enigma. I don't like letting anyone in – not even a man to read a meter.

'I want you to go back to who you were, El,' Charlie says.

'Who was that?' I ask.

'Like Lissy. You were out playing sport all the time, you were drawing and painting,' he replies. 'And bright! Oh, you were bright!'

I lick my lips.

He shakes his head sadly. 'What you saw with your dad. It was . . . unspeakable.'

'Please don't say it,' I say quickly.

He nods. 'Right,' he says, and stands up.

'Are you leaving?' I ask. 'You've been here five minutes. Do you want to stay for dinner?'

'I've said my piece,' he says. 'Don't dwell on the past. OK? And the air in this city is like tar, so I'm going.'

He nods at me, walks back down the corridor and opens the door.

'See you in a few days for Christmas, girl,' he says.

I watch him leave and then I close the door and I sit at the table again, flick my eyes to the laptop. If anything, Charlie's unexpected and clumsy visit has validated my anger.

I *was* once like Lissy, confident and extroverted, but our lives have turned out very differently. We both lost our parents, but Lissy has risen like a phoenix out of tragic embers. She knows where she's going and she can breathe, whereas I'm trapped under a thick blanket and it's suffocating me, but the worst thing is that I'm holding it over my own face. What would happen if I let the blanket go and I came up for air? Who would I be? After all these years hiding from myself and everyone else, I'm scared to answer this question, but I'm going to.

I open the laptop lid, install a VPN and link to a server in Beijing. Then I lean back, heart hammering, worried that it's about to siren and call the police on me, but it doesn't, obviously. I hover between standing and sitting and making tea and then I think I'm being ridiculous, because I've done nothing illegal after all. But am I going to do anything illegal? Of course not. I just want some guidance, some advice.

I open the web browser Anon once again and I spend an hour clicking back and forth between threads of conversation. Discussions are happening in real time and I watch plans unfold like films running in front of my eyes. It still feels wrong to be here, yet here I am, investing in angst and anger and finding that I'm rooting for the people who want revenge. I wonder if they could root for me too? Would anyone pitch in to help me?

I create a profile, change my name several times before calling myself 'Top Step'. I don't even know where the name comes from, but it's non-gender-specific, mundane and invisible. The website doesn't ask me anything else. No contact details, no age, no gender. I suppose this is why it's called Anon.

I click on the, 'New Conversation' button and I type in 'HELP' in the subject line.

'Come on, El,' I say to myself. 'Take the initiative.'

I hover the mouse over the button that says 'Confirm'. My heart is drumming, but I press enter on the keyboard and let out a shuddering breath.

I get up, go to the kettle and make a cup of tea. Steam rises from the cup and I pour slowly, letting it warm my face, like a bath. I close my eyes for a second, then a loud bleep emits from my laptop. I spin to face the screen to see that there's a comment to my thread. An invite to a private message.

I stare at it. From the time it took me to post the thread to that bleep couldn't have been longer than a minute. I look around the flat like there's someone in here with me and the camera lens in my laptop winks in the soft glow of the oven light. I rip a front page from a book on the shelf behind the table, grab some duct tape and stick it over the camera on the front of the laptop, and then I sit down and look at the message.

Horsehead: How can I help you, friend?

Top Step: I wasn't expecting a reply so soon??

Horsehead: The internet is a magical place. There's always someone awake, somewhere in the world.

Top Step: Where are you?

Horsehead: The Black Hills, South Dakota. You been?

Top Step: No.

Horsehead: But you've seen films, right? It's trees, mountains, horse leather, grit and a lot of Native American history. Where are you at?

Top Step: Should I be telling you where I live?

Horsehead: Shall I guess then? Could be a long night!

Top Step: The UK.

Horsehead: Ace. I fucking love the Brits!

Top Step: What does Horsehead mean? Is it from *The Godfather*?

Horsehead: Yes! Love that scene. Everyone loves a severed head, right?

Top Step: I can't say I've seen many?!

Horsehead: Yeah, nor me. And I'm no *Godfather* either. I'm a regular John Doe. You a John or a Jane?

Top Step: Should I be disclosing this?

Horsehead: You're a girl then. A British chick! Nice! What's your Calamity, Jane? What do you need help with?

Top Step: I'm here for some advice really.

Horsehead: Give me the lowdown.

Top Step: I need to get even with a man, but I have no idea how to do it. I don't know much about anything like this.

Horsehead: OK, standard revenge story. Sounds right up my street. You want to fuck this guy up? Be a hunter?

Top Step: Is that what you do? You help people on this website get even with people you don't know?

Horsehead: That's correct, my friend. For a fee, I'm here as a mentor for fuck-uppery. Good, right?? So tell me the deal. You love this guy and he cheated?

Top Step: No.

Horsehead: He's your evil boss? Your evil pimp?

Top Step: Not a boss or a friend or relative or a pimp. Actually he's quite a difficult target.

Horsehead: How so?

Top Step: He moves in very elite circles, which is why I came to this website. But I don't know anything about him apart from what's online, which isn't much. And where he works and where he lives.

Horsehead: Who's the guy?

Top Step: Do I tell you?

Horsehead: Well now might be the time? Do you want help or not?

Top Step: OK. I just . . . I've never done anything like this before.

Horsehead: This isn't confession, doll.

Top Step: I don't know if I should be doing this.

Horsehead: Of course you *shouldn't* be doing this. But you *are* doing this. So spill.

Top Step: His name is Jim Valente and he's in the media industry here in the UK. His company makes a programme called *Pranksters*, which is basically pranking the public for entertainment and my dad got caught up in it. On its own, it seems such a trivial reason why I want to do this, but it inadvertently led to his death.

Horsehead: Your dad died???

Top Step: The programme is all about exploiting a person's good nature. It made my dad second-guess himself a few weeks after when a guy died in front of him. My dad could have saved him, but he stopped himself.

Horsehead: OK, so this guy Jim Valente. He's the top of the food chain? He's the one you want to go after?

Top Step: I found letters between him and my dad. My dad pleaded with him not to air the episode that he got caught up in. He didn't want my sister and me to watch it. I don't know why, perhaps he felt too embarrassed? Maybe he thought we'd be made fun of at school? Maybe he worried for his own reputation as a children's writer? Anyway, Jim threatened him with legal action. It's his company, it was his decision.

Horsehead: You gotta give me everything from start to finish.

Top Step: It's late here, Horsehead.

Horsehead: So go make yourself a cup of tea. Isn't that what you Brits do?

It's two in the morning when I switch off the computer and I should be exhausted, but I'm buzzing. I've never written so many words before to anyone, let alone a stranger. They poured out of me, a waterfall from a dam I didn't know was overflowing.

Horsehead watched Episode 32 and was silent as I told him about Christopher Barrows and how it connected the depressive episode which spiralled Dad out of control with guilt. He said he thought it was terrible, that we'd suffered for the price of cheap entertainment, and we ended the conversation with him saying he would wait for me to contact him again, should I want to formulate any sort of a revenge plan. He made me feel validated, reassured me that I would be doing the right thing if I chose to go ahead.

I wonder what Horsehead looks like. I imagine him with sharp cheekbones, deep-set eyes, a shading of stubble around the mouth. Perhaps his skin is pitted in the cheeks. A straight nose, thin lips, wry smile. Perhaps he's Native American. He'll have nice teeth, thick hair. I wonder what his family is like, if he has pets, what his friends do. I like him and I like what he's proposing to do for me.

Revenge is supposed to be a bad thing to crave, and taking an eye for an eye will only make the world blind. But I feel that my eyes have been opened to blazing colours. I feel alive.

EIGHT

I look at the lights strung across the village's pretty streets. It's Christmas morning and it's a fresh, bright day with a wind in the air. I inhale deeply. I've been to church, and even though I don't know what I believe, sitting in that building and hearing the voices lift in Christmas cheer gave me energy.

'Merry Christmas!' someone calls from across the road and I lift my hand in greeting but fail to speak, carrying on without seeing who it even was.

Christmas was Dad's favourite time of year. He loved the necklaces of lights in the towns and villages, the pearly coloured beads around the trees, decorations in the store windows and industrial-sized tubs of Twiglets. We had our traditions – decorating the tree, making mince pies and cards out of sugar paper and glitter pens. The little plastic reindeers which had been cake decorations years ago would appear a week before Christmas and Dad would put them and a few of Lissy's special teddies in the living room in a circle with a tea set and then move them every night until Christmas Eve, when they'd dangle precariously from the tree branches, looking like they were trying to steal presents.

I tilt my head up to the sky. Is Dad up there? Is Mum? Can you see me? What should I do? But the sky is silent, bright blue and dazzling.

'Shut the effing door!' Lissy squeals as I come into the kitchen. 'It's freezing!'

She's dressed in a short blue dress and black tights with tiny elves on them and she's sipping from a champagne flute.

'You've started already?' I say.

She shrugs. 'Of course! Did you sing "Come All Ye Faithful" in church? I love that one.'

'If you'd come with me, you could have sung it too,' I reply, and pull off my boots.

'It's Christmas Day,' she says. 'I watched *The Muppet Christmas Carol*.'

'Is that because you're a muppet?' I tease.

'Shut up,' she says, but she's smiling and she puts down her glass. 'I made gingerbread bells too, look?'

'I love your gingerbread,' I say.

'I know,' she replies. 'It's why I make it every year. Mum's recipe.'

I pick one up from the table and it's still warm and melts in my mouth.

Uncle Charlie appears from the living room with a glass of expensive fizz in each hand. 'You're having one, El, yes?' he says, handing me one. 'We've got to do things properly, haven't we?'

Charlie always tries to go the extra mile at Christmas because he wants to both honour and protect us from Dad, who hangs, spectre-like, above the day.

'Can I do anything?' I ask.

'I've burnt the potatoes,' he replies. 'But what's new?'

I smile and think how lucky I am to have Charlie in my life, even if he burns potatoes.

'Have a gingerbread bell, Charlie,' says Lissy, and gives him one.

'Very good,' he says.

She pulls both of us towards her into a scrum and then from her pocket she pulls a party popper.

'Happy Christmas, bitches!' she shouts, and let's it go at Charlie's head.

Polo barks from under the table and Charlie sighs, hair streamered with coloured paper ribbons. He raises his glass to the middle of our little group of three and Lissy grabs her glass and clinks his violently. I lift mine to join theirs. Every year everyone pretends.

In bed, I think of Horsehead and wonder how he might have spent Christmas. We've not been in contact since our conversation because I haven't known what I've wanted to do and a prick of anxiety has burst my initial bubble of euphoria.

There's a noise outside and my sister creeps into my room. She doesn't turn the light on and I sit up.

'What are you doing?' I ask her.

'I couldn't sleep,' she says.

She gets into my bed and cuddles into my side like a little monkey. Her feet are glacial and she warms them on my legs and I let her. I lean my cheek against her head, breathe in the smell of her hair: Moroccan oil shampoo.

'Too excited about your gorilla?' I tease.

'Thanks for my necklace,' she says. 'I'm glad it's not a gorilla. It would never write to me anyway.'

I laugh but she doesn't. I feel her body shiver.

'Are you OK?' I ask.

'Sometimes I get sad,' she says after a moment. 'I wish he was here.'

All day, like every Christmas day, she's been bouncy and loud and happy. She sang all the carols, stood for the Queen's Christmas Message because she knows Charlie and I find it funny, and insisted on watching the Christmas *EastEnders* episode. At four, she changed into a unicorn onesie and made dangerously strong eggnog and got tipsy after one glass and then, on our post-lunch walk around the village, she wore Uncle Charlie's hat made of faux fur and feathers that she'd ridiculed only days previously. Sometimes I'm guilty of forgetting that her heart is as full of holes as mine is. She just hides it better.

I find her hand under the covers.

'I do, too,' I say.

'And I wish Mum was here,' she whispers.

I'm quiet because Mum is the ghost we don't talk about.

'Thank God for Charlie,' Lissy adds.

'And each other,' I say. 'I couldn't live without you, Lissy.'

'You can be so dramatic,' she groans. 'Like Dad.'

But she smiles in the dark; I know because I can see the silhouetted curve of her cheek and I'm glad to make her smile because that's all I've ever wanted for her. To smile and be free of the pain I carry.

I spend three days with Lissy, Charlie and Polo in an indulgent loop of TV programmes, winter walks and boxes of Christmas chocolates, but I'm glad to have the excuse of shifts at the restaurant so I can leave.

It's New Year's Eve now. It's five o'clock and we've only just finished the lunch shift, which has been long with raucous groups of friends and cawing family reunions, and will soon be full again for the evening. Usually I request the late service because it gives me an excuse for why I'm spending New Year alone, but tonight I'm going out.

'Do you want a quick drink before you go?' David asks.

I shake my head and put on my coat. 'I've got somewhere to be,' I say and smile at him. 'Happy New Year.'

'*Bonne année*,' he says.

I head out into the cold, pull my coat collar up and walk to where I shouldn't be: Belgravia.

I suspected Jim and Lucinda might host a party but didn't know it for a fact. They could have jetted off halfway round the world to see the New Year in from a boat deck or roof terrace somewhere, but here they are.

I stand across the street, shadowed from the glare of their window. The kitchen curtains are open, theatre-like, to show the outside world all the fun they're having, and bright lights catch all the jewels dripping from the decorated throats and hands below. Cocktail dresses and loud open-collar shirts press against one another, shiny eyes and white teeth flash, hair flicks, cigars smoulder.

I see them in the middle of the room: Lucinda in an elegant high-neck violet dress and Jim beside her in a white shirt and black jeans. He drapes his arm around her and I watch Lucinda smile easily up at him as he holds court over the room. Everyone inside looks happy and in love, on top of their lives and on top of each other, and I feel my hands clench. Jim doesn't deserve this indulgent lifestyle when my sister and I are trying to heal scars that he played a part in delivering. I need to go back online, seek Horsehead's counsel into how I could get close enough to prank Jim.

THE PRANK

*

Horsehead: Happy New Year, doll!

Top Step: Hi, Horsehead. How are you?

Horsehead: It's been a while. I was wondering if you'd got cold feet and I thought that was sad because I liked the sound of your Jim Valente. Pure revenge gold potential.

Top Step: I was thinking about our conversation. I didn't know if I wanted to do anything.

Horsehead: But you know now?

Top Step: I think so?

Horsehead: Christmas is a hard time without your loved ones, right? Did that sway you?

Top Step: Partly, I suppose.

Horsehead: Tell me about your Xmas, Top Step? You spend it with your boyfriend?

Top Step: I don't have a boyfriend. I spent it with my little sister and my uncle. Are you in a relationship?

Horsehead: No way. I'm a lone wolf.

Top Step: So how did you spend your Christmas?

Horsehead: Alone.

Top Step: You don't have family?

Horsehead: Dad passed on. Mom is a bitter and twisted old sow because he left a LOT of debts. She lives about four hours' drive away.

Top Step: I'm really sorry to hear that.

Horsehead: Nah, it's OK. I fought crime in the neighborhood, jerked off to girls online. At one in the morning, I heard my housemate have sex with his doll.

Top Step: I'm sorry??

65

Horsehead: He's got one of those life-size dolls he ordered from the internet.

Top Step: That's disgusting!

Horsehead: I know, right?

Top Step: Are you friends with this guy??

Horsehead: Jeez, no. He was an internet find, but we've been together for years. Sometimes you get stuck with people, right? But he's got a sick mother. I know, I've checked her accounts. So it might be worth sticking out.

Top Step: You've checked her accounts??

Horsehead: Sure. Pure interest, obviously. Not stealing any inheritances. Yet. In other news, you know what I read over the last few days?

Top Step: What?

Horsehead: I read up a little on your friend Jim Valente. Read that he picked up a funding worth $2m from investors this month for a series he's commissioned. He's sitting pretty in that company, right?

Top Step: Yes, he is.

Horsehead: He's been elected member of the Board of Media Regulation. And he's taking the family on vacation to Miami in the spring. *And* Cyclops's share profit has rocketed over the last five years.

Top Step: Do you see what I mean? He has this perfect life, he's untouchable. How do I solicit any sort of plan when we don't move in the same circles? I'd have to infiltrate his life somehow! But how unless I tried to – I don't know – work with him or something?

Horsehead: Now there's an interesting idea.

Top Step: And completely bonkers.

Horsehead: Is it though?

Top Step: I mean what would I do? Clean his house or something? Something in his company?

Horsehead: I read they're looking to fulfill a role.

Top Step: The host for *Pranksters*? There's no way I could do that. No way I would want to. And I have zero qualifications for what his company does. I didn't go to university, unlike my sister. I barely scraped school to be honest. After Dad died, I wasn't interested in learning. I *couldn't* learn, you know? I was too busy just trying to survive. I can waitress and tinker on the computer and speak French. Those are my life skills. Forget the glamorous host, the best I could be for him would be a PA!

Horsehead: His PA?? YES!

Top Step: No, I was joking. I can't do that, Horsehead.

Horsehead: You could, actually. And wouldn't it be the best sort of prank? You'd be the closest person to him day in and day out!

Top Step: No, I couldn't do it and I'd be completely exposed. He could link my name back to my dad.

Horsehead: Amateur! We'd lift you an identity.

Top Step: You can do that?

Horsehead: It's my bread and butter, doll. That's my job, right? I'm a white hat. Professionally I'm a good guy and I sort out online problems for businesses or private or whatever.

Top Step: Really?

Horsehead: Yep. But at night, I'm a black hat. You know what that means?

Top Step: You're a hacker?

Horsehead: Correct! And I like to play digital games. I'd need to do some jiggery-pokery on arranging for Jim Valente's current PA to not work there any more, but if I could do that, I'm in a good position to arrange for you to take that job.

Top Step: No, I really couldn't. He's seen me before.

Horsehead: Seen you?

Top Step: Briefly. I went to his house to return his credit card. He left it at the restaurant that I waitress at. That's what started the whole thing.

Horsehead: You think he'd remember you?

Top Step: I don't know? I suppose looks can be changed?

Horsehead: Now you're thinking. I could sort you references, if you give me basics, and then I'd handle your entire application.

Top Step: No, really. I couldn't. Also that would be a massive gamble for you.

Horsehead: I know how to cover my own tracks. I'm a maverick, doll. But you'd need to pay me, obviously.

Top Step: How much?

Horsehead: $1,000

Top Step: I don't have that sort of money, Horsehead. I'm sorry.

Horsehead: So take out a little loan. Or, you could pay me $400 upfront and then transfer the rest in weekly instalments. Could that work?

Top Step: I don't think I could do this. I don't know you.

Horsehead: You don't have to *know* me. You just have to trust me.

Top Step: Have you got . . .

Horsehead: References??! Ha! Is that what you were going to ask? References from revenge-happy clients?

Top Step: This is all a bit foreign to me.

Horsehead: Sure it is and if it was a friend asking if they should hand over $1000 to a guy I'd spoken to twice, I'd say, are you *insane,* brother?? But I'm legit. I actually am.

Top Step: How do I know?

Horsehead: Because I'm telling you. Listen, all you would need to do is give me a CV and a black and white photo of you and your middle name so I can send you a new ID. I'll do that for free, OK? And then you can see if I'm true to my word. If you like it, you send me $400 and away we go.

Top Step: Do you actually think this could work?

Horsehead: 'We are inclined to believe those whom we do not know because they have never deceived us.' Quote Samuel Johnson. Why don't you sit back and watch me do some magic?

Top Step: I've never done anything like this in my life.

Horsehead: That's what all the virgins on here say.

Top Step: What if I'm caught?

Horsehead: You won't get caught if I'm playing your fairy godmother.

Top Step: Or *The Godfather* after all?

Horsehead: Right! Fairy Godfather! Yes! Ha! I missed a trick there! But you won't. No, no. Your tricks are just beginning.

NINE

I'm thankful to close the front door behind me tonight. The last few nights I've been dreaming about Episode 32 and the look of devastation on my dad's face has etched inside my eyelids. I drifted throughout the shift today and made clumsy mistakes, which Wendy was forced to pick up for me.

'Would you get on the ball today?' she said. 'You've forgotten an entire main meal on table six.'

'I have?'

'Pork belly. I've just told the kitchen for you,' she sighed.

'Sorry, thank you.'

'And table fifteen are still waiting on their bill.'

I sift through the letters on the doormat, bunch my upstairs neighbours' together for them and take my own inside the flat, turn on the light and look at them. An electricity bill, a pizza pamphlet and then, something entirely different.

I blink. It's only been three days since my conversation with Horsehead, but I've been sent some post from the agent who looks after Pudding Cottage and I know what it is instantly. I didn't want to give Horsehead my address here in London, and definitely not Charlie's in the village, so I settled on the agency, who would forward anything to me. I open the small white jiffy bag and pull out an ID with a black and white picture of my face on it and a name along-side. Matilda Evans.

I sit at the kitchen table, which is dark save for a lamp in the corner of the room, and stare at the ID. What I'm proposing to take on feels immediate and suddenly very real. Horsehead can do this for me. Can I do it for myself?

I feel the urge to draw Jim; him and me, together.

When I was younger, I had a recurring nightmare where I had to hide under a table from a lion that was going to eat me. I told Dad one night as we sat on my bed in the dark and he cradled my head while I wiped my tears with the sleeve of my pyjama top.

'I've got an idea,' he said, and he went out of the room and came back with a pen and paper and switched on my bedside lamp.

'Not a story, Dad,' I groaned.

'Draw the lion,' he said, 'as a tiny kitten and then draw yourself as a warrior princess.'

'I can't draw, Dad.'

'Yes, you can,' he replied. 'It's in your genes, isn't it? It doesn't matter how good it is. In fact, the funnier it looks the better. Name the lion. What's he called?'

'I don't know?' I said.

'Gary?' he suggested. 'Nigel?'

I laughed. 'Nigel?'

'Nigel the lion isn't scary, is he?'

'No.'

He handed me the pen and the paper. 'Draw it. Anything in life that scares you, you draw it, you sing a silly song about it, you write about it. It makes it feel smaller.'

71

He patted my arm, left me with the paper, and I set to draw Nigel the lion. I drew him as a tiny cat wearing a bonnet and looking ridiculous. I laughed at it and after that I never had the nightmare again.

I start to draw Jim. I draw him as a micro man pinned to the ground with my boot heel. I draw him being flushed down a toilet, falling off a cliff. I draw fast, bold lines, get lost in this release, and then I lean back in my chair. He *does* deserve this anger and he *does* deserve my time and money in making him pay the price. This anger takes me to the memory of the last time I saw my dad and it's always unwelcome, always so vivid.

The sun had disappeared beyond the fields and a grey blanket of clouds was rolling in. I could smell rain in the air. I was supposed to be in the car with Uncle Charlie and Lissy and Dad was going to join us in the pub an hour away for the three-course Christmas lunch with cousins over from Canada. But at the last minute I'd pleaded with Charlie to leave me at Pudding Cottage.

'I'll drive with Dad,' I'd said, standing on the driveway with Charlie. 'I don't want him to be lonely in the car. And he might forget to set the alarm. Or leave the door unlocked.'

He'd done both previously and the truth was that I was worried about him because he had been acting increasingly strangely, switching from erratically happy to morose in a matter of seconds. I'd caught him looking at pictures of Mum and at newspaper cuttings of Christopher Barrows, and whenever I'd see the latter, the knot of guilt I'd carried in my stomach since it happened tightened its hold.

Charlie rolled his mouth, unsure. 'He was saying he wanted to finish his chapter and meet us at the pub, El.'

'I'll be quiet, Charlie,' I replied. 'I'll walk down to the stream and give Dad an hour for his book. And then I'll come back and we can meet you.'

Charlie glanced back at the car, where Lissy was sitting and staring out of the window at us and looking impatient.

'OK,' Charlie said. 'See you there, girl.'

I didn't go back in to tell Dad I was staying. Instead, I walked straight to the stream and, in the pale light before the rain came, I played Poohsticks with myself and spoke to the birds that landed on the branches above me. I took out the little toy horse I had in my pocket, galloped it up and down the riverbank, until the mud stuck to its plastic legs and made it too heavy. I cleaned it with leaves. I watched for the heron who sometimes came looking for fish, though it didn't come that day.

I was out there for a long time before I thought to look at my watch. When I did, I saw that almost two hours had passed. My heart quickened. Had Dad left without me? If he hadn't, we were definitely going to be late for the lunch.

I remember the sound of my trainers on the grass and the mud. Soft, squelching thuds. I ran into the house, kicked my shoes off and went up the stairs and called his name, but there was no answer. I went down again, still calling, and opened the kitchen door. Then my breath was snatched away from me.

It wasn't supposed to be me who found him lying face down on the table – I guess we'll never know who Dad intended that to be – but I was the one. I must have called 999, must have called Uncle Charlie, but I can't remember any of that. I only remember screaming and clawing at my own face with my nails and then collapsing to the floor and wrapping myself around Dad's leg. Did the paramedics unwrap me from that position? Did Uncle Charlie?

I lay my pencil down on the page, stare at Jim's face and then back to the ID. I'm going to do it; I'm going to pay Horsehead his $1000 and I'm going to try to get into Cyclops.

I've run to Belgravia again and I stretch my legs down the street from the house.

It's been three days since I sent Horsehead the money. He hasn't been in touch since I transferred it and now I feel foolish because the chances are that he's cut and run and I'm never going to be able to hurt Jim the way he's hurt me. But what if he is legitimate? What if he's trying to find a way to remove Jim's current PA?

I've been looking at her profile on their company website; she's called Christine and she looks smart and she looks nice, so how on earth would Horsehead go about getting rid of her? And if he was successful, how would he manipulate it so that I got an interview? How good would he have to be to fool Jim's HR team and how good would I have to be to fool Jim in order to get the job? Could I really work alongside him every day without exposing who I really am? The thought causes my heart to skip. How could I be in such close proximity, knowing what I know?

I daydream about the possibilities of what I could do if I worked with him. Tear up all his schedules? Send him to false meetings? Cancel all his important client dinners? Leak information about his actors? I could unearth secret love affairs, I could muck up a crucial deal, I could embarrass him in front of significant others. But these small things would mean I could be very easily caught out and thrown out of the company. Besides, if I want to do something big, I'd need to bed in and be clever.

I hear a door open and see a woman and a young boy coming out of the Valentes' house. The boy must be Benjamin, Jim's son. I turn my head until they're walking away from me and I start to walk after them.

'We will be late,' says the woman. I remember her from the first time I saw Jim at his door. She took the little dog, Gertie, back into the house so she couldn't run out to me. Her accent is Eastern European and she is heavily built, tall and blocky with smooth hair slicked into a neat bun at the nape of her neck.

'It's a pool, Sylvie,' the boy says cheerfully.

Sylvie, that was her name.

The boy bounces along beside her. His hair is dark, floppy. He's wearing shorts and a sweatshirt, despite the cold. She's dressed in a coat, but it's short and I can see she's wearing cycling shorts and trainers on her feet.

'I need to be back for eleven,' she says. 'And start on lunch, yes? Why do we have this conversation every week? The butcher is coming this morning with the beef.'

'OK,' he says.

'And your mother needs the vitamins on the way back. We must stop at the pharmacy.'

'Yup,' he replies. He swings his bag on his arm, scuffs it on the ground.

'And she needs me to arrange the flowers for next week, all right? I cannot forget. Do not let me.'

I think she must be a nanny or a housekeeper. Whoever she is, she sounds like she runs a tight ship.

75

'Yup,' he says again. He seems apparently used to this running commentary.

'Do not drag your bag, Benji,' she scolds. 'That one was expensive, yes?'

'I've got three the same,' he says blithely.

She shakes her head.

'Your father is at golf until four,' she continues. 'He will miss you going back to school.'

He shrugs. 'That's OK,' he says. 'He's never around when I go back.'

'No,' she replies, and then she puts her hand to his head. 'We will get ice cream after swimming, yes?'

He looks up at her and smiles. 'An ice cream?'

'You think I should not spoil you?' she says, and smiles back at him.

They walk up to Wilton Place and, after three minutes, we all arrive in front of the doors of The Berkeley Hotel and Spa. They stride in and leave me gazing after them in awe and then I feel a vibration from the pocket of my leggings. I take out my phone. It's a message from Horsehead.

Top Step: You got me an interview??

Horsehead: I did.

Top Step: But it's only been a few days since I sent you the money!

Horsehead: What can I say? I'm a very efficient worker. His PA is gone and important, busy people need PAs quick.

Top Step: Oh my God! Are you serious?

Horsehead: Deadly.

Top Step: What happened to the PA, Horsehead?

Horsehead: Let's just say that people should be more careful with their profiles online. There was a HR issue with some of her media posts. Some comments about the company, a leak here and there about finances.

Top Step: You hacked her social media accounts?

Horsehead: I might have done.

Top Step: Do I want to know how you get to do these things?

Horsehead: Probably best not to ask.

Top Step: Nothing dodgy?

Horsehead: Are you listening to yourself? Of course it's dodgy! (LOVE that word btw!) But a gentleman never tells.

Top Step: Are you a gentleman?

Horsehead: How you wound me, doll! And we barely know each other.

Top Step: But nothing you said was true on her account, was it? It couldn't have been?

Horsehead: Ah, but the mere suggestion of going against your boss or his company was enough. A man like Jim wouldn't like it if people spoke against what he holds close, right? No one does, but especially not an alpha male like that. It's about pushing buttons. In this case, quite literally.

Top Step: But she'll defend herself, surely?

Horsehead: Of course she will. She probably did. But he fired her anyway.

Top Step: I feel a bit . . . numb? Shocked. It's been, I don't know, five weeks since I saw him in the restaurant and it's turned my life upside down.

Horsehead: People's lives can change in a matter of moments. Surely you of all people know that. But you can do this, OK?

Top Step: OK.

Horsehead: I'm pinging you the CV I wrote you. Open it.

Top Step: OK.

Horsehead: You got it?

Top Step: I worked at a publisher in the US?

Horsehead: Correct. A tiny independent called Squid Ink. In Boston. And guess who's the CEO?

Top Step: You?

Horsehead: Me. And I've given you an awesome reference.

Top Step: You've made up a whole company??

Horsehead: A little website smokescreen. Nothing fancy. Borrowed a few authors and books from other places, nothing he'll recognize and I doubt he'd do the research.

Top Step: What about HR? They'd do the research.

Horsehead: HR is a stretched department in every company I've ever known. Maybe it's different over in the UK, but I doubt it. They'll check out the website most likely, but they're busy people, right? They're not going to check up on authors, especially US ones that don't have established names in the UK. I've kept everything else as close to the truth as possible. Your name is Matilda, as per the ID, your real middle name, and you'll see that you went to France for school, etc. etc. Now, listen. I've done the best I can do in deleting applicants, but I can't delete them all and leave little old you, because that would be too obvious. There are five people in the running.

Top Step: You hacked the application process??

Horsehead: Cyclops use an independent recruitment website. That was the easiest bit.

Top Step: What if the other applicants have loads of experience?

Horsehead: They haven't, because I deleted those ones. Now, you need a cover story about your personal life.

Top Step: My personal life? You think he'll ask me about that?

Horsehead: Yes! Smarten up, doll. Right, I've done my bit, now it's your turn. You gotta ACT because this could be the moment the tide turns for you.

Top Step: Have you got any advice??

Horsehead: Laugh, because a rich man's joke is always funny.

I leave the restaurant after my lunch shift and go to a store that I googled last night after my conversation with Horsehead.

'Looks good, that one,' the proprietor says.

I stare at myself. The eyes in the mirror are my eyes, the nose and lips are mine, but the wig has changed me completely. A short, dark, sleek bob accentuates my jawline and my cheekbones. I look like a 1940s cabaret dancer.

'You're lucky to have dark eyebrows and eyelashes, being a redhead,' she says. She holds up the soft brown wig, long and silky with a fringe. It matches the texture of my own hair. 'You wanted to try this one as well?'

I nod and take it from her, though I'm reluctant to remove the bobbed wig because I like it so much. It's like I've been given a second chance to be someone else. Is that what I want to do? To become someone else, or to live the life I should have led if Jim hadn't taken my father away?

'Yes please,' I say.

The proprietor smiles, pleased. 'What's your party on the weekend then?' she asks.

'Bond theme,' I reply as I lay the bob down and begin tucking my hair into the brown wig.

The shop owner takes a hairpin, secures it for me and then lets the brown hair fall softly around my shoulders. It's beautiful, shiny and soft with a thick fringe, and I run my fingers through the hair.

'Cute,' she says. 'A bit Miss Moneypenny. You could team it up with a little suit and heels and glasses?'

'It's really nice,' I say.

'And I'll fetch you the blonde one from the window you wanted to look at.'

I play with the brown wig in the mirror, tie it up, let it down again. Is it the right one for an interview? The fringe really changes my face, hides more of me and my scar, of course, and that brings me confidence. Could I be the person that I came up with last night in this wig? A young woman who worked for a company in Boston, who has a brother called Tom, who likes baking cakes and who is called Matilda Evans?

'Here,' the woman says, holding the blonde wig out for me. 'This will change you entirely.'

I put it on.

'Wow,' she exclaims. 'I like that a lot.'

I'm surprised that I like it too. Darker roots with beach blonde hair, wavy and thick to my shoulders. Who could I be in this? I think. Someone wild, who says outrageous things and sings on crowded buses without a care in the world? Someone like Lissy?

The owner picks up the other two wigs, strokes them. 'You can curl all of these pieces and straighten them if you're careful. And you can wash them normally, too. That's why they're much more expensive than your average party-shop wig.'

It's like I've put on three different personalities in the space of twenty minutes.

'I'll take all three,' I say. 'For all eventualities.'

Though what those might be, I don't yet know.

TEN

'Here we go,' the Uber driver says.

The wipers screech on the car's windscreen as I look through it and up at the building in front of us. It appears dramatic and foreboding, with its tall, glass-panelled exterior having taken on the moody grey of the sky, at odds with the stone buildings around it.

'Can you come back for me?' I ask the driver.

'You can call another car, love,' he replies.

'But can you . . . would you wait for me?' I say.

I don't really know why I'm asking this of him. Maybe because this man seems nice and is smiling back at me from the rear-view mirror. He's middle-aged and his eyes are owl-brown and kind-looking. He told me stories as we drove through the streets; about his pick-ups, his obsession with Lenny Kravitz, and his sister who collects seashells.

'How long are you going to be?' he asks.

'I don't know,' I say.

'Listen, if I'm still about, you can call me if you need a lift home, yeah?' He reaches to his glovebox, takes out a card and twists around. His leather jacket squeaks against the seat. 'Here.'

I take the card. 'Thanks,' I say and glance down at it, 'Euey.'

'No problem,' he replies.

'I'm Eleanor,' I say.

'OK, Eleanor.' He smiles.

I open the car door and walk to the entrance of the building. Although it's cold, I'm sweating with worry that Jim might recognise me from that one moment we had just over a month ago at his door. I told him my name. I wish I hadn't done that. This morning, I spent half an hour caking on make-up to hide my freckles and the scar on my forehead, despite most of it being covered by the fringe of the wig. I've fastened on the wig within an inch of its life, and it's hot. The confidence I felt in the store is failing me. The wig, which looks soft and brown on the surface, claws at my scalp; the fringe, which had made me feel hidden and strong, now feels hot and sticky against my forehead. I rearrange it over my shoulders, once, twice, three times, because I'm so nervous.

There's a security guard on the door dressed in a black suit, and a girl about my age behind a white gloss reception desk tapping away on a keyboard. She's wearing a headset and I can tell she's listening to music because she's rocking her head to a beat. Behind her on a matt-black wall is a six-foot silver eye, the same logo I found on the letter to my dad.

'Hi,' I say, tentatively. 'I'm Matilda Evans. I'm here to see Mr Valente.'

She removes an earphone and nods. 'Sure. Take a seat.'

'Thanks,' I say, and sit on one of the bright blue sofas. Like his eyes, I think. I glance back at the huge Cyclops eye on the wall. His eyes are everywhere.

The coffee table in front of me and the doors are all glass and white gloss finish. There is deco lighting and tall plants, black and white photographs of programmes, actors and directors on the walls. It's overwhelming, intimidating. I wring my hands, sit on them and then drum them on my knees – do anything to try to distract myself.

'Matilda Evans?'

That's me. I have to remember that's my name now. I look to the receptionist, who points to double doors behind me, and I stand up. I hope I don't slip up with remembering my name. What if I tell someone my real name by mistake? How would I cover it? A tidal wave of anxiety rolls over me. I haven't even made it out of the lobby yet.

'Second door on the left,' the receptionist says. 'Yolanda from HR will meet you and take you to Mr Valente.'

She presses a button so that a glass barrier opens for me and I walk through it and push open a door, where a young woman greets me wearing a black suit, a red shirt and a smile.

'In here,' she says and she opens another door.

I take a deep breath. He's in here and there's no going back now. I follow her through and there he is, sitting behind a table with my CV in front of him.

'Mr Valente,' Yolanda says. 'This is Matilda.'

I lock eyes with him. He's here, he's real and I am quaking in front of him. My mouth has gone dry but I can't lose my nerve now. I have to act, step outside of myself, become someone else. Yes, I'm Matilda Evans and I worked for Squid Ink, I have a brother called Tom, I like to bake cakes. I lived in France.

'Hello, Mr Valente,' I say, and step forward and hold out my hand.

Jim takes me in, a sweep of my body with his eyes as he did the first time we met, and I stiffen again under this physical scrutiny but keep my eyes focused on him. I'm wearing a high-collar white shirt, high-waisted black trousers and blue heels. He pauses at the heels before snapping his eyes upwards again.

'Welcome, Matilda,' he smiles. 'Call me Jim.'

He takes my offered hand, winks at me.

'Sit,' he says.

I sit down in front of him and Yolanda takes a seat beside him. There's a glass of water on the table in front of me and it's cold as I reach for it and even colder on my teeth as I drink it.

He tilts his head at me, parts his lips slightly.

'I recognise you,' he says.

Adrenaline is pumping through my body so hard that I think he must be able to see the veins in my neck throbbing.

'Have you auditioned for me before?' he asks.

'No,' I say. 'I'm a terrible actor.'

But I've never acted so hard in my life. Jim laughs but doesn't say anything for a moment and I'm chewing the inside of my mouth, can feel the flesh begin to soften. I know it'll hurt later on, but I can't stop myself. I'm screaming inside my head. It's all over before it began.

'Oh,' he says with a shrug and he looks down at the CV in front of him.

I swallow. Is that it? He's taken my answer about never seeing me before as the truth? Breathe, I tell myself.

'I can see that you've already worked for a CEO,' he continues. 'In Boston?'

'Yes,' I say. 'I like to travel.'

'And why did you move back?' he asks.

'I saw and did a lot of things out there and I gained a lot of different experiences and perspectives. But it was time to get my teeth into something bigger back home.'

He raises an eyebrow. 'Something bigger meaning Cyclops?'

'I saw the advert on a website and I thought it looked like too good an opportunity to miss,' I say.

He nods.

'What do you know about the company, Matilda?' Yolanda asks.

'I know that it was founded in 2002 by three guys uploading skits and sketches from their basements online for their friends,' I reply. 'Their ideas earned them viewers and a great reputation. I've seen Markus and Sean give a lot of interviews online.'

'Those two were the showmen,' Jim nods. 'They were smart with what they did and they got a lot of attention and that attracted private investors. I was one of them and joined them in 2003.' Here he smiles. 'It went from three people and now we have over two hundred. Most are freelancers, of course, that's the nature of the game in production, but I pay people well and they like to keep coming back. I get people on good contracts. Speaks volumes about the company's faith in employees.'

'Can you tell us about your last boss, Matilda?' Yolanda says.

I think of Horsehead. 'He's very talented,' I comment. 'Organised and efficient.'

And fraudulent.

'He said the same about you,' Jim says. 'We've had correspondence over email.'

I would smile if I wasn't feeling so terrified. Oh my God. Jim does his homework. Has Horsehead managed to cover his tracks? What about the website he made for Squid Ink? Would Jim have pored over that, too?

'What did you like about working for him?' he asks.

I clear my throat. 'He taught me business ethics, relationship building, how departments work together,' I say.

'And you think you can learn from me?' Jim says.

'Yes,' I reply.

'What do you think I can teach you?'

I look at him coolly. 'Anything you want to,' I say.

'And why in this industry?' Yolanda asks, glancing sideways at Jim, whose lips have curled upwards into a wolf-like smile at me.

'Because it has edge,' I say. 'Glamour.'

'The world of television production *is* glamorous,' Jim says. 'But behind the glamour is grit. It can be demanding.'

'I like a professional challenge,' I reply.

'And *I* can be demanding,' he continues.

'I like a personal challenge,' I say.

I'm waiting to crumble at any moment and give myself up, but Jim smiles at that because I've amused him. I take a sip of the water and try to calm my heart rate.

He studies me for a moment. 'This job is demanding, but it can be dull as hell,' he says. 'And you seem like you've got a bit of spirit about you. Your boss in Boston seemed to think so. You think I should employ you above the others? Give me the reason.'

'I have a fetish for printers?' I say.

He laughs that loud booming laugh that I remember first hearing at The Cello; his whole face is transformed by this golden smile.

'We'll see then, shall we, kid?' he says. 'When can you start?'

I blink. 'What?'

'Start?' Yolanda says at the same time.

Jim nods. 'I'm a busy man and I have no more time to be wasting on interviews. Yolanda, this kid is the best of the bunch so far.'

Yolanda clears her throat. 'Jim, we have the final applicant waiting in the lobby—'

'But I like *this* one, Yolanda. She's smart, and she made me laugh,' Jim says. 'You know how I like to laugh, so you'll deal with the applicant most delicately, won't you?'

She pauses. 'I will,' she replies.

He turns his blue eyes on to me. 'Provided you accept, obviously. You want the job, yes?'

'I do,' I say.

He nods. 'Yolanda will get you a contract on your way out. You'll start on Monday. Have a good weekend.'

I look at Yolanda, who has her eyebrows raised at Jim, but she smiles at me widely when she realises I'm looking at her. 'Congratulations,' she says.

Is it? I wonder.

She stands up, opens the door for me and I go to follow her.

'One more thing,' Jim says, and both of us turn at the doorway. 'It said on your CV that you speak French, Matilda?'

'Yes,' I reply.

He smiles. 'I like that.'

I wait for him to say more, but he doesn't. He turns to the window and I understand that I'm dismissed.

I stagger out of the building, try to gulp in breaths of cold air because it feels like I've been suffocated of oxygen. I walk down to Embankment Gardens and lean my head against the cold black iron railings to try to quiet my mind.

This is all for you, Dad. I have to be strong to do this for you. And for me.

I don't know how long I'm there before someone touches my shoulder.

'Are you all right?'

I turn my head to see a woman with smart, short black hair in a blue coat. She is looking at me, concerned.

'I'm fine, thank you,' I say and I step away from the railings, wobble on my heels.

A few paces down the pathway, I get out my phone and call Euey. He picks up after three rings.

'Euey,' I say. 'It's Eleanor, you dropped me off at the Cyclops building this morning.'

'All right, love? How are you doing?'

'Can you come and get me?' I ask. I don't really know why I'm asking. To see a friendly face? And what does it say about me if the friendly face is an Uber driver whom I first met only hours ago?

'I'm dropping someone at Warren Street,' he says. 'Where are you?'

'I'm going to walk to Trafalgar Square. Can you come there?'

'Give me ten minutes?'

'OK,' I say.

I walk out of the park and up Villiers Street, manage to get to Trafalgar Square, where I perch on the edge of the wall and stare at the huge lion fountains. Ten minutes later, a horn beeps.

'You all right?' Euey asks as I climb inside.

'Yes,' I say. 'No.'

I catch his eyes in the rear-view mirror.

'I'm not really sure I know what I'm doing.'

'Nor do any of us, love,' he says. 'That's life, isn't it?'

ELEVEN

I wait until the end of my Friday-night shift before I tell David that I'm leaving.

We sit at the bar, where Pavel darts around like a hummingbird, cleaning and positioning glasses. The restaurant is empty of diners, but we can hear the kitchen staff laughing while doing the clean-up, and Wendy and Kobi are setting out for the lunchtime service tomorrow. David drinks a cold white wine and I drink gin. The lime is fresh in my mouth and the ice is cooling. I can't even taste the alcohol, but I know Pavel poured me a double.

'You wanted to talk to me?' David says.

'Yes,' I say. 'I'm handing in my resignation.'

I slide a letter on the bar towards him and I'm sad as I do it. The restaurant has been my security blanket for five years and the people in it have been warm to me, even when I've held them at arm's-length.

He stares at me. '*Pourquoi*?'

'I've got a new job,' I reply.

'A new job where?' he asks.

'Not waitressing,' I say, but I don't offer him any more.

David taps the letter with his thumb and sighs. 'I knew I would not be able to keep you here for ever,' he says. 'You are too smart.'

'That's sweet of you to say,' I reply. I'm flattered that he could think of me as some sort of pearl waiting to be scooped out of the silt and shucked.

'Is there anything I can do to change your mind?' David asks. 'A promotion?'

I shake my head. Finding Jim, the letters between him and my dad, Horsehead. One by one, they've all opened my eyes, and I can't ignore them.

'David, thank you,' I say, 'but I've accepted this new role. It would be unfair for me to go back on it.'

'I wish you had told me you were unhappy,' he says, and he sounds hurt. He drinks his wine.

'I wasn't,' I reply. I feel like I'm breaking up with him. 'I'm sorry, David, really.'

He nods. 'You want to try new things, *oui*?'

'I guess that's it,' I say. 'I can work nights for as long as you need me to.'

'When do you start your new job?' he asks.

I grimace. 'Monday. I'm sorry.'

'Oh,' he says. '*Oui*, that is soon, isn't it? You cannot do two jobs. I can juggle the shifts.'

'I can work some weekends,' I offer, but he shakes his head.

'That is OK,' he says, smiling at me.

'I'm sorry to do this to you.'

'We will miss you,' he adds. 'You are a real solid part of the team, *oui*?'

'Thanks,' I say, because I'm genuinely touched at his words.

'I will organise a leaving party,' he says, and stands up.

'No, no. Please don't do that.'

'Let me,' he says. He puts a hand to my arm and I let him. 'I want everyone to be able to say a proper goodbye. Does Wendy know?'

'Does Wendy know what?' Wendy says and sits down beside me.

'I'm leaving the restaurant,' I say.

'You're doing what now?'

'An office job,' I say. 'I applied for it and I . . . I got it.'

'Aren't you the dark horse?' she says. 'Office job? Sounds *sparkling*.'

She laughs and so do I and then I'm suddenly overwhelmingly sad to be leaving them.

'There will always be a place for you here,' David says. 'You know this, *oui*? You are family.'

Lissy has come to see me in London for the weekend and we walk from Hyde Park to the Serpentine and sit on the bench overlooking the trees and the high-rises of Kensington and Knightsbridge. This was one of Dad's favourite places to come and so we visit regularly, enjoying the view throughout the seasons.

Lissy looks out at the still water. 'Will you tell me again,' she says quietly. 'Tell me Dad's story about the trolls and the goats.'

I smile. A favourite story of ours. Lissy used to make Dad and me tell it over and over.

'You know the troll story as well as I do,' I say.

'But I like the way you tell it,' she replies. 'Because you were there.'

I look to the island in the middle of the lake, where the trees are dense, and I recall the conversation with Dad when I was seven.

'OK,' I say, and I begin the story.

'Who lives there?' I had asked Dad as we walked the park that summer.

'Trolls,' Dad answered without a pause in thought. 'Banished from the park to live in misery and squalor on the isle.'

I remember that even at seven I threw him a look of disdain. 'Trolls aren't real, Dad.'

He looked wounded. 'They are. And goblins and faeries.'

'Do they live on the island too?'

'No, no,' Dad replied, as if I'd said something ridiculous. 'Only the trolls and the odd goat to keep them in check.'

'Like the story,' I smiled.

'Billy Goats Gruff was no story, Ellie,' Dad said. 'It's legend. The biggest defeat in Troll history.'

Lissy laughs. Sometimes, when I'm retelling our stories, I'm pained thinking about him and our years together. As if she realises, Lissy takes my hand and together we look at that island. I wonder if the trolls are in there, huddled up, all of them frightened of the goats that are patrolling.

'I love that story,' she sighs. 'I loved all his stories.'

'That's the beauty of a good storyteller,' I say. 'Taking people with you.'

'He didn't take us with him on his final chapter though,' she whispers.

I look at her. 'No,' I say. 'He went where we couldn't follow.'

'Do you ever get angry?' she asks. 'About what he did?'

'I get very angry,' I reply.

'I write to get rid of my anger,' she says. 'What do you do? Paint? Why don't you draw more, El? You're so good, you could *do* something with it.'

I ignore this, look to the lake. 'I used to put my anger in a box,' I admit. 'But I've decided not to do that any more.'

She looks at me curiously, but I stand up.

'I'm going to leave The Cello,' I announce.

She stands too. 'You're leaving the restaurant? Why? What are you doing?'

'Getting myself out of the box,' I say.

TWELVE

I thought it would be Yolanda or someone else junior who would walk me through the different floors of the building, but to my surprise it's Jim himself who introduces me to his departments. He places his hand on the small of my back, steers me like I'm his ventriloquist's dummy, and I can feel the heat of him against my skin through the blouse I'm wearing. I'm holding my coat and wish I could put it on again so I don't have to feel his fingers on me.

His teams are loud and vibrant and they all wear the creative uniform: skinny jeans and pointy shoes and short skirts and boots and big hair and thick-rimmed glasses, individually exactly the same. Their pods are littered with tiny designer coffee machines and papers and coloured pens and plants. There are toy animals, Lego characters stuck on screens, Post-its. Everyone is friendly; they wave and they smile, but of course they would smile, because Jim is behind me and he's watching them.

We have a tour of five floors before he takes me up to the top of the building, to a small square roof terrace that overlooks the river. The stone tiles are a beautiful dove-belly grey and in the centre of them is a white metal table and four chairs. Lining the glass barrier and along the sides are a haphazard collection of vast terracotta pots: winter heather, ornamental purple cabbage and thin dogwood which stems upwards in a firework display of oranges and reds.

'This is only for my use,' Jim says. 'Look at the view.'

His hand is still on my back and I turn to face him so that it drops off.

'It's lovely,' I reply.

His chest is inches from me, but he doesn't move back. Instead, he leans across me.

'See the London Eye? I like to think it's the Cyclops eye mirrored over the river.'

'Yes,' I say. I don't want to breathe because inflating my lungs will mean my chest making contact with his.

'You wait,' he says, and he beckons me back towards the lift. 'My floor is the best of all. Let's take the stairs.'

We walk down two short flights of stairs and arrive at the seventh floor, the end of the tour. Jim has the entire top floor of the building and it's made up of a huge entrance hall with white marble flooring and white walls and a colossal office straight ahead. His PA's desk – my desk – is on guard outside it, with a tall filing cabinet behind it and a smaller cabinet with a printer on top. Further along is a grey sofa for waiting clients and a bathroom opposite.

'Wow,' I exclaim.

'Hang your coat there,' he says, and gestures to a black coat stand outside his door.

'You've built yourself a wonderful place,' I say.

'And how does that make you feel?' he asks. 'Being part of it?'

'Privileged,' I say because that's what he'll want to hear.

He smiles at me and looks pleased.

'You're the face of the company and myself,' he says, and gestures for me to come into his striped frosted-and-clear-glass office. 'Here's my office.'

We walk inside and immediately a little dog shoots towards me like a rocket.

'Oh, yes,' Jim smiles. 'Matilda, meet Gertie my dog.'

I remember this dog from when she bolted at me through Jim's door in Belgravia. She's small and dainty and covered in fluffy honey-coloured fur and she barks excitedly.

'She's a German Spitz,' Jim says.

'She's lovely,' I reply, and go to stroke her head. A little bell chimes from the collar she is wearing that I can't even see beneath the thick fur. 'Hi, girl.'

'She likes you,' he says, as she licks at my fingers. 'And she's very particular, aren't you, mutt?'

'Does she come here all the time? You don't leave her at home with Lucinda?' I ask. 'Or Sylvie?'

As soon as I've said it, I know it was a mistake. Jim looks at me oddly.

'Sylvie is your . . .' I gabble. 'Housekeeper? Is that right?'

'She is,' he says.

'I read about her in an article,' I say, trying to sound casual.

'Good to know you've researched,' he replies. He looks back at Gertie. 'Lucinda doesn't like the dog – hates her, actually. And Sylvie is allergic to dogs. Which is why I have her with me most days, except for Wednesdays. We have cleaners then and they can take her out and it frees me up a bit. I like her here.' He bends down, scratches behind Gertie's ears. 'She's my confidante. Knows everything.'

'Oh,' I say.

He straightens. 'Come inside,' he says.

In the centre of his office is a solid black wooden desk, on top of which sits a large white Apple monitor, along with an in-tray and several hefty-looking files. Behind it is a huge white filing cabinet, and shelves lined with countless books and awards and more files. There is a big yucca plant in one corner, a charcoal sofa on one side by the window, with a huge silver-framed mirror hanging above it. Everywhere there are framed stills of shows on the walls and I think some must be of *Pranksters*, but I haven't ever seen any episodes other than 32. I realise that I should have done my homework; I'll have to watch some so I can pass any questions Jim might test me on.

'You're the barrier between me and the people who want to see me,' Jim says. He nods to the sofa and I sit, but he remains standing above me. 'That's an enormous amount of power to hold. The people you need to free my time for are the heads of departments: Marketing, Finance, Writers, Production, Sales, Concepts.'

'Do I have an allotted time with you?' I ask.

He looks at me. 'You can see me whenever you want. You run my life here. I have to see you whenever you say so.'

The way he smiles at me when he says this makes my skin itch.

'I'll schedule fifteen minutes in with you every day. Does ten o'clock suit?'

'You tell me,' he says pointedly.

We fall into a silence and my heart is thudding so loudly that I think he might be able to hear it. Gertie jumps up at me.

'What can I help you with first, Mr Valente?' I ask.

He laughs softly. 'I wasn't planning to call you Miss Evans for the duration,' he says. 'Unless that's something you like?'

I bite my lip. 'Er?'

'Call me Jim,' he replies. 'And I'll call you Matilda. Yes?'

I take a breath and smile brightly, though my chest is tight. 'Yes,' I say. 'So what can I help you with first, Jim?'

He smiles, nods and then hands me a list of paper from his desk. 'Actually,' he says, 'I want you to pick your favourite name.'

The paper has twelve names on it, with their roles but nothing more. I look at him, but he nods at me encouragingly.

'My disciples,' he says. 'Who's your favourite?'

'My favourite?'

'What's the best name on there?'

I look back at the paper. 'I suppose Justin Goldstein is a nice name?' I say. 'Junior marketing manager.'

'Excellent. We'll start with Justin then. Can you call him in?'

'Sure.'

'And Yolanda from HR.'

'OK.'

'Poor Justin. It's always tough for the first one.'

I frown. 'First one to what?'

'Get fired.'

I stare at him. 'You're going to fire him?'

'The others on the list follow,' he adds. 'Set up half-hour slots with each of them and Yolanda until lunchtime. I run a tight ship, you understand? An agile company needs to be lean and efficient. There's no room for dead wood.'

I swallow hard, feeling guilty towards Justin even though I've never met him.

I get up from the sofa to leave Jim's office.

'I like coffee in the morning, Matilda,' he says quietly, and I turn to face him again. 'And I like efficiency. I like people going the extra mile. I want you to ensure that nothing is ever an issue, everything is fine, you hear me? I want to reschedule that meeting that you spent all yesterday fixing up for fifteen people to attend? No problem. I want you to pick me up a coffee while you run down to the press office? Absolutely you will. I haven't got time to order the Christmas present for my father from Fortnum & Mason? You'll do it for me, of course. You'll pick up my dry cleaning, my wife's vitamins from the pharmacy. You'll flirt with my clients, you'll tease my staff, but you'll be aloof and detached. You are here to reflect me. You're charming, attractive, ruthless. Prove yourself indispensable. Understand?'

I feel sick. 'I understand,' I say.

'And I like pink lipstick.'

'Sorry?'

'Pink lipstick,' he repeats. 'You need pink lipstick. Think of it like a uniform.' He winks at me. 'Compulsory.'

I don't know if he's joking or not.

'OK,' I say.

I walk out of his office and go to sit at my shiny white desk outside. I look at him through the glass, leaning back in his leather chair and smiling at me. I force myself to smile back at him and then I breathe out. I boot up my computer, put the phone headset on and hunt out Justin Goldstein's extension number.

I'm exhausted after my first day. I've spent my time setting up my systems, learning names, grappling with the amount of corporate jargon Jim throws at me through the door when he wants something but doesn't explain it.

The woman at the till at the pharmacy takes the lipsticks from me to scan them. 'We have a fiver off perfumes, diffusers and colognes,' she says, dully, and goes to hand me a voucher.

'No thanks,' I start, and wave it away, but then I close my mouth and take it from her. 'Actually, yes, I'll take a look.'

Top Step: Today has been one of the most difficult things I've ever done.

Horsehead: You OK?

Top Step: He makes me feel sick and I don't really know what I'm doing there. I feel like I'm living in some sort of film.

Horsehead: What was he like?

Top Step: Authoritative. Considered. Intelligent.

Horsehead: Hot damn, that's a good three words. What would mine be? So, fucking, sexy. Oh, that was easy.

Top Step: I was so scared, Horsehead. The whole time. I really don't know if I can do this.

Horsehead: It's natural to feel anxious, doll. You're way out of your comfort zone and it feels dangerous, right? But you did it and now it can get even more interesting! Take your time and look for things you can easily sabotage. Meeting confusion, send him the wrong way in a cab, cancel a lunch, whatever.

Top Step: I did think of things like that, but I don't want to get fired for incompetence.

Horsehead: But you can have some fun! Walk the tightrope of the thin line (and all other similes).

Top Step: You're a literature nerd as well as an IT nerd?

Horsehead: Not literature. Can't spel.

Top Step: I've decided on two things. One – I need to make friends here and, two – I need access to all of Jim's emails – so I need to befriend the IT crowd.

Horsehead: Nice, doll! You're thinking right. IT is the HUB of a company.

Top Step: Is it strange that I've spoken more words to you than anyone else for a long, long time?

Horsehead: Does that mean we're soulmates?

Top Step: Do you believe in that?

Horsehead: Sure! For larks, why not?

THIRTEEN

I know Jim likes the lipstick because when I arrive at the office the next day he stares at my lips and then smiles to himself like he's won a prize. It makes me feel unclean.

'I was joking about the lipstick,' he says.

'Oh,' I reply. 'That was a test?'

'Not really,' he says. 'But if it had been, you passed with flying colours.'

I'm embarrassed. Is that what he wanted? To embarrass me?

'I'm a joker,' he smiles.

I nod, wipe at the lipstick. 'I see.'

He opens a drawer of his huge desk. 'This is my trinket drawer,' he explains. 'All my little gems are in here.' He pulls out some huge red shoes. 'I'm a clown.'

I recognise them immediately. 'Are those . . . those are used in the *Pranksters* episodes.'

'That's right,' he says. 'It's my favourite show and these are my favourite prop. I keep them here. And soon, with the new series launching again, they'll be out to play once more!'

I bite on my tongue hard as I watch him kick off his loafers, slip on the clown shoes and flop around the office in them. He's expecting me to laugh, but my throat has constricted because I'm thinking about Episode 32, how my dad didn't see them, how he only saw the little girl in trouble.

'You don't like them?' Jim asks.

I force myself to laugh like Horsehead told me. 'They suit you,' I say.

'The trick of being a good CEO,' he says, walking circles around his desk, 'is to keep everyone on their toes. Be the smartest, be the funniest, be the most ruthless. Keep them all guessing, yes?' He smiles at me. 'Do you have any surprises, Matilda?'

I swallow. 'No,' I reply.

'No dark sides?'

'No,' I say quietly.

'Well, that's good *and* bad,' he remarks. 'I like a good girl. But everyone has shades of grey, don't they?'

I clear my throat. 'I got you a present last night, Jim,' I say, and hand him a bag. 'So I do have a sort of surprise.'

Jim looks amused. 'A little early in our relationship for presents, isn't it?'

'It's a thank you for hiring me,' I explain.

He looks into the bag and then up at me. 'Sandalwood?' He takes the diffuser out of the bag. 'I like sandalwood.'

'You do?' I feign amazement.

He nods. 'It's a good present.'

I offer my hand for the diffuser. 'Shall I plug it in for you?'

He nods. 'Over there.'

I laugh gaily, walk over to the plug and bend over, knowing he's watching.

I'm doing this for you, Dad, I think. Yet even though I've set out to avenge him, I know Dad would be so ashamed of me if he could see this – his daughter in a skirt inches above her knees, pink lipstick smeared on her lips and bending over in front of a man who looks at her like a piece of meat.

'It's the biannual briefing this morning,' Jim says when I stand up again.

He walks to the lift, still in the red shoes, and it dings immediately and the doors open. He steps inside, calls to Gertie and she bounds in to join him.

'Ready?' he says to me.

The auditorium is a lecture theatre with white wood surrounds and a curved black ceiling. It's decked with glossy white seats, is lit with white spotlights, and has huge white speakers along the walls. It feels like a cinema, which I suppose is the intention. My attention is drawn towards the stage, where there's a big screen blazing with the Cyclops silver eye.

Most of the seats are already filled, so I perch on the edge of an empty aisle seat at the back just as Jim comes on to the stage with Gertie at his heels. He's wearing the shoes and immediately everyone in the full auditorium starts to applaud and stamp their feet. He looks ridiculous in them, creepy even, but I look like the only one who can be thinking it. I pretend to clap but stop my hands from meeting each time, because to clap will feel like a betrayal.

'Welcome to the first briefing of the year!' Jim begins, and people start to whoop and shout. I watch the smile on his face widen. 'What a good time we had last year! We have been awarded with Editing House of the Year, Branded Content of the Year and Best Independent Production Company. I am also now on the UK Creative Board, as well as Media Regulation. Well done us!'

Shrill whistles zip across the curved ceiling and I want to cover my ears.

'You know the drill,' Jim continues. 'These briefings are for the teams to talk about the new creatives coming up and for you to have your priorities laid out for the year ahead. Andrea is going to talk about some new programmes.'

A woman has taken the stage alongside Jim. She looks incredible in a silver dress, sequinned like fish scales, and silver earrings. She glimmers and shines in the lights. Her hair is a mass of glossy dark curls, tossed casually over one shoulder. She has a clicker and she motions to the screen.

'We have some treats in store,' she says. 'We have progressed with a few of our initiatives from last year. The two that we're going full steam ahead with for this year are *The Underground Girl* and *Mr Cut and Wren Darby*.' There are catcalls and cheers. 'For those of you who don't recall, or haven't been privy to the early concept meetings, I'll talk you through them.'

She clicks on a remote and the screen behind her shows a young girl, sitting cross-legged in tatty clothes against the white wall of an Underground station.

'*The Underground Girl* is about Polly. She's twelve and she lives in a disused Tube station, busking and stealing money and avoiding getting caught by social services. Her single objective in life is to find her little brother, Sam, who was taken into foster care, and eventually she finds someone to help her. Amir promises to find Sam if Polly gives him her extraordinary knowledge of the Underground and how to move around it undetected. What she doesn't know is that Amir is a terrorist.'

There is whooping and cheering and Andrea smiles and then continues to talk about the next programme, and after that Jim stands up and takes the floor once again.

'Ladies and gents, your esteemed Head of Marketing and best pitcher I know, Andrea Rubins.'

He smiles at her and she smiles back, blows him a kiss and someone wolf-whistles as she departs the stage, and I think how pretentious this corporate gathering feels, exactly like the shows it produces.

'And now,' Jim says, 'while the concepts team set up for the second-tier programmes, I want to talk to you about what's starting up again this year. I've saved the best of the new initiatives for last and you all know what it is, don't you? It's the new series of *Pranksters*.'

I watch the atmosphere, which is already charged, go electric and people start to stamp their feet.

Jim waits for a moment before he raises his hands.

'You know that this is our biggest programme. It's *the* biggest commissioning series for the broadcaster. We've had writers working all year in the break since our beloved Jemima died. But this year our new host will come. *This* year will be a new golden era. But that's enough titillation for you. Enjoy our evergreen montage.'

Circus-clown music fills the room and the screen behind Jim bursts into life with clips of close-up bemused and befuddled faces. An actor hits himself on a swimming pool diving board and his victim belly-flops in after him to help; an old lady blows out a candle on a cake and her teeth are falling out because they've been replaced by ones that don't fit.

My hand flies to my mouth. What if the woman who dived in after the actor couldn't swim properly? What if that old lady was embarrassed by her teeth falling out and now hides her smile behind her hands? What happened to people being kind to each other?

A teenager wears a dress that says 'I buy fur!' on the back of it and someone lobs a banana at her head; a man on a motorbike is blasted with foam bubbles from a car in front of him and weaves dangerously into the verge; a boy jumps into a lake and screams when he sees the multiple sedated crocodiles in it. Streamers fall into the faces of all these poor people who've been trapped. Their awkward laughter when they realise they've been pranked and the shame in their eyes when they look dead into the camera makes me want to cry.

I find myself clenched, consumed by violent heat, but the entire auditorium around me is laughing. I feel like the only one who doesn't understand, except that I know I'm the only person who actually *does*. What would happen if I said it? What if I stood up and called them all up on it? Gave them the dark side of this programme? Would they listen? Would they care?

I look back at the screen with hatred and wish for it all to burn. I stand up, lurch to the side.

'You OK?' someone says.

But I can't talk. I stagger to the door and push through it to the other side, where I try and choke back sobs, but I can't.

At lunch, I go to Hungerford Bridge and stare into the river below, watching it swirl restlessly beneath my feet. Sometimes I wonder what it would be like to slip inside it, feel its cold embrace and lose myself like Dad did.

A boat passes underneath on its way to Greenwich and its echoing hum drowns out the ringing laughter in my head for a moment. How can everyone but me find it all so funny?

A voice speaks. 'I sometimes wonder if I could bunk work for an afternoon in the summer and pitch up a tent down there.'

THE PRANK

I jolt out of my thoughts and turn to a man standing not a metre next to me who's looking at the triangle of beach down below us. He looks like he's mid-thirties and is casually handsome, with olive skin and dark hair. I wonder why he's on the bridge and why he's talking to me, but I don't feel threatened by him.

He leans over the rails. 'You think I could do it?' he asks. 'I could become a writer in residence.'

'What happens when the tide comes in?' I say.

'I'd get wet,' he replies.

I smile.

'You can be anything in London,' he says. 'It's paved with gold.'

'Apparently that's actually true if you scrape hard enough,' I reply. 'My dad told me that there are people who collect dust from the cracks outside the old jewellers' shops to find quantities of gold and silver there.'

He looks at me then, a smile on his face. 'For real?'

'We tried it once, but we didn't find any,' I say.

'Only broken dreams?' he asks.

Everything is broken.

'You know what my favourite thing about London is?' he says. 'There's always someone fun to talk to. What's your favourite thing?'

'Anonymity,' I reply and smile to show him I'm not completely devoid of warmth.

He laughs and I like this laugh; it's light and musical and chisels his face. I want to draw him.

'I'm Bobby Walters,' he says.

'I'm . . .'

'I work at Cyclops,' he adds.

My heart jackhammers because I was about to tell him my real name. I swallow it back quickly. 'I'm Matilda Evans,' I say.

'I know who you are,' he replies with a grin. 'See you around.'

He gives me a little wave and walks away and I'm left staring after him. I almost gave myself away. I've got to be careful.

FOURTEEN

This morning, Jim has blocked out an hour for a meeting in his office with Andrea Rubins, the woman who spoke yesterday at the briefing, and so I use the opportunity to run an errand.

Last night, I spent an hour practising Jim's signature from his letter to Dad that I took from Pudding Cottage. I've printed a letter I've written on headed paper as if from Jim and, at the bottom, I've signed it. It's almost a flawless replica. I take the lift all the way down to the basement, to the one department that Jim didn't bother introducing me to. IT.

I knock on the open door. 'Hello?'

There are two men inside the room, each at a large desk with several monitors casting a blue glow over their faces. One is slight with dark hair and a beard framing a narrow face and deep-set, gunmetal-grey eyes; the other is large-framed with a soft face and mutton-chop sideburns. Both of them are dressed in jeans and casual T-shirts – none of the frills and fancies of the floors above.

They look up at me at the same time. This is a big moment and I have to get it right. I have to get them onside. My hair is sticking to the back of my neck because I'm hot and my knitted dress is sticking to my ribs.

"'Lo! A visitor, Eric!' the slight, bearded man says.

'A visitor, Paul!' Eric affirms. There's a gap in between his front teeth which makes him look childlike.

'You don't get many visitors?' I ask.

'People think we're virtual, like we actually live in the interwebs,' Eric replies.

'Like we're the paperclip help icon from days of yore,' Paul adds. 'I miss him, don't you?'

'What's the paperclip—' I start.

'Oh, please don't mock us with your youth,' Paul says. 'Come in, come in.'

I step inside, look around. Everything is neat, orderly and I can hear the gentle hum of computers in the background.

'I came to say hello,' I say. 'I'm Matilda Evans, Jim Valente's new PA.'

'Jim's new PA!' Eric gives me a dramatic bow. 'Our pleasure to receive you. Are you in some sort of IT jeopardy?'

'Have you tried switching the computer off and on?' Paul asks.

'Have you tried kicking it? We get some of that here.'

'Poor old Mac 12,' Paul says. 'God rest its soul.'

They both cross themselves and I laugh.

'No, really,' Eric says, 'how can we help? We do IT and I also dabble in some production shizzle from time to time. I'm multitalented, but I can't speak for Paul.'

'I only operate in zeros and ones,' Paul replies. 'Nothing fancy here.'

I smile. 'There are a couple of things I need a steer on with Outlook,' I say. 'How to link my account with Jim's, as per his last PA? Did she have that?'

They nod. 'Yes,' Paul says. 'But we'll need written permission from Jim.'

'After what happened with Christine, he was adamant no one else would have access,' Eric adds.

'What *did* happen?' I ask.

'She put some pretty stupid comments up online,' Eric says. 'Error!'

'Oh,' I say, and feel guilty.

'Can you come back with a signature?' Paul asks.

'I've got one,' I reply, and give Eric the paper with my forged signature on it. 'Is this OK?'

Eric raises his eyebrows. He looks at it for a moment and I think he's going to shake his head, tell me he knows the stunt I'm trying to pull, but then he nods. 'Give us a couple of hours to set this up, Matilda. We'll give you a ting-a-ling when it's done.'

'Perhaps I can buy you both a coffee as a thank you?' I suggest. 'Take you to a cafe down the road?'

They stare at me.

'We can't leave the basement!' Eric exclaims. 'We'd burn up in the light!'

'He means yes,' Paul says. 'And thank you, that's kind. No one ever says thank you to the IT geeks.'

'Which is exceptionally narrow-minded,' Eric says, 'because we could pull the plug any moment.'

I smile and think that Horsehead would like these two.

I spend hours relearning all the Office programmes I haven't used since I left school and navigating Jim's calendar and contact list that he's *actually* allowed me access to. I answer calls and print things he barks through the door to be printed, scan things he wants scanned after many failed attempts. He tells me to read all the news on the internal website, 'The Eye', as it's called here, and so I do that, try to appease him, but he's going at a hundred miles an hour and I'm struggling to keep up. This is a different world from the restaurant and I miss it, miss Wendy and David and the colonel and the Turkish poet.

Throughout the day, people come and go through Jim's office and introduce themselves to me with varying levels of warmth. I skip lunch. I do everything right because I can't afford to put a foot wrong. I need to learn. Regularly, I pinch myself because I can't believe I'm here, that I'm Jim Valente's PA, sat at a shiny white desk. I own his life here, as terrifying as that is.

It's five in the afternoon when the phone finally rings. It makes me jump. I connect it to my headset and clear my throat. 'Hello?'

'Matilda?' says a male voice. 'It's Paul from IT.'

'Hi, Paul,' I say.

'Sorry about the delay, but we've waved the magic tech wand,' he says. 'You should be able to access Jim's inbox now.'

I glance at Jim's office door, see him inside with his head bent low. 'Thank you so much,' I whisper.

'You're welcome,' he replies. 'Have a lovely evening.'

He hangs up and I lunge forward to the laptop, refresh my email and there it is – Jim's inbox. I click on it and watch excitedly as folders begin to line up, but my excitement is cowed by the volume of them loading – there are hundreds of them. I dare to click inside one and see, to my dismay, hundreds of subfolders, too.

I start doggedly clicking through them, hopeful that he might have some personal emails that I can use against him in some way. But I scan email after email about marketing campaigns and budgets and see nothing interesting. I try another tack, clicking on the folder entitled 'Personal: House Finances; Personal Finances; Houses; General Admin; Benjamin School Fees'. I click them one by one, but none offers anything interesting. I feel overwhelmed. I had no idea there would be so much – but then, how did I not realise?

'Finishing for the day?'

I look up. Jim is at his door. He can't see my screen, it faces the wall, but I minimise it quickly.

'I might stay and type up some of the minutes you wanted doing,' I say.

'No, no,' he says. 'That can be done tomorrow. You don't stay later than me unless I tell you to.'

I nod, trying to conceal my disappointment.

'I leave the office very late some days,' he explains. 'Sometimes I stay until it's the next day.' He smiles. 'How did you enjoy the briefing yesterday?'

'So great,' I say.

He smiles his handsome, practised smile, but it doesn't reach his eyes and I'm nervous. 'It was a good presentation,' he says. 'Wasn't it?'

'Really great,' I say again.

'Tell me your favourite bit,' he demands.

'All of it,' I reply, quickly. 'But I liked the montage. The evergreen brands.'

'The montage,' he says. 'Of *Pranksters*?'

'Yes.'

He looks like he's studying me. 'But you left halfway through it.'

I gawk at him.

'I saw you leave, Matilda, and you didn't come back.'

I lick my lips, because what can I say?

'Jim, I'm sorry,' I say. 'I . . . It was women's things.'

He waves it away. 'Listen, it's your first week and already Wednesday and we haven't had a welcome lunch, have we?' he says. 'You're wondering where my manners are. Tomorrow. Clear my diary. I'm assuming yours is free.'

'I'm free,' I confirm.

'I know a good place,' he continues. He nods to my computer. 'Close that up,' he says. 'Go home.'

It's like he knows.

FIFTEEN

This morning, I've been spending half my time printing out documents for Jim and the other half wrestling with his enormous inbox, and I'm so caught up in the monotony of clicking that when the file thuds on my desk it makes me jump.

'My expenses,' Jim says above me.

I hurriedly click out of his inbox and I open the file. The top page is his bank statement and my eyes widen. Seven thousand pounds for December.

'And that's been thin,' he says, noting my look.

'Oh,' I reply.

'I'll take Gertie and give her a walk for half an hour and then you meet me for lunch, yes?'

He goes to leave and I watch him and can't believe my fortune. I'll be alone on the entire top floor for thirty minutes. I suppose this is normal; I suppose a PA would have access to whatever their charge has. Would I dare to look inside his office for something that might give me evidence of an Achilles heel? Perhaps there's something inside that 'trinket drawer' where he keeps the red shoes that I could look at? Maybe there's evidence of something unsavoury, something unprofessional, that he's hiding in there? My eyes flick towards it, but no sooner than they have, Jim has produced a key from his inside jacket pocket and locks the door. The balloon of excitement in my lungs deflates instantly.

'See you there,' he says, and the key disappears into his pocket.

The lift comes up. He and Gertie step inside and the doors close.

I wait for ten seconds before I pick up my phone.

'Hi, Facilities?'

'Hello, Miss Evans.'

'Hi, I'm trying to get into Jim Valente's office – have you got a spare key for it? I've got to get a document typed up for him which is on his desk and I can't get in.'

'No spare key for that office, I'm afraid, Miss Evans.'

I double-take. 'No spare?'

'Mr Valente's instruction.'

'Right,' I say flatly. 'Thanks.'

I put down the phone, stare at the office door and then I randomly cancel a meeting in his diary next month. It's small and petty, but I feel frustrated. Jim's a step ahead of me in a game he doesn't even know he's playing.

Jim pours himself a large glass of wine. We're in a neat little restaurant above Covent Garden's cobbled streets with lots of costly glassware and pristine white linen. Gertie lies underneath us, her warm weight against my legs.

I feel as if I'm floating above myself looking in. I can feel every part of my body, every limb present at the table because I'm so rigid. This is the longest I will have spent with Jim and I'm not sure how I'm going to focus to keep myself together.

'There's the worst-kept secret in media,' Jim says. 'Miranda Ford and Jason Lawal in the corner.'

I look around to see two people at a table talking softly to one another, his hand curled around hers, ebony on porcelain white. I don't recognise either.

'They're together?' I ask.

'Exactly,' Jim says. 'Miranda is married to Michael Wang, that celebrity chef, and Jason is with that blonde model.' He nods towards them. 'But it's in the interest of a fine restaurant or hotel to protect many illustrious affairs. Reputation is everything.'

I think of the couple at The Cello who stole kisses at that back table and I wonder about how we in the restaurant all played a part in their complexities.

'I'm trying to land Miranda in one of my shows,' Jim continues. 'Having her in the picture will attract some others. I'm this close to getting her – this close.' He has his finger and thumb an inch apart.

'I hope it works out,' I say, because I don't know what else to offer.

I pick at my bread roll. I feel so out of my depth with Jim, with being in this world, that I'm even more shut into myself than I ever have been. I need to *act*, like Horsehead told me to. I need for Jim to trust me, to like me. I smile at him.

He leans forward. 'It's time to tell me a little bit about yourself.'

I swallow. 'What do you want to know about me?'

'Your personal life.' He gives me a wide, shark-like smile. 'Hopes, dreams, ambitions. What's the end goal?'

'The end goal?'

He smiles. 'Perhaps you *could* be an actor if you wanted to be. So many of the girls, and the men too, Matilda, join my company or freelance for me because they want to get in front

119

of the screen. But some people have it and some don't.' He picks up his wine glass and studies me over the rim of it like I'm prey. 'You have something. Rawness.'

'I don't want to be an actress, Jim.'

'What do you want then?'

I stall with my reply because all I want, all I've wanted for years, is my dad back in my life. I want to laugh easily like I used to.

Our starters arrive.

'A man? Have you got a lonely heart?' he smiles and begins his scallops.

'Oh, no,' I say. 'I don't have anyone. I mean . . .'

'Too busy partying hard?'

Gertie barks as if she feels my discomfort and Jim looks away from me to her.

'You're right, beast,' Jim says, chewing. 'We need to talk business.'

He's a fast eater and he finishes the scallops, clutters his cutlery together and then sweeps bread-roll crumbs from his napkin for Gertie, who makes a noise underneath us like a hoover. I eat my goat's cheese tart hurriedly, my fingers hot around my knife and fork.

'The industry awards ceremony is in a month,' Jim says. 'I need my regular seats, I need to sample the wines for the after-party, I need to choose who I'm seen with in front of the press when I'm going in. You need to call Natalie Lewis there. She's in the events team at the theatre. Arrange a meeting with her.'

'Right,' I say and I get my phone from my bag and make a note of the name. 'Yes, I'll call her.'

'And there's the memorial service for Jemima Mataya in a fortnight at Claridge's,' he explains. 'I need you to print a load of documents I have on the computer about her career. A refresher for my speech.'

'Was she the girl from *Pranksters*?' I ask, recalling my conversation with Wendy.

He nods. 'Such a talent,' he says. 'Such a waste!'

'I read about her,' I reply.

'She built the brand,' he explains. 'She was the host for eighteen years. You grew up with her, am I right? *Pranksters* was successful because of her and, obviously, because it's hysterical. It's my cash cow, my true love. Everyone needs to laugh. My father was hard-working, but he was straight. You know what I mean by that, Matilda? He never had *fun* and people need to laugh because there's enough depressing shit in the world, isn't there?'

I nod.

'Hard work got my father nowhere, too. He worked so hard, never saw his family, never took a holiday, was never financially rewarded. He retired at sixty-five and died three months later. And you know what? I didn't see him smile all those sixty-five years. Never saw him laugh because he wasn't that type of man. A sense of humour sets us apart, don't you think? I'm hard-working, but I know when to laugh.'

I'm silenced.

'The long and short of it is that I don't like earnest people, Matilda,' he says. 'They bore me. My old man was a bore. He could have done with a shock to his system, a yank on his chain.' He laughs softly. 'Listen to me. All my "daddy issues". What about you?'

I'm taken aback by his words. 'Me? Have I got . . . have I got daddy issues?'

He laughs loudly. 'No, I meant, can you laugh?'

'Yes,' I say, though I'm far from it.

'Anyway,' he says. 'The memorial is important because it marks the end of the grieving for our beloved Jems and it's a start for someone new. A new era for *Pranksters*. We halted production for a year after Jemima died, but now it's time for the rebrand. More pranks, more fun, and the industry awards is important because that's when I'll be announcing who's the successful candidate for the host. You need to talk to marketing, who are putting together everything for the memorial, and get the speech running order together so I know when I'm talking,' he concludes. 'Gwendolen Harris is arranging it.'

'OK,' I say, and I add her name to my phone notes. 'Who is she?'

'She's one of my freelance marketing managers, but she's on constant roll so she works in the building. Catch her first thing Monday.'

'I'll get on to it,' I say.

The waiter comes to our table. 'Are you ready for your main course?' he asks.

'Bring it on,' Jim says, and then he looks at me with those blue eyes. His words feel like a direct challenge to me and I'm not sure I can meet it.

>Horsehead: Ooo, your first proper date with Jim!
>Top Step: Please don't call it that.
>Horsehead: Are you compatible?
>Top Step: Seriously, please stop talking like that.
>Horsehead: But it's important you're compatible because he'll need to trust you enough so that you can do little things that teeter on the edge of sackable without being sacked.

Top Step: It went OK.

Horsehead: Your first week is almost done. I'm proud of you, doll. It can't be easy being there.

Top Step: Strangely, it feels good.

Horsehead: And you got access to his emails?

Top Step: Yes.

Horsehead: What have you found?

Top Step: So far nothing because there are thousands of them.

Horsehead: Baby steps. Shall we download the inbox to your personal computer?

Top Step: Should we? Can we?

Horsehead: It's possible. How confident are you in the IT crowd?

Top Step: I don't know? They're pretty geeky?

Horsehead: How confident are you in me?

Top Step: I think you're the god of the digital sphere.

Horsehead: Yeah, I am. But for now, perhaps we go careful. An IT hack should never underestimate another IT hack. It's Friday tomorrow. You could take the day off from your evil doing.

Top Step: I'm exhausted, Horsehead. I could sleep for weeks and I've only done four days there.

Horsehead: Go easy, doll.

Top Step: On Monday I've got to meet with a girl called Gwendolen Harris. I'm logging on to the company profiles right now. No idea what she looks like, but apparently she works on *Pranksters* and I need to speak to her anyway about some memorial.

Horsehead: A memorial?

Top Step: The host of *Pranksters* died a year ago. Her name was Jemima Mataya. They're replacing her but are going to hold a sort of closure for her.

Horsehead: She was a big deal?

Top Step: She hosted it for ages, 18 years or something. She was this child star that they, I don't know, cultivated.

Horsehead: Sounds sorta creepy. Anyway, send me the link to the profiles. Let me see Gwendolen.

Top Step: www.CyclopsProductions.co.uk/ourcompany/ourpeople

Horsehead: Man, this is good. Look at these people! Photos like they're all film stars?! Who looks young and stupid on here? Shit, they all do.

Top Step: Horsehead, you can't judge that from their photos.

Horsehead: Mila Jackson, screenwriter. Or no, Gary Pollock. Pollock?? Like bollock? You need to befriend him just for the name. WOWSERS. Check out Andrea Rubins. She's hot! OK, I've found Gwendolen. Gwendolen Harris, right? Chubby little honey with a face like a kicked puppy.

Top Step: Horsehead, don't be mean.

Horsehead: Doll, are you kidding? You and me met on a *revenge* website. She probably spends her Friday nights eating Ben and Jerry's with her cats licking the spoon.

Top Step: Play nice.

Horsehead: And where did that ever get anybody?

SIXTEEN

It's my leaving party tonight at the restaurant and I've roped in Lissy to make it more bearable, because the thought of being the centre of attention – even if to everyone else it's just an excuse to get drunk – doesn't sit well with me.

I'm reading on the bedroom floor, having done my hair and make-up in five minutes. Lissy, however, is sprawled on the bed, surrounded by an array of cosmetics and hairspray because, to her, any night out in London is worth dolling herself up for.

'It's in the restaurant,' I say for the hundredth time.

'I know,' Lissy replies, applying a third layer of mascara.

'There's no one there you'd be remotely interested in.'

'It's not about me being interested in *them*,' she says. 'It's about them being interested in *me*. Every world is a stage, El, and that means your restaurant, too. Make an impression and the world will open up for you.'

I can't argue with her when she's in performance mode. I watch her as she clicks and clacks her compacts, applies glitter to her cheeks and then drops it all over my bed, and then I turn my attention back to my book. It's by the Turkish poet from the restaurant. I found him on social media and bought his translated collection.

I haven't got any social media presence; I wonder what sort of thing I would post and who would ever both reading them anyway. Would I post my drawings? Would I write about the people I've met? The things I've seen? Would I post anonymously about Jim? Would I write about finding my dad slumped across the kitchen table?

'What are these?'

I look over to Lissy and see that, in the short time I've lost myself in the book, she's stolen into my wardrobe. I snap my book shut.

'What are all these, sis? Where did you get these from?' She brings out the short, dark wig. 'Can I wear this?'

She puts it on before I say 'no', and it suits her. She turns about in front of the mirror and pouts.

'Hawt! I could take this to the—'

'You're not taking it anywhere,' I say.

'Come on, El! I could wear it at Max's party next month!'

'Get ready, will you?'

'All right, keep your hair on.' She laughs and holds up her hands. She sits back down on the bed cross-legged and takes up her brushes again.

I stand to get my jacket and bag from the back of the door when a loud bleep emits from my laptop.

'You've got a message,' she says, and drags my laptop to her lap and opens the screen.

Only one person messages me. Horsehead. I lunge over, snap the laptop shut on her fingers.

'Ouch!' She looks at me, wounded.

'Lissy, that's private.'

'I didn't see what they wrote,' she says, and then she looks guilty. 'I'm sorry, I shouldn't have looked.'

'You're so nosey,' I say.

She hops off the bed. 'El, I'm sorry.'

'OK, it's fine,' I reply.

'Can you tell me who the message is from?'

'Just a guy,' I say, impatiently. 'Come on, we're going.'

Her face lights up. 'A guy? A boyfriend?'

'No,' I say. 'Get your coat.'

'What's with the secrecy? Is he married?'

'Would you shut up? He's in a completely different country.'

She smiles. 'Aw! You have a pen pal? That's so nineties!'

It's strange being in the restaurant as a customer, especially when all the actual customers have left. Wendy, Pavel and the others join Lissy and me at the bar in their black and white starched uniforms and I feel out of place here in black jeans and a blue silk top.

'It's weird seeing you as a proper person here,' Wendy says. 'I'm not going to wait on you.'

I smile. 'Not even for a tip?'

She laughs. 'You're not rich enough for me, babe.'

'Oh my God, I love this place,' Lissy says next to me. 'Why did you never take me here before?'

'It's a hundred and seventy-five pounds for a four-course meal,' I tell her. 'Without drinks.'

Her eyes widen and she stares around in awe at the plush decor, fingering the embroidery of her chair. 'For my birthday, though?' she says.

'Still no.'

David joins us, air-kisses both my cheeks and sits next to me. 'How are you, El?' he asks. 'How is the new job?'

'It's good, David, thanks,' I reply.

'*Bien,*' he says.

I've been deliberately vague with anyone who asks me about what I'm doing now. Even Lissy and Charlie are in the dark; all I've offered them is that I got a job as a PA in the city because it pays more and I'd like to get a flat of my own. I appealed to Charlie's sensibilities and he bought it and then I felt bad for lying.

'Thank you for tonight,' I say.

'We miss you,' he replies.

'Don't give her delusions of grandeur, David, please,' Wendy teases.

Lissy sticks out her hand to David. 'I'm Lissy,' she says, flicking her hair. 'Eleanor's sister.'

'It is a pleasure to meet you,' he says, ignoring her hand and kissing her.

'Wow, your accent,' she gushes. '*Je parle français.*'

He smiles, delighted. 'But of course, you speak it too!'

'David is the restaurant manager here,' I say.

'You'd give us mates' rates though, wouldn't you?' my sister asks. 'If we came here to eat?'

He looks amused. 'Of course. With your family?'

'Just me and sis,' Lissy replies blithely. 'We're orphans.'

David looks over her head at me. 'Orphans?' he says.

'Both our parents died when we were younger,' she explains.

He keeps his eyes on me. 'I am so sorry,' he replies, more to me than to Lissy. 'I had no idea.'

I nod my head, a silent appreciation of his respect.

'My sister doesn't talk much, does she?' Lissy says.

'Would you like another drink, El?' David asks, reading my discomfort.

'Thanks,' I say.

He signals to Pavel to pour me another glass and I look at Lissy with warning in my eyes. She either doesn't notice or chooses to ignore me, because as soon as he comes back, she is still full of smiles and joviality. I watch her lean on the bar and cup her chin in her hand.

'Tell me everything about *you*, David,' she says.

The night passes easily because of my sister. I watch her, this teenager, as she charms her way into the hearts of the people I've known for years. She asks them questions, keeps eye contact with them, tilts her head and smiles encouragingly when they speak. She laughs in all the right places, she interjects with relevant and well-timed quips. She's open about her life, what she's doing and what she hopes to do, but she doesn't over-talk. She walks the thin line of self-deprecating yet confident and her manner is utterly bewitching. I sit and watch her and wonder how she was able to navigate her way around social etiquette but I somehow missed out on the training. Is this how she genuinely feels, I wonder. Unguarded and at ease? Out of nowhere, I feel a pang of discontentment. I'm a failure not to live a life like my sister's.

SEVENTEEN

The canteen has harsh fluorescent lights which hurt my eyes. Gwendolen Harris, who is early forties, has tortoise-shell glasses and glossy nude lips, sits at a table and in front of her is a chocolate muffin and a frothy hot chocolate, in which the tips of her fine blonde hair dangle. She doesn't notice.

I wait for her to finish shuffling her papers around.

'I'm usually a bit more organised,' she says. 'Shoot, I'm sorry. I've had a lot on recently. And it's Monday so that's why I'm having lots of chocolate. Heavy weekend – you know what it's like.'

'I don't judge on chocolate consumption,' I say and try to smile at her as my sister would smile at a stranger.

'Don't report me back to Jim for being disorganised!' she says.

'I promise,' I reply.

'This wasn't actually my project, this memorial,' she explains. 'But it's taken over the whole department lately and apparently I'm the organised one. You wouldn't know it right now.' She clips some pages together and then hands them to me. 'A copy for you. Sorry, I should have done this before our meeting. I don't know where the time's gone recently. You're going to think I'm a real klutz. And a chocoholic.'

'It's fine,' I say, still smiling. My jaw aches with it and I wonder if I can really be so out of practice. I thought I smiled with customers all the time at The Cello, but maybe I didn't.

'So. Drinks and a reception at Claridge's a week on Wednesday,' she explains. 'All the heads of department go and the direct marketing and PR people and then the broadcasters and a whole lot of journalists. I'm going because I've ended up organising most of it.' She pauses. 'I'm not sure if that's a blessing or a curse to be honest! Usually I wouldn't be invited to this kind of thing, ever.'

'I'm sure it'll go perfectly,' I say.

'Thanks for the vote of confidence,' she says. She looks at her schedule. 'It starts at six and finishes at ten. There's a clip of Jemima's work to be played in the background on a loop. I've got that here and I'll send you the link in case Jim wants to see it. The rest of all these papers are the who's who of people coming, the list of canapés, the wine selected, that sort of thing. Page four has the timings. Jim will speak at eight-thirty; there will be champagne for his toast. And there will be a microphone.' She flicks through the rest of the pages. 'I think that's what you need to know in a nutshell.'

'This is great, Gwendolen, thank you so much.'

'Call me Gwen,' she says.

'OK,' I reply. 'Did you ever meet Jemima?'

'Oh yes,' Gwendolen says enthusiastically. 'She was the face of *Pranksters*, obviously, and she'd always be in and around the office. She could have made it to Hollywood, though, everyone said it. Everyone wanted her. It was always her intention to go back to America, but she was ours, you know? She loved it here.'

'She was the face for a long time, wasn't she?'

Gwendolen nods. 'Eighteen years,' she says. 'And it's taken a year to even *get* to a place where we can look for another host for *Pranksters*, you know? I still can't believe she's died. I saw her boyfriend launched a drugs-awareness foundation a few months ago. He's been hit hard after there were rumours they'd had an argument the night she took the overdose.' Her phone beeps and I watch her get it out and read an email. 'Sorry. Another thing I need to do. Some of my campaigns are big. It's actually totally exhausting. By the end of the week, I'm eating ice cream in front of the TV.'

I think of how Horsehead described her.

'Ben and Jerry's?' I ask.

'Always, one hundred per cent,' she says.

I want to smile and ask if she has a cat, but I refrain.

'Is Jim any closer to choosing the new host for *Pranksters* yet?' asks Gwendolen, clicking off her phone.

'I'm not sure,' I say.

'I'll ask Bobby,' she says. 'He knows everything about that show.'

'Bobby?' I ask. I think of the man on the bridge and feel immediately nauseous at how I almost told him my real name. 'Bobby Walters?'

'That's him,' she replies. 'You've met him?'

'Yes,' I say.

'I wouldn't kick him out of bed,' she says and gives me a conspiratorial wink.

I look down to the documents so I don't meet her eyes. I've never had anyone in my bed. Ever. The thought of him – anyone – in my bed makes me flush.

'Thanks,' I say. 'I'd better go now.'

*

I return to my desk. I hope to spend more time on Jim's emails and also figure out how I can cancel the meeting that he has with the actor Miranda Ford with the minimum amount of suspicion. It would be a tiny bullet to chink his golden armour, but I want to feel that I'm hurting him somehow. I also have something else I can get to work on: Gwendolen has unknowingly told me how I can get more information on *Pranksters*, and if that programme is Jim's 'true love', knowing everything about it is what I should dedicate some time to. Perhaps there have been others like me who have been upended by one of its episodes.

I pause. People like me. Is that what I should be looking for? Victims of pranks that have gone wrong?

Excitedly, I write Bobby Walters an email and ask if he'd be free to meet me for lunch. A second later, I pick up the phone before I register who's calling me.

'I got your email,' Bobby says without a hello. 'You want to buy me lunch?'

He's direct but his voice is playful and I feel flustered at this combination.

'I . . . yes,' I say. 'Gwendolen Harris said you were the person to speak to about *Pranksters*.'

'*Pranksters*?'

'Yes,' I say. 'Is that OK? I wanted to talk to someone about it.'

'Is this about Jim's host?' he asks, but doesn't wait for my answer. 'Tomorrow, twelve-thirty in the lobby.'

'OK, good,' I reply.

'See you,' he says and hangs up.

'Busy making friends?'

Startled, I look up to see Jim in front of me, with a pretty young woman by his side. I hadn't heard the lift so he must have been with her on the roof terrace and they've come down by the stairs.

'Who was that on the phone?' Jim asks.

'Er, Bobby Walters,' I say. 'I'm . . . we're having lunch tomorrow.'

He smiles. 'Interesting,' he says.

I don't know what he means by that, or by the smile, and he doesn't offer an explanation for either.

'You need to get my guest some coffee,' he says.

The pretty young woman smiles at me and I smile back. She can't be older than twenty, has dyed blonde hair and dark red lips. She's wearing a blue dungaree dress over an open-neck white silk blouse and manages to look both feminine and edgy.

'Of course,' I reply. 'Sorry, Jim, I didn't know anyone was coming in. I'll cancel your next meeting.'

'Do that,' he says and he goes to turn and then he stops. 'Wait, not coffee. Hot chocolate. Because isn't this girl just delicious?'

I look to the young woman and she smiles bashfully at Jim. I'm shocked that he didn't ask her what she wanted to drink first, but why would a man like him assume anyone else has an opinion? And why would she question him when he'd disarmed her first with his oddly shaped compliment?

I look back at him. 'Same for you, Jim?' I enquire. 'Hot chocolate?'

'You think *I'm* delicious?' he asks, but he doesn't wait for my answer. 'Yes, make it two.'

He walks into his office and she trots after him and I get up and go down to the canteen.

THE PRANK

When I return, Jim meets me at the door and takes the hot chocolates. I go back behind my desk and glance at them intermittently and wonder who she is. I see her talking animatedly to him and him watching her intently. Once or twice I see his hand graze her thigh, but she doesn't move away and I wonder if she's noticed because she's smiling – but how could she not? How is it that Jim can act like this and she's saying nothing? Is that how it works to get somewhere in this business, really? After I see it happen a fourth time, I get up and march to the door, knock violently and then open it.

'Jim,' I say. 'I need a signature on a document pretty urgently.'

He looks annoyed at my intrusion. 'What?'

'It's a contract from . . . Feico,' I explain.

He rolls his eyes. 'That can wait.'

'Right,' I say. 'Sorry.' I look at the young woman. 'Can I get you anything else?'

She stands. 'Actually I could use the bathroom,' she says and I note a French lilt in her accent.

'Right opposite my desk,' I gesture and she nods and walks towards me. I hold the door for her and, as she passes, I glance over at Jim, who looks thunderous. 'Anything for you, Jim?'

'A moment's fucking peace?' he snaps.

'Sorry,' I say.

He sighs, stretches his arms either side of the sofa. 'Antoinette applied for the *Pranksters* host,' he explains.

'Oh,' I say.

'She's French. You lived in France for a while. I remember from your CV.'

'Yes,' I say.

135

'It's such a beautiful language,' he adds. 'But I don't understand a word of it. Tell me something in French.'

'What do you want to hear?' I ask.

'Tell me I'm incredibly beautiful,' he says, and laughs.

I bite my tongue.

'*Tu es incroyablement beau*,' I reply.

'Tell me I'm the funniest person you know,' he says.

'*Tu es la personne la plus drôle que je connaisse.*'

'Tell me that you would do anything for me,' he says.

I pause, but he stares, unblinkingly, at me.

'*J'ai envie de te gifler*,' I say.

He laughs, none the wiser that I've told him I want to slap him.

'Tell Antoinette that I'm done with her now,' he says. 'You can take her downstairs. She's not the one. Too shy. Not *receptive* enough. Do you know what I mean?'

I think I do. I close his door and breathe a sigh of relief for Antoinette because she's escaped him.

When I come back from the lift, I see Jim standing in his doorway. He beckons me with his finger.

'So now we've eliminated Antoinette, I need you to help me,' he says. 'We're going to play a little game and it's called "Mirror, Mirror".'

I frown. 'Mirror, Mirror?'

'Come on,' he says.

I follow him into his office and he gestures to his desk, where he's got five pictures of young women fanned out. All of them are blonde and bear a striking resemblance to Jemima Mataya, just as Antoinette did. I didn't think of it at the time. Now it makes sense.

'Who's the fairest of them all?' Jim says.

I look up at him. 'What do you mean?'

'I've been interviewing these girls for the last month,' he explains. 'And I can't decide who's best for the role of host.'

'For *Pranksters?*' I ask.

'Correct,' he says.

I look at them again. 'I couldn't possibly pick one of these women out,' I say.

He smiles. 'Yes, you could. Crush a dream, raise a hope. It's very empowering.'

'But I don't know anything about them, Jim,' I add. 'I don't like this game.'

'You're thinking of Justin Goldstein,' he says.

'I feel like I'm playing your weekly roulette game.'

'You don't like the responsibility?' he asks.

'No,' I say.

'You know, in the sixties there was a psychological experiment that focused on the conflict between obedience to authority and personal conscience. It was found that most people obeyed authority and transferred their personal responsibility upwards and therefore freed their consciences to go on and administer electric shocks to people.'

'I know that experiment,' I say. 'Milgram. People gave fake shocks to "victims" even when they knew the voltage would be fatal.'

'Isn't it interesting?' he muses.

'It was very unethical.'

'But didn't we learn a lot about authority and conformity?' he says. 'Anyway, I'm not asking you to electrocute anyone. All these girls have done audition tapes, they all can front a camera well. There's no right or wrong answer here.'

'Still,' I say, 'I can't just—'

He grabs my arm and I inhale through my teeth in shock.

'Calm down,' he says with a laugh. 'I'm going to help you. Close your eyes.'

I don't want him touching me. His fingers are cold and I pull away from him, but he tightens his grip.

'Close your eyes,' he repeats.

My heart is pounding. 'Why?'

'Close them,' he says and there's something threatening in his voice.

Perhaps if I close them he will let go of me, but he doesn't. He jerks me forward and then moves my arm from side to side.

'It can be like pin the tail on the donkey,' he says. 'You tell me where to stop.'

'Jim . . .' I begin, but my voice is weak.

Don't touch me, my body is screaming. Don't touch me!

'Call out stop,' he says.

'Stop!' I say. 'Stop!'

He lets go immediately and I open my eyes, draw my arm into my chest. He doesn't notice, scoops up a picture and waves it at me. 'Marie Jarski!' he announces.

I look at the picture.

'The Chosen One!' Jim says.

'OK,' I reply. I feel faint, need to get out of here.

'Call her agent,' he says.

I look at the young woman, her heart-shaped face, blonde hair and bright smile, and I want to apologise to her picture.

'OK,' I repeat and go to walk out of his office, relieved to get away from him, but he starts talking again.

'Matilda?'

I turn to face him.

'Your skin,' he says. 'It's so soft. Like cream.'

*

It's the end of the day and I stand at the bus stop and look at my phone. I've been waiting for the bus for twenty minutes and all I've been thinking about are those words.

Soft like cream.

I want to be home as quickly as I can because I want to wash them off me. I waver on the decision to walk home, but I haven't got my trainers. I call Euey, but he's at Heathrow doing an airport pickup. I could call another Uber, but I can't rally the energy to make conversation with someone. I could take the Underground – it would be quicker – but I haven't been in the tunnels for years.

I recall a memory from when I was six. I stood with my dad on the platform at Embankment and I held his hand and we waited for the train.

'He breaths in and fills his lungs with dank air and waits.'

I looked up at Dad. I knew at this young age that the third-person narrative meant the introduction of a story. There was a rush of air and a low growl of the train from within the tunnel. The metal tracks started to hop with electricity.

'This is it,' Dad said. 'The beast's eyes flash from out of the darkness; they will be the last eyes he will see.'

The train breath whipped up my hair and I watched the mouth of the tunnel, waiting for the beast's grand reveal.

'The man has been ill for years. Ill in the head and ill in the heart,' he said softly. 'Too late for medicine, for cures, for saving.'

I looked up at him, tugged on his sleeve. 'What about the beast, Daddy? His teeth! Is he a dragon? Or a wolf?'

'Timing will be everything,' Dad continued as if he didn't hear me. 'As the train surges into the station, he will jump

139

like a moth into the light, straight into its jaws. He will be obliterated instantly. Bones splintering, flesh tearing, insides turning outward. The train brakes, people inside are lurched forward.'

It was a different story from the others. It wasn't fun and I was starting to panic. I didn't even know why. I couldn't understand the concept of it all, but I could hear his delivery and it was ominous.

'There's a moment of silence and then there is chaos. Shouting and screaming outside the carriages, frightened faces inside looking out, catching panic. A stampede of frightened people. Some move forward to helplessly help. Some run away, up the stairs, up into the world where they can pretend they didn't see. Some are stunned into statues.'

'Daddy?'

He looked at me then, but he didn't see me. He was lost in narration.

'The little girl melts backwards with her hands out behind her, feeling for the cold curve of the station wall. Her eyes are tightly shut and she doesn't know when to open them. She thinks when people are barging into her and she cannot keep herself upright that this is the time and she snaps them open. She sees only a sea of people next to the train. She quickly walks away from the scene, up the stairs and on to the streets. She has a fine spray of blood on her face. Nobody notices.'

'Daddy.' I was crying then because he was scaring me.

My tears brought him back to me and he knelt down. 'Darling, sorry, darling. It was nothing. A book idea.'

But I was inconsolable for a week after that and forbade my dad to take the Tube for a month. I was young and I didn't

understand why I banned him exactly, but even at six I knew
this wasn't a story but a fantasy.

I found his suicide note at Pudding Cottage that day, fourteen years ago. To this day, no one else knows anything about
it. Not Uncle Charlie, not Liss. I plucked it from the table with
fingers that weren't my own, white and shaking, and I put it
somewhere safe. For my eyes only. I read it that once on the
day I found him and then I put it away in my bedside drawer
and I've not laid eyes on it since, because for all the words he
wrote over his lifetime, he had only written us the date, the
time and a few lines.

Forgive me for what I will do today. I am a coward, but
I love you all and never forget it.

He called himself a coward because he couldn't help
Christopher Barrows, but he was always a hero in my eyes.

It's time for the letter to come out again because Jim should
know that his pranks lead to the most horrific consequences.
He should know that not everyone will be silent about them.

EIGHTEEN

Bobby leans against the wall of the reception. He's wearing a heavy tan coat with faux fur along the top of it and a smile as he looks down at my feet.

'Did any animals get harmed in the process of making those boots?' he asks as I bleep my badge and walk through the glass barrier.

'They're snow boots,' I reply.

Lissy picked them for me to wear outdoors. They're light grey and fuzzy with fur around the edges.

'Cute.'

I laugh, self-consciously because I'm not sure any man has ever called my clothes cute before, even nonchalantly like that.

'Let's go,' he says.

Bobby takes me to a Vietnamese deli on Seven Dials for lunch, trendy without being inflated, and we order pork and dumpling stew and sit at one of the cheap, lightweight metal tables. The waitress brings over our drinks and the lemonade stings my tongue.

'Are you enjoying the job?' he asks.

I nod. 'Jim is exactly what I thought he would be. He's a bit of a circus ringmaster, isn't he?'

'And what does that make all of us?'

'Performing monkeys?'

He laughs and I notice for the first time his very dark moss-green eyes. 'Profitable monkeys, at least. Give him his due, Jim's grown the company massively from when he took it over all those years ago.'

'What happened to the founders?' I ask.

'They were boys,' Bobby says, and drinks his lemonade. 'They hit the big time. I think Jim came at the right moment and he was cash-rich. He cleaned them out after a few years. They left, did other things.'

'That seems a bit unfair,' I say.

'Life's a bitch,' he replies. 'And Jim's a winner.'

'Is he?'

'Ruthless but charming. When it suits him, Jim likes anyone and everyone. But we have big rows.'

'About what?'

'I put my twopence in about how to spend the money. He likes to blow a lot.'

'Has he got more money than sense?' I ask.

Bobby shakes his head. 'He's got an abundance of both. So mind yourself.'

'What do you do, then?' I ask as the waitress delivers two large portions of rich dark stew and places them in front of us. 'Apart from talk to strangers on bridges?'

He smiles and picks up his cutlery. He holds his knife and fork the opposite way round. I always notice how people eat. A service life.

'I'm in concepts,' he says.

I blow the steam rising from the bowl. 'Oh,' I say. 'Like ideas?'

'Yeah,' he replies. 'Not that I have many. You wanted to talk about *Pranksters*? I hear you got to choose the host.'

I feel disgust at the memory of Jim's hands guiding mine over the pictures of the young women.

'Yes,' I say. 'A girl called Marie.'

'And it's Jemima Mataya's memorial next week,' he adds. 'It's no coincidence that Jim's putting that on in the same few weeks that he'll be announcing Marie.' He takes a mouthful of stew. 'All a PR stunt. So why the interest in the programme?'

'It's the company's most valuable asset,' I say. 'And I find it interesting. Members of the public are so gullible, aren't they?'

'Everyone can be fooled, given the right environment for deception.'

I raise my eyebrows because I wasn't expecting this eloquence of words.

'You think it's funny?' he asks. 'The programme.'

'I think it's interesting,' I repeat.

'You know, I read once that laughter is an evolutionary social bonding tool,' he says. 'There was this study that showed that when gangs attack someone, they're often reported to laugh while doing it. It's the power of shared laughter that connects the group. Conformity.'

I think of Jim's words about authority and conformity. He's happiest when he's in control and he likes holding the strings.

Bobby drinks. 'I've also read that people laugh when there's an unexpected surprise. Like a clever joke, or when they feel scared or relieved. People laugh because they don't know how to react.'

'I think that's true of *Pranksters*,' I say.

'That people don't know how to react to it?' he says. 'Yeah, I agree with you. It's pretty merciless. Some of the stuff on it I could either laugh or cry at.'

I think of my dad.

'What if you did have someone cry?' I ask. 'Would you put that on air?'

'Depends,' he says with a shrug. 'But you can never judge someone's reaction to it, that's true. I've read some horrific things online about pranks that go wrong. Mostly in the US. Americans tend to supersize things, though. They're extremists. I read about these kids who threw eggs at cars for a laugh and one day they picked the wrong car and one of them got shot, straight out of the window.'

'Because of an egg?' I ask.

'Because of an egg.'

'Eggstremists,' I say.

He laughs and then eats another dumpling. 'Anything that involves the public has a heavy weight of uncertainty,' he comments, chewing as he speaks.

'And responsibility,' I say. 'How can you be sure that a set-up works?'

'Careful planning,' he replies. 'And that's up to the production team.'

'What if it's not careful enough?' I probe.

'Then you can get into hot water. And need a watertight legal team. But luckily we haven't had too much happen to involve the legal team,' he says. 'No death by egg.'

'No death at all?'

He looks at me funnily. 'No.'

I smile but it's devoid of feeling this time. 'Glad to hear it,' I say, and bite into a sodden dumpling. It's tacky in my mouth.

'Go halves with me on that cheesecake,' he says.

'OK,' I reply.

He nods happily and gets up to order the cheesecake.

'I have a question,' I say on his return. 'Why does Jim lock his office?'

He laughs but shakes his head. 'It's a mystery to us all. I've thought about breaking in to it. We all have.'

The waitress comes over and hands Bobby a slice of vanilla cheesecake. He thanks her. And she leaves.

'Does Jim have trust issues?' I ask.

'Jim trusts no one,' Bobby replies, and digs a fork into the cheesecake. 'You'd be wise to remember that. Look what happened to his last PA.'

'What *did* happen to her?' I ask.

He shrugs. 'Honestly? I don't know. She was with him for years. She'll have a hard time finding a new job for a while.'

I look at the cheesecake in front of me and have suddenly lost my appetite for it.

NINETEEN

It's Wednesday and there's a stack of letters on my desk when I come in after lunch. I glance at them without interest until I see a letter wedged in the pile that I recognise. It's the letter I posted on Monday night. A flutter of excitement thrums inside my chest. I place it at the top of the pile, go to knock on Jim's door.

'I have your post, Jim.'

'Come in.'

He takes the mail from my hand and pulls the letter – my letter – from its envelope.

I hold my breath as I watch him skim the words on the page.

A copy of my dad's letter and one sentence, block capitals, that I've written:

THIS IS WHAT PRANKSTERS DID TO HIM.

A frown line appears on Jim's forehead. He snaps the paper straight and reads it more carefully. Then he slams the letter down on the desk, making me start.

'Why are people such fuckwits, Matilda?' he says.

'Sorry, Jim?'

'Do you know how many letters I get like this about *Pranksters*?'

I lick my lips. 'What is it?'

'It's someone with an agenda. Probably someone who thinks they can squeeze money out of me.' He pauses. 'Like so many of them try to. It's probably not even real.'

'What does it say?'

He ignores my question. 'Why do people blame their unfortunate little lives on others?' he says. 'Tiresome.'

'Are you . . . are you upset?' I ask.

'I don't let people *upset* me,' he replies. 'You'll always have people laughing at others, Matilda, because it makes them feel better about themselves. That's what *Pranksters* is all about.'

'Maybe some people see the programme as exploitative?' I suggest.

'And they'd be absolutely right,' he says. 'Exploitation is always a money-spinner. You've seen *The Wolf of Wall Street*, haven't you? Getting rich off someone's blind trust in you. Who's in the wrong, though?'

'That's obvious,' I say.

'Is it?' he replies. 'It's evolutionary to get ahead.'

He crumples the letter in his hand and I want to cry out and press it to my heart.

'I write some of the episodes myself, you know that?' he says. 'The ideas meetings are the only meetings I attend. I never miss them.'

I wonder if my dad's episode had Jim's mark on it and feel a tight fury coil itself in my chest.

'Jim, are you free?' says a female voice. 'I can't get hold of your bloody PA.'

I look at the door and see Andrea Rubins dressed in a black silk jumpsuit and blue spiky heels. Her hair is thick and long and dark and her eyes are catwalk smoky.

'That's because my "bloody PA" is in here with me,' Jim retorts. 'Have the two of you met?'

This woman looks at me with undisguised boredom.

'Matilda, this is Andrea Rubins,' Jim says.

'Hello,' I say.

'Yeah,' she replies, and then looks back at Jim. 'Have you got five minutes?'

Jim looks at me. 'Get us some coffee, Matilda,' he says. He throws the crumpled letter carelessly to the floor, where it rolls under his feet like rubbish. I stare at it, any hope of satisfaction I had now crushed and lying beside it. 'Matilda?'

I look up from the letter on the floor. 'Sorry?'

'Coffee,' Jim says.

'Mine is an espresso, double shot,' Andrea says, sitting herself on the sofa opposite Jim.

I leave his office, snatch my bag but leave my coat because my body feels like it's blistering with heat. I go straight to the lift and then, when the doors are closed, I heave great breaths which reverberate around the walls because I can't let the pain out yet. I get out my phone and I log in to the forum.

Please be there. I need you.

Horsehead: You did what?!

Top Step: I sent him the copy of my dad's letter.

Horsehead: What letter?

Top Step: His suicide note.

Horsehead: His suicide note?? What the fuck? Why did you do that! You've literally arrived at the place and Jim will turn his big Cyclops eye straight on you!

When you get home, you're going to slap yourself in the face with a fucking fish because you've been a prick.

Top Step: I wanted to see his face, Horsehead. I wanted to hear what he'd say! This is why I'm here. To *do* something! Revenge!

Horsehead: But not *that*, doll! Jeez. So what did he say?

Top Step: Nothing. He threw the letter on the floor like it was nothing.

Horsehead: Top Step, Top Step. Don't be so naive.

Top Step: I wish you were here with me. I feel like I've taken on Goliath.

Horsehead: David killed Goliath, remember? Hey, you could shoot him and save yourself all this trouble? With a gun though, not a pebble from a slingshot.

Top Step: We don't have guns on hand in this country.

Horsehead: *You* wouldn't, obviously, you're a middle-class white chick who drinks tea. It's not hard to ask for one though.

Top Step: Have you got a gun?

Horsehead: What do you think?

Top Step: Have you ever shot anything?

Horsehead: Yes.

Top Step: You've shot someone??

Horsehead: Empty beer cans on a wall. I'm American not a fucking murderer. Stop watching *CSI*.

TWENTY

The next day, Jim picks up the coffee I bought him from the canteen and he knocks it back like it's a shot of vodka. I asked for it to be extra hot and as soon as he swallows, his eyes bulge.

'Shit!'

The brown liquid dribbles down his chin and Gertie barks from the sofa opposite my desk.

'New barista,' I say, and I take the moment to enjoy that it has scalded him.

He snatches up a tissue from a box on my desk and dabs at his mouth. 'Not for long,' he growls, and drops it to the floor for me to pick up. 'Book me into the golf club for a week on Sunday.'

I nod, click into his calendar. 'Oh, I think you have your son's cross-country race on that Sunday?' I say.

'Book golf anyway,' Jim replies. 'I have a client I need to win round. And you need to get a present for my wife for her birthday. You choose.'

'A . . . a present? What does she like?'

'A spa in the New Forest, a new silk dressing gown, lingerie, whatever you want,' he says.

I swallow. I can't imagine choosing a gift so intimate for anyone, let alone Lucinda Kit.

151

'And don't let on if my wife calls about Sunday,' he says. 'I hate Ben's races. I hate all the bloody school events.'

He disappears into his office and leaves me thinking that my dad never had the chance to go to many of my or Lissy's school events. I think how proud of us he would have been if he'd ever got to tell us.

While Jim's busy, I turn my attention to the relentless list of folders in his inbox and click solidly for an hour, reading, skimming documents and pages of correspondence between all and sundry.

I hover over the next one in the list – 'Forecasting'. I groan internally and begin clicking through graphs and spreadsheets and forecast analyses.

But there is one email halfway down the list where a name appears that is unfamiliar and is not from a work address. It was received yesterday.

From: Oliver Kealey

To: Jim Valente

Date: 27 January 2021, 15:34:51

Regarding this letter with the alleged suicide note. There doesn't appear to be any considerable link for you to pay attention. It's essentially emotional blackmail without detail so is utterly harmless. Not like the others. Don't pay heed to it.

But while we're on the subject, your question re: *Pranksters* – we WILL need to keep up the contract with McManus. That, I regret to say, might be a debt you will pay for ever. We should have heard about the date in advance from the courts, but we didn't. Judge didn't keep his word; I will speak to him.

I'm in Italy but back next week. Meet me Tuesday 2nd – Covent Garden Hotel, 8 p.m.

I look to Jim's office door. He's inside, head bent low and scratching red pen through documents. I take my phone from my bag.

Horsehead: 'Oliver Kealey'. I can see what you can see online – he's a private lawyer, used to be a barrister and now retired. Does he do any legal stuff with Cyclops?

Top Step: We have a legal team here. And we also have an independent legal counsel called Thacker and Isle. I checked with HR on the pretence of a legal question.

Horsehead: So we have an Oliver Twist in the plot? Lovely.

Top Step: What else can you find on Oliver?

Horsehead: Nothing else of note on him. No physical address, zilch.

Top Step: It reads like my letter triggered this. I didn't think it had had any effect, but it did, Horsehead. And it's led us here! To names. McManus.

Horsehead: Yeah it does, doll, I'll concede that. So what's your next step?

Top Step: I've searched all the folders for the names, but there's nothing else from Oliver Kealey and nothing with 'McManus' on it.

Horsehead: Try the vaults?

Top Step: The what?

Horsehead: The archive vaults. Ask your IT nerds.

Top Step: You think? So soon after I asked them for Jim's inbox?

Horsehead: Sure!

Top Step: What if I get them fired?

Horsehead: Casualties in warfare. Don't worry about the IT nerds. They're part of the game.

Top Step: Are they?

Horsehead: They are now! You can't worry about anyone there. You've found out what to focus on. McManus.

Top Step: I'm going to go to the Covent Garden Hotel, Horsehead. Next week. I'm going to go.

Horsehead: Really?? You're going to crash their meeting like some sort of terrible undercover cop??

Top Step: Yes.

Horsehead: Shit, that's big, doll. Jim CANNOT see you.

Top Step: I know.

Horsehead: How you going to do this?

Top Step: I'll dress up.

Horsehead: Seriously? Like what? You got another wig?

Top Step: I have three.

Horsehead: Hell, you *are* prepared. Why don't you add a comedy fucking nose and really go to town.

Top Step: You don't like the idea.

Horsehead: No! Jeez! If he saw you, it could be game over.

Top Step: Or it could be something I can use? The email mentioned *Pranksters*. That Jim's forever going to pay for it. I want to find pranks that have gone wrong and this could be one of them!

Horsehead: I mean, yeah, shit. It could be. Just be fucking careful, yeah?

154

*

I sit on my bed in my pyjamas with my laptop on my knees and I FaceTime Lissy.

'How was your day?' she asks. She's propped her phone up on her TV stand in her university room and I can see she's painting her nails on the bed. Her room is a messy love child of Aladdin and Father Christmas. There are tacked posters on the wall: one of Maria Alexandrova, the Russian ballet dancer, and one of a cat licking its behind.

'It was fine,' I reply. 'I'm sitting down a lot.'

'You'll develop a shelf-butt,' she says.

'Thanks,' I say. 'I'll log that away. How's everything with you?'

She shrugs, not looking at me because she's being careful with her nails. 'Good,' she answers. 'I'm writing more sad poetry.'

'Which is weird, Liss, because you're a happy person.'

'Am I?' she says. She gives a little laugh, but I don't know if it's a laugh that says she's joking or a laugh that affirms she's sad. 'I'm writing about Mum,' she adds.

I inhale sharply and then she looks straight into the camera of her phone.

'I know,' she says. 'Sorry, but I am. It's nice to release it.'

I say nothing.

'It's good to release things, isn't it?' she presses. 'Why don't you talk about her?'

'Why would I?' I reply.

'El,' she starts.

'I've got to go, Liss,' I say, and hang up.

TWENTY-ONE

Signing myself into Jim's inbox was risky enough, but to ask for access to old emails is a step further and I have to be careful not to raise suspicion.

It's Friday, eleven in the morning, and Jim is out at a meeting with Andrea Rubins. I take the lift down to the basement and walk into the IT room. Paul is hunched over a screen and his fingers are typing faster than I think humanly possible. Eric is nowhere to be seen.

'Hi,' I say, walking towards Paul. It's so dark in the basement that I can barely make my way over to his desk. Even his face is in darkness. 'Don't you want the main light on?'

He mock gasps and looks up at me; his eyes are illuminated in the blue light of the screen. 'And see the world in cruel technicolour?' he says.

'Where's Eric?' I ask.

'He's upstairs fixing a computer,' he replies. 'We played rock, paper, scissors for it. He lost.'

'OK,' I say, and think maybe that's better. Two people might be harder to convince. 'You really like the basement that much that you don't like leaving it?'

'Real people scare me. That's why you won't see me at any of those shitty briefings.' He smiles to show me he's joking, but I nod because I agree with him. 'So what's up?'

'Jim has a missing-emails issue,' I say. 'Can you help me get into the historical vaults? Jim doesn't know anything about them and nor do I, but I'm pretty certain you'd be able to help me?'

'You've come to the right place,' he replies. 'What are you looking for?'

'Specifically a couple of names.'

'OK?'

'Oliver Kealey,' I say. 'And the name "McManus".'

'McManus,' he repeats, already beginning to type. 'No first name?'

'Jim's forgotten it,' I say.

'OK,' he replies.

I touch his shoulder lightly, think of Wendy. She would be proud of me.

'Thank you so much,' I say.

He hits enter and in seconds I see emails start to appear, but as soon as I begin to get excited, they stop. There are only five and they're old, from 2004, and all in quick succession.

'OK?' Paul says. 'Is that what you want?'

I peer at the screen.

'I'll give you some room to check,' he offers.

I skim-read them and he averts his eyes, busying himself with another screen.

From: Oliver Kealey

To: Jim Valente

Date: 13 October 2004, 13:26:57

The legalities around this are interesting and difficult. How are the boys on this? Keep them informed. There might be a significant fallout and they'll need to know how to respond.

From: Oliver Kealey
To: Jim Valente
Date: 13 October 2004, 13:46:21
Yes, this is sensible. Have you seen the family? What's the condition at the moment?

From: Oliver Kealey
To: Jim Valente
Date: 13 October 2004, 14:04:12
Send him to them. What do you feel is a reasonable sum?

From: Oliver Kealey
To: Jim Valente
Date: 13 October 2004, 14:48:39
You could wrap up the programme, but if not, I suggest we arrange the contract between ourselves. Personal to personal, agreed?

My mind is whirring with questions. What has happened? Whose condition and who are the boys? What contract are they arranging?

I click on the last email, hoping that it might give me some clue.

From: Oliver Kealey
To: Jim Valente
Date: 14 October 2004, 15:28:20
I am conscious of doing this over email if you're not wanting to go the other route via T&I and can't use your home address. Let's meet at the usual, and discuss further?

And then there's nothing, a dead end. I suck my teeth, frustrated. Where are all the replies to these emails?

'Paul?' I say. 'I can't see the correspondence from Jim on this email chain. Is that something you can help me with?'

He turns around, takes the mouse from me and starts to click. 'Huh,' he says. 'Yeah, that's weird. You want me to keep digging? We have our vaults accessible for ten years – I'm not sure how these slipped through the net – but if you need more information, we can pay for access?'

I weigh it up, but I'm worried that too many questions might be asked. 'No, don't worry. Thanks for trying,' I say.

'I did find this, though,' Paul continues. 'There was another name in these emails you wanted to look at, right? McManus?'

There's no one in the office other than us, but hearing the name aloud causes a flutter of anxiety in my chest.

'Yes,' I reply.

'It appears in one email,' Paul explains. 'I searched the entire system.'

'Just one?'

'Yes,' he says.

'OK, can you forward all these on to me, Paul?' I ask.

'Sure,' he replies.

'Thanks,' I say. 'I owe you.'

'That coffee,' he suggests.

'Absolutely,' I reply.

I wait until I'm home that night before reading the McManus email. As soon as I returned to my desk and saw them in my inbox, I printed them out and deleted them, too afraid to read them anywhere other than in the safety of my own flat.

Whatever is written in this email, I dare to hope it could expose Jim somehow and in turn help me structure his downfall.

I sit on the sofa and I unfold the paper.

From: Tess McManus
To: Jim Valente
Date: 21 December 2004, 11:08:46
Mr Valente.
We've talked as a family and we've decided to accept your pro-
posal on Episode 8: Skating. We don't want courts and Chloe
doesn't want to be in newspapers any more than she has to be.
We'll meet to discuss the conditions – Oliver Kealey wrote in his
letter dated 3 November 2004 that you'll set up the account.
We'll keep our silence, but know this – we will never forgive you.
What you do, what you stand for, everything about your com-
pany and *Pranksters* is dark and my daughter paid the price for it.
You stop paying, we go to the press.
Tess McManus.

A shot of euphoria floods my veins. Was this Episode 8 of
Pranksters? Surely yes.

I open my laptop and in a website browser, I write 'Pranksters, episode 8, skating' and hit go. To my surprise, however, there are no matches. I add 'McManus' alongside it, but
again, the infinite resource of the internet turns up all episodes
but this one. I frown, confused. Was this episode never aired?

I spend more than an hour composing one short line to
Tess McManus. I ask to meet her.

Horsehead: How did you find this gold dust??

Top Step: The IT department. Though I'm a little
worried the guys there might become suspicious of
what I'm doing.

Horsehead: I told you – they won't question you.
Hell, they've probably never talked to a real girl before.

Top Step: You're being cruel.

Horsehead: It's probably the truth, but we're digressing.

Top Step: I need to find this footage, Horsehead. This could be how I can take Jim down in the best way ever!

Horsehead: Hold your horses there, doll. If any prank had gone so bad, any evidence would have been destroyed.

Top Step: The only evidence I would need is Chloe's account of what happened, though, wouldn't I? So I need to talk to her and to her parents. And I need to find out more about what the 'account' means. I can only think that Jim's paying them. And there must be physical archives, Horsehead, right? Of all their programmes? I could find that one and more!

Horsehead: Look at you.

Top Step: What?

Horsehead: I'm like a proud parent, doll. You've become a hunter.

TWENTY-TWO

'I like your pyjamas,' I say.

Lissy's pyjamas are pink with white and yellow dancing circus ponies.

'Thanks,' she replies. 'You look like a convict.'

She's right. Mine are boringly grey and white striped. I take the tea she's made and shift on the bed to make room for her. We're at Charlie's for the weekend and Polo is asleep on the carpet below us, smelling of weeds and mud.

I almost made my excuses not to come to Charlie's this weekend, because since I read those emails, I've been desperate to spend every spare minute solidly searching online for anything to do with the McManus family. I've dug up hundreds of Chloe McManus profiles on social media sites, all of which I'm checking through, but there's absolutely nothing on any Tess McManus. Can people be that invisible? Surely in this day and age all people leave digital footprints? That said, I have kept myself hidden well enough.

I check my emails every few minutes to update them in case Tess has written back to me, but each time I'm met with silence. I'm afraid that she won't email or that she's decided that life has moved on and, if that's the case, then that lead is dead.

'Why are we watching this?' Lissy asks.

THE PRANK

We're watching *Pranksters* on Lissy's tablet. Finding out about Episode 8 has spurred me on to looking into more of them. From what I've already seen, all episodes blur the line of what's acceptable ethically, but there must be one that's so off the wall that I can delve into its archives and see if I can contact the person who fell victim to it, see if they would be willing to talk about their experience. It could turn out to be a needle in-a-haystack exercise, but I need to be prepared to go down any route, because I might not be able to find Chloe or hear from Tess McManus.

'My friend recommended it,' I say.

Lissy nods and then laughs loudly at the screen. 'Ha! I love that one,' she says.

'You think these are good?' I ask.

She snorts. 'Isn't that why we're watching them?'

'It's schadenfreude,' I say. 'Laughing at someone else's misfortune.'

'Oh totally,' she agrees. 'But that guy pranked for thinking a ferret can talk is an idiot and deserves ridicule.'

'Do you think he felt embarrassed?' I say.

'Are you kidding?' she replies. 'People will probably call him Ferret Man for the rest of his life. Hope he's got a sense of humour.'

'I feel sorry for him,' I admit.

'You'd feel sorry for a frog in the rain,' she counters. 'Some of this is a little dark, but that's life, right?'

'You blindly accept that life should be like that?'

'Oh God, El,' she laughs. 'Not all of us have got your viewpoint.'

'What's my viewpoint?'

'Ethical superiority,' she says. 'I love you, but you do tend to sit on your high horse and judge the rest of us for having a bit of a laugh at people.'

'Do I?' I say, because this is news to me.

'Yeah,' she replies.

'Don't I have a sense of humour?'

She reaches for me. 'Of course you do,' she soothes. 'You're one of the funniest people I know, but you can be oversensitive to things since . . .' She trails off, but she doesn't need to finish the rest of the sentence. We both know when I became hyper-sensitive – but how has she not become the same? I move my arm away from her fingertips and she picks up the remote and pauses the programme.

'Can I ask you something?' she says. 'Serious now.'

'Yeah?'

She sucks on her bottom lip, studies me. 'Will you tell me about her? About Mum?'

It's like she's hit me. 'About Mum? Why are you suddenly wanting to talk about her?'

'I'm always wanting to talk about her,' she says quietly. 'I miss her so much.' She sighs. 'You have all these amazing stories about Dad but never any about Mum.'

'I only have one story about Mum,' I say.

She smiles, oblivious to my tone. 'OK, is it one I don't know?'

I scowl. 'Once upon a time, there was a woman who had a family, a husband, a little girl and a toddler. One day she had an affair with a guy called William and then she left.'

'El . . .' Lissy says.

'She went to America,' I continue. 'For a year, she wrote to her daughters, *wrote* to them. Dad said she never called, just wrote. What kind of a mother doesn't want to talk to her kids?'

The day she left, Mum went shopping with the duck-yellow canvas bag. I'll always remember that detail, strange as it is. Yellow is the first colour the eye sees and therefore the colour of warning signs. Perhaps I should have read into this more, that Mum chose that bag. I wanted to go with her, but she was adamant that she wanted to go alone, and we later learnt that she took the train to Wiltshire with William and a week after that they left together for America. Such a simplistic plan, but so calculated.

'It's not you girls, all right?' Dad said. He'd discovered a note from Mum in their bedroom, but we were forbidden to see it. 'It's because of me. Never you, OK?'

'Will she come back?' I asked, because she had always come back.

But he stared into the middle distance and in the weeks that followed he sank into a state so low I didn't think he was going to make it to the other side. He stayed in bed with the curtains drawn and I brought him sandwiches and cups of tea until we ran out of both. After twelve long days, I picked up the phone and I called Uncle Charlie and when he came, all the pain that I had held in to look after Dad came out. I was hysterical and raving.

'And then she died. Left and then *died*.'

Lissy's face has creased, like she's about to cry, but I feel angry – no, worse – furious.

'She could have given us *good* memories,' I add. 'Instead of a few letters she sent from California.'

Lissy's eyes are filmed with tears and my fury dissipates. I reach across to her, hold her hand.

'Sorry,' I say. 'Sorry. But I never thought Mum could up and leave us and she did and that's when I first realised that the people you love can *hurt* you. I'll never forgive that. Never. Her leaving us was a massive part of what happened to Dad. His depressive episodes got worse after she left, you know that. And then . . .'

I swallow down a sob that threatens to spill over because I can't mention the prank to her, or anything afterwards.

'Then we were left by both of them,' I add.

'Do you blame Dad for what he did to himself?'

'Of course not,' I say. I grind my teeth. 'He was pushed to do it.'

'By who?' my sister asks, but I don't answer her aloud.

Pranksters. Jim.

'We should go to sleep,' I say.

'Don't you want to carry on watching this?' she says. 'Take our minds off it?'

'No,' I reply. 'Definitely not this.'

Lissy is in my bed, wrapped up in sleep. I wonder if she dreams like I dream – about events from the worst years of my life, in vivid colours – or if she's spared these things. I wonder if she dreams of laughter and impromptu song lyrics, of summer-faded grass and stolen kisses with all the boys she talks to me about.

I go to the kitchen and sit quietly at the table. One of Charlie's ferns trails green fingers along the wood grain and on to a sheet of white paper. I move the paper towards me, then reach behind for a pencil from the cluttered dresser. Before my brain registers what I'm doing, my pencil has started to draw a face. The shape of it first, strong and square, and then the hairline. I stroke the lead over the page to take time on the strands of thick, dark hair and then I draw the eyes, close-set, intelligent. I flick a dimple in a cheek, sweep the laughter lines around his mouth. I make Jim handsome because he is. I take my time over it. It's a good portrait and I feel small again because nothing I've done has made any difference to this titan of a man.

I hold my head in my hands, breathe out and then I turn the paper over and start to draw a slender frame, a jewel-like face. I line out beautiful wavy hair and a full beaming smile, eyes that are creased in laughter. I draw her bending at the waist, with her arms outstretched the way I remember when I ran into them. I'm hit with paralysing sorrow because I've drawn Mum. She was the one who inspired my love of art.

'Poetry in colours for me, poetry in words for your dad,' she used to say.

I rip the paper, ball it and the noise tears into the silence.

Horsehead: Why are you awake at this time of night? Isn't it two in the morning over there? Have you transformed into an owl? I'd like to transform into animals. What could I be?

Top Step: I don't know.

Horsehead: Play the game.

Top Step: A duck-billed platypus.

Horsehead: Come on now. I need claws.

Top Step: They do have claws.

Horsehead: They have flippers.

Top Step: They have claws.

Horsehead: Shit, I looked it up. They do. You're pretty clued up on your platypuses. Platypi?

Top Step: I'm a bit sad.

Horsehead: Sad, angelfish? Why?

Top Step: I've had a bit of a strange conversation with my sister about our mum.

Horsehead: What's the deal with your mom?

Top Step: You said that you weren't close to your family, is that right?

Horsehead: Correct. Bunch of – what's that Irish word? – eejits.

Top Step: We're also dysfunctional. Mum had an affair and moved to America and then she became really ill. She died, actually. It was a year before our dad died.

Horsehead: What happened to her?

Top Step: She had cancer.

Horsehead: Aw, I'm sorry. So you guys don't have anyone?

Top Step: We have our uncle.

Horsehead: I'm really sorry, doll. Truly. What was she like, your mom? She give you good hugs? She sing you lullabies? Kiss your knees when you fell over?

Top Step: I guess she did all those things.

Horsehead: Makes it harder when they leave you. Tell me about her.

Top Step: I don't know where to start . . . She read us books, took us to the woods, picked out shells at the beach for us. She always had a chocolate bar in her bag for when things got bad.

Horsehead: Bad?

Top Step: Like when I realised I'd never become a Ninja Turtle.

Horsehead: You sound like you were a deluded kid, but your mom sounds real nice.

Top Step: I didn't think she'd ever leave. Not properly. Dad had episodes of depression and Mum used to leave him for days, weeks at a time, but she always came back. And then she just didn't. She died and never said goodbye to us. Anyway, the point is that Lissy seems to have this whole other viewpoint of Mum. She's younger than me, has a completely different history with her, you know? She wants to be able to remember the good and I can't. I was so angry when I found out she'd died. Not upset but angry. I never forgave her for leaving and when Dad died, I transferred that anger and guilt over to Mum too. I couldn't be angry at Dad, so I directed it to her.

Horsehead: Why couldn't you be angry at him?

Top Step: Because he was my everything.

Horsehead: Maybe you need to grieve for your mom?

Top Step: Trust me, I can't do any more grief. I don't know if my heart has the capacity.

Horsehead: The heart can always give more.

Top Step: Enough of me.

Horsehead: No, not enough of you. You're in a strange place, doll. Rally your friends around you. You need a bit of TLC, right?

Top Step: I don't have any friends, Horsehead.

Horsehead: Sure you do.

Top Step: No, I don't think I do. I keep everyone at arm's-length, even the people who I worked with for years at the restaurant. They were so good to me and I never let them in.

Horsehead: Why not?

Top Step: Because why get close to anyone?

Horsehead: Oh jeez. I'm playing the world's smallest violin over here.

Top Step: Do you know what, that's the first time I've ever thought about it. I'm completely devoid of friends, except for my sister. She's the only one who really knows me and I even pretend with her! I pretend everything is OK because I don't want her to suffer like I have.

Horsehead: What am I then, if you have no friends?

Top Step: You're invisible. A man online who I've never even seen.

Horsehead: Oh hell, Top Step. Don't make me spend all my savings on a plane ride over to see you. I'd only slap you round the face with a fish and fish don't travel well. Let people in then. See how that goes for you.

Top Step: OK. Thanks for listening to me. I'm not sure that's what the $1000 was for, was it? :)

Horsehead: Please don't emoji me.

Top Step: Sorry ;)

TWENTY-THREE

Gwen and I ride the lift down to the first floor together where all the physical content archives are kept under lock and key.

'Thanks for taking me down to the archives,' I say.

'Pleasure to help,' she replies. 'What are you looking for?'

'Profit and loss statements for a few of the early episodes,' I say, hoping that sounds like the right jargon.

She looks surprised. 'Wouldn't Finance have all that? You don't need the physical content. Although I suppose all the contracts and things are kept in the folder alongside the footage.'

'Right,' I reply, cursing myself. I can't mess this up, I can't risk losing Gwen as an informant. 'I think Jim wants to go through everything for audit purposes.'

'OK,' she says, but her brow furrows. 'I would have thought he had people doing that sort of thing for him? I suppose keeping his eye on the details has got him all his money and where he is today.'

'That must be it,' I say.

I'm nervous, have started wringing my hands, but the lift doors open and save me from saying anything else. Gwen steps out first and buzzes with her ID card on to a steel plate on the wall. I watch her punch in four digits and the lock on the doors clicks. The inside of the vault looks like a huge warehouse, with bare polished-concrete flooring and floor-to-ceiling silver shelves as far as I can see packed with files and books. The air in here is cold and smells of metal.

'We have digital copies of everything, obviously, but the physical stuff is stored here, for various uses,' she explains as we walk forward. Our footsteps echo. 'We also have a secure lock-up in Fulham for the confidential, as-yet-unscreened material.'

'It's amazing in here,' I say, looking around as we pass shelves. 'How do you find anything?'

'It's all alphabetical but, like a library, it has its own system and it's sort of complicated to work out. So it's a good thing you asked me.'

We appear to be the only two people in here.

'It's not monitored by anyone?' I ask.

Gwen shakes her head. 'No.'

We round a corner.

'Here,' she says. '*Pranksters*. Organised by episode, first series is at the end there and then it moves downwards and then across. The black folders have the footage and everything else in it. Script, expenditure, sign-off, everything like that.'

My heart leaps. 'Brilliant,' I exclaim. 'Thanks so much.'

She nods. 'OK,' she says. 'To get out just sweep your pass. You don't need the code.'

'OK,' I say.

She gives me a little wave. 'Bye then.'

'Thanks for all your help,' I say.

I watch her walk back until she's out of sight, listening to her kitten heels clack to fade. The doors close behind her and I'm left alone. I jog to the end of the aisle, stand on tiptoes and trace the printed words on the first reel in its box: *Pranksters*

Episode 1: 'The Clown' / 'Heidi and the Bear' / 'The Farmer's Crop'. Three pranks per episode.

I skip over the boxes to look for Episode 8. It's halfway down or, rather, it should be. I can find Episodes 7 and 9, but Episode 8 is missing from between them. I frown. Perhaps it's been put out of sequence.

I go back to the first shelf again and scour the boxes, but all other episodes are in order. I begin to look further on, past 9, all the way to 20, in case it's been categorised as 18 by mistake, but it's not here. My breath snags. I'm only metres away from the file that must contain my dad's footage, Episode 32, 'The Lost Child'. Before I ask myself if I'm OK with looking at it, I've reached up, taken it down and opened it. There's a clean copy of the script, though I've seen the episode so many times I could almost recite it word for word. Seeing it in black and white makes me feel ill.

I put the script back, look at the finance records, which detail the costs for the actors, the location, the set-up of the cameras on council property and a payout to the coffee shop for use of their premises on screen. There's a payment to my dad for £300 and, with this, a stapled sheet – the contract with Dad's shaky signature, his name in print and the date next to it. I read about the details of the campaign around it, the tags online, the payments to and from the broadcaster for snippet adverts, for rights to air and repeats. All this money for such cheap entertainment.

There is no copy of the letters my dad sent Jim, nor Jim's replies. The folder appears squeaky clean, just another episode quietly sitting for audit purposes.

'What are you doing?'

The voice echoes around the floor and I twist round to see Andrea practically on top of me. I open my mouth, dumbfounded that I've not heard her. She's wearing ballet shoes and a silken black dress and has glided, wraithlike, through the aisles without notice.

'I was looking for—'

'Is this about the awards ceremony montage? For his announcement about his new host?' she asks. 'Because that's why I'm here. You tell him.'

'Tell . . . ?'

'Jim!' she says. 'He doesn't need to go fishing to see I've done it.'

I nod. 'The awards ceremony. Right. Yes, it is.'

'Tell him I'm getting it. Literally here getting it now.' She sighs. 'In fact, you can help me. What's that one you have there?'

'This?'

'I need five episodes for the clip and the digital ones are god knows where in god knows what folder,' she continues. 'We'll cut them all down tomorrow. No one has a bloody ounce of time.'

I stare at her dumbly.

'Give it to me then,' she says and reaches her hand out for the file.

I have it clutched to my chest like a child would a beloved toy. I hold it out reluctantly and she takes it, looks at the writing.

'"Lost Child". Yes, good.' She turns to the shelves, looks at labels. '"The Hotel Inspector",' she says. 'Yes, that was a good one. "Rip Tide", that one, yes.'

I'm staring at Episode 32 in her hands. I feel an over-whelming lurch of protection over it and want to take it back from her.

She looks at me. 'Two more.'

'Two more,' I repeat stupidly. I reach across, blindly take one from the shelf. 'Here,' I say.

'"Treasure Island", OK. And that one as well,' she says, picking one from the opposite side. She reads its print. '"Fran's Invisible Furies". Right. Come on, then.' She uses a voice she would use for a dog. She turns on her slippered heel and stalks towards the door.

TWENTY-FOUR

It's Tuesday night and I'm wearing the sleek bob wig, bright red lipstick and a blue collared dress that I found at the back of the wardrobe and which I'll have to throw away after this because I'll need to be doubly sure I don't wear it again, ever.

Euey has picked me up from my flat and he looks confused as I get inside.

'Eleanor?' he says.

'Yes,' I say. 'It's me. I . . . I'm meeting a friend and we thought it would be fun to dress up. Nineteen-forties sort of thing.'

I see Euey's head bob in a nod and he pulls away from the curb. 'Oh, great,' he replies.

We drive in silence and I'm glad I called him, and even gladder that he was available. I like him, and I feel safe with him somehow.

'Here we go,' Euey says after fifteen minutes. 'Covent Garden Hotel.'

My throat is dry. I open the car door and pause.

'Are you around to take me home?'

He shakes his head. 'Aw, I'm sorry, love. I've got to get home now.'

'OK,' I say, and suddenly feel very alone.

The hotel bar is small and intimate, with dark-framed art on the walls and jazz playing. I wonder where Jim and Oliver might sit. I scan the free tables – there are several at the back and some by the windows. I go to the bar and order a red wine, considering my options on where to sit or whether to hover here. Then I panic that perhaps they're having dinner in the brasserie and won't come to the bar at all.

'Six seventy-five,' the barman says.

He looks a bit like Pavel from The Cello, or maybe I just want him to. I pay him.

'Take a seat and I'll bring it over,' he says. 'Would you like olives? Nuts?'

'Oh,' I say, because now it's obvious that he doesn't expect me to stay here at the bar. 'Right. No, thank you. Just the drink.'

I go to the back of the bar and seat myself at one of the empty tables. It's louder here because it's closer to the entrance of the restaurant. Should I have picked differently? I could always move.

I take out my phone to fiddle with because I think I must look suspicious here, alone. I should have thought to bring a book or a magazine.

'Madam?'

The barman has appeared with my drink.

'Thank you,' I say.

My words are snatched away because Jim walks through the door, and seeing him causes my skin to prickle with heat. I pick up my phone again as the barman places my wine on a delicate paper coaster for me.

'Excuse me?'

It's Jim's voice. It seems to be directed towards me and I keep my head low.

'Be with you in a moment, sir,' the barman replies.

'It's a Merlot with two glasses,' says Jim.

'Certainly, sir.'

In my agitated state, my phone slips through my fingers and I drop it to the table, where it clatters loudly before I sweep it up again. I hide my face behind the bob wig and pretend to be looking in my bag, but between the curtains of hair, I see Jim remain near my table. For an alarming moment, I think he's going to sit with me, at my very table, but he stops and stands at the table in front of mine. He throws his jacket over the back of the chair and then sits, facing away from me. If ever I believed in luck, this very moment has confirmed it.

'Oliver, over here.'

I look at a man who is walking towards Jim. He looks less tailored than Jim, as though his suit was expensive at the time of purchase but is now past its best. His hair is white at the temples, too long at the back, and he has purple bags under his eyes. The men say nothing to one another, not even a greeting, while a waiter places a bottle and glasses between them.

'OK?' the man, Oliver, asks when the waiter has left them.

'I'm getting sick of spinning these plates,' Jim says.

'Aye,' agrees Oliver. 'But that's the price, isn't it? That was always the choice you made.'

'Some of the payments are too heavy. You need to reduce the amounts.'

Oliver purses his lips. 'That will be difficult.'

'What do I pay you for, then?' Jim snaps.

Oliver doesn't answer. He pours the wine into each of the glasses and then sits back with one.

'More importantly,' Jim says, 'is that you need to work out what to do with McManus now.'

He reaches around to his jacket, removes a small object from the inside pocket and both Oliver and I look, but I can't see what it is.

'She almost found it,' Jim adds. 'Sylvie. So I want you to keep it for a while.'

'No,' Oliver replies.

'No?' Jim says.

I see that they're staring at each other. Jim twists the thing round in his covered fist and I will him to open his palm, because I'm gambling with my time looking up at them without being noticed. My heart is now jabbing so hard in my chest that my lungs feel as if they're being punctured from within. I sip at the wine to moisten my mouth but want to spit it out because the taste has increased tenfold with the pressure of this moment – it's tangy, sharp and bitter.

'That's yours to keep,' Oliver says. 'Everything on it is for you to keep track of.'

'It's like a fucking grenade,' Jim curses.

'Not if I wrap it all up in legal talk,' Oliver explains. '*That's* what you pay me for.'

They're both silent for a moment and Jim snatches his hand closed and drops whatever it is back into his pocket. He drinks from the glass that Oliver has poured for him.

'I've kept it all on there,' he says.

Oliver glances around the bar and I avert my eyes to avoid his. 'If you've got any sense, Jim,' he says, 'you'll delete all that shit and just keep the spreadsheets.'

'It's like some weird sort of souvenir,' Jim remarks. 'I don't like being tricked, Oliver.'

'That's rich coming from you, Jim. Isn't a tenth of your profit derived from that programme? *Pranksters*?'

'But this wasn't funny,' Jim replies.

There's a moment's silence.

'I still don't know what happened to her fucking phone,' Jim says. 'And that's the missing piece.'

'Forget about it,' Oliver says.

They don't say anything for a while and when they start a conversation again, it's about golf, the theatre, Oliver's estranged wife, a charity gala next month.

I stay for ten minutes more. Then, as subtly as I can, I get up and walk out of the bar.

Top Step: They mentioned *Pranksters*. That's what makes me think whatever he had in his hand could be interesting to me.

Horsehead: It had information on it, right? That's what the other guy said? Spreadsheets?

Top Step: Yes.

Horsehead: So it's going to be a USB then. Or a microchip.

Top Step: Whatever it is, his housekeeper Sylvie almost found it and that's telling me whatever the thing is, it's at their house.

Horsehead: But if she nearly found it, he might have moved it.

Top Step: True. Maybe his office.

Horsehead: Right. So you need to get inside.

Top Step: But it's locked, remember?

Horsehead: Can't you figure out a way to undress him of his jacket?

Top Step: Undress him?

Horsehead: Who knows what you'll resort to? You could get into his, whaddya call them over there? Knickers.

Top Step: Horsehead! I'm not going anywhere near that!

Horsehead: Ha! I love winding you up. Look, it's fine. Pick the lock.

Top Step: I can't pick locks!

Horsehead: How do you know if you've never tried? It's easy. Anyone can spring a lock when you practice.

Top Step: Are you serious?

Horsehead: Locks provide an illusion of security, doll. They make everyone feel safe at night, but if someone really wanted to get in your house, they could.

Top Step: That's really NOT reassuring, Horsehead.

Horsehead: Yeah I know, but how about this, right? Locks are shit at keeping you safe and that's scary, but it's also sort of heartening! It means that most people are actually good people and don't go around creeping inside houses.

Top Step: What *we're* proposing isn't good. We are *not* the good people.

Horsehead: Yeah, I mean, not us. We met on a revenge website. So for picking locks you'll need a tension wrench and pick rakes – you can order them online. Something wallet-sized. This one looks good – https://multipicklock.com/lock-manipulation And there are websites to show you how to do it, OK? It's more art than science, so you've got to practice, right? You have to develop a feel for it and each lock is different, but the same basic principles apply to all of them.

Top Step: This feels way out of my depth, Horsehead.

Horsehead: Come on, doll. Anyone can do it.

Top Step: How would I get in? He always leaves the office after me. Deliberately.

Horsehead: Dead of night? Don't media junkies ever pull all-nighters?

Top Step: The building has security at night.

Horsehead: You'll think of something.

Top Step: And what about the phone, Horsehead? 'Her phone'. Jim called it the missing piece.

Horsehead: Fuck knows. Keep cranking the wheel, doll. Do some crazy shit. Remember that the best ideas and the best outcomes are born from insanity. Don't be an unlikeable heroine. You gotta be brave, yeah? In the meantime, we'll both look for things on the McManus family because they sound fun times.

TWENTY-FIVE

My computer and the lights are off because I haven't yet turned them on and everything is quiet. I've come early to the office because I've wanted to take a look at Jim's office door. How easy would it be, really, to pick a lock?

I bend down, am about to put my eye to it, when a scratching noise makes me jolt backwards in panic. I see Gertie on the other side of the frosted glass, pawing at it, and I frown, confused, because how could she have been here all night?

I stand straight and go to turn the handle when I feel a hot breath at the back of my neck. I touch my hand to it and then turn around to see Jim inches from my face and I yelp with shock.

'Where were you going?' he asks.

'Jim!' I say. 'You scared me.'

He smiles at me, and I look to where he came from. Not the bathroom because I would have seen the lights; not the lift because I would have heard it arrive. Did he take the stairs? Surely I would have heard him? Where then but behind the tall cabinet behind my desk? I shiver at the understanding. Was he here, watching me, silent in the dark?

'I saw Gertie,' I say. 'I was worried that maybe . . .'

'Gertie is fine,' he replies. 'Why are you here so early?'

'I came in early to finish the minutes you wanted for your finance meeting,' I say.

'Admirable,' he says, and he slides past me and opens the office door. 'Come through.'

I hover at the doorway, watching Gertie nuzzle into Jim's palm, the bell on her collar clinking. She jogs over to me.

'I'm here early to escape my family,' he explains.

'Oh,' I reply.

'There's always a bill to be paid, a holiday to be booked, things to buy.' He sighs. 'Take a seat on the couch and tell me about your family. Tell me about the holidays you all go on.'

I blink. 'Family holidays?'

I search my head for the fictional life story. I made pages of notes during the days when Horsehead was putting the application together and yet I feel unprepared to take this stage. I have a brother, I like cakes, I like – what else?

'Sit,' he says.

I perch on the edge of his sofa and Gertie jumps up to join me. She lies down with her head on my lap. My fingers work into her fur like it's a stress ball.

'We all go camping,' I say. 'The three of us, my dad and my brother in Yorkshire. Or we go to the coast.'

'That's nice,' he says. 'Your mother doesn't go with you? Doesn't enjoy camping?'

'My mother?' I stutter over the word.

'Maybe she prefers glamping?' he suggests.

I falter. Why had I not thought to paint a picture of a mother? I am staring at him stupidly while he watches me. My conversation with Lissy is still so fresh in my head. 'She . . . she left us,' I whisper and then I kick myself internally.

'Is that why you're like you are?' he says.

'Like I am – what?'

'Mysterious,' he says. 'Aloof. Detached.'

'I don't think I am, Jim,' I reply.

We watch each other and Gertie lifts her head, senses tension and barks. Andrea Rubins is standing at the door in a dress that's a devastating shade of emerald.

'I thought we were meeting for breakfast?' she says.

'I thought you were going to call?' he counters.

'I can't call very easily,' she says. 'Can I?' She flicks her eyes at me. 'Goodbye, Matilda.'

I'm dismissed, and relieved beyond words.

'Excuse me,' Jim says quietly. '*I* dismiss my own PA from my own office.'

Andrea recognises the undertone of warning in his voice. She has overstepped the mark and she folds her arms, exhales out of her nose. I look between them, unsure.

'Take my dry cleaning to my house,' he says and nods to the back of his door where a suit bag is hanging. 'It's Jemima's memorial tonight and that's the suit.'

'OK,' I say.

'And you're dismissed,' he adds.

Despite the cold, I feel like Icarus flying towards the sun with wings that will catch light and burn. I don't want to step inside this house and yet there's an opportunity to be had here. I want to see the house, want to see Jim's most private quarters and also take stock of where – if anywhere – a USB might be hiding if it's still kept here.

I ring the bell and stand back. I can hear someone approach the door and then I see Ben, Jim's son, dressed in dark jeans and a green polo shirt.

'Hi!' he says brightly.

'Hello,' I reply. 'I'm . . . I'm Matilda. I'm your dad's PA.'

'Oh!' he mutters. 'Right!'

'I've been asked to drop some dry cleaning for him for tonight,' I explain.

'Come in!' he says.

'Am I allowed to . . . ?'

But he has already bounded across the hallway, to the kitchen door, and so I walk inside, gazing upwards and around. Their house is even more beautiful than I imagined it could be: light and clean and smelling of furniture polish.

'Do you want coffee?' he calls like a grown-up.

'I . . . Sure?' I say.

I cross the hall to join him, glancing into the living room as I walk past to see moss-green chesterfield sofas and an Edwardian writing desk. Next to it, on a little ebony table, is a vase of fresh flowers: baby's breath and roses.

'You're not in school?' I say.

'Inset day,' he explains. 'But I normally board three days a week.'

'Bradbury's,' I say.

'That's right,' he replies, and seems pleased that I know.

He drags a chair to the counter and climbs on top of it to open one of the mounted cupboards and take out a coffee pod.

'Milk?' he asks, and I smile because I can see that he's enjoying playing host.

'A little bit, thanks,' I say. 'Where's your mum?'

'She's out,' he replies as he reaches to press the button for the espresso machine. 'I'm supposed to be doing maths.'

'I won't tell,' I say.

It's strange being in the house like this with Jim's son. He seems sweet, almost naive, and I wonder if he'll grow up to be like Jim or if he'll be like Lucinda. Perhaps he'll be nothing like either of them.

'This is a lovely house,' I say.

The kitchen is bigger than it looked when I saw it through the window on New Year's Eve, but then it was crammed full of people. Looking at it now, I can see that the room is easily the size of my flat.

'Do you want to see the rest of the house?' he asks. He stirs the coffee with a silver spoon.

'Can I?'

'I'm the best tour guide,' he says, and holds out the coffee cup for me. I recognise it as Emma Bridgewater, and it has tiny spots on it. My mum used to covet these. 'Everyone says so.'

I take the coffee from him. In my other hand, I still carry the dry cleaning. The hanger tops are beginning to imprint in my palms because it's heavy, but I don't want him to reconsider this casual gesture.

'People come over from Dad's work all the time,' he adds. 'Christine, his last PA, was over a lot. His friend Andrea, too. She's Mum's friend as well.'

He leads me up the stairs, past the pictures mounted on the landing walls of fine ink drawings of London, of Ben beaming out of a frame holding a trophy for junior football and a colourful blast of what I recognise as a Hockney.

'Is that a real Hockney?' I ask before I can stop myself.

'Yeah?' he says.

Mum would have loved that too.

'There's the house in Suffolk.' He points out an aerial photograph of a huge plot surrounded by trees and fields beyond.

'Do you have horses?' I ask.

'Mum does,' he replies. 'Dad doesn't like animals. Only
Gertie.'

I tarry as I walk, absorbing their whole life on these walls.
What would Jim think if he knew what I'm doing? Would he
be angry? Would he care? Would he ever find out?

We walk along the corridor of the third floor, pass a
bathroom where I spot scented candles, Burberry, mosaic
tiles and cornflower-blue towels.

'My room,' Ben exclaims, stopping abruptly and sweeping
an arm out. 'I've got a Marvel duvet. Do you like Marvel?'

'I love it,' I say.

He beckons me inside and I step forward. 'I painted this,'
he says. He jogs over to a desk by the window and picks up a
crudely made cardboard rocket. 'Do you like it?'

'It's great,' I enthuse.

My eyes scan his room: his navy curtains, elaborate Lego
Star Wars sets on shelves, books on planets and tigers and
football, photographs on his walls. There are three of him and
Lucinda together: hand in hand and smiling on a beach with
Gertie, on horseback together in woodland and one where
he's a baby and she's holding him with her eyes closed and her
forehead pressed to his.

'Those are nice,' I say.

'Yeah,' he replies. 'I love my mum.'

I didn't expect such rawness and it causes me to smile.

'That's a nice thing to say.'

I wonder if he feels the same about Jim.

'Is there a closet I should put this in?' I ask, and then trip over myself. 'Or has your dad got a study? I wouldn't want to put this in his bedroom. He'd probably not appreciate that.'

'Oh, he won't mind,' Ben says. 'I'll take you up to their room and you can hang it. Christine used to come up all the time.'

I follow him up another flight of stairs to the top and he opens the door and I feel my throat closing up. The room is flooded with light and full of sharp edges, glass and polished metal. A piece of art hangs above the bed – a tree bending in a storm. The lights are wired on dimmers, the blinds are electronic, the curtains look heavy and expensive. The coving on the high ceiling looks like a piece of art on its own. Jim sleeps here. He gets undressed here. I stare at their impeccably made bed, the spotless ironed duck-egg duvet and goose-down pillows.

I want to stay in their room and examine everything. I want to smell inside their wardrobe, get down on the floor, under the bed and see what they keep there. I want to remove my shoes and feel the carpet pile under my bare feet, look out of the windows they look out of every morning. I want to see what books they have in their bedside drawers, examine anything inside. Being here in this most private of rooms gives me a buzz.

'You can put it in there,' Ben says.

I open a full wardrobe with a mirrored exterior that takes up one side of the room and am dazzled by the clothes, so many clothes. Hers – power dresses, cashmere, pashminas, White Company shirts, black leather trousers, print skirts. On his side, dark running and workout clothes, soft sweaters, a staggering number of suits. I hang the dry cleaning up and close the doors.

'Want to see the bathroom?' Ben asks. 'There's a jacuzzi!'

The en suite has underfloor heated white tiles and blue walls and William Morris-design towels, duck egg in colour to match the bed linen. A bath big enough for two with jacuzzi jets, a shower big enough for six. A dressing table and stool with a mirror atop it and, in the middle of it, an elegant wooden jewellery box, rosewood with a mother-of-pearl inlay. My mum had one like this.

'The phone's ringing,' Ben says and, before I know it, he's shot out of the room and I'm left alone.

I know I should follow him, but I cross the room, put my cup down and open the jewellery box. Pink suede lines the inside and it smells of Dior perfume. There are four compartments, all crammed full of rings, brooches, necklaces and bracelets which sparkle seductively. There's a ring beneath a couple of necklaces. I reach inside and take it out. It's simple and slim but with a bright sapphire within it and two diamonds on either side. It looks like a ring that Dad gave Mum for her engagement. It's bigger than Mum's certainly, and tarnished with age and neglect, but the cut is exact. I feel unbearably sad. Mum used to worship her ring and took it to be professionally cleaned every year. She hasn't got the ring any more, though. No one has. I turn it over in my palm and watch it dully sparkle in the bathroom downlights before I hear feet approaching.

'Who are you?'

I jump, and turn to see a solid mountain of a woman in the door frame. I recognise her immediately. Sylvie gives me a full-body sweep like I'm going through airport security. The ring is still in my closed hand by my side.

'Oh, hi,' I say. 'I'm Jim's PA. Matilda.'

'Why are you in *here*?' she says. She wears a plain black top, black trousers and sensible flat brown shoes. Her thin eyebrows are high from her hairline being pulled tight by her severe bun. 'You should *not* be in here!'

'I made her a coffee,' Ben smiles, coming into the bathroom behind Sylvie.

I pick up the cup that I've left on the dressing table. 'I'm delivering Jim's dry cleaning,' I explain.

Sylvie glowers at Ben. 'This girl is new,' she says crossly. 'She doesn't come into this house and have *coffee*. She does not come up here into your mother's rooms.'

Ben blows out his lips, dismisses her. 'Pfff, come on, Sylv. She thought my rocket was awesome.'

'I did,' I say.

Sylvie's eyes narrow. 'Where is it?' she asks. 'The cleaning?'

'In the wardrobe,' I say.

'Please leave,' she says, and she turns on her heel. She marches to the top of the stairs, where she stops and spins back to look at me.

'Oh,' I mutter. 'Right. OK.'

'Sylvie!' Ben says, disappointed. 'I didn't even get to show her the robot Mum got me for Christmas!'

'Your mother would not appreciate you inviting people for tea parties,' Sylvie replies.

'It's not tea,' he counters. 'It's coffee.'

I nod. 'No, Sylvie is right,' I say to Ben, because Sylvie seems fearsome and not to be got on the wrong side of. 'I shouldn't have accepted coffee.'

'No,' Sylvie affirms. 'You should not. And you should never wear heeled shoes in this house, let alone in this room!' She glares at Ben. 'There is a *boot room*, Benjamin.'

'My bad,' he says with a shrug. He waves at me. 'Bye!'

'Bye, Ben,' I say.

Sylvie snaps her fingers as I pass and I give her the coffee cup. 'Wait,' she says. 'Have we met before?'

How would she think she knows me? The only other time she's seen me was at Jim's door when I delivered his credit card and it was only for the briefest of moments.

'No,' I answer.

She purses her lips in doubt. 'Goodbye,' she says.

Jim is thankfully at meetings for the rest of the day and I'm glad because, after what happened this morning, I don't want to be alone with him. I can still feel the shiver of his breath against my neck.

For the rest of the day, I sit in the office with Gertie at my feet and spend the hours scrolling through the profiles for Chloe McManus and wondering how Horsehead might be getting on with finding her. I still haven't heard from Tess McManus and wonder if I should send her another email or wait.

From time to time, I glance in my bag and look at the ring I've taken. I know I should give it back, but it looks more and more like Mum's ring. Mum had left her ring for Lissy and me, originally. I found it on her bedside cabinet the day after she walked out and I took it and hid it in a cupboard in my doll's house. I didn't tell Dad because this was the first time she'd ever removed the ring and I knew that it meant something significant. For a month, it stayed there and it winked at me whenever I opened the doors of the house in the middle of the night, sat on my haunches on my floor with my torch. After two months, when Mum still hadn't come back for it, or us, I gave it to Dad.

He was sitting at the kitchen table one morning, staring into nothingness, and I pulled gently on the sleeve of his shirt and opened my hand. He looked at me and then at the ring I was holding out to him. He gasped before snatching it out of my palm and closing his fist around it and moaning, as if it was me who had wounded him.

'Dad, I'm sorry,' I said. 'I shouldn't have done it.'

He stood abruptly and marched out of the room. I followed him.

'Dad?'

He went into the bathroom and banged the door closed behind him, but he didn't lock it. I pushed it open, cautious because I thought he would be crying. And I was right, he was, but there was also fury in his eyes as he stood above the toilet and threw the ring inside. It clinked on the enamel and down into the water.

'Dad!'

I ran up beside him, but he flushed it, crashed down the lid and looked at me.

'There,' he said. 'Down the toilet, along with everything else that I held sacred.'

We both cried that night, but alone, in separate rooms. I heard him and he heard me, I'm sure, but neither of us said a word the next morning or any day afterwards.

I experience the memory as keenly as yesterday. Before nausea threatens to unfurl itself out of me, I look back at my screen.

'Chloe McManus, where are you?' I say aloud.

Gertie lifts her head and the side of my foot is suddenly cool. The lift doors are opening and Bobby Walters walks towards me, smiling.

'Hi,' he says.

'Oh, hello,' I say, going to click out of the account. 'Are you here for Jim? Because he's out at the—'

'I was actually after you,' he replies.

'Oh.'

'Do you want to have dinner tomorrow night?' he asks.

I'm thrown off guard because I haven't seen or spoken to him since our lunch last week, but he's smiling.

'Why?' I say.

He laughs. '*Why?*'

'I mean . . .'

'No,' he says. 'I like "why". Let's see. Because I liked talking with you over lunch? Because you seem vaguely smart? Because I like your eyes? Because you made an egg joke that I thought was funny? How many reasons should I list?'

'I think that's enough,' I say. I'm blushing, but I hope he can't see it over the amount of make-up I have to put on to cover my freckles.

'Great,' he says. He turns to leave but then stops. 'See you tonight at the memorial. Gwen said you were coming.' He walks towards the lift and presses the button just as the doors open.

'Bobby?' Jim says. 'You were looking for me?'

'Nope,' Bobby replies and, waving goodbye, disappears into the lift.

Jim stares at me for a moment. 'What did he want?'

'He wanted to talk about the memorial tonight,' I say.

He nods. 'You delivered my suit?'

'I did.' I hand him the post. 'I met your son.'

'Did you?' he asks, flicking through it.

'And Sylvie.'

He looks up from the letters. 'Oh, Sylvie. She doesn't like me very much, but she's very useful, even if she does look like Alice the Goon from *Popeye*.'

TWENTY-SIX

I imagine what Wendy might say if she knew I was here at Jemima Mataya's memorial. If she was here in my place, she would be standing on a chair in the middle of the room so she could spot every single famous face in the bar, then asking them to sign her chest.

'Matilda!'

I turn to see Gwen walking towards me in a black dress and gold heels and holding a champagne glass.

'You look amazing,' I say.

She waves my compliment away and drinks her champagne, getting the ends of her hair in it. This, I've come to realise, is an unfortunate signature characteristic of hers and yet one I find increasingly endearing. I could draw Gwen a hundred times and not tire of her.

'You've got a glass,' she notes. 'Good. This is already my third! It's so hot in here!'

I nod in agreement. The bar is stifling; it's crammed with people and the heating is on full. I can already feel that my tongue is ridged at the edges and curling in from dehydration. I wonder how long I have to be here for. I wonder where Bobby is.

'There are a lot of people here,' I say.

'Yes,' she replies. 'They're all people who worked with Jemima.'

'You've done a great job.'

'I don't think I'll be praised for it,' she says, and flicks her eyes towards the left.

I follow them to see Andrea sailing through the door in a glorious floor-length, flame-orange, sweeping gown, hair swept up in a mass of waves on top of her head. Her smile, when directed to those she needs to impress, is megawatt.

'She's really come down on me about this whole thing, like I haven't already got enough of her shit to deal with,' Gwen says.

I realise she's beyond tipsy.

'You know, she once suggested I work out a fitness programme.'

'Really?'

'And one time, she took me up to Jim's office so I could explain to him why a marketing campaign hadn't gone the way we thought it would. I stood in the middle of that room while she listed all the mistakes I'd made.'

She looks daggers at Andrea, who seems to sense it. She looks around at us and Gwen smiles and waves. Andrea does neither and turns away again.

'Are you surprised?' she says.

'No.'

She laughs. 'You know, so many times I've drafted things, emails, feeds on my platforms about what she's done and what she's said to people. She hates me too, it's no secret.'

'She might be a bad enemy,' I say, 'considering how close she is with Jim.'

'Close!' she laughs. 'That's one word for it.'

THE PRANK

I balance my wine glass on a shallow sill. 'Gwen,' I say, 'I'd really appreciate your help with the archives. I couldn't find one of the episodes I was looking for. Do people take them out regularly?'

'No,' she replies. 'But some footage that's recorded isn't used. We have to keep them number-sequenced, though, for audit purposes.'

'Why aren't some of them used?' I ask.

'Oh, you know,' she says. 'Like people who've clocked on, or not had the type of reaction we've wanted. They've shouted or cried or something.' She smiles. 'Not great for TV.'

'What happens to the footage?' I ask.

But she doesn't answer; she's looking at her watch.

'Shoot, it's nearly eight-thirty,' she says. 'Jim's speech. I've got to go and ready his microphone.'

'OK,' I say, and watch her leave.

I'm about to turn on my heel and escape the building when I hear the tap of a silver spoon against a crystal glass and the room quietens. How can I leave? I scan a route through two huddles of people to the door, but someone moves and it's closed to me. I realise that I can't go anywhere; I'm trapped.

Jim comes to the front and motions to the screen behind him. It flashes to life with a close-up still of Jemima Mataya – so distinctive with that alabaster skin and red lips, the white-blonde hair.

'Jemima Mataya,' Jim says, 'was a rare talent. An icon for so many years. She could be sarcastic, wildly inappropriate, obscene to journalists because she liked to tease. A party girl, a confidante, a weapon. She came to us as a victim herself, a girl we pranked and who delighted in it so much that her naive

197

performance stole the entire episode. She endeared herself to the nation and we saw the value in her. She became the host, the "girl with the microphone" and then she became even bigger than that. She was the heart of the show, the entire *brand*.'

He pauses and I see that his jaw clenches. Is he upset? Jim? Around me, other people look sad, but all I can think about is Jemima Mataya in that red jumpsuit saying to my dad that *Pranksters* is as 'cruel as fuck', and I don't feel anything but rage towards her.

'I'll not forget the night I heard,' Jim continues. 'I was with our marketing manager, Andrea.'

I see her near the front of the crowd and she nods slowly at him.

'We were devastated. As were you all, because it was an absolute tragedy that she died. It's often the most vivacious that we overlook as carefree but who are hiding the deepest, most traumatic problems. She had left the world a TV star, but she could have been more, everyone knows that. She had Hollywood knocking at her door, but she loved us and we loved her. She wanted us.'

Behind me, someone is crying.

'We'll never forget the talent that we have raised. We share with them the successes that they have with us. And we'll never forget those who have fallen, like our Jemima Mataya, but we continue. There will always be others to grow, to keep, to flourish. We've left it a year before recruiting another host, but now the time has come to find our new "Jem". We will be announcing her arrival very soon.'

At this, there is a murmur around the room. Jim has thrown all the journalists a titbit that will have created tweets and gossip-magazine articles by the morning.

'We all need closure,' Jim adds. He raises his glass and the collective do the same. 'Here's to you then, dear kid,' he says, and we all drink.

I leave the moment I can, checking my coat and bag out from the cloakroom. I have a message on my phone and I drop it from shock. It clangs on the floor. It's an email from Tess McManus.

Top Step: Tess McManus wrote to me.

Horsehead: Fuck! What'd she say?

Top Step: She doesn't want to talk to me.

Horsehead: Fucking typical.

Top Step: Of her?

Horsehead: The situation, durr. I don't know the woman! Thought she might bite though. After all these years, after whatever it was that happened, you'd think she might help you. What did she say?

Top Step: I'll paste the email. *Eleanor, I don't know how you got my email, but I don't want to know who you are. What happened to my family is PRIVATE and we don't talk about Jim Valente and his company with anyone. You say your family was pranked. I have nothing to say to you. He's not a nice man. Delete this address and never contact me again. Tess McManus.*

Horsehead: To the point, isn't it?

Top Step: Very much.

Horsehead: But it narrows things down nicely then, right? It leaves you with one choice on the McManus front.

Top Step: I go after Chloe. But how do I find her? I've been trying ever since IT gave me the email.

Horsehead: Do I have to do everything?

Top Step: Can you?

Horsehead: I've been trying too.

Top Step: Why are you so nice to me?

Horsehead: Because you're my Julia Roberts?

Top Step: Julia Roberts??

Horsehead: Your life – *Erin Brockovich*. If this was a novel or a film or whatever, that could be your pitch. Finding all the people that Jim's done wrong by and bringing him to justice for all of them.

Top Step: I'm flattered, except that I'm not that tall. I'm a poor man's Julia Roberts.

Horsehead: Not to me.

Top Step: Seriously, though. You're very good to me.

Horsehead: I'm good to you because I also don't like people being exploited. Also you paid me.

Top Step: What happened to you, Horsehead? Why are you on this site? I don't know why I've never asked you. Did someone exploit you?

Horsehead: You really wanna know?

Top Step: If you want to tell me?

Horsehead: What happened is that I messed up, Top Step. I set light to some fucker's crib.

Top Step: You committed arson?

Horsehead: It was revenge, Top Step, for exploitation.

Top Step: What happened?

Horsehead: I paid for it, that's what. Not that I was put away for that. They couldn't prove it was me.

Top Step: But you went to prison?

Horsehead: Mike Durfee State Prison. I got five years. It's a shithole in Springfield. I was set up on a robbery six months after the arson and guess who it was in my court-room? The guy I did the arson on, smiling like a fucking Cheshire cat. He'd stitched me up. So now I'm living in this shitty apartment in the middle of the Hills (not the Beverly ones, obviously) with BO Boy and his dolls. I was supposed to disappear, get to Vegas and live my life in the penthouse suite of The Venetian, waste money on the machines, on ladies! Or go to Mexico and live on the beach and my only worry would be if the tide was gonna reach my toes.

Top Step: What a pair we make.

Horsehead: What a sorry fucking pair.

Top Step: Can I ask you a question, Horsehead?

Horsehead: What?

Top Step: Are you sorting anyone else out on this forum?

Horsehead: Are you asking whether we're exclusive, doll? Ha! That's a new one.

Top Step: You've helped me beyond my wildest hope. Given me so much time, so much help.

Horsehead: Your case is cool, doll. Like a real-life movie. All the rest of them have fallen by the wayside. I flutter in and out of other people's convos, as you'll see if you go on the website, but I'm not stinging, if you catch my drift.

Top Step: Thank you, Horsehead. For everything. I mean it.

Horsehead: You cherub. You don't need to thank me. To be frank, you've given my life a bit of spark again.

Top Step: An arson joke?

Horsehead: Ha! And you're sort of funny.

Top Step: I went to Jim's house, you know that?

Horsehead: You did?

Top Step: I didn't have a chance to look round, but I . . . I know I shouldn't have, but I took a ring from their house.

Horsehead: A ring?

Top Step: It's Lucinda's ring. It's gold and sapphire.

Horsehead: You stole a ring from her? Are you insane? Why did you do that?

Top Step: Because it looks like my mum's ring.

Horsehead: I'm all for crazy shit, but you need to put that back ASAP, doll, because that could get your ass fired in a heartbeat.

Top Step: I know, I know. I will somehow. Anyway, I didn't have the chance to go looking for anything.

Horsehead: It's fine – keep to the agenda. You're building trust with Jim. You're looking for the things amiss. You're looking for that USB. We're looking for Chloe McManus. You're gonna pick his lock. You're gonna pour some wee or something in his coffee.

Top Step: I'm not doing that last one.

Horsehead: Who knows.

TWENTY-SEVEN

It's six in the evening and I'm exhausted after a day of fielding calls from excited journalists who were at the memorial last night.

'Can you give us a comment about the new host for *Pranksters*?'

'Have you met the new Jemima?'

'Can you describe her for me?'

'Is it likely that she will be as close to Jim as Jemima was?'

I haven't had a moment to look any more for Chloe McManus and it's put me in a bad mood. I put an updated printout of Jim's diary for next week in a folder for him.

'Are you done?' he asks, as I walk into his office.

'I think so,' I say, and hand over the folder.

'Did you sort Lucinda's present?' he asks.

'I ordered her a Gucci bag and a silk scarf from Liberty,' I reply. 'They're coming here tomorrow. Would you like me to deliver them to the house for you?'

'No,' he says. 'I'll take them. That way it looks like I bought them.'

'OK,' I say, disappointed.

'We also need a welcome present for Marie Jarski,' he says. 'Order her a necklace from Tiffany and have it delivered to her agent.'

'OK,' I repeat.

'She's going to be a star,' he adds. 'The next season of *Pranksters* is going to be a hit. It turns a bit darker this year.'

'Darker how?' I ask.

'Bit less slapstick, bit more edgy,' he replies.

'It's already quite dark, isn't it?' I say.

'We live in dark times,' he remarks. 'And some people come from dark places, so we need to give them comedy they can escape to. You and me, we come from a position of privilege. Contented childhoods, right?'

'Mine wasn't always content,' I say.

'But you knew love, yes?' he says. 'You had a good family?' I think of Dad. 'I knew love,' I agree.

'So you know what "normal" should look like,' he adds. 'But "normal" for some people is neglect and abandonment, and *Pranksters* provides relief,' he says. 'Dark relief for people in dark places.'

'Hey, Matilda. You ready?'

Jim and I look to the door and see Bobby standing there.

'Ready for what?' Jim asks.

'I'm taking Matilda out for dinner,' Bobby replies.

Jim looks at Bobby and then at me and then he laughs. 'Oh, are you?' he says. 'Excellent.'

I find myself winding between Soho's alleyways with Bobby, listening to him chatter. I almost slip in my boots because the pavement is icy. I grab hold of his arm.

'Steady,' he says.

I let go at once, embarrassed.

'Your terrible snow boots again,' he laughs.

'I'll feed that back to my sister.'

'Is she responsible for your footwear?'

'And many other fashion errors.'

'You'd look good in a bin liner,' he says.

'That sounds . . . murdery?'

He laughs and I realise I haven't let go of his arm. I let go.

I breathe in the sights and sounds and smells of the city: laughter from groups of friends, an echo of a brawl down the street, the neon lights of clubs, chargrilled ribs and cigarette ash, a siren wailing in the distance.

Bobby takes me to a Lebanese restaurant located next to Soho's red-light district and I say how much it reminds me of the food in Tel Aviv and Dubai. I talk about Slovenia's winding river in Ljubljana, with the beautiful market at the foot of the castle on the hilltop. I talk about Budapest, Malta, Vienna. All this information I've got from books and from Dad's travel journals.

Bobby asks me questions and I answer them, lying through my teeth because I'm drinking wine too fast. I shouldn't be drinking like this, maybe not even at all, but I'm nervous. Bobby's eyes are fixed on me and his smile is full and he thinks I've lived life and that I'm an interesting person, when neither is the case.

I learn about him. He's well read and well travelled and well mannered. He's close to his family, has two brothers who work in advertising and music and he wants a dog to go running with. He co-founded a sports charity, sits on the board of a creative arts group and speaks Spanish.

We talk about London and the desire of leaving it and I tell him about a book I saw called *Cabin Porn*, which has photographs of people's tree houses and woodland cabins and huts in fields.

'That's exactly what I want,' he says. 'Sometimes I want to forget everything I ever started.'

'Which is what?'

'City living.'

'Where do you live?' I ask. 'A big city apartment?'

'Actually I live on a barge,' he says. 'I can unshackle myself whenever it gets too much.'

'And have you?'

He leans back and wipes his hands with his napkin. 'No,' he laughs. 'I've been there nine years because I have a good mooring rate. I'm moored in Little Venice. Self-named Admiral of the Canal.'

'Ah, the seven seas,' I reply.

He grins. 'Next bar?' He touches my fingers briefly and they ignite from his contact.

'OK,' I say, wondering who I am, because this isn't me. I don't let people touch me; I don't have male friends. No friends at all except Lissy and Horsehead. Would I call Wendy and David and everyone at The Cello my friends? They don't know me. Should I have let them know me?

We pull on our coats, walk up towards Warren Street and stop for a drink at a tiny pub on a corner.

'You ever been in here?' Bobby asks. 'It does pies upstairs. Only pies. Phenomenal.'

'Like, custard pies?'

He bursts out laughing. 'What are you? A clown?'

'What is with those shoes Jim likes to wear?' I say.

'The clown shoes from *Pranksters*?' he replies. 'I know. It's like a fetish. He signs off every single episode. Nothing is aired without his say-so. You've got to make him laugh. It's getting harder and harder, actually. It's like he's been seasoned by weirdness and so each new episode gets more and more strange.'

Bobby orders himself a pint, me a glass of wine, and while he waits, I find a table in the corner of the bar and watch him, his easy smile at the barman, his easy stance, easy manner. He's cut from the same cloth as my sister and I am a fraud, a liar and, most recently, a thief.

'Jim *is* pretty strange,' I say when he returns with our drinks.

'Unhinged,' Bobby nods. 'Why are you so interested in *Pranksters*, anyway?'

'Am I?' I ask.

'You went down to the archives,' he says. 'Gwen told me. Why?'

I feel my body grow tense. 'I was having a look,' I say.

'Right,' he replies.

I smile in a hopefully innocent way.

'To be honest,' Bobby adds, 'sometimes I hate that we make that programme.'

I wasn't expecting that from him. 'Really?' I say. 'Why?'

He sighs. 'Because for every ten pranks that are genuinely hysterical, there's one that feels . . . I don't know . . .' He trails off, seeming lost for the word.

'Cruel?' I offer.

He nods slowly. 'Yeah. I guess that's it. Over the years, there's been the pressure of bettering the previous season's success. That means bigger and bolder ideas and, I don't know . . . some of the pranks have gone beyond funny. I looked this up too, right? The dictionary definition of a prank is "a practical joke or mischievous act". And that implies something light-hearted, right? The definitions for "trick", however, are many. "A skilful act performed for entertainment or amusement, or a characteristic habit or mannerism." But its primary definition is "a cunning act or scheme intended to deceive or outwit someone". And that's what we do. We deceive people.'

He's said exactly what I feel about it. It's as if he's read me, pulled out my sadness and fury and laid it bare, unpicked and understood it all.

'Jim loves the company. He's obsessive about it and what's his,' he continues. 'If people leave Cyclops to work elsewhere, he goes mad about it. Actors who have chosen another project over his he writes off totally.'

'How do you know all this?' I ask.

'Part of the rich tapestry of my life in the company,' he replies. 'Because I'm a wise old owl and I've heard things.'

I pause, weighing up my next question. Should I ask him outright about McManus?

'You've got to tell me all you know,' I say.

Bobby laughs. 'Fine. Next bar I'll tell you all about Maureen from the canteen and her tiddlywink collection.'

'Please,' I say.

'Or the post boy, Mark. He goes out every Sunday to his parents' for a roast and then has the leftovers on Monday, whizzed up in a flask.'

'That's gross,' I say.

'I know!' he agrees. 'I fucking love people.'

We continue in bars and pubs along Warren Street and I keep on drinking. At midnight, we're in a tiny bar which is playing live folk music and Bobby drags me up from my seat and his hand catches mine and he's twirling me around and it feels so good to be like this. Free? What is the feeling? Loss of inhibition? I have a glass in my hand and my wine is sloshing all over the wooden floor, but no one seems to mind because lots of people are dancing and everyone is drunk, including me. I shouldn't have drunk so much, I'll tell him something I shouldn't, but he spins me into him and my body is touching his. He has the big thigh muscles of a runner; they strain through his jeans and they excite me. I put my hands up under his shirt and I feel his surprise, a little ripple of his skin as my fingers graze his back. Is this what it's like to touch someone? To feel their electricity beneath your fingertips? To have them respond to you?

'Are you manhandling me?' he asks in my ear.

'Sorry,' I say and I remove my hand, suddenly sharply sober and embarrassed.

'You can,' he says.

He kisses me. I'm not prepared for it, I still have my glass in my hand and I'm tilting it and the remnants of the wine run droplets down my legs. I'm screaming no in my head, because this wasn't the plan. I should get away from him and never find myself in this situation again because I didn't embark on this dangerous journey for this.

I draw away from him.

'It's late,' I say.

'Your name isn't really Matilda, is it?' he says.

I freeze. 'What?'

'It's Cinderella,' he replies.

He leads me back to the table where our coats are slung over the backs of the chairs, whips them up and holds mine out for me.

'You're getting the Tube?' he asks as we step outside.

'I don't ride the Tube unless I can help it,' I say.

'Scared of the dark?' he grins.

'Close,' I say, and think of my dad's story. I smooth my coat. 'I prefer the bus.'

'Fair enough,' he replies. 'I'm thinking we should go out again. Next weekend? You could come for dinner on my boat.'

'Would I have to wear a pirate hat?' I ask.

He laughs. 'Only if that's what you're into.'

'Can I . . . can I let you know?' I say, because I'm hit with an overwhelming sense of guilt and falsity. This man doesn't know anything real about me; not even my real name. I'm also more terrified than ever of myself. I don't go on dates or kiss people. I don't get invited to men's houses or boats.

'Sure,' he says and he leans in again and kisses me very gently on the mouth.

On the bus home, three boys get on and one is sick on the floor by my feet, but I barely register it. I'm too busy reprimanding myself for feeling something foreign – a creeping happiness which I don't deserve and which I certainly don't have the capacity to deal with. I won't do this again.

I open my bag and slip my hand inside it, feeling the smooth stone of Lucinda's ring.

Horsehead: Where have you been?

Top Step: Out.

Horsehead: Out where?

Top Step: With my sister.

Horsehead: Liar. She'll be at university in the week.

Top Step: Wow, you do pay attention.

Horsehead: So that can only mean one thing. You hooked up!

Top Step: No, I didn't.

Horsehead: You did! You're being all weird.

Top Step: How can you get that over a message? I didn't hook up, all right?

Horsehead: OK. However you guys say it over there then – 'you had a cup of tea and a scone'. Who's the guy?

Top Step: No one you know, obviously.

Horsehead: Ah! So you did then.

Top Step: I got the lock-picking tools you sent me.

Horsehead: Changing the subject!

Top Step: I thought I'd try doing it tonight.

Horsehead: Drunk?

Top Step: I'm not drunk.

Horsehead: Good. And don't you go skipping into the sunset farting glitter with a boy. We've got a job to do.

Top Step: I won't!

Horsehead: Well, I didn't think you'd go stealing rings and go for night-time dances with boys. My virtual girlfriend is cheating on me!

Top Step: Actually you're truly the only one who knows who I am at the moment.

Horsehead: Given that I'm here and you're there, your fluffy words are hardly consolation.

Top Step: I'm laughing.

Horsehead: So am I :)

Top Step: You did an emoji!

Horsehead: Oh my God. I did. Urgh, who am I?

I hold the tools in my mouth and try to slide the wrench in to engage the mechanism and the pick above it, but they're slick in my clammy fingers as I force them into the right position. I'm drunk and my fingers are clumsy, but I know that even if I'd been completely sober there'd be no way

I'd be able to do it and this makes me feel even more the failure.

I click on another set of instructions, kneel bare-legged on the bathroom floor and peer into the lock.

'Tension wrench,' I say to myself. 'At the bottom. Slight pressure. OK.'

I glance at the instructions again.

Let the driver pins come above the shear line. Use equal force and give so that when the pins start to drop, the driver can catch the plug as the lock begins to rotate.

'What does that even mean?'

I insert the pick at the top of the lock and slide it all the way in. I wonder if this is how surgeons start out feeling; that they're fiddling about with a mechanism that they can't even see properly and getting a 'feel' for what's right.

I spend a useless hour trying to pick it and then I throw the entire pick set across the room, where the tools clang loudly against the bath. Who am I, trying to pick a lock? Who am I, getting people fired so I can take their jobs, going out for dinners with men like Bobby, stealing rings and getting involved with things over my head? I lean my head against the wall. I suppose that's always been the problem – I don't really know who I am.

I go into the bedroom, collapse into bed and roll so I'm facing the bedside cabinet. Lucinda's sapphire ring glints at me accusingly, but I put it on anyway and fall asleep, dream of Mum.

TWENTY-EIGHT

'Did we really have to do this in the deep midwinter?' Lissy asks. She stands in the middle of the garage, arms across her chest, shivering. The naked light bulb swings above our heads.

Uncle Charlie nods. 'Yes.'

'Could you at least have put a heater in here?' Lissy whines.

'Could you at least have put on a jumper?' Charlie replies.

My sister snorts. 'Sadist.'

'We're selling the cottage,' Charlie says, handing me a roll of black bin bags. 'And I don't have the room to store the furniture and everything else here, with all your old stuff from school *and* your dad's old rental in London cluttering the place.'

'But all this is sentimental,' my sister wails.

'Oh, really?' he says. 'And how often have you looked through a box of pictures you drew when you were five, Elizabeth?'

'I remember drawing some pretty good cats at that age,' she replies. She looks at a tower of boxes. 'Where do we even start with this lot?'

Charlie takes off a musty fleece which is covered in dog hair. 'You start by putting this on.'

'Oh my God, that's gross, Charlie,' she says. 'When did you last wash this? 1874? I'd rather freeze.'

Charlie ignores her. 'And then you can get on to the clothes, seeing as so many of the boxes are full of yours. El will do the books and the old CDs and DVDs. Lots can go to the charity shops.'

'And what about you, Charlie?' Lissy asks. 'Which box are you tackling?'

'I'm going to make dinner,' Charlie says. 'Don't be such a cheeky mare or I'll lock you in here.'

'I'll call social services,' Lissy remarks.

'Good, they can finally take you off my hands,' he retorts.

I listen to my sister and uncle spar and think that if anyone was listening to us they'd believe we were a normal family doing a normal New Year clear-out of a garage. They'd think we have good, easy banter together, but if they scratched a little more, they'd find three people acutely anxious about the task ahead because of all the memories it's going to uncover.

Charlie leaves us and Lissy looks at me and puffs out air so that the hair at the front of her face flicks upwards. 'We'll do half an hour, right?' she says. 'Then we'll go in and watch *Eastenders*.'

'I'm not sure thirty minutes will scratch the surface,' I say. I snap open a bin bag for her and then I drag a box over and crouch over it. 'Look, Liss! Books we used to have when we were little. Nursery rhymes.'

'Miss Moppet with her spider?'

'Miss Muffet,' I correct her. 'Look, and the Blue Rabbit and Pink Rabbit.'

'Blue Rabbit was racist,' she says, pulling out a box labelled "clothes". 'Page three. I remember.'

I laugh. 'What are we doing tonight?'

'I'm going out with Ginger tonight,' she says, head buried inside the box. 'She's back from uni this weekend too and we're going to meet in town for a Thai.'

'OK.' I try not to let my disappointment show because it's not her fault that she has a ton of other friends and I don't.

'Sorry,' she says. 'Let's go out next Saturday night in London and get home late and order Indian takeaway from Light of Bengal and overdose on poppadoms and then eat mini Magnums we'll have bought on the way home in a multi-box. We'll watch some shitty film and eat all of them and then we'll fall asleep on the sofa. I'll wear your dressing gown and your bed socks.' She laughs, light like a fairy sprinkling dust. 'Gags.'

'Next Saturday?' I say. 'I'm not sure.'

She stops, looks at me. 'Have you got plans?' she asks.

'I . . . I don't know,' I say.

Her eyes widen. 'A date?'

'No . . .'

She grins. 'Oh my God, you're seeing someone, aren't you? I *knew* it! Ever since the wigs and your pen pal!'

'I'm not seeing anyone,' I reply, but Bobby's face flashes in front of my eyes.

'Are you gay? It's cool if you are. Is it Wendy? I loved her. You'd make a great couple.'

'I'm not gay,' I say. 'And nor is Wendy, but thanks for your support.'

'Why don't you want to tell me who it is?' she asks.

'Because it's no one,' I reply.

She looks unconvinced. 'Is it that guy David?' she probes. 'My ex-manager David?'

'He was sort of cute, right?' she says.

'I'm not in a secret relationship with David,' I say. 'Can you drop it?'

'OK, OK,' she says. 'Hey, look at this number!' She holds up a tiny red velvet dress with cream lace detail. 'Was this mine? What a slut.'

I think of Bobby as I sift through the boxes. I wonder if he would like me if he knew the real me. I open another box of books – Roald Dahl, *Harry Potter*.

'Liss, look here.' She doesn't answer. 'Liss?' I look over to her. She's riffling through a box with a frown on her face. 'What's that?'

'What?' she says, closing the box. 'What did you say?'

I turn back to the box of books. 'Over here . . .'

But she's not listening. She stands up with the box. 'I'm going to take this lot inside a sec,' she says. 'And get a jumper.'

'What? We've literally done five minutes. Charlie will lock us in!'

But she doesn't answer. She leaves and I carry on with sorting through the garage. I find a box with a book of short stories that Dad wrote, his first kids' book – all the stories he made up for Lissy and me and then published for the world's kids to enjoy. I sit and read about the old witch who lived in a burnt-out, gnarled stump in the woods and immerse myself in the place Dad was happiest – fiction.

I put it down and dig deeper into the box to find our holiday albums and open one absently before realising which it is. I'm looking at photos of Athens, the last holiday the three of us had taken together.

Athens had been warm in mid-November. Dad had booked it last minute, a luxurious hotel with a marble lobby, a swimming pool and spa facilities. We had walked everywhere, filled every day wandering streets, finding little churches and restaurants. We went to the Parthenon and the ruins and museums, spent lazy hours in the squares, us kids eating copious amounts of ice cream which they sold year-round and Dad drinking strong coffee and writing in his notebooks. He found a little independent bookshop that sold English books. We went there every morning and he would talk with the bookseller while Lissy and I each chose a new book because we read everything so quickly.

'My girls,' he said proudly, every day.

We hadn't ever had a holiday like that before and I remember thinking at the time how extravagant it was, but Dad told us he wanted to treat us. He was so happy that week, and interested in everything. He would stop by a flower at the side of the road, a weed, and point it out to us like Uncle Charlie would have done. He would marvel at every new flavour of a dish he tried and brandish his fork at each of us and badger us to try it. He would read everything he could about a site we visited until we dragged him away, bored.

The last photograph of Dad that I have is one of him sitting at a table in an Athens cafe. He's beaming because he'd sampled the cheese soufflé and declared it the best thing he'd eaten – ever. He's wearing the 'holiday' T-shirt that he'd bought from a market stall and I had ridiculed him for it.

'Dad looks like a giant banana,' I said, and Lissy, six, found it so funny that she snorted lemonade out of her nose.

Remembering that holiday brings me an equal measure of happiness and sadness. Happiness because the week was almost magical; Dad was sunny and warm and witty and brilliant. Sadness because in Athens he tricked us: a month after we'd returned, he killed himself. I think he knew what he was going to do and wanted us to have amazing memories to look back on.

It's half an hour before I realise that Lissy hasn't returned. I bet she's in the warm, her shoes kicked off, eating chocolate. I unfold my legs, walk out of the garage and back into the house to chide her, but she's not in the kitchen. I'm about to call for her when I hear her voice, raised, in the lounge.

'You didn't know? How could you not know! It was in your garage!'

'I swear, Lissy,' Charlie says. 'I didn't! All those boxes came from London.'

'What does this mean now?' Lissy says.

'Can we sit and talk about it?' Charlie's voice is pleading and this alarms me over anything else. 'Can I see them?'

'No!' Lissy yells and I hear her storm out. I come to meet her at the foot of the stairs and she stops dead when she sees me.

'Liss? I heard you going at Charlie,' I whisper, nodding my head towards the lounge. 'What's happened?'

She shakes her head and can barely speak, and I think she's going to cry.

'Liss?'

'He . . . he put all my bears in a box which has been eaten by moths and God knows what else.'

'Your bears?'

She nods. 'The little ones, you know, the ones Dad bought me.'

Lissy used to sleep with all her little bears on her bed. She used to tie them together by their paws with scarves and dressing-gown cords so that if there was ever an emergency, she would take one and the others would follow.

I throw my arm around her shoulder. I'm touched by this display of loyalty to the things Dad bought her. 'Oh, I'm sorry, Liss. Can any of them be rescued?'

'I don't know,' she says.

'Winston? Patch?'

She shrugs my arm off. 'It's fine. I should get ready to meet Ginger.'

'Now?' I say.

'I don't want to stay here,' she replies. 'But don't mention anything to Charlie, OK? I feel bad for having a go at him. Stupid old ape.'

I nod and she goes upstairs.

'OK, El?' Charlie says brightly, walking through.

I look to Lissy who, on hearing Charlie, appears around the corner at the top of the stairs and calls out to us, 'Charlie, I told her about the bears, OK? It doesn't matter.'

My uncle seems to falter. 'What? The . . . the bears?'

'The bears in the box,' Lissy says.

Charlie looks at me and then back at Lissy. 'Yes,' he says. 'The bears.'

I frown and Charlie goes back into the kitchen. I hear him calling for the dog.

Top Step: What did you used to do on holiday?

Horsehead: It's 'vacation.'

Top Step: It's not, actually. Just like pavement isn't sidewalk, lift isn't elevator and jumper isn't sweater.

Horsehead: Except when they are.

Top Step: Tell me what you did on holiday.

Horsehead: How is this relevant to anything?

219

Top Step: It's called making conversation.

Horsehead: OK. We went west. Wyoming, Montana and shit. The four of us. Camper vans, baseball caps. Sandals. We went hiking, stayed in tents in the mountains. My sister and I used to try to spot bears and cougars.

Top Step: You didn't say you had a sister. Is she older or younger?

Horsehead: Younger than me and thinks she owns the world.

Top Step: She sounds like Lissy. Do you get on?

Horsehead: We were close, yeah. Less so now. Where did you go on vacation?

Top Step: We used to go to Yorkshire.

Horsehead: The place with the tea?

Top Step: And the train museum.

Horsehead: Rock. The Hell. On.

Top Step: And Norfolk. My dad and uncle lived there with their parents and they turned it into a rental when my grandparents died.

Horsehead: Don't they have webbed feet there?

Top Step: No! It's very beautiful.

Horsehead: You're a European, doll. Surely you've been to more exotic places than places with tea and trains and trolls?

Top Step: We went to Spain a couple of times. We stayed in a villa with a pool and goats that went by on top of the hill every evening. They used to wear bells.

Horsehead: Love a goat with a bell.

Top Step: And Athens, we went to Athens once.

Horsehead: I wanna go there someday. All that history, doll. The myths, the legends, the gods. Neat place, right?

Top Step: Not for me.

Horsehead: Whatever. Listen to your Godfather here, right? You have another shot at the McManus pie because I am a genius. I've found Chloe for you. She works at a leisure center in Saffron Walden in Essex, wherever the hell that is. There's a really old turf maze. Like, the oldest in the world.

Top Step: Horsehead! How did you find out??

Horsehead: The turf maze? Looked it up. 1699!! Was that when dinosaurs ruled the earth? Dragons?

Top Step: I mean, how did you find out about Chloe!

Horsehead: I chased Tess McManus down online.

Top Step: You found Tess McManus??

Horsehead: Obviously you had her email address. I did a bit of stalking, looked at where she hung out online. We met on Mumsnet.

Top Step: Seriously? Don't people hide their names on there?

Horsehead: Black hat, hello? She's pretty cagey online, but everyone needs an outlet right? We've become friends. My name is VioletRobinson101.

Top Step: That's sort of creepy, Horsehead, to invent a personality like that.

Horsehead: Do you need me to point out how you're sitting in your little job as PA to Jim Valente?

Top Step: OK, point taken.

Horsehead: Tess McManus came good to old Violet Robinson. Took me seventeen private emails, but think I got enough to know where she's at.

Top Step: Did she tell you what happened to Chloe?

Horsehead: There was an accident at an ice rink in 2004. Skating, doll! That's why Episode 8 was called 'Skating'. Chloe was fourteen. Tess didn't mention the word 'prank' to me and she didn't mention exactly what happened, but that must be it, right?

Top Step: It has to be!

Horsehead: When will you go and see her?

Top Step: Sunday, tomorrow. But what if Chloe doesn't want to talk? It was so long ago, she was so young, she'd have to dig up so much trauma – what if she doesn't want to help me?

Horsehead: As soon as she hears your story, how can she not? According to that letter from Tess to Jim, he ruined Chloe's life and she decided to stay silent. She should've crucified the guy, I know I would have done. She was a coward, but you're not gonna be.

Top Step: This is great, Horsehead. You're amazing.

Horsehead: I know. You making any progress on picking locks?

Top Step: I brought a padlock with me to my uncle's house and I've been spending every spare moment trying to pick it.

Horsehead: Nice.

Top Step: It's not going brilliantly.

Horsehead: Just keep at it.

Top Step: OK, I'm going to go to bed.

Horsehead: Wait, I've got an important question before you go.

Top Step: What?

Horsehead: Do you think I need a penis beaker for my bedside table?

Top Step: I'm sorry, what??

Horsehead: The chats on Mumsnet. Fucking brilliant. I'm gonna become a regular.

TWENTY-NINE

The leisure centre is a large concrete building which boasts an 'Olympic-sized pool, a spa and facilities to match all sporting levels and developmental needs' on a fading blue plaque. I go inside and am greeted with a blast of hot air and the unique smell of all leisure centres: moist lockers, chlorine and fusty equipment, all discernible even over bleach.

I wait for the man on reception to finish with a customer, pick up a flyer of activities during the week and I spot Chloe's name on the staff list. She teaches indoor netball, basketball, rehabilitation swimming and she's in charge of membership admin.

'Can I help?' the receptionist asks.

I stuff the flyer into my bag.

'I'm looking for Chloe McManus?' I say. 'To ... talk about membership.'

'In her office,' he replies. 'If you hurry, you'll be able to catch her before her class starts. Second door on the left.'

I thank him and wander down the corridor to the office with her name on the door. I can't believe Horsehead has found her, can't believe I'm lucky enough to have someone fight my corner as he's doing. This could be a huge step if I get it right.

I knock on the door and hear a voice from within.

'Come in?'

I push open the door and a woman looks up at me from behind a desk wearing a navy polo shirt with an orange diamond emblem on it. She's early thirties with mouse-brown curls and a smattering of freckles on her face and she looks friendly.

'Hi,' she says. 'Can I help you?'

'Chloe McManus?' I say.

'Yeah,' she replies. 'Have you come to talk about a membership?'

I gesture to the empty chair opposite her. 'Can I sit down? This will only take a moment, I know you have a class.'

'Sure,' she says.

'I'm not here about a membership,' I begin. 'My name is Eleanor Greene and I was hoping you might be able to help me.'

She frowns now, confused. 'I can try?'

I take in a breath. 'This is going to sound strange.'

'OK?' She leans forward now and she's still smiling, but there's a flicker of uncertainty in it.

'I found an email between your mother and Jim Valente.'

Her smile vanishes and she snaps backwards, widens any friendly starting gap we had between us.

'You're a reporter,' she says.

'No,' I reply. 'I'm not.'

'If you're not a reporter then how did you find an email? How did you find me? My mum would have told me if someone had contacted her.'

'I did contact her,' I say.

'How did you find me?' she demands. 'You want money? Is that it?'

'No, no,' I say. 'Please, Chloe, listen to what I have to say.'

She folds her arms and I grit my teeth because I should have prepared better and I'm floundering.

'I'm someone like you,' I say. 'I mean, my family was affected the same way. By *Pranksters*.'

She twists her mouth. 'I can't talk about this,' she says.

'Whatever happened to you, Chloe, could help me put right the wrongs that Jim and Cyclops did to you.'

'No way,' she replies, shaking her head. 'No fucking way.'

'Please,' I say. 'I want to expose all the pranks that Jim Valente and his company might have covered up. Because there must be so many!'

She laughs, loudly and with scorn.

'You think you're the first person who's tried to really break him?' she says. 'He's untouchable, you get me?'

'No, Chloe,' I plead. 'He's just got a lot of money—'

'And a lot of money can help a lot of people,' she counters. 'You see what I'm saying?'

'He *bought* your silence,' I say.

I see her tongue run over her teeth behind her closed lips.

'Chloe, please.'

'Jim and I have an agreement,' she says sharply. 'And I can't talk about it, OK? I'm legally bound not to. You know a lot more than you should know given that nothing has been in the paper, on TV, nowhere.'

'But it's blackmail, Chloe, can't you see?'

'I wanted to move on from what happened,' she replies. 'I wanted to *live* and his money helped me. It helped way beyond that. His money made my whole family comfortable. It was a . . . blessing.'

I'm losing ground with her.

'What happened to you?' I ask. 'At the ice rink? Will you tell me? I need people, Chloe, real people, to rally with me against him and against the company! Don't you want to bring him to justice?'

'You can't!' she says, and her voice begins to rise. 'You can't! Not even with the USB, with everything—'

There's a knock on her door.

'Clo?' A man opens the door, pokes his head inside. 'It's eleven-thirty. Everyone's in the hall.'

'I'm coming,' she replies and he disappears again.

'A USB?' I say.

But the interruption has been enough for her to compose herself. She looks back at me. 'I don't know what happened to you,' she says. 'Whatever it is must be bad enough for you to track me down here. But what I went through later became even more complicated. Jim and that company owed me, but now my family owes him.'

'I don't follow,' I say.

She pauses. 'We're locked in. After my accident, there was another . . . incident. Forget anything you read and move on.'

'Can you tell me about the USB?'

She licks her lips. 'Someone tried to do exactly what you're doing. Someone who was close to him tried to expose him but couldn't do it. And you have nothing, so stop trying because he will ruin you.'

'Who? Who tried?'

'Please leave,' she says.

'Can I give you my number?' I ask. I grab a pen and write it hurriedly on one of her papers.

She looks at it and then sweeps it to one side. 'I'd get up and see you out,' she says. 'Except, as you'll probably know from all your research about me, I can't.'

I'm confused for a moment until her eyes drop down to her waist and then I realise that all this time she's been sitting in a wheelchair.

Top Step: A wheelchair, Horsehead! That must have been the consequence of whatever happened at the ice rink.

Horsehead: You think the prank put her in a wheelchair?

Top Step: Yes!

Horsehead: No wonder Jim wanted to pay the money and settle out of court and the papers.

Top Step: She mentioned a USB, Horsehead! And that someone else tried to expose him but couldn't.

Horsehead: Who?

Top Step: She didn't say who. Someone close to him.

Horsehead: Hmmm.

Top Step: The issue is that she's reluctant to help me. She said the situation has become complicated. For all Jim and the company owe her, her family now owes the company. Whatever that means.

Horsehead: OK, but she's still worth pursuing then, right? You've got to see her again and work at this relationship, OK? She's in a wheelchair FFS! This is the big break you were looking for in terms of pranks going wrong and you blew it!

Top Step: I went unprepared. I came across too strong, maybe. I begged.

Horsehead: Jeez, do I need to fly over, don some boobs and a wig and pretend to be you so we can get this job done properly? Why don't you just knock on his door right now and turn yourself in?

Top Step: Horsehead, please. I'm trying.

Horsehead: I'm trying harder than you are, doll, sitting here in my underpants while you flit around on dates and shit.

Top Step: What would you suggest?

Horsehead: See her again. Work on her. And I don't know, go over to Jim's house and think about your next steps. Scale the house, break into the office! *Do* something!

He's right to have berated me. I've screwed up a potentially huge breakthrough.

The edges of my forefingers turn red with the repetition and my wrists begin to ache. After an hour, I throw down the lock-picking tools and slump against the wall. Why am I even doing this? I shove them back into my bag and get up, put on my running shoes and my warmest running top and then I punish myself by pounding the streets, thinking about how on earth I'm going to make any sort of dent in talking to Chloe or find out how to unearth this USB or whatever it was Jim held in his hand. Do I dare believe that the USB she spoke of could be the same as the one I overhead mentioned in conversation between Jim and Oliver?

I stand across the road from the house on Wilton Crescent, masked behind the trees of the private gardens for half an hour. My feet have gone numb and any warmth my body built up from the run has faded.

From the sliver of open kitchen curtain, a movement catches my eye and I see a dark-haired woman dressed in red. It's not Lucinda and it's too lithe to be Sylvie. I squint to see better.

It's Andrea Rubins.

Jim comes into my view and I watch as he hands her a glass of red wine. The two of them flit in and out of my sight, drinking their wine and talking, and I watch them for a few minutes, thinking I should leave in case one of them looks my way. Then I witness something I was not expecting. Jim goes towards her, puts his hands on her shoulders and he kisses her neck.

'Shit!' I whisper aloud.

I think how Gwen laughed at my description of Andrea and Jim being close. She obviously knows they are having an affair. Where's Lucinda? She can't be in the house, surely? They wouldn't be so brazen?

I grapple for my phone in the pocket of my leggings. My fingers clumsily tap on the screen to awaken the camera. I watch them as they stand close together, talking again, and I wonder if I've missed my chance, wonder if they'll move to another room and that would be it. Where would they go where I'd be able to photograph them? I almost miss Andrea leaning in to kiss him.

I click the phone and it flashes violently. I crouch down, alarmed that they might have seen it, and curse myself for not thinking, in my haste, to turn off the auto-flash. I wait for ten seconds before raising my head again but see that Jim and Andrea are still there, still kissing. I turn off the flash and go to take another photo. But as I do, there's movement in the window above the kitchen. It's a figure – a tall frame, black against the light of the room, stock-still. It's Sylvie and she's looking right at me.

I duck. Did she see me? I peer around. There are no street lights above me to unmask me, but I stay hunched, praying she might have taken that moment to shut her curtains and didn't see the flash of my camera with that first photo.

After five minutes, my legs start to seize and I dare to stand and look at the window. She's gone. But so too are Jim and Andrea. Have they been warned by Sylvie? Is Jim about to come out of the house and catch me? Wherever they all are, I can't stay here any longer. I jog away, heart punching in my chest.

THIRTY

I stare at The London Palladium's enormous stage, unable
to imagine anything more terrifying than being up there with
hundreds of pairs of eyes on me. Jim, however, is a creature
used to the spotlight. He strides up the steps to the stage and
parades across it, with Gertie trotting alongside him. Andrea
joins them from the other side. Her open-toe boot heels click
on the floor and her silken black dress swishes against long
bare legs. I can't help but stare up at her, though she looks
down at me with a vulturine glower. It feels strange to know
what I know when she has no idea of it.

'Mr Valente, you'll be doing the keynote from the left
side,' Natalie says, walking up to join him. Natalie Lewis is
the events coordinator and is wearing a headset, a smart grey
suit and tortoiseshell glasses. She's carrying a clipboard and
has a clipped South African accent. She points with a pencil
stage left. 'You'll be miked, unless you prefer the lectern this
year?'

'You know I like to walk the stage, Natalie,' Jim replies.

'That I do, Jim,' she says. 'You'll be coming out halfway
through your introductory montage – is that correct?'

'Correct. I'm announcing the new Jemima Mataya. You
might have seen it in some of the gossip mags. I'll be in the
green room and then will come up onstage from there once

the footage is running.' He looks to me. 'Andrea will be giving the footage to IT.'

'Right,' I say.

Natalie nods. 'All fine,' she says. 'And afterwards, you'll join your team third row from front, stage left.'

'Yes,' he replies.

'Can I check the numbers for your contingent?' she asks.

'Nine,' I answer.

'No more?' she asks, and looks at Jim sideways. 'I only ask because they seem to change every year.'

'Not this year, Natalie,' Jim says, and then he looks at me. 'You want to come, Matilda?'

Andrea rolls her eyes.

Jim smiles. 'Why not? It's not *all* about the printers, is it?'

'I—'

'Ten then,' Natalie says and writes it down. 'Fine. Good.'

Jim looks back at her. 'Though one thing I do need is absolute control of the sound and lighting desk for when I'm talking. I want my technical people in it and no one else.'

'Our technicians at the theatre are very accomplished and absolutely trustworthy for all your production needs, Mr Valente.'

'Of course they are, Natalie,' Jim says. 'But I need my own crew.'

She taps at her clipboard. 'I see.'

'It's because of the confidentiality of this footage I'll be presenting,' he explains. 'It was Bobby Walters' suggestion and a good one. So that's what we need. That's not a problem, is it?'

'If you are on stage first – which can be arranged, I'm sure – then your team will be able to have exclusive use of the facilities on site for the duration of your speech, Mr Valente,' she replies smartly, clearly used to Jim's whims after so many years. 'No problem at all.'

Jim looks to me. 'Matilda, can you schedule a meeting for the head of IT so we can talk it through? He'll need to brief his lot.'

I nod. 'I'll arrange for Eric to see you next week.'

He looks baffled.

'Eric,' I say. 'The head of IT?'

'I always forget their names,' he says.

Andrea walks over to him and touches his arm gently. 'We need to go,' she says.

'Yes,' he agrees. 'Flag a taxi, Matilda. We're going to lunch.'

'Are we?' I say.

'Not you.' Andrea laughs.

'Take Gertie back,' Jim says, giving Gertie a gentle nudge with his shoe. She skits towards me and I pick her up. She's like a huge furry baby. She licks my face and smells of digestive biscuits.

When I come up from the lift, the first thing I see is that Eric and Paul are at my computer and I'm flooded with terror.

'What are you doing?' I ask, trying to sound bright.

Gertie takes up residence under my desk.

Eric moans. His mutton chops are freshly trimmed. 'Configuring! 'Tis the day of configuring doom! And as you're the most important, we start with you and Jim.'

'I'm more or less finished with yours now,' Paul says. 'I checked Jim's office, but it's locked so we'll have to come back to his. Is he here now?'

'No,' I say. 'He's at lunch, so you can't get in unless you can pick a lock.'

Paul stares at me and I clear my throat.

'I'm joking,' I say. 'Why wasn't I told about this configuring thing happening?'

'Did you not get the company-wide email we sent out?' Paul asks.

I bite my lip. 'Was there one?'

'From IT Helpdesk, entitled "Service Updates",' Paul says. 'Unforgettable, surely?'

'I'm sorry,' I reply. 'I might have deleted it.' Or they're not telling me the truth. Perhaps Jim has asked them to investigate me.

'No one cares about us, Eric,' Paul says.

'Told you,' Eric says. He looks at me. 'Every three months there are updates.'

'You do updates manually?' I ask.

'Most are automatic,' Paul replies. 'But occasionally the leprechauns need a bit of hand-holding.'

I hover beside them, lift a pen on the desk and put it down again. 'How long will you be?' I ask. 'Shall I stay?'

'If you want to watch us typing some code that won't make sense to you,' Paul says.

What can they access on my computer? What can they see that I've been doing? I've been looking for Chloe on this computer. How could I have been so stupid?

'OK, I'll stay,' I reply. I eye my computer warily. 'Actually,' I say, 'I did need to talk to you both. It's about the awards ceremony in a couple of weeks. Jim needs you to do his sound and lighting at The London Palladium. For his announcement.'

'What's the announcement?' Paul asks.

'The new host for *Pranksters*,' I say. 'Jim needs one of you at the ceremony. He doesn't want to use the technical team at the theatre.'

Eric rolls his eyes. 'Diva.'

'I'm no sound and lighting engineer?' Paul says and looks worried.

'Please,' Eric says. 'I've done enough of these. It's clicking a button for him, but the man likes to have the control.'

'I'll set up a meeting for you and Jim,' I say to Eric. 'Have you finished with my computer?'

'Yes,' Paul replies.

The lift dings and we all jump, but it's not Jim who comes out, it's Gwen.

'Matilda!' she says.

She looks red-faced and puffy-eyed and her hands are worrying the ends of her hair.

'I hate this place,' she says. 'I hate it!'

'What's happened?' I ask.

'What hasn't happened?' she says. 'Andrea emailing from God knows where she is, picking apart one of my campaigns. She's CC'd the entire department.'

'Oh, Gwen,' I say.

'Think this is our cue to leave,' Paul says. He and Eric wave at me and walk to the lift.

'I've had it,' Gwen says. 'Honestly. I have. How much of my soul does this company want? I am so embarrassed! I've been here *years* and she treats me so badly!'

It's then that I have the idea.

'Let's go out, Gwen,' I say. 'Tonight.'

It's ten at night and I've spent three hours with Gwen in a throbbing bruise of a club in Soho. Blue and purple neon lights rove against black walls and hundreds of tiny disco balls throw diamond shards across a sticky dance floor. There are groups of students on a night out, party-going office workers and tourists, and I watch Gwen cram up against some burly guy, limbs flailing and tangled.

'This is what I needed,' she sighs, slumping down next to me. 'A fucking *break*.'

'You deserve it,' I say and hand her a drink.

'You know what?' she replies, smiling widely. 'I do.' She gulps down the cocktail because she's thirsty and it's sugary-sweet like cola. 'What's this?'

'It's called an Angel's Tit,' I say.

She giggles madly. 'Brilliant,' she says. 'Why aren't you dancing?'

'I'm not a good dancer.'

'Come on,' she pleads.

'No, really,' I say. 'I've never liked dancing.'

'Who doesn't like dancing?' she counters.

I smile. 'My sister would agree with you there,' I say. 'I don't . . . I don't like being touched.'

But I think of Bobby, of his hands on me, of his lips on mine. I did like being touched by him. I liked touching him. Somewhere along the line I have forgotten what it feels like to feel someone else's warmth.

Gwen grins, head lolling slightly as she drinks again. 'What present did Jim get Marie as her welcome gift? There were rumours going about the office.'

'A Tiffany necklace,' I say. 'It was more than my month's salary and some.'

'He treated Jemima like a princess because she was the brand. He'll do the same with Marie. He managed Jemima, you know that?'

'He did?' I say.

'I think they had a sort of love–hate relationship,' she explains. 'But I can imagine Jim thrives on things like that.'

I nod. 'I think you're probably right there.'

Gwen takes a long drink. 'You wanted to know what happens to the footage we don't use in *Pranksters*,' she says.

I look at her.

'You asked me at the memorial and I didn't answer.'

'Right,' I say. 'I was only making conversation.'

'The truth is that it gets deleted,' she says.

I stare at her. 'Really?'

She nods, sucks on the cocktail straw. 'Wiped,' she adds.

'But what about the audit trail you mentioned?' I ask.

'The script is kept, the records of the finances put against it are kept, but not the actual material. Why would we keep it?'

'The episode I was looking for didn't have a file at all. It was gone.'

She frowns. 'Don't know what to tell you on that one. Was it a super early one?'

'Yes,' I say.

'Maybe it was a bad one,' she laughs. 'Maybe someone complained about it.'

'Do you get many complaints about *Pranksters*?'

'Oh, I think so,' she replies. 'I don't handle that side, obviously. But everyone knows that *Pranksters* is all in the name of fun.'

I bite my tongue. 'Yeah,' I say, and then I sigh. 'To be honest, Gwen, I don't like it. I don't like that programme.'

'Do you know what?' she says. 'Nor do I.'

'I can't believe that it gets deleted,' I say.

'Can't you?' she replies with a laugh. 'Don't you *know* Jim by now? If he doesn't like something, he gets rid of it.'

*

The cab driver helps me take Gwen to her front door and I fish her keys out of her bag and pull her inside.

'I'll wait in the car,' the driver says, eyes squinting because of the rain.

'I'll put her in bed,' I say, switching on a hallway light. 'Won't be a moment.'

He nods and jogs back to the car. Without his help, I'm short of breath almost immediately. Gwen's arm is like lead around my neck and her legs drag heavily and uselessly along the floor.

I blow on her face. 'Come on, Gwen,' I whisper. 'Help me out a bit.'

She picks up her feet but wheels them around like a cartoon character. 'Is Caroline here?' she slurs.

'Caroline?'

'She's my roomie,' she says.

I hadn't factored in any housemates or friends.

'Isn't it sad? I'm forty-one and I have a housemate! She's twenty-five. She's like you, got her whole life ahead of her, while I go from one project to another at work, micromanaged by the Wicked Witch of the West, and fuck about with nice boys who aren't men and appropriately aged men who act like stupid boys.'

'You could leave, Gwen,' I say. 'The company.'

'It's my ball and chain,' she replies.

'But it makes you so upset,' I say. 'Andrea is horrible to you. And Jim is controlling – it goes from top down.'

'He gets away with so much, I can't even begin to tell you,' she says, and then hiccups. 'Don't tell Caroline I'm drunk. She's a nurse and she doesn't really drink. She thinks I'm abhorrent.'

'Where's your bedroom?' I ask.

She lifts an arm, zombie-like, to the left. 'It's purple,' she giggles.

I lug her towards the room she's vaguely motioned to and I kick the door open, click on the light with my shoulder. It's girlie but fitting for her; the walls are painted purple and it smells of roses. It's tidy and neat; she has decorative storage boxes and books in colour order on her shelf.

I drop her bag and her coat to the floor and heft her towards the bed, where she promptly crashes face down on to the duvet, her hair fanning out on the pillow like spun gold. I turn her on her side, lift her feet up and remove her shoes. She's breathing heavily and her eyelids are beginning to flutter, almost completely asleep already.

I stand straight, look at her for a second and then at the door. The flat is quiet. I'll take my chances with Caroline. Watching Gwen for any flicker of movement, I go to her closet, riffle for any sort of hat and scarf combination she might have, a coat at the back of the wardrobe she won't miss. Then I bend down and crouch like an animal to the carpet and remove her work badge out of her bag.

I lift an umbrella that's hanging on the back of her door and glance back at Gwen. It's now or never.

'I have to go back to work,' I say to the driver when I open the cab door again.

'Now?' he says.

'Now,' I reply. 'My office is in Central.'

'You city types,' he says and he turns the car around.

THIRTY-ONE

Rain streams from the tips of the umbrella like jellyfish tendrils, but I'm glad of the weather because it's added a layer of invisibility for me. I use the umbrella as a shield as I come into the lobby of the office, shaking it out in front of me. There's a man dressed in a black shirt at the desk used by the receptionist and he glances up at me as I enter.

'Hi,' I say, giving him a brassy smile. I'm wearing Gwen's mustard-coloured 1920s cloche hat with the brown wig tucked underneath and a houndstooth scarf. Though there's a slim possibility of looking anything like Gwendolen, I definitely don't look like me.

The security guard grunts a reply in my direction and lowers his eyes to the screen in front of him. I can hear gunshots and American accents blaring from it, which means he's occupied, but I can't run the risk that he's not diligent in his job.

I bleep the security badge and green writing appears on the screen of the turnstile.

Welcome, Gwendolen.

There's a light which flashes as the system recognises the code on the badge and the glass doors swing open to let me through.

I call the lift and try to look casual. The building is silent, save for the quiet movie and the thudding rain on the glass

241

panes. I wonder how many other people might work so late at night like this? Surely no one will be here at all? I shift my weight from foot to foot and then stand still because I'm nervous that I look nervous. The lift doors open and I press the button to the third floor for Marketing so that I appear authentic. Not that I think this security guard would check, but what if he does?

At floor three, the doors open and I peer out cautiously but am greeted with nothing but dark pods. I turn left and take the stairs. I've never done this before. The stairwell is badly lit and smells dank, like Uncle Charlie's garage, and I suddenly want to be there, in safety and familiarity, and not here.

My heels and my breath are sharp sounds in my ears and I stop to remove my shoes before I push open the door to the seventh floor to pad across the marble flooring. The sensor lights come on and I feel exposed, vulnerable, but I walk towards my desk, drop my heels and the wet umbrella underneath it, out of sight, and go to Jim's door.

From my bag, I fish out the tools from the wallet and I crouch at the lock. How long will this take me? Will I be able to do it? I start with the tension wrench at the bottom of the keyhole and am surprised that it doesn't feel remotely familiar. Then I realise it's because Jim's office door is already unlocked.

My head whips round. Is Jim here? A shiver runs along my spine. His office is dark, but could he be hiding in the shadows like he was that morning I came in early? I pick up the wallet, move quickly backwards towards my desk and hunch there for a moment, breathing fast. My eyes sweep the cabinet next to my desk, but there's nothing behind it but its own shadow. Is he sleeping inside his office?

I move back towards it, peer through one of the clear glass strips, but the sofa is empty, as is his chair, and I can't see Gertie. Could he be out walking around the block at this time of night? Why would he be here?

I move away again, creep over to the bathroom and open the door. I check every stall, but they're all empty. I release a breath and look back at the office door. I wouldn't have to unlock this door with the tools and waste time, but do I take this chance? Did Jim leave it unlocked by mistake, tonight of all nights? Such a coincidence seems unlikely, but it *is* a chance to get into his office, and I could be quick to look around. I set the alarm on my phone – twenty minutes is all I will allow myself.

I open the door, turn on the lights and run straight to his desk. I begin to finger frantically through its drawers before pausing to think. Jim is a smart man and would know instantly if a page were out of place. I breathe in and out before recommencing, going through things slowly this time. In the drawers, there are stapled papers, golf balls, pens, historic schedules and neatly organised contracts, but no memory sticks or microchips. Is that definitely what I'm looking for? I close the drawer softly, open another, carefully removing books, receipts and papers, and then another, until I get to the last – his *trinket* drawer – where the disgusting *Pranksters* red shoes yawn out at me. I take them out and look to see what's beneath them. There's a file with a sticker on it that reads 'Pranksters Host'. I open it, leaf through red-inked application forms that Jim had fanned out for me to choose Marie Jarski from. Why does he still have all these?

I go to put them back, but the file gets wedged against something at the back of the drawer. I bend down to move whatever it is. It's a packet of condoms. I let go immediately, feeling sick.

I replace the file, retrieve the vile shoes and shut the drawer. I stand, go to his filing cabinet in the corner of the room and finger through blotter pads, pens, calculator, invoices, statements, stapled correspondence. There are embossed cards kept in alphabetical order: agents, creatives, solicitors, lawyers, journalists, MPs, actors, sportspeople – he knows them all. But there is no memory stick or USB in here, either.

I spot an unframed photograph in one of the files. It's of Jim, shaking hands with three men. One of them is Bobby, and he's very young. I frown, confused, just as my phone beeps with the alarm. Twenty minutes have already gone and I can't risk being here too much longer. Will I have to leave empty-handed? I'm crushed by bitter disappointment. It feels like Jim outsmarts me at every step.

I shut the drawers gently and look around. Beside the filing cabinet is Jim's briefcase. I freeze. He always takes it home, so that means he's here somewhere. But where? I look beyond the door, to the lift, but it's silent, so I pull the briefcase open and look inside. There are files of programming schedules, his Moleskine notebook and calendar, his calculator, his ink pens. I begin to remove the layers. Historical sales and purchase ledgers from 2015 through to 2020. Another file, more sheets, more jargon. No memory sticks. I go to close it, frustration mounting, when I notice a file entitled 'Jemima'.

I printed a load of documents for Jim before her memorial. There's no reason for me to open this and yet she's related to *Pranksters* so I do it anyway because I'm starting to get desperate. I skim them, read how she was first a victim of one of the pranks – Episode 3: 'Postcards From Deirdre' – and how her reaction stole the nation's hearts. She rose to stardom, became an advocate for the programme despite a questionable private life of drugs and alcoholism. I read how her boyfriend at the time was questioned in relation to her death – even though she died of an overdose, alone – because her laptop and her phone were missing and were never found. Her boyfriend denied taking them.

The phone. Could Jim's conversation with Oliver Kealey have been referencing this phone? Was Jemima's phone the 'missing piece' and, if so, the missing piece to what? I think about my conversation with Chloe McManus. The person who tried to expose Jim was close to him, and who would have been closer to Jim than Jemima if he managed her for eighteen years? Was it her that tried to expose Jim somehow? My head feels blurry and I rub at my eyes and it's at that moment that I hear an echo of voices drift from the stairwell. Jim is coming.

For a moment I'm too stunned to do anything but gape, and then my legs kick into action and I skid towards his desk and crouch in the hole where the chair fits inside and reach to bring it back in to hide me as the door opens.

I've left the lights on.

I hold my breath. There are two sets of steady clicking footsteps on the marble. Sweat begins to bead on my forehead. I lower myself, contorting my body to be as small as possible in the tiny space. I exhale through my mouth slowly, painfully, before inhaling again.

'Thank you for giving me the tour,' a young voice says. 'I love your cute roof terrace!'

'You're welcome, Marie,' Jim replies.

Jim has brought Marie Jarski here at night for a tour of the office?

'Where do I need to sign?' she asks.

'Over here, on the desk,' he says. 'I've got it ready for you.'

From a small gap between the swivel chair and the side of the desk, I see him round towards me and I clamp my hand over my mouth, but he doesn't move the chair.

'I can't believe I'm going to be like Jemima Mataya,' she says, and I hear the scratch of a pen on paper above me.

'It's a big step,' he replies.

'I'm ready,' she says.

'Ripe,' he says.

'Right,' she laughs and I grimace on behalf of the both of us.

'So,' he continues. 'You'll come here on the night of the awards and we will get a taxi together. We'll go straight to the green room – I've asked for it to be clear just for us and private – and we'll drink champagne until we're ready to take you out onstage.'

'Oh my God!' she squeals. 'I feel so nervous!'

'Don't feel nervous,' he says. 'Your life is about to begin. Think of the parties and all the people you're going to meet.'

'I have big shoes to fill,' she adds.

He laughs softly. 'You want to see big shoes?'

Inches next to my head, he opens one of the desk drawers and I see a sliver of red as he removes the *Pranksters* shoes.

'Oh!' Marie exclaims, delighted. 'You keep them in here?'

I hear him taking off his shoes and putting the long, patent red ones on. 'Everyone likes a clown,' he says.

She giggles. 'You look too funny!'

I can hear the comical flip-flop of the shoes around the office as she laughs and claps him. I'm stiflingly hot in the coat; my forehead is pouring sweat under the wig and hat.

'They keep me young,' he says. 'I like feeling young. People like you keep me young.'

'Can I try them?' she asks.

'Of course,' he replies. 'Like an initiation!'

I hear him take them off and her put them on.

'You look fabulous,' he purrs. 'You know what would finish the look?'

'What's that?' she says.

'Pink lipstick.'

'Pink lipstick?' She laughs because she thinks he's joking, and I want to gag.

'That could be your signature,' he adds.

'You think?' she says.

'Jemima's was red. Yours should be pink.'

I bite at my bottom lip so as not to make a sound as he returns the shoes and slams shut the drawer next to my ear.

'I'm glad to have you on board,' Jim continues. 'We've gone a year without Jemima, but we need to reinvent.'

'I am sorry about Jemima,' Marie says. 'She really *was* the programme after so many years.'

'Don't be sorry,' Jim replies. 'Jemima is history, kid, and you are the future.'

He gestures for her to walk out of the office, and he makes to follow her but pauses. Then I realise what's going to happen. He switches off the light and I hear him lock the door.

I wait a full thirty minutes before I come out from beneath the desk and for a moment I stand, uselessly, in the dark. Oh my God.

I don't dare turn on the lights when I reach the door. Instead, I light the torch on my phone and position it like a spotlight. I riffle in my bag for my lock-pick wallet and then I go to work.

For the next hour, I sit twisting and turning and flexing and bending. I change position over and over, upright, kneeling, head bent over so I'm practically upside down, put my face right up to the lock to see better, but my breath condensates the glass.

'Please,' I whisper, but the tools don't turn.

The minutes tick on as I fiddle and tilt and bumble. I look at my phone, see that it's nearly one in the morning, and I dry my clammy hands on my thighs. It's slowly dawning on me that I won't be able to do this and Jim will find me tomorrow, locked in his office.

I move position again and my knees crack and then I hear a familiar whirring noise. The lift is coming up. I grab the tools and run back to the desk to contort myself. As the door opens, I moan internally. If Jim is coming back he'll sit at his desk. But I don't have time to move. I sit tight and hear a soft thud of shoes on the marble before they stop.

'Hello? Is anyone in here?'

It's the security guard. I exhale with relief.

'Gwendolen Harris?' he says, uncertainly.

I see the light snap on in the bathroom as he goes in to check it, before moving to the office door. He tries it and, satisfied it's locked, turns back again. I hear him whistle as he steps into the lift and the doors close to go down again. Will he be looking for 'Gwen' all night or will I have to chance that he might believe I would leave the building while he's looking for me? Will he have access to who's in or out of the building?

I go back to the lock. The tools continue to slip for another half-hour. I rub my eyes because they've become blurry with concentration as I try once, twice, three times, four. Am I going to have to ring security and ask him to break this glass? How would I explain that to Jim?

'Come on, El,' I hiss furiously, then I feel the lock move.

The pins turn and I open the door, giddy with relief. I unfold myself to standing and it hurts to be straight again after all this time. I close the door behind me, kneel and work it backwards to lock it, but after another hour, I have to give up. My fingers and my head are swirling with exhaustion and I have to hope that Jim will think he didn't lock it, that he was too engrossed in Marie.

It's three in the morning. Can I go back downstairs and leave without arousing the security guard's suspicion as to where I've been all this time or should I wait until six, when the security shifts change?

I walk up the stairs to the roof terrace and look out over the river. The city is sleeping, but there are still cars on the roads, still planes blinking in the sky, still the blare of sirens somewhere below. The wind whips up the ends of Gwen's scarf and I wrap it around myself more tightly, glad of it and the coat and hat and the umbrella. Tomorrow I can run to the shops and get something to wear so no one is suspicious because I'm wearing the same clothes as I wore yesterday. I'll then need to stuff Gwen's belongings in my drawers and dispose of them somehow.

I pull out one of the white chairs, dig my hands into the pockets of Gwen's coat and shut my eyes, but I don't sleep because all I can think of is the phone.

Her phone, her phone, her phone.

At six, I come cautiously downstairs to the lobby, find that the security guard has changed and I bleep through the glass gate, waving at him cheerfully as I continue towards the door.

'You're here early?' he says.

'Yeah!' I say. 'Been in for an hour! Just getting a coffee.'

'Careful!' he says.

I frown at his warning but then feel myself crash into someone coming the other way and I drop my bag with shock.

'Paul!' I say.

'Hi,' he says. 'You're coming out?'

'Yeah,' I say. 'I came in early to do a few things.'

I bend to pick up my bag and scoop everything inside. Paul bends down to help.

'Thanks,' I say, and feel my stomach plummet as he hands me the wallet of lock-picking tools. I snatch it from him, smiling through clenched jaws, but he's picking up something else, too.

Gwen's ID badge. I hadn't even noticed I dropped it.

'Oh,' I say, lightly. 'I was . . . I found this in the lift. I was going to pop it on the reception desk.'

'Right,' he says. He looks at me for what I feel is a very long time before handing it back.

'I never took you for that coffee,' I say quickly. 'You want to come out with me now?'

He shakes his head. 'No, you're all right,' he replies.

I swallow. 'Another time?'

'Sure,' he says.

'Bye.' I smile at him, but his expression remains decidedly neutral and he says nothing.

I turn and walk briskly to the reception desk, where I make a show of scrawling a note on the desk and putting the badge on top of it. We've only met a few times, but going round in my head is the thought that Paul can see me, the real me, behind the mask.

THIRTY-TWO

I hand Gwen a coffee. She looks puce.

'I was so drunk,' she says. 'Was I really drunk on a Monday night?'

'You were quite drunk,' I reply.

'Shoot, I feel *awful*,' she whines. 'But I remember I had a good time.'

'I think you did,' I say. 'If it makes you feel better, I'm pretty tired today, too.'

The truth is that despite the lack of sleep I've had, I'm wired. It's nine in the morning and as soon as I'm done with Gwen, I'm going to call Chloe McManus.

'I've got meetings back to back today,' she says. 'Thanks for the coffee. It's really nice to have a new ally in this place.'

Ally. I swallow.

'You can trust me,' I say.

She pauses. 'I think I told you something about *Pranksters* last night that I shouldn't have.'

'*Pranksters*?' I ask.

'About footage that is . . . objectionable.'

'I don't remember talking about *Pranksters*,' I say. 'I remember talking about cocktails that sounded like erotic movies.'

She licks her lips. 'Oh,' she says, and laughs timidly. 'I thought I remembered . . . but no. OK. Fine.' She smiles. 'I don't want to speak badly of the company.'

'You haven't,' I reply. 'Only of Andrea—'

'There you are,' says a clipped voice.

Andrea is marching towards us with a face like Medusa and I try to catch Gwen's eye to laugh at the timing, but Gwen visibly shrinks.

'Is everything OK, Andrea?' she asks.

'We have a meeting in an hour and you've not printed anything out for me,' she says. 'And where are all the campaign ideas for *The Underground Girl*?'

'I've got them on a PowerPoint presentation,' says Gwen. 'I thought it might be a good idea to—'

'I'm not asking you what you *think*,' Andrea says. 'I'm telling you to *do*.'

I look at her scowling face and Gwen's crushed one and in that moment I decide that Lucinda should know about her friend and her husband sleeping together. I need to give Gwen a little something back for getting her blind drunk and stealing her pass and this is the perfect gift. I *can* be her ally.

I offer to take Gertie for a walk after lunch and as she snuffles along in the flower beds of Embankments Gardens, I take my phone from my bag.

'Is Chloe McManus working today, please?' I say when the call is picked up.

'Yes. Can I ask who's calling?'

'My name is . . . Matilda Evans,' I reply. 'I'm ringing about my membership.'

'I'll put you through.' I'm put on hold for a moment until the line clicks.

'Hello?' Chloe says.

'Chloe?'

'Yeah, speaking,' she replies. 'Can I help?'

'It's Eleanor Greene,' I say.

'Sorry?' she says. 'Mark said . . .'

'I came to see you about Jim Valente,' I say.

'Oh God, you,' she replies. 'I told you. I have nothing to say.'

She hangs up and I call straight back. I'm put on to the receptionist again, who innocently transfers me, believing my story that we were cut off.

'Hello?' Chloe says.

'Chloe, listen . . .' I begin.

'Why won't *you* listen—' she says.

'Jemima Mataya,' I say at the same time.

There's a beat of silence.

'What about Jemima?' she says, but the tone of her voice has changed from angry to cautious.

'Was it Jemima who tried to expose Jim?'

There's silence.

'Chloe? Was it? Why did she want to expose him?'

'Your number is getting blocked,' she hisses, and slams down the phone.

Horsehead: Why haven't you messaged me? It's TUESDAY, dude, nearly a whole week since we spoke and I've been sitting here waiting like, how do you Brits say it? Like a fucking lemon. Shit, what does that even mean? What have you been doing??

Top Step: I got into his office. Jim's office.

Horsehead: You did??? How?

Top Step: I took Gwendolen Harris's badge.

Horsehead: Oh! Clever girl! So what happened? Did you find anything?

Top Step: I think the phone that Jim and Oliver talked about is Jemima Mataya's phone.

Horsehead: I'm sorry, I don't follow. What exactly are we investigating here? I thought you were looking for a memory stick/USB or whatever, not a phone? And you gotta remind me who Jemima Mataya is.

Top Step: She was the host of *Pranksters*.

Horsehead: OK, yeah, I read up on her a bit. She liked a drink, didn't she?

Top Step: I think that Jemima had tried – somehow – to expose Jim and I think it was with something on a USB.

Horsehead: You know this for a fact?

Top Step: Not a fact, no. It's an assumption. I think Chloe McManus knew about what Jemima was planning to do.

Horsehead: You think that the USB was Jemima's and Jim took it from her?

Top Step: Yes.

Horsehead: She was the host of *Pranksters*, his most valuable asset, so why would she want to expose Jim?

Top Step: That's the $64,000,000 question.

Horsehead: We could play a few games with this if you like?

Top Step: Don't do anything with this, Horsehead, not yet. I need to be a good PA for the rest of the week while I work all this out.

Horsehead: Sure, no way. Aye, Captain!

THIRTY-THREE

It's Friday and tonight I know that Jim is out with Andrea at a charity gala, so there's no chance of him marring what I've set out to do.

I'm wearing all black: a black hat to cover my hair, black leggings, black long-sleeved top and a black rucksack. A block before Wilton Crescent I stop to put on a navy jacket to bulk myself out. It feels like a lifetime ago that I was first here. I'm invested now, so deeply entrenched by my loathing for Jim that I can hardly remember the girl who ran here that first night, who handed Jim that white envelope with his card inside.

Tonight I'm delivering a very different kind of envelope.

I walk slowly to Jim's front door, taking a brown envelope from the rucksack, and lay it on the doorstep. I put my finger to the gold doorbell before sprinting down the road. I run towards the back of Wilton Crescent garden, where I turn and watch from behind the curved railings.

I'm expecting Sylvie, but it's Lucinda who answers the door in fashion leggings and an oversized cashmere top. Her loose blonde hair flies back with a gust of wind and her arms fold across her body. I hear her call out as she searches from side to side, then she takes a step out. Her feet must be cold on the chequered tiles, but she takes a second step to look further down the road. It's then that she looks down because she's trodden on the envelope. She picks it up and peers around again before opening it. She takes out the three A4 photographs and studies each one. Her mouth draws into a tight line as her eyes take in the images. She looks out at the street again and then disappears into the house and slams the door. I see her standing in the kitchen for ten long minutes before she closes all the curtains in the house – every single one downstairs and then upstairs. Does she know I'm here watching her?

I want to imagine what she's doing, what she's feeling. Perhaps she's laughing at these photographs, has known about Jim and Andrea all along and will shrug it off like it's nothing. Perhaps she's already burnt the pictures in the wood burner, has opened another bottle of wine and taken up nail varnish to paint her toenails in the bath.

Or maybe she's thinking about all the times she's invited Andrea into her home, about Andrea at work with Jim. Maybe she's crying. I feel the sharpness of guilt because I'm destroying her life alongside Jim's. Have I done the right thing? I think of Gwen. Let Jim and Andrea explain themselves to Lucinda. Let Gwen have a moment of peace.

On Saturday evening, Bobby meets me at a bus stop near Warwick Avenue. I tell myself that I'm here because I want to know more about Jemima Mataya and her relationship with Jim, but I'd be lying to myself if it was only for that reason. Bobby makes me feel normal and like I deserve a moment out of the life I've lived in grief to break out and open my wings, though I know nothing good can come from spending time with him. He's too close to Jim and, when I'm done, what else is there but to say goodbye to every element of this lie?

We walk side by side and he tells me about upcoming shows, about a member of his team who has a phobia of skittles and about the many names Andrea has which she doesn't know about. His stories are entertaining and I listen, happily, because I have nothing to offer of my own. I worry he might ask me about one of the places I said I'd been. I'm worried he'll find out that I'm just a boring girl with nothing about her.

We reach the canal and I gape at it from the bridge before we walk down the stone steps. It's dark, but I can see lights from the lines of boats on both sides of the canal, all different sizes and styles and colours. I can see the trees drifting their fingers in the water. The wind skims across the water and picks up the chill of the air, but I can't feel its cold.

There are five elderly men on the towpath on fold-out chairs outside their boats, sharing a box of old mince pies, and a young couple lying on their deck wrapped up in coats and each other.

'Stargazing,' Bobby says, looking at me watch them.

'I was looking at the old blokes with the mince pies,' I say.

He laughs. I like making him laugh. I thought I only made Lissy laugh and that she only laughs because she's my sister.

We walk a few more steps before he stops and smiles at me. 'This is my humble abode,' he says.

We're in front of a classic barge, painted charcoal and white with plant pots on the top of it. I can smell thyme and mint.

'You grow thyme and mint?' I ask.

'What? You think I don't look like the type to grow herbs? I was going to cook you dinner.' He steps on to the boat and reaches for my hand. 'In through the hatchway!'

'You don't say "door"?' I say, amused.

'One must use the correct terminology, otherwise one must not enter,' he says.

'Must one?'

'Yeah.' He grins.

I take his hand – how I love the touch of this hand – and he gives me the tour. The boat is compact but luxurious, kitted with a sleek white galley kitchen, a dining area and a lounge. At the front is a spacious bedroom where I see a sheepskin rug on the floor, and a blue duvet. Seeing where he sleeps – as with Jim – feels incredibly intimate, but I don't feel worried about being here, and then I wonder if I should.

'It's very clean in here,' I say.

'You should have seen it an hour ago.'

In the living space, he's got a bookcase and I'm drawn to it because I can see that he's bought this year's Booker Prize winner, Dad's favourite writer. I take it out.

'You like books?' he asks.

'Words are worlds,' I say, echoing my dad.

'Please note also my worthy collection of horse brasses on top of the bookshelf.'

I look up. 'Horse brasses?'

'My nan collected them,' he says.

I graze my fingers over one of them – a smooth, circular cast of a shire horse's head with a wheat sheaf curved around it.

'Nice,' I say.

'Apparently they date back to the Roman age,' he explains. 'Nan really knew how to banter.'

I laugh and then sit on the sofa.

'Oh, hold up.' Bobby leans over me to switch on a lamp and its ray streams on to my legs. I'm wearing black sheer tights and a tartan skirt and now I worry that I look stupidly young. He's in his mid-thirties, a decade older than me, and probably used to more sophisticated women. 'I was going to cook for you,' he says, moving away again and getting plates out of a cupboard. 'With herbs. But it took me so long to clean that I had to order a Domino's instead.' He smiles apologetically. 'I'm sorry. Is that OK? And it's really boring – margherita – because I didn't want to gamble on anything outrageous.'

'Like pineapple?' I say.

'I actually don't have a problem with pineapple on pizza,' he replies.

'Nor do I,' I say.

'Shit.' He looks around. 'I've got a lemon we could slice and put on top of it?'

I laugh. 'Margherita is OK, minus lemon,' I say.

I like that it's how we're going to spend tonight – relaxed and informal. I don't know if I would have managed another charade like last time. This feels like an evening I could be having with my sister. Is this what it feels like to be with friends? With a lover? I think of Gwendolen's comment about not kicking him out of bed and feel myself redden. I hope he doesn't notice under the heavy foundation I've layered.

'Do you want a drink?' he asks. 'Wine?'

'Sure,' I say.

'White?'

'Fine.'

He nods and uncorks a bottle.

'How was your week?' he asks.

'Oh, you know,' I reply. 'Stressful. I find I'm second-guessing Jim's moods a lot.'

'I think most people do that most of the time,' he says. He pours the wine and hands me one.

There's a shout from outside the boat and Bobby gets up.

'Our exotic dinner!' he beams.

He leaves and I stare about his boat some more until my eyes rest on the horse brasses on the shelf. Behind one is a half-obscured photo, and I reach to pull it out. It's Bobby and a young woman with their arms slung around each other, smiling at the camera.

'You have a picture of Jemima Mataya on your wall,' I say as he comes back through the hatchway holding a pizza box.

'Yeah,' he says.

'You were close?'

'Yeah.'

'Oh,' I say. 'I'm really sorry. I didn't realise.'

He busies himself opening the little boxes of sauces.

'I miss her,' he says. 'She was great. Truly. One of those genuine bright sparks. And she lived for that show. She made friends easily.'

'Was her death a real shock?' I ask.

He shrugs. 'She flirted with a lot of drugs,' he replies. 'That was no secret. She was catapulted into the public eye when she was seventeen and she partied hard and with a lot of people she shouldn't have partied with. Her family were in America and she didn't have many people to anchor her, you know what I mean? Garlic dip?'

'I didn't realise that Jim managed Jemima,' I say. 'Gwen told me.'

'Oh, yeah,' Bobby says. 'She didn't even have an agent originally because we found her on the programme. Then she found Bill, an agent who massively took advantage of her, never taught her the dos and don'ts of public life, and then Jim convinced her to leave him.'

'And that was good?'

'It was good to get away from Bill, but it wasn't good that Jim managed her himself. They had quite a toxic relationship. To be honest, after eighteen years, I think she wanted to get out.'

'Why didn't she?' I ask.

'Do people get to leave Jim?' he says.

'What does that mean?'

But he only shakes his head. 'Cheers.' He clinks his wine glass to mine and I know that he's not going to answer any more of my questions. I wonder which one I've upset him with. If he was close to Jemima, possibly all of them.

I smile at him. 'Sorry. I didn't mean to talk work. It's a nice photo, though.'

'Dig in,' he says.

I take a slice of pizza. 'You don't have any others in your boat?'

'Photos? Some. Look, there I am as a very awkward twelve-year-old – and shit, why didn't I see that before now and what are those trousers I'm wearing?'

I laugh.

'Most of my photos are actually in albums,' he adds. 'I'm retro. Besides, you'd want me to have a picture of my mother in my bedroom or something?'

I smile, but it fades as I think of my own mum, documented nowhere but in my head, like a fluttering candle flame that I can't obliterate however hard I try. I need to return that ring. It's in my bag still. Close to me.

'What's she like?' I ask. 'Your mum?'

'She's great,' he says. 'She's a teacher. She tells me her eight-year-olds are more mature than I am.'

'What about your dad?'

He smiles. 'Dad's Dad. He worked on an oil rig for thirty years, got a lot of funny stories. What's your family like?'

The pizza I'm eating turns fleshy in my mouth, loses its flavour immediately. I put down the slice. 'My mum wasn't great, but at least I had my dad. He was wonderful.'

He frowns. '*Was* wonderful?'

I don't say anything for a moment, but it's just the two of us here and the silence becomes heavy.

'They're both dead,' I say.

His shock is held in a split second of silence before he speaks. 'Oh shit,' he says, exhaling. 'I'm sorry.'

'It was a long time ago,' I say. 'My mum wasn't with us when she died. She was abroad with her new partner and she fell ill. And then my dad – he committed suicide a year later.'

I swallow. It feels so blunt saying it like this. Like I'm reading the news. My chin is trembling and I feel myself collapsing into Bobby's arms and he holds me tightly. I can't remember the last time someone held me while I cried.

'Matilda,' he says. 'God, I'm sorry.'

This man knows a desperate truth about me, is the first person I've trusted outside the tight circle of my family, yet he doesn't even know my name, and that makes me cry harder.

'Do you want to talk about them?' he asks.

'No.'

'I'm sorry.'

He reaches to stroke my hair and I tense up because not even the hair is mine. It's held in rigid, but what if it moves? I edge away from him.

'Please don't tell anyone they're dead,' I say quickly. 'At work.'

'That is in no way my information to tell,' he replies. 'You can trust me.'

He's looking at me with concern, and with that look, a single tear drips from my face on to his T-shirt. He takes my face in his hands, rolls me over gently and cradles me and we lie wrapped up in one another on his sofa and listen to the sound of the water licking at the side of the boat.

I leave early; I don't even wake him. I retrieve my boots and coat and slip out of the hatch into a black morning along the towpath. I look at the river below; watch as eddies curl around the plant life that sprouts from the bank, then vanish.

I feel strange; both liberated by speaking the truth about Dad and yet weighed down by it. I've stayed all night with Bobby, even though we didn't come close to doing anything physical. He held me for hours and then at midnight we sat up, ate the pizza and watched *Lost in Translation*, curled up together, before falling asleep again in our clothes. He understood and that should feel incredible, but it only makes me feel sad. I've made myself vulnerable and now I have to claw it back in again.

I need to see Chloe and get some answers about Jemima.

THIRTY-FOUR

I can feel Jim's hot breath on my neck. He's standing above me, leaning on my desk with his arms either side of me. I'm trying to make myself as small as possible by tucking my arms in, but I feel like his prisoner. Gertie is beneath my chair.

'No, not that one,' he says.

I keep scrolling.

'That one?' I ask.

'Not short enough,' he replies.

'That one?'

'I don't like the colour.'

'What colour do you want?' I ask.

'Pink,' he says.

I grit my teeth. We're on a website I've never even heard of and he's choosing something for Marie Jarski to wear at the industry awards ceremony next week. She sent her choice over yesterday – a long yellow dress with a high neck – but Jim has dismissed it as too chaste.

'The programme is young and dark and edgy,' he says. 'She has to fit the cast.'

'Right,' I reply, and carry on scrolling.

'That one,' he exclaims, pointing to a strapped, sheer, doll-like dress.

'I wouldn't go to bed wearing that, Jim,' I say.

He laughs. 'Ring the designer,' he says. 'Pick it up this week.'

'We should check with Marie first, shouldn't we?' I ask. 'She'd need to feel comfortable in . . .'

The lift doors open and Andrea strides out, heels clicking. I catch her eye and they throw knives out at me before she looks at Jim.

'Jim, I need to talk to you,' she says.

He doesn't even look at her from the screen, but I see that his expression is one of irritation. 'We've had the conversation already,' he says.

'It's not about Lucinda,' she replies.

I see his eyes flick to me and I realise then that Lucinda has confronted him on those photos, perhaps she's confronted the both of them.

'What then?' he says.

'There's an article been published online,' Andrea says.

Jim sighs and looks up at her. 'And?'

'It's about Cyclops,' Andrea says. 'It's on the *Reel Event*. It's incriminating.'

He makes a dismissive noise. 'The *Reel Event* is tiny. I have a communications department to sort this kind of thing, Andrea. You think journalists don't have a sulk now and then and contact these minute companies for a couple of hundred quid?'

'It's gone on to the French media website, *De Plume*.'

'Again, small,' he replies.

'Jim,' Andrea says. 'It suggests that *Pranksters* is "unclean".'

'*Unclean*?' He sighs and turns back to me. 'Get the *Reel Event* up and write my name in the search icon.'

I nod. 'OK.' I type clumsily because they're both watching me.

'Show me,' Jim says.

I turn the screen towards him and he bends down again and takes control of the mouse to scroll through the article. I watch as his expression turns from mild annoyance to fury in a matter of seconds and I flick my eyes to the screen.

It's time to talk about the things we brush under the red carpet.

It's difficult to build up a sufficient claim against a man so well known and so well loved within his field, but there has to be one person to start it all. I am that person and I'm stating my truth against him, Jim Valente. His money-spinning programme, *Pranksters*, has got long-standing secrets. Did they die with Jemima Mataya a year ago?

I get no further reading it because Jim slams his fist down on my desk.

'What is this unfounded piece of crap?' he yells.

Under my desk, Gertie bangs her head and barks with shock.

'I have alerts on my company name set up for things like this!' he shouts. He glares at me. 'Call a company meeting in the auditorium, *now*.'

I nod and he clicks off the article, wanting to remove it from his sight. I go to take the mouse from his hand, except he pauses.

'Why is my inbox folder in your emails?' he says quietly.

Dread steals over my body. 'Sorry?'

'There.' He points. 'That's my inbox.'

'Is it?' I say, swallowing and willing myself not to be sick. 'I've never noticed it there. I'm so sorry – should I have been doing something with it?'

He turns to me then and our proximity is unbearably close. I can feel the heat of his breath and the blue of his eyes on me is almost blinding.

'How did you get my inbox?' he asks.

'I don't know,' I stammer. 'I guess . . . I guess it's always been there.'

'No,' he says. 'I don't think so.'

I shrug, not trusting myself to say anything.

'You shouldn't have access to that,' he says. 'Delete it. Right now.'

I nod my head fast. 'Sure.' I take the mouse and click the folder and it disappears.

'My email correspondence is confidential,' he adds.

'Absolutely, yes,' I reply. 'I didn't know it was there, Jim. I'm sorry.'

I try to look innocent, but this is the first time I've felt aggression from Jim and it's making me overheat. What has Horsehead done? Because who else would have written this article but him?

'Company meeting at ten,' Jim says. 'Whoever is responsible for writing this is going to have to find themselves a very good lawyer.'

He goes into his office, slams the door and Andrea and I remain.

'I don't like you very much,' she says.

Jim stands on the stage and snaps his eyes at the last few members of staff to come in. He looks tall and strong in his suit, like the world could shoot at him and he'd be able to take the bullets.

'Pay attention,' he says, though everyone already is because they're wondering why they've been called here out of the blue. 'This will take five minutes, but it's important we're all together. Because that's what we do here, we all muck in. This is a great and powerful company and its reputation for professionalism, for tenacity, for passion within the media industry is top. And it's you. You who make it what it is.'

From my seat at the back of the auditorium, I see people turn to each other and lift their eyebrows.

'But,' Jim continues, 'there are some people who like to disrupt this reputation. I want to draw your attention to an article published this morning on the *Reel Event*. It's a tiny website – some of you won't even know what it is, some of you may have seen an article published on it. Whichever way, after this briefing, you'll never see it because I've arranged for it to be taken down and the company behind the website will be sued for slander. The piece was written anonymously, by a coward, by someone who doesn't know what they're talking about. They wrote that *Pranksters* is corrupt, that it's *unclean*. Are we going to let that stand? Our programme? *Our* baby?'

At the same time as feeling terrified that any moment I'll be exposed for all this, a part of me is exhilarated to witness his display of anger. At last I've found a splinter in Jim's shining armour. His reputation is the thing he cares about, his weakness.

'You might think we're too big and I'm too busy to draw attention to so small a thing. But the reason why I'm telling you about it is because slander is not to be taken lightly. I won't stand for anyone smearing the company that we all work so hard to build and maintain together. You get somewhere by working *hard*. By thinking outside the box to win marketing campaigns, striving for the best possible relationships with the broadcasters. Creating unique talent programmes, stretching our budgets so they deliver. Bulldozing our competition.'

He looks around the room and I see that he's impressive, despite his underlying rage.

'Make yourselves proud of being part of this. Make *me* proud. And in case it was any of you in this fucking room who wrote that article, if you don't like the way we've done something, then you leave,' he says, quietly. 'But never go to the press. Because guess what? I own them all. One way or another. Everyone gives me their pound of flesh.'

The energy in the room switches at once. Nervousness flutters like a hundred trapped butterflies above our heads.

'Dismissed,' Jim says with a cheerful smile, as if it's a joke. There's a peel of anxious laughter across the auditorium and then people start to get up.

I stand up and start to file out alongside the silent company, but I hear my name called – loud, slow, deliberate.

'Matilda,' Jim says. 'Stay here.'

I walk down the stairs to the stage and stop short a few metres from him. He glowers at me and then steps closer to close the gap between us.

'Are you OK, Jim?' I ask.

The door closes behind the last of the employees and the sound reverberates around the auditorium.

'I fired my last PA,' he says, 'because after years she proved untrustworthy.'

I say nothing.

'I've had a strange couple of weeks,' he continues. 'This article, a letter I received a couple of weeks ago, some post my wife received, and a phone call from an old friend.'

His blue eyes are burning into me. He knows I'm to blame.

'An . . . an old friend?' I say.

'Something feels *off*,' he says. 'Keep your eyes peeled for me, there's a good girl.'

'Of course, Jim,' I reply.

'*Personne ne me prend pour un con*,' he whispers, and I can't help it – my eyes widen.

No one makes a fool of me.

He speaks French. He tricked me.

Top Step: Why did you write that? Are you crazy?

Horsehead: Bored.

Top Step: You've made Jim suspicious of *me*.

Horsehead: No, I've made him suspicious of *everyone*. Isn't that part of the plan? We need to take him down, right? So let's enjoy it along the way, because we don't know this is going to have a grand finale, do we? Why not take the opportunities while we have them? I thought you were into risks?

Top Step: I've only just come on board with your 'risks', Horsehead, but this was stupidity. And I think Andrea is suspicious of me!

Horsehead: Why?

Top Step: She doesn't miss a trick.

Horsehead: But nor do I.

Top Step: You're not *here*, Horsehead. You're not living it. You have no idea how scary it is to be doing this! You promised not to act on what I'd told you and then you did it anyway and threw me under a bus!

Horsehead: Stop being so dramatic, doll. It riled him. We need more anonymous little knives to get under his skin.

Top Step: I'm trying! I feel like we're on top of something. Wait, do you have the article you can send me? Or evidence that it got on those websites?

Horsehead: Like a screen print or whatever?

Top Step: I'm going to send it to Chloe and I'm going to take responsibility for it. Maybe she'll take the bait if she knows she doesn't have to be dragged into it with me, that she only needs to talk to me.

Horsehead: A good plan! I'll send it now. See?? I HELPED.

THIRTY-FIVE

It's Wednesday and Jim and I walk towards Soho Square for lunch. Our breath merges in the air as we go and I move apart from him slightly because I don't like feeling like any part of me overlaps with him. I'm glad of the noise of the streets because Jim is quiet next to me and I've realised that, unless he's working, he's seldom quiet. I sneak a glance at him and see that his face mirrors the sky, an angry blanket of grey. Gertie trots alongside us, snuffling at the ground, the bell on her collar tinkling.

I use his silence to mull over what I'm going to do about Chloe. It's been two days since I found her work email address and sent her the article Horsehead wrote, but I haven't yet heard anything back from her. I don't even know if it would have reached her or gone straight into a junk inbox. Perhaps she's deleted it and blocked my email address.

'The Mayfair Hotel called twenty minutes ago,' I say brightly, trying to read his mood. 'Your suit will be delivered from Henry Poole and Co. to your room. Are you staying there at the moment?'

'I moved in last weekend,' he says. 'Why not be decadent?'

'Lovely location for your wife to go shopping,' I dare to say.

He sucks his teeth. 'Indeed,' he replies.

I sneak a look at him. He is always the showman, but I see that his jaw is set tightly.

'I'll be staying there for the next few nights,' he says. 'Until after the awards ceremony next Tuesday.'

'Are you OK, Jim?' I ask.

'Oh, I'm dandy,' he replies. 'Hundreds of articles on Jemima this morning. Have you seen them? A lot of questions raised about her.'

'Yes, I've seen them.'

'But all PR is good PR,' he says.

'Is it?'

'That's the fucking spin,' he growls.

We reach the restaurant and Jim opens the door for me. Inside, it's small and refined, with dimly lit globe lights and exquisite antique furniture. It's an obvious hint that the menu will be of the same quality as the interior: stately. Jim doesn't bat an eyelid because this elegance is Jim Valente's everyday.

He orders a bottle of red wine, a venison starter and a rump roast, and I order a salad and then spinach dumplings, which are the first things I see on the menu. The wine comes and we are silent as the waiter pours it into our glasses. Jim taps on his phone and lays it face up on the table.

'We need to talk, don't we?' he says as the waiter leaves.

I sit on my hands and my throat constricts. He's found me out. 'We do?'

'About the industry awards,' he continues.

'Right,' I say, breathe again.

'Has Natalie Lewis sorted the sound and lighting desk requirement?' he asks.

'Yes,' I say. 'Our guys have the exclusive use of the desk. It's behind the stalls and is lockable. Eric is seeing you this afternoon about the final arrangements and timings.'

'Eric?' he says, looking vague.

'Head of IT,' I remind him for the second time. 'He's the one who knows how to operate the desk.'

He picks up his wine glass. 'Tell me again about your last boss.'

His tone has changed. His voice is soft.

'My . . . In America?'

'That's right,' he says.

I close my eyes a beat. This is it, then. It's all over. I pick up my wine glass and swill it around. It looks like blood.

'What do you want to know?' I ask.

'He emailed me,' Jim says. 'Last night.'

I stare at him. 'He did?'

'He's a character, isn't he?'

I can't believe what I'm hearing. My God, Horsehead. What are you doing?

'He certainly is,' I manage to say.

'He misses you,' Jim says. 'He asked how you were getting on.'

'What did you say?' I ask.

'In a world that can't stop talking, you're delightfully to the point,' he says. 'You get on and do.'

'That's all he wanted to know?'

Jim nods. 'And if I thought you were up to par. I said yes. For now.'

Did Horsehead email Jim because he wants to make sure I'm on track and that Jim doesn't suspect me of anything? I gulp back some wine, choke on it and cough. The waiter comes with our starters and then leaves. The salad looks crisp and fresh but cold, and I shiver. I need to log on to the forum right now and ask Horsehead what he's playing at.

'He also asked me if you had a boyfriend,' Jim says.

'He what?'

'Is that the American way?' Jim asks. 'Should I be concerned about your love life?'

'No,' I reply. 'Definitely not.'

'I told him about Bobby,' Jim says. He picks up his cutlery and cuts into the venison.

'What about Bobby?'

'That you seem close,' Jim adds. He smiles and the dimple in his cheek is pronounced. 'Someone has finally wooed him, it seems.'

'I don't think that—'

But Jim interrupts me. 'There have been countless other girls, you see,' he says, chewing. 'Bobby and I go back a long way, so I've seen all the others fall.'

I pick up my fork and play with a bit of lettuce. Jim drains the glass of wine and pours more for himself, doesn't wait for the waiter. He's watching me for a reaction. I can feel those intelligent eyes on my face.

'He's a bit old for you, isn't he?'

'Perhaps we should change the subject,' I suggest.

'Certainly,' he says. 'I shouldn't have brought up past office conquests.'

I breathe in, trying to calm myself down, and start to eat. A cherry tomato bursts in my mouth. How many others has Bobby been with in the office? I'm upset with myself for having created a weakness in this life when I should be strong and emotionless. Should I stop seeing Bobby outside work? Before

I even finish asking myself the question, I know the answer is yes. I'm a fool for thinking it could be anything other than what it should be. He's a contact, someone who has answers to questions about *Pranksters*. He should be nothing more. And yet, the touch of his hands. Touch is what I've been missing for so many years. Such a simple human connection.

'Does it make you uncomfortable?' Jim says. 'Talking about your sex life?'

I look at him. 'About as comfortable as asking me to wear pink lipstick for you, Jim, or picking out Marie, or choosing her dress.'

'And yet you did it. You did all those things that I asked of you.'

My skin is on fire. I'm scared, but I'm also livid. 'I'm very obedient.'

He laughs again. 'I like you, kid. My other PAs have been pretty, but you're sharp, too, aren't you? So my advice is this. Only regret the things you don't do, not the things you do.'

I clear my throat. 'What about you, Jim?' I say. 'Do you have regrets?'

He laughs now and I watch as he rolls his tongue around the question like it's an amuse-bouche between courses. 'What would I have to regret?'

'Anything you could have done differently?'

He takes another mouthful of venison, chews it thoughtfully and leans back in his chair. 'Things I could have done differently.' He pauses. 'There was someone who pushed me to a limit I didn't know I was capable of.'

'What happened?'

He goes for another bite of the venison. 'I ended their career.'

'Oh,' I say.

'Talking of which,' he says. 'I fired Gwendolen Harris today.'

My mouth falls in shock. 'Gwen? Why?'

'It was her that wrote the article,' he replies. 'She denies it, but we found out that it was from her work IP address. Stupid cow.'

'That's not possible,' I whisper.

'Except that it *is* possible,' he says. 'She and Andrea have had cat fights for years. And what happened at my house a few nights ago with the photos that . . .'

He stops suddenly and my heart skips. He was about to tell me about the photographs I delivered to Lucinda and I realise with a sinking feeling that he thinks it was Gwen who sent them. My plan to help her has completely backfired.

'Anyway, I've been looking for a reason to axe her,' he continues.

'But she must have denied it?' I say.

He nods. 'She did,' he replies. 'But further investigation revealed that last week she came to the office at gone eleven at night. Why? What was she doing?'

'That could have been for anything,' I say.

He smiles. 'You liked her, didn't you?'

I look down at my plate, feeling sick with guilt.

'And that's a shame,' he says. 'But now, more than ever, I need everything watertight, you understand? The awards are next week. I don't need traitorous bullshit like that in my own damn company.'

'No,' I reply.

'Did you know?' he asks. 'That she'd written it?'

'No,' I say. 'I swear.'

'Because you're on my side,' he says.

I nod quickly, a car-shelf dog.

'I'm on your side, Jim,' I echo.

'I sincerely hope you are on my side,' he says. 'Even if you do want to slap me.'

'Jim . . .' I say. 'You speak French.'

He smiles, but it's brief. 'I deserved the sharp end of your tongue on that one,' he comments. 'I went too far. Jokes sometimes go too far and you pay for them for a very long time.'

I meet his eyes, nod.

'You remember that whenever you decide to play a joke on someone,' he says.

'I'll remember,' I reply.

'*Bien*,' he says. 'I didn't realise you could be feisty.'

I suck at my teeth.

'My wife needs a present,' he says, changing the subject. 'I'm in the fucking doghouse.'

'OK,' I say.

'Jewellery,' he says. 'That's how you cover your tracks.'

Top Step: Why did you frame Gwen, Horsehead? You've completely destroyed her career!

Horsehead: You said Jim was getting suspicious of you.

Top Step: Yes, but that didn't mean I wanted you to sacrifice Gwen!

Horsehead: Right, so you've got a conscience now?

Top Step: I don't like what you're doing.

Horsehead: Relax, doll! She wanted out anyway, right? Don't feel bad for Gwen. She can now get her cats! Yay!

Top Step: And do NOT email Jim again. What were you thinking?

Horsehead: Oh, that was fun times! He's actually pretty witty, but also sorta gross. He said he had a hunch about who'd been in your panties.

Top Step: That's horrible.

Horsehead: I know. Don't you just want to *destroy* that guy??

On Friday afternoon, I take Gertie on a walk around Embankment Gardens. I have lots to do today ahead of the awards ceremony next week, but I needed the air. I need to remind myself why I'm doing this, settle the gnaw of unease that's creeping up my spine when I go to sleep at night. I feel so close to something and yet dangerously blind.

The gardens are comforting. Dad loved green spaces. There were some nights where he would finally stop writing at one in the morning and, in his energetic buzz, rouse us from our beds and put our coats on over our pyjamas and lead us out of the front door on a night walk. We'd always end up somewhere green, even if it was a roundabout. We were pirates digging for treasure, we were explorers looking for creatures of the dark, we were botanists off to tame man-eating plants. I never realised how strange that was until I grew up.

I wish I'd never grown up.

I think about Gwen and how she's been destroyed by my and Horsehead's actions. I never meant for her to get the blame for what I'd done. Should I get in contact with her and explain myself?

'Hey.'

I turn to see Bobby behind me.

'I saw you come out here from my window,' he says. 'You OK?'

'Yeah,' I reply.

'I heard about Gwen,' he says.

'Oh God, Bobby,' I say. 'I don't think she wrote it.'

'She didn't,' he says. Then he looks at me, mute, for a very long time.

'Have you spoken to her?' I ask.

He nods. 'She thinks someone set her up.'

'Really?' I say meekly, and I feel like I'm going to unravel, right here on the grass, but he takes my hand and squeezes it.

'Do you want to come to mine tomorrow night?' he asks. 'I'll cook. With *herbs*.'

My relief floods out, full force, into a smile. 'Yes,' I say. 'That sounds good.'

He leaves me and I feel dizzy with the emotion. Guilt, fear and excitement all in a matter of moments.

I look at my phone again and my breath catches in my throat. I have a text from Chloe. I forgot that I wrote down my number for her.

You're serious about this? If you are, come and see me tomorrow morning and we'll talk.

Finally, I'm getting somewhere.

THIRTY-SIX

I sit opposite her in her office. She's wearing an ironed blue polo shirt with a red bib over it and she eyes me suspiciously.

'I've got ten minutes before a game,' Chloe says.

'OK.'

'You really want to do this?' she asks. 'Try to take Jim on?'

'I do.'

'You wrote that article?'

'Yes,' I lie. 'Finding out about you, Chloe, and finding out that Jemima Mataya might have tried to expose Jim the same way I want to, is what I need to help me. But it's all confused. I need some details.'

I see her move her bottom jaw, grind her teeth.

'I can't be seen to have anything to do with any of this,' she says. 'You understand?'

'OK,' I reply.

She studies me for a moment and then she speaks. 'You guessed right. Jemima had been controlled by Jim for years and she wanted to leave him and the company and move back to America. So she tried to expose him the only way she knew how. By *Pranksters*. She knew all the people affected by it, like me, because she'd been on every shoot, you understand? She'd witnessed all the fallouts, and she was threatening to go to press with all the details unless he released her from her contract. She wanted to go to Hollywood.'

'What did she do?' I ask.

'She put everyone's names on a USB and then confronted Jim with it.'

'He's got the USB,' I say. 'At least, I think he does.'

'But there was something else, too.'

She opens one of her desk drawers and takes out a silver phone and places it face down. On its protective backing is a printed picture of Jemima Mataya with sunglasses on, her tongue out and doing the V peace sign.

I stare at Chloe.

'What's . . . what's this?'

'Her phone.'

Her phone, her phone. White noise fills in my ears.

'Shouldn't this be with the police?' I ask.

'Jemima died from an overdose,' Chloe says. 'To them and to the world, that's the end of it. And how would I explain my part in having it for an entire year? I don't – *can't* – have anything to do with this. You understand? And how would you explain yourself? You admitted to me that you're work- ing with Jim under a false name. If you want to do this, you have to be careful.'

'How have you got the phone?' I ask. 'Why?'

'Jemima hid this phone and filmed Jim when she went to confront him with the USB. He admitted on camera that he bought people off, but he realised she was filming him and he went mad. She fled without the USB, but she managed to take the phone and she texted me that night, telling me she was going to stick it in a postbox and mail it to me. She told me the PIN code and told me to do what she started but couldn't finish. She told me to take him down at all costs, that *I* was evidence enough and didn't need the USB full of other stuff he'd taken.'

'Then what?'

'Then the next day I read that she'd overdosed,' she says. She looks for a minute like she's going to cry. 'It was horrible. She'd texted me all of that, she went out and she mailed the phone, and then went back to her house and overdosed.'

'Jim said that he was with Andrea Rubins the night Jemima died,' I note. 'I remember him saying that at the memorial.'

'He might have been anywhere with anyone later,' she says. 'But he was definitely with Jemima earlier in the evening.'

'But you didn't do it,' I say. 'You didn't expose him.'

'I didn't do it,' she says quietly, and I can see emotion flit over her face. Guilt? Remorse? Fear? 'The money . . .' She shakes her head. 'The money was too precious to my family.'

'But you could come forward now, couldn't you?'

'No,' she says. 'I can't.'

'Chloe . . .'

'I *can't* go out publicly with any of this. I risk repaying everything he ever gave me.'

'Even if all this went to court?'

She shakes her head. 'Please,' she says. 'I can't.'

'OK,' I say. 'Can you tell me what's on the USB?'

She shrugs. 'Names, transactions? I don't know exactly.'

'But whatever it is, Jemima thought it was enough to ruin him.'

'Do you know what it looks like?' I ask.

'Jemima hid it in her jewellery box,' she says. 'It's a tiny USB in a locket.'

Would Jim have kept it in the locket? Do I remember seeing any jewellery in his office that night I broke in? It could be anywhere.

'Surely she had a copy of all this information?' I say.

Chloe closes her eyes, exhales and then snaps them back open. 'Her laptop was never found,' she replies. 'But I know that Jim had it.'

'How do you know that?' I ask.

'Because she had it with her the night she went to him and she didn't go back home with it.' She looks at the phone. 'You'll see for yourself when you watch the video.'

'Wow, OK.'

'You'd make a storm with what's on the phone on its own. But with whatever is on the USB, it would be even bigger. That's what she told me.'

I don't want this phone and yet she's sliding it over to me and I'm putting it into my bag alongside Lucinda's ring, and I realise that I'm in so deep now. I've committed to this.

'The code for her phone is 100784,' Chloe says. 'Her birthday. And I don't want to see you ever again. Really. I said that things got complicated for me and I meant that. I don't want to go down that road again.'

'Right,' I say, just as someone knocks on the door and we both turn to it in surprise.

'You ready for me to kick your ass on wheels again this week?'

I know that voice. Bobby is standing at Chloe's door.

We lock eyes and my stomach feels like it drops straight through the floor. I'm not wearing my wig or any make-up, but by the shock on his face, he knows it's me.

'Oh, sorry, Clo,' he says, carefully. 'I didn't realise you had company.'

He's wearing a blue bib, the same as Chloe's, over shorts and a blue sports T-shirt.

'It's fine,' Chloe replies. 'We're finished.'

'Yes,' I say, and I stand up.

We're face to face, so close that I could reach up and touch his face, and his eyes are penetrating. My legs are shaking. Has Jim sent him here? Have I miscalculated and all this time Jim has had him following me? How can I have got this so wrong?

'I'll go,' I say.

But as I try to slip past him, I feel his hand grip my wrist.

'I'm going to give the first game over to Ray, Clo, OK?' he says to her over my shoulder. 'I've got to make a call for half an hour.'

'Oh shit, really? Ray's not as fast as you in a chair,' Chloe replies.

'I'll see you in a bit,' he says, and then he follows me out of the office.

I don't want to look at him, but he is close behind me. We walk out of the building.

'Who are you?' he asks.

I turn to him, rooted by his voice to the ground, like it's magnetised.

'What happened to your hair?' he says. 'And your face? You have a scar?'

I've never felt so naked as I do now, fully clothed, in front of him. 'I . . . I came to see Chloe,' I say.

My words seem to burn him. 'Oh, I get it,' he says. 'You're a reporter.'

'I'm not a reporter,' I reply. 'I read an email in Jim's archives about Chloe weeks ago. I don't know her. I was . . . I was following up on something that didn't feel right.'

He shakes his head. 'If that were true, why would you come into work with brown hair and cover up your face? You came to work from day one with something to hide, so what is it?'

He's angry because I've cheated him. I can see the muscles working in his jaw.

'Please, Bobby,' I say. 'Please don't tell Jim that I'm here.'

'Why shouldn't I?' he says.

'Because I was just trying . . . It's complicated, Bobby. *Pranksters*. I have nothing to do with Chloe, but I . . . I'm working for Jim for myself. I . . . I don't even know how I can begin to explain.'

'Try,' he says.

What do I say? How can I work my way out of this? Do I dare tell him the truth?

'I came to work for Jim because . . . because I'm working out something that happened to my dad and I thought Chloe might be able to help me.'

The anger on his face wavers. 'Was your dad involved in that episode?' he asks.

I blink. Has Bobby just given me a cover story I can run with? 'He was a cameraman,' I say. 'Yes. But he . . . he never worked again after what happened to Chloe. And he . . . he would never tell me why or what happened. I applied for a job with Jim because I wanted to go into the industry, same as my dad. I never thought I'd get in, but I got the role and then I just blindly tried to stumble around in the dark with it all.'

I stop talking, look at him and silently plead that he will believe my lie.

'Oh,' he says, and he seems to slump, his expression melting into one of grief.

'I'm sorry I didn't tell you,' I say.

He shakes his head. 'You wanted to find out the truth. That's fair.' He looks me straight in the eyes. 'The truth is that it was my fault. There it is. My fault that Chloe's in that wheelchair.'

I'm confused. 'Your fault? What do you mean?'

A sudden sadness replaces his anger. 'I even took the episode from the archives. I couldn't bear for anyone to look at it again. It's been in my office for years.' He puts his head in his hands. 'The footage has been deleted, but all the other things, the script, the costs, I've got them. Is that what you were looking for? Are you wanting to go after me?'

That explains where the physical file has been all this time. 'After you? No! Why would you think that?'

'You want me to go over it again? The upset that I caused to Chloe's mum, her brother? I can't undo it, Matilda! I can't say sorry enough! I've started the charity for Chloe, I come here every month to play basketball, we're *friends* now.'

I frown. 'Bobby, I don't understand what you're saying.'

'You know who I am?' he says. 'I'm the third founder of the company. The one who stayed.'

I'm not sure I've heard him correctly. 'You . . . you founded Cyclops?'

'Me, Markus and Sean,' he says. 'RSM Media. They left and I should have left with them. Jim bought out the company in its early years, but he convinced me to stay. He loved my ideas and I thought it would be good to work with him.'

That photograph of him and the two others that I found in the filing cabinet in Jim's office. I *did* recognise them. Markus and Sean.

'What's this got to do with Chloe's accident?' I say, but I think that the truth of the answer is forming on my own tongue and I feel sick.

'I wish they'd stopped making it, but it had become so successful by then. *Too* successful. *Pranksters*.' His voice breaks with emotion. 'It was my concept right from the beginning. I thought of most of the pranks. And the prank that left Chloe in a wheelchair, it was my idea. I was eighteen and a stupid kid.'

My tongue has stuck in my mouth. I reel back from him, actually physically reel so I stumble a little. 'What?' I ask, even though I heard him and I don't need to hear it again. I'm hyperventilating. '*Pranksters?* Your idea?'

'Head of Concepts,' he says. 'That's my title. I was always the ideas guy of the three of us when we founded it.'

I'm screaming. 'You said you hated it! *Pranksters!* You hated it!'

'Hey, hey,' he says, looking up at me, shocked at my anger. 'Why are you screaming?'

'You think Chloe was the only one who got injured by that programme?' I shout. 'Oh my God! You don't have a *clue* what that programme is! It's a sick mindfuck for innocent people!'

'Matilda, calm down,' he says and he's scowling now. 'Why are you shouting at me? Let's talk about this?'

But I shake my head. I have to get away from him. He doesn't follow me.

There's only me and one other person on the platform waiting for the train. He sits on a bench scrolling on his phone and I stand a few metres away from him against the railings and stare at the ground. The concrete is cracked below my feet and the pale light of the afternoon falls on the weeds and scrub that poke out in the gaps between rusted iron bars. My breath frosts in the air. I can hear birds singing somewhere above me and the tap-tapping sound of the man typing on his phone.

I can feel physically the impact of Bobby's revelation, a deep aching punch in the stomach that hurts when I move. I think back to the emails I found between Jim and Oliver Kealey and what they meant.

> The legalities around this are interesting and difficult. How are the boys around this? Keep them informed. There might be a significant fallout and they'll need to know how to respond.

The boys were the three of them – Bobby, Markus and Sean. They would have been frightened after what happened to Chloe. Now it makes sense. But it didn't stop them making more of those disgusting episodes. Have I been chasing the wrong person all this time? Jim never came up with the prank himself – was it Bobby who was responsible for the prank that caused my dad to second-guess himself with Christopher Barrows? I close my eyes, can't bear the thought of it. Would Bobby have relinquished the footage if my dad had written to him and begged?

I'm exhausted by my anger and my shame. I should have known better than to trust anyone, especially anyone at Cyclops. What was I thinking? That I could serve revenge cold to Jim and walk away into the sunset with Bobby? No good comes of trusting people, because they just leave you.

The train rushes into the station. I should forget about all of this, but Jemima's phone feels heavy in my bag. Do I owe it to my dad to see this through, come hell or high water? Do I owe it to Chloe? To Jemima? And would I even have the chance if Bobby tells Jim about me?

Horsehead: Seriously, doll. Did you kill Tamagotchi when they were a thing? I've been waiting for you to reply to my messages! Are you the world's worst cliff-hanger or what??

Top Step: Things have become complicated. In so many ways.

Horsehead: Did Chloe reply to your email?

Top Step: I saw her.

Horsehead: YUSSSSSS. Is she going to play ball? Will she help us?

Top Step: She *did* help us.

Horsehead: How?

Top Step: If I tell you, you've got to promise not to do anything stupid with it.

Horsehead: WHAT?

Top Step: You didn't promise.

Horsehead: Hope to die, stick a needle in my eye. How did she help?

Top Step: She gave me Jemima Mataya's phone.

Horsehead: I'm sorry? What now?

Top Step: Chloe has had Jemima's phone for a year.

Horsehead: Son of a bitch! Why has she got a dead girl's phone??

Top Step: Jemima mailed it to her the night she died. Jemima saw Jim the night she overdosed. She tried to confront him. She filmed it on the phone.

Horsehead: OMG. Can you open it?

Top Step: Chloe gave me her code. It's her birthday.

Horsehead: What's on it? Have you seen it?

Top Step: Not yet.

Horsehead: Upload it for me!!

Top Step: You are NOT putting this anywhere, Horsehead. It's in my bedside cabinet, SAFE. There's more I need to find out before you go trigger-happy on this. Apparently the USB that Jim has is kept in a locket.

Horsehead: A locket? It must be tiny!

Top Step: I know.

Horsehead: What's on it?

Top Step: I don't know. And Chloe didn't know either.

Horsehead: Shit. This has turned into something bigger than you thought, hasn't it? Jim's star tried to take him down and then she died?? Please, please, send me the files on that phone!

Top Step: No.

Horsehead: Oh, you're no fun anymore.

THIRTY-SEVEN

Dust particles rain through the curtain slit and on to my face where I lie on my bed and stare at the ceiling. I grip Jemima Mataya's phone in my hand. I didn't switch it on last night; I could only stare fearfully at it. It feels alive and dangerous and it belongs to the police or at the bottom of a river, anywhere but in my shaking hand. I can't put off looking at what's on it indefinitely, though, and where else could I dare look at it but here, in the sanctuary of my flat?

Now or never.

I turn the phone on, tap out the PIN and the screen bursts into life. There's a black and white background picture of Jemima with a puppy on her lap and she looks happy. The battery is full. I see that she has 722 unread emails and several thousand social media notifications. I feel like I'm exhuming a corpse.

I swallow, click on to the gallery app and scroll through the videos to the last one, dated 20 January 2020. The day she died. Bile crawls up my throat. I put down the phone and look away for a moment. Do I want to watch this? What does this mean? What is this leading to? Horsehead was right; this is far bigger than anything I ever expected to find.

I close my eyes and click on the video and squint. Immediately, I see the white table on the rooftop of the Cyclops building. On it is a bottle of white wine and two glasses. The view is slightly wonky and the picture distorted by what looks like reeds before I realise that the phone must be wedged in the long-stemmed dogwood.

'Jim Valente is coming up here to meet me,' comes Jemima's voice, and her face appears on the screen. Her face is made-up, but up close I can see ageing lines around her eyes and mouth. Her pupils are large, dilated, and her lips are twitchy. She's dressed in a white coat with grey faux-fur trim and a black polo neck underneath. She reaches her hands out to adjust the phone. 'And then the whole world will know what he does.'

She goes to sit down on one of the chairs and looks back at the phone. Then she pours the wine from the bottle and I wait with her as she waits for Jim.

I forward the video along ten minutes until I see him come into view.

'Jim,' she says, and hands him a glass of wine as he sits opposite her. 'I've got to talk to you.'

Jim sits down. 'You sound serious,' he says, taking the wine. 'What's the matter?'

'It's about my contract.'

He laughs. 'This chat is becoming far too frequent for my liking, Jemima.'

'I'm too old for *Pranksters*,' she says.

'You're the entire programme,' he replies. 'Your magic is that you make it so palatable. You dumb down the dark.'

'But I see things differently now,' she says. 'Cheap laughs come at a price. You exploit people, Jim, for the sake of entertainment. I'm thirty-five and I've grown up and you've had all my best years.'

'Your best years,' he says, 'which were down to me and which you've happily cashed in on.'

She's silent for a moment. 'You know what this is about, Jim,' she adds. 'I want to go back to America and now's the time.'

'Oh, this has nothing to do with Fox knocking at my door a month ago?' he says. 'Because suddenly someone wants you?'

'It's a film part, Jim. It would be good for me.'

'But it wouldn't benefit *me*, Jemima. So I have a problem with it, see? You flirt with my money and my patience and you go talking to studios without my knowledge when I'm your manager and I own your time.'

'You treat me like a child,' she says.

'Because you act like one,' he retorts. 'All those parties, all those terrible mistakes you make over and over and over that I have to smooth over for you in the press. You're a functioning alcoholic and a user.'

'You can't keep me for ever, Jim.'

He sips his wine. 'Do you forget that I know everything about you, kid?' he says. 'The stint in prison you did in Utah for drug use when you were sixteen? Your mother's welfare fraud? Your father's indiscretions?'

'You're one to talk about *them*, Jim,' she says.

'I know all the things you never want to come out,' he threatens.

'But I have something on you that could trump all of those things,' she says. 'So I think you'll give me what I want.'

He smiles. 'Is that right?' he asks.

I can feel my heartbeat accelerate and I lean in closer to the screen.

'I have all the evidence.' Jemima reaches into her coat, takes out a locket on a chain and shows him. 'Of all the nasty little surprises you've hurt people with. Right here.'

The buzzer for the front door rings and I jump. I switch off the phone, shove it in my beside cabinet and walk out to it, place my hands to the wood.

'Hello?' I say.

'Sis? It's me.'

The sound of Lissy's voice transports me to safety and I open the door. She stands in front of me, a bouquet of bright pink flowers in her hand. Behind her, I can see that frost has kissed the pavements overnight.

'I messaged last night and this morning,' she says and hands me the flowers. 'Thought I'd chance it that you'd be here.'

I take the flowers. 'Why did you bring me these?'

She shrugs. 'Because I thought you'd like them? Can I come in or what?'

'Sorry,' I say. I stand aside and we walk down the little corridor to my flat. 'I've been . . . I was busy. I . . . Do you want . . . How long are you here for?'

She stops at the door. 'I don't know,' she says. 'Are you busy?'

'No,' I reply quickly. 'I mean, sort of.'

'I feel a bit . . . I wanted to do something normal with you,' she says. 'That OK?'

'Normal,' I repeat. 'Yes, I want that too.'

I want to forget that video, want to forget everything I've ever started.

'Let's go out,' I say and open my door. 'I'll grab my coat and my phone, OK? And put these in water.'

I open my flat door, go to the kitchen and put the flowers in the sink and then grab my coat and phone from the bedroom. I notice that Bobby has bombarded me with messages.

I'm sorry I'm not who you thought I was. Can you forgive me?
Please can we talk? There's so much more that I want to
say to you.
I've gone over the file. Which cameraman was your dad?
What happened when he died?

'What's that?' Lissy asks.

'What's what?' I say, following her voice to the kitchen.

'That ring,' she says. 'Is that Mum's ring?'

She's looking at Lucinda's ring, which I've stupidly left on the table. Had I been wearing it and hadn't even noticed and just put it down casually? Had I been wearing it yesterday?

'It's not Mum's,' I reply, scooping it up and putting it on. 'I found it at the market.'

'Are you . . . are you sure?' she says. 'It's OK if it is. In fact, I'd *want* it to be hers.'

'It's not hers,' I repeat. I go towards the door and hear her follow me. 'I wouldn't want anything of hers, anyway.'

'Why do you hate on her all the time?' she asks angrily.

'Calm down,' I say. 'I thought you wanted to do something normal? I don't want to fight with you.'

'I want to love her,' she says.

I take out my hat from my bag. 'Let's go.'

We walk along Oxford Street together, abnormally quiet. I wish Lissy wasn't here and, at the same time, I want to pull her tightly into my side and never let her go.

'How's your job?' she asks.

'It's good.'

'You seem a bit manic.'

'I'm very busy,' I say.

'You're not yourself.'

'I *am*,' I insist. 'You know when I said I was getting myself out of the box? This job is about that. This job is about Dad.'

She frowns. 'What does that mean? Your job is related to Dad?'

'Exactly,' I say.

'Like publishing?'

'No.' I stop walking. 'Look, Liss. There were people responsible for how Dad died. And I'm working through that.'

She looks completely bewildered. 'What are you talking about?' she says.

'It's all a bit complicated.'

I carry on walking, but she's not following and I look back at her. She's looking at me intently.

'I can't talk about it really,' I say. 'OK? I'm sorry. I know we don't have secrets, but this . . .'

'I need to talk to you, sis,' she says, stepping forward and reaching for my hands. 'About Dad. About Mum.'

'What about them?'

'Look,' she says. 'I know you have this golden image of Dad, but he made a conscious decision to leave us to deal with everything because he couldn't cope.'

'Depression is an illness, Liss,' I say. 'You know that.'

'But he could have got treatment. Counselling. Drugs. He could have *done* something.' She sighs. 'I think you loved Dad in a different way than I did.'

I frown. 'What's that supposed to mean?'

'I think your love for him turned you down a particular path. Didn't it? I don't think you're who you should have been.'

I'm angry and I realise it's because she's spoken the absolute truth. I'm not who I could have been. Because of Jim.

'How does anyone know what they *should* have been?' I snap at her. 'You become who you are from the life you have.'

But she folds her arms. 'You've let Dad's memory over-shadow you. And he's not an innocent party.'

'He *was* an innocent party, Liss. You have *no* idea.'

'Matilda?'

Someone is in front of me and my brain takes a second to catch up with my eyes. When it does, I almost have a heart attack.

'Ben!' I say. 'What are you doing here?'

'I *thought* it was you!' he says.

Thank God I'm wearing a hat so he can't see my real hair, but my freckles and the scar on my forehead must be obvious.

'I'm shopping for some school shoes with Sylvie,' he says and, like a shadow, Sylvie appears at his shoulder.

'Matilda,' she says stiffly.

My sister looks at me quizzically. 'Who's—'

I force my cheeks to lift into a smile. 'This is my sister, Lissy,' I say.

'Hi,' my sister says.

Sylvie nods but doesn't blink, like some sort of reptile.

'We're going to have breakfast at the Breakfast Club in Soho,' Ben says. 'That's our favourite, isn't it, Sylvie?'

'It is our favourite,' she replies.

'Sometimes we go after swimming,' he adds. 'And Mum meets us there. How's Dad?'

I frown. 'You haven't spoken to him?'

'He and Mum aren't talking,' he says.

'Benjamin,' Sylvie's timbre is low with warning.

'Did you read that article about *Pranksters*?' Ben asks. 'Mum didn't let me see it, but someone I know at school—'

'*Benjamin!*'

Lissy looks at me and I avoid her eyes and the four of us stand awkwardly.

'We'd better go,' I say after a moment.

'OK, bye! Come round again sometime?' Ben says.

'Sure,' I reply.

'See you,' Lissy says, and when they leave, she turns to me. 'Who's Matilda?'

'I am,' I say. 'I mean – in my job. They know me as Matilda.'

'Your middle name?'

'That's right,' I say.

'Why? And who's the boy?'

'My boss's son. Shall we go to Topshop?'

I start walking and she jogs to catch up.

'What job have you got, exactly?' she asks. 'And why is it connected to Dad?'

'I'm a PA,' I say. 'Shall we carry on having our nice normal day?'

'What's going on, El?' she presses. 'The boy said something about that programme. *Pranksters.* The one you made me watch the other weekend.'

I clench my fist, bring my knuckles to my mouth.

'Do you know what, actually I think I need to get on with some things today,' I say.

She frowns. 'What?'

'I'm busy,' I say. 'I'm busy, Liss, OK? And I can't . . . This is about Dad, what happened to him. Do you understand?'

'Dad was a liar,' she says. 'You don't need to do things for him.'

I'm shocked by the viciousness in her voice. 'What? Why are you talking like this about him?'

'I need to show you something,' she says. 'Something I found. You're not going to like it.'

'So don't show me,' I reply.

She stares at me. 'You have to *know*.'

'Please, Lissy,' I say. 'I can't deal with the bullshit you think you have on Dad. Let me keep his memory. Let me do the thing I need to do. For him and for myself.'

A tear pearls on her cheek and then she turns and walks away from me and I watch her go.

THIRTY-EIGHT

I stare out of the bus window as it pulls up at the stop opposite the office. Why have I come to work? I could turn around right now and get on a train to Charlie's house, but my feet are taking me off the bus and walking me through to reception, through the glass barriers and into the lift. I've come too far to give up now.

Yesterday, when I returned from being out with Lissy, I sat on my bed and I opened the beside cabinet and I stared at Jemima's phone until the light faded in the room and I shut the drawer again. Tonight I'll make myself watch the video.

The lift doors open and Jim is standing at my desk holding three huge black files. Gertie is asleep under my desk.

'Good morning,' Jim says.

'Is it?'

'Oh dear,' he says. 'How I hate gloom. That's not what I pay you for, you know.'

I hang my coat on the stand.

'Trouble in paradise?' he asks. 'Man trouble?'

'Everything is fine,' I reply. 'How was your weekend?'

'Excellent,' he says. 'My room was upgraded.'

'Good.'

'I spoke to Ben last night on the phone,' he says, putting the files down next to my phone. 'He's very taken with you, you know that? He says he saw you in town with your sister.'

His phone starts to ring and he's looking at me and my eyes are frozen to his face.

'With your sister,' he repeats. 'Now, correct me if I'm wrong, but I'm certain you told me you had a brother.'

'That's right,' I say. 'I have a brother *and* a sister.'

'Lissy,' he says, pronouncing the double 's' in her name like a snake.

'Yes,' I reply.

'And why didn't you mention her before, when I asked you about your family?' he asks.

'I forgot?'

He laughs wolfishly. 'Are you so forgetful?'

'I'm closest to Tom,' I say. 'Lissy is five years younger than me. I . . . sometimes I forget . . .'

'You forget,' he says. 'That's careless. Would you ever forget me?'

'It's unlikely,' I say.

'It sure is,' he replies, and he turns and walks back into his office and closes the door.

I sit at my desk, gripping the edge, and load my computer.

'You're brunette today, I see.'

I look up to find Bobby standing in front of me.

'Not answering my emails or my texts?' he asks.

My eyes are on Jim's closed door. 'Bobby . . .'

'Will you come and talk with me?'

'I can't,' I say.

'Please, Matilda,' he says.

'That's not my name,' I whisper.

He frowns. 'What?'

'Do you still write any of the material that's used in *Pranksters*?' I ask. 'You said you came up with the idea. Do you still write any of it?'

'Not after what happened to Chloe.'

'Why wasn't the show wound up after what happened to her?' I say. 'How could you let it run on? People have paid the price for a cheap laugh and yet every year it was remade and it's disgusting.'

'I agree with you,' he says. 'I do.'

My desk phone starts to ring but I ignore it.

'You know Jim bought her off? Chloe?'

'Yes,' he answers.

'And you're still *here*?' I say. 'You *work* here and you know he does that?'

'I'm tied here,' he says. 'To the company. And to Jim.'

'If you wanted to leave the company you could leave it,' I say.

'No,' he replies. 'It's not like that with Jim.'

'Why don't you *say* something?' I ask. 'To the press?'

'I don't think you realise how much power Jim has.'

The phone is insistent, its shrill tone matching my own.

'I don't think you realise how much *you* could have if you were brave enough to risk meeting him head-on,' I say.

'Is that what you're doing?' he asks. 'What happened to your dad, Matilda? Really? Because I can't find him on the records. I've rung every single cameraman and woman listed.'

I blanch. 'He's . . .'

His voice drops to a whisper. 'He was harmed by a prank, wasn't he? He wasn't working for Jim.'

His stare burns straight through me.

'What's your name?' he asks.

'Matilda!' Jim's voice pierces the air. 'Pick up the fucking phone! What do I pay you for? Are you two having a fucking private party out there?'

I look at Bobby and pick up the phone and he waits for a beat and then walks away. I watch him go to the lift and press the button.

'Hello?' someone says. 'Are foo there?'

'Jim Valente's office?' I say. I watch Bobby step into the lift and the doors close.

'Geth Jim on the fon!'

The voice is female but sounds muffled, drunken.

'Sorry?'

'Jim!' the voice screeches. 'Geth him on the foooon!'

'Andrea?' I say.

'Yeth!' she says.

'Are you all right?'

'Path me over!' she says thickly. 'Whyth he not answering hith mobile?'

I press to transfer the call to Jim's office and see him through the glass as he shoots me a look and puts down his pen.

I look back to the lift, see the doors close behind Bobby and feel my chest deflate with sadness.

'Someone broke into Andrea's house last night,' Jim says, coming out of his office. 'She's in hospital with a broken cheek.'

'A broken cheek? That's awful,' I say.

'You're fucking telling me. The awards ceremony is tomorrow and she was going to co-announce Marie's position. I'm going to see how bad she is.'

He whistles at Gertie, who comes speeding out of his office and jumps up at me.

'Take Gertie home for me, I can't take her into the hospital,' he says, pulling on his coat and locking the door. 'And tell my wife that I expect to see her tomorrow night on the red carpet.'

His shoes clack on the marble flooring and he doesn't even wait for the lift, instead disappearing down the stairwell.

Gertie whines softly and I lift her up and put her over my shoulder, as though she's a baby. She licks my neck.

'Ouch, Gertie.'

I think she's nipped me because I'm holding her too tight, but I realise that it's not teeth but something hard that's jutted into my shoulder. I push her fur out of the way to reveal her collar underneath.

I never looked closely at it, but I do now. There's the little silver bell, an emerald gemstone and a tiny locket.

Gertie's my confidante here. Knows everything.

Jewellery. That's how you cover your tracks.

'Hold still,' I say to Gertie, and I unclip the collar as she licks at my face.

I lay the collar flat on my desk and slip the locket from it. I prise it open with my fingernails. Inside is a tiny USB.

'Oh my God,' I whisper.

Gertie woofs at my feet and I look down at her. I have Jemima Mataya's phone and the USB and whatever they contain has the power to blow Jim apart. My heart starts to hammer. Knowing that I could set a bomb under him doesn't make me feel strong but incredibly small and I suddenly want to walk away without ever knowing what's on either of them. I could resign, move back to Charlie's and help him tend plants and drink fizz at Christmastime. I could go back to being Eleanor – but do I want to go back to being that grey shade of me?

I grab a new memory stick from my drawer, go to jam it into my computer, but then I stop. What if Eric and Paul could access this computer? What if that's what they were doing that day when I came out of the lift and found them?

I nod at Gertie. 'We need to go.'

We walk to Charing Cross Library, which is the only place I can think to go that is anonymous and allows dogs. I sit at one of the computers.

'All this time, Gertie,' I say to her, and she snuffles at my hand and wags her tail.

I glance across to the other people working on computers around me, conscious all of a sudden of being here in such an open environment. They have CCTV in this library. But who's going to know where to look for me?

I download the contents of the locket USB into a temporary folder on the desktop and then clip it back to Gertie's collar before uploading the files on my new memory stick. As the files appear in the new memory stick, I almost tip the desk over. Here, in digital form, laid out and ordered by date, are historical transactions between bank accounts – Jim's personal account and various beneficiaries: *Miss C McManus, Mrs Stilwell, Mr Shah, Mr Land, Miss N Castledine.* This is how Jim keeps track of them all?

Another file is labelled 'Video Footage'. I open it and see thirty folders lining up. *Pranksters* Episode 8: 'Skating'; *Pranksters* Episode 16: 'Tool Kit'; *Pranksters* Episode 23: 'The Thing You Never Said'; *Pranksters* Episode 31: 'Secret Police', and on and on. Are these all the episodes related to pranks that went wrong?

My finger is on the mouse and I hover the arrow over the file, about to click into one, when Gertie headbutts me on the leg and I give myself a sense check. I look again at the people beside me. An elderly man looks up from his screen and meets my eyes. It's not safe to open the files here. I close down my computer and yank out the memory stick, zip it into the pocket of my bag and we leave the library.

I need to take Gertie back to Wilton Crescent. I wonder how much time I'll have before Jim is back in the office. I wonder if I might have time to go home and download this to my computer before I have to return to the office. I want to tell Horsehead, form a plan. I'm dizzy with the thought of it. But then it slowly becomes clouded and a cold coil of unease wraps itself around my body. I told Horsehead that I thought Andrea was suspicious of me, but surely her attack can't have anything to do with him? He's miles away, in another country. He isn't violent, isn't involved.

'Come on, Gertie,' I say. 'Let's go.'

Top Step: I've got the memory stick.

Horsehead: What? *The* memory stick?!

Top Step: On the dog's collar, all this time!

Horsehead: The dog?!

Top Step: Jim's dog! Can you believe this, Horsehead? All that time, Gertie had it? All the times I was in the office alone with her asleep on my feet! Jim told me, too! I remember he said that she was his confidante here.

Horsehead: What's on it??

Top Step: I think it's footage from all the pranks that have gone wrong. All the pranks that Gwen told me got deleted.

Horsehead: FUUUUUUUUUCCCCK. Send whatever is on it to me.

Top Step: I'm in a taxi to Jim's house taking Gertie back, and then I'll log on back home again.

Horsehead: Go jolly!!

Top Step: Horsehead, Andrea was burgled last night.

Horsehead: Seriously?

Top Step: She got hurt actually.

Horsehead: Maybe that's a good thing. She was a bitch.

Top Step: I feel bad. Like it was my fault or something. You didn't work your magic there, did you?

Horsehead: Doll! Ha! I'm actually charmed that you think so highly of my capabilities, but I can't commit physical harm all the way from the Black Hills!!

Top Step: I'm sorry, Horsehead. But you said it yourself, we met on a revenge website. I wondered if you'd got someone to follow her . . . I don't know. Forget I said anything. I'm sorry.

Horsehead: My tentacles don't reach across the Atlantic.

Top Step: OK.

Horsehead: Yet.

Gertie puts her head up to rest it in my lap, but I'm physically bouncing up and down on the seat of the black cab, contracting my glute muscles. Her head keeps jerking and she looks at me crossly and I can only shake my head in apology and put my hands under my thighs until we reach the crescent. I look at my bag next to me on the seat. I feel like the memory stick is burning a hole through it.

When we get out, I ring the golden bell and step back with Gertie in my arms as the door opens. Lucinda stands there, dressed in a crew-neck grey T-shirt, covered over with a chunky-knit white cardigan. Her hair is up in a messy bun and her eyes are made-up, smoky.

'Who are you?' she asks and then her eyes register Gertie. 'And why have you got our dog?'

'I'm . . . I'm Jim's PA,' I reply. 'Matilda.'

She twists her lip in a sneer. 'Of course you are,' she says. 'Look at you. How old are you?'

'Jim has to . . . I'm twenty-five.'

'Twenty-five!'

I hold Gertie out to her. 'Jim wanted to keep Gertie here for a couple of days,' I say. 'Until after the awards ceremony.'

'Oh, did he? He's too busy with third parties, is he?' she says scornfully.

'I don't know,' I say.

Gertie is dangling in the air halfway between Lucinda and me and I draw her back into me.

'I thought you were supposed to be his PA,' she snaps. 'You're supposed to know his every move, aren't you? Do you know where he is now?'

'He's . . . he's with Andrea Rubins,' I say.

'Oh!' She laughs bitterly. 'Of course he is!'

'Her house was broken into last night,' I explain. 'She's in hospital.'

'So Jim's gone to play hero, has he? Oh, I was the last to know about that affair, but do you all think I don't know about all his other indiscretions?' she says. 'Jemima Mataya, she was one, did you know that? Did he tell you all about the things I keep out of the press for him? All his affairs, all his *everything*?'

She releases this torrent of anger so close to me that I back away from her.

'He makes so many friends across the world, but he makes enemies too, you know that?' she continues. 'People don't want to work with him. He owes people money. Someone threw a firebomb through our kitchen window once, you know that? He doesn't do the things he says he will and he does the things he says he won't. He doesn't engage with Ben, he doesn't *care* about anyone but himself!'

Behind Lucinda I see Sylvie hovering in the hallway and I try to catch her eye, but she stays silent. Gertie whines in my arms.

'Tell him I'm not coming to his ceremony, all right?' Lucinda spits. 'I won't be there smiling like a fucking doll on his arm because I know what he's announcing there – it's his new Jemima, isn't it? Well, good *luck* to her!' She glares at Gertie. 'Ben's not back for a few days so you can keep the damn dog.'

She slams the door in my face and the force of it sends gooseflesh down my arms, even though I'm wearing a coat. Gertie barks and I stroke her as we walk back towards the cab.

'Matilda,' says a voice.

I turn to see Sylvie pulling the front door closed. She walks hurriedly to catch up with me. I stop and hold out Gertie.

'I am allergic,' she says. 'And Lucinda is angry. You will keep the dog. But we need to talk, do we not? Because I saw you that night, taking photos of Jim and of Andrea.'

I hold my breath.

'And I saw you even before you got the job with Jim,' she says. 'Red-headed. I remember seeing you when you returned his credit card.'

She's wrong-footed me completely.

'And I have tried to find out about you, but nothing comes up.' She glowers at me. 'You tell me what you want from this family?'

'Nothing,' I say. 'I don't know what you're talking about.'

'I think you do,' she replies. 'Do you want for me to call the police?'

I lick my lips.

Her eyes narrow. 'Lucinda and Ben are my life,' she says. 'You understand? It is my job to protect them at all costs.'

'I'm . . . I'm not interested in them,' I say.

'What *are* you interested in?' she asks. 'Jim?'

I don't answer.

'Because he will only take,' she says. 'You do not want anything from that man. He destroys girls like you. I have seen it! I have seen it with Lucinda here.'

'That's not what I meant,' I say. 'I don't want him like that. I want . . . I want to ruin him.'

She leans in to me and takes my arm and I think that from her fierce grip on my skin she's about to march me straight to a police station. But she stares into my eyes and a sly smile creeps onto her lips.

'Take him for all he is worth,' she says. Then she turns and closes the door behind her.

THIRTY-NINE

I have a message from Jim that he's with Andrea in hospital for another hour and so I decide to divert to my flat before going back to the office. In the kitchen, I take two bowls from the cupboard and put some dry cereal in one and water in the other for Gertie, and as she starts to eat, I realise that I have two pieces of evidence with me now: the locket USB on Gertie and the memory stick I copied the files on to. Perhaps this will work in my favour if I need to hide anything. I sit at the kitchen table and I put the recorded stick into the laptop and twitch my legs as it loads.

Immediately, the video files start to load: *Pranksters* Episode 8: 'Skating'; *Pranksters* Episode 16: 'Tool Kit'; *Pranksters* Episode 23: 'The Thing You Never Said'; *Pranksters* Episode 31: 'Secret Police'; *Pranksters* Episode 66: 'Moi'; *Pranksters* Episode 75: 'The Screw Loose'.

I click on Episode 8, but just as it starts to play, the frame freezes. I look down at the screen, thinking I've nudged the pause button, but I haven't. I double-click on it, but it remains still. I look at the scroll bar; there are three minutes on the file. I click again, but it stays where it is. I take my hand from the mouse – perhaps it's buffering and needs to be left alone. I wait for ten seconds and I click it again and then again, but it doesn't move. I take out the memory stick, reinsert it and restart loading the folder and file. But this time, it freezes at nine seconds.

I click out again and open another file. The video looks funny and then it goes blank. It's corrupted. Sweat sticks to my skin. I go back to the video, manically tap the mouse to 'play', but it doesn't even open. I start demonically clicking every document I can, but nothing is loading. The whole memory stick is frozen, dead.

I look at Gertie.

'Come here, girl,' I say.

I unclip her collar, take the memory stick from the locket once again and plug it in. At once, the files start to line up like jewels and I exhale, relieved. I don't wait for them all to download, am hungry to open one, but as I do, they all disappear.

'What's going on?' I say.

I reload the memory stick, but there's nothing on it. I sit back in the chair, feeling a cold sweat of fear on the back of my neck. Something is wrong with my computer; something feels very wrong full stop. I go to log on to the forum to see if Horsehead can help me. But then there's a knock at my door and I turn my head sharply towards it.

I haven't buzzed anyone in, so who is it? I slam the laptop shut as Gertie barks nervously. I quickly reattach her collar with the USB inside before getting up and creeping to the door.

'Hello?'

'El?' says my sister.

I jerk back from the door as if she's scalded me through it and I tear at my wig, wincing with pain as the carefully placed pins rip at my hair.

'Your upstairs neighbour let me in,' she says. 'I thought you might have left a spare key under your door or something and I could wait. What are you doing? Can you let me in?'

I toss the wig into the open doorway of my room and lean to shut it before I open the door to her. 'I . . . Shouldn't you be in Southampton?'

'Shouldn't you be at work?' she says but stops when she sees Gertie at my feet. 'What's with the dog?'

'Come here, Gertie,' I say, grabbing her collar to stop her jumping at my sister.

'Why do you . . . ?' she starts. But she shakes her head and steps into my flat. 'I've got something important to say,' she begins. 'And I should have said it yesterday. It's why I came, really, but I . . . I have to tell you now.'

My shoulders slump and I follow her to the kitchen. 'Liss, really? Now? I have to go back to work in a minute, I only came back to get something, so it's not really a good time—'

She whirls around. 'Yes, now!' she yells, and I'm shocked into silence. 'Hear me out, OK? You know that argument I had with Charlie the other weekend?'

'What?' I say. My head is fuzzy and I'm restless. Why aren't those memory sticks working? Is Jim going to know that it was me who has wiped the information off the locket USB when I return Gertie?

'About the bears!' Lissy says.

'What about the bears?' I ask.

'The box of my bears. I lied about them,' she says. 'It wasn't what I found.'

She takes one of my hands and starts playing with my fingers. They're clammy and cold and suddenly I've got a burning headache. I feel totally apart from my sister for the first time in so many years and yet she's dragging me back to her.

'I've really weighed up talking to you about this,' she says.

'What, Liss? What is it? Because I really don't have the time right now, OK?'

She drops my hand. 'Too busy?' she says with a snarl.

'Yes,' I reply.

'Then *un*busy yourself,' she says. 'Because here's the thing. I found *letters* in a box in the garage. Letters from Mum to Dad and then from William, her boyfriend. Before Mum died. And I think you should see them.'

She opens her bag, hands me a bound pile of letters and I physically move away from them.

'I don't want to see any of them! Not from her!' I shout. 'She left us!'

'Dad knew Mum was ill and she wanted us to come to America to see her before she died.'

My throat constricts. 'No, she didn't,' I say.

'Yes!' She thrusts one of the letters towards me.

I can see the writing. I'd forgotten Mum's beautiful curved lettering, joined by curling vines. And then I smell something so familiar that it punches me in the gut. She used to spray her letters with perfume – Chanel. I lurch sideways, away from the letter, covering my mouth with my hand. Gertie whines under the kitchen table and I wonder if she can sense my anxiety.

'I know it's hard,' Lissy says. 'But you need to read this, El.'

'Liss,' I say. 'No.'

But she nods at me. 'Please, El.'

I take it from her and read the words.

Girls, I can't travel, I'm so very tired with the illness now. I have emailed, William has emailed and we've called. Countless times, girls, and I miss your voices. I love you, I'm sorry I've disappointed you. Please come to see me. xxx

I look at Lissy, who nods at me and silently hands me another letter.

'I don't want this,' I say, because the writing is different and I know who it's from.

'Please,' she says again. 'You have to understand.'

Stephen, Kirsty is too unwell to call and you're ignoring our voice-mails as well as our emails, so I'm appealing to you like this, through a letter, which will take days to reach you. These are days that Kirsty doesn't have time to waste because she's going to die and soon. Whatever your grievances with me and with my rela-tionship with Kirsty, for the sake of your girls, you need to bring them out here. I'm begging you. Stop this selfishness and let them say goodbye to their mother. William.

I am gripping the letters very hard.

'She died ten days after this was posted,' Lissy says.

There's a sound in my ears, an incoherent gurgling, and I realise it's me, that I'm moaning. Lissy puts her hand to my arm, but I can't feel it. I look at it dumbly.

'I talked to Charlie,' she continues. 'He told me about *Pranksters*. And then I understood. You understand too now, don't you? Dad's suicide wasn't about Christopher Barrows, not really. The *Pranksters* episode that fucked Dad up was about a child never being able to say goodbye to her mother before she died. Just like what happened to us. The woman in white, the girl's mother, even had *red* hair for God's sake! Just like Mum! It was too much for Dad. His guilt had completely resurfaced by then and it was going to kill him long before Christopher Barrows ever went running through that traffic light. You understand me? Charlie told me that Dad wrote to Cyclops, the company that made the programme, begged the CEO – Jim Valente! – not to air the episode because we might guess, we might find out what he'd hidden for an entire year.'

It's as if I'm underwater. My sister is talking to me from above and I can't decipher any of her words.

'No,' I say, but the word comes out small and crumples uselessly to the floor and I physically follow it. A lifetime of love and trust for Dad is splintering into a thousand pieces and I'm heaving for breath. *I cannot have my girls see this.* Was Dad worried that we'd find out what he'd done if we saw it? Would his own guilt speak out and force him to tell us what had really happened to Mum?

She reaches for me. 'El, I'm sorry. I never wanted to hurt you, but you had to know the truth. All your life you've lived under his shadow and you've been acting really strange since you mentioned Jim Valente that weekend before Christmas. When I found the letters and then I met that boy in town called Ben and he mentioned *Pranksters* too, I started putting it all together. That they're father and son, aren't they? And you, out of nowhere, work for him! Why are you working for Jim Valente, El?'

'I was just . . . I was trying to make things right,' I say and I stand up. My legs feel numb. 'I . . . I had to . . . I've got to go now.'

'Where are you going?' she asks.

'I need to breathe,' I say. 'Come here, Gertie.'

Gertie peeks out from underneath the kitchen table and comes to me.

'Can you leave, Liss, please? I need you to go.'

'Wait, El, I'm *worried* about you,' she says, but I'm already out of the door.

I don't return to the office. I've wandered, drunk on grief, and found myself at a park.

The gates are shut, but I jump over the iron railings. My coat tears on the spikes – when did I put a coat on? – and I look back at it, pull myself free and then waver. For a terrible moment, I think I'll pass out on top of them and bayonet myself, but I land with a soft thud in the mush of leaves. Gertie whines from the other side of the railings and I realise that she can't fit through the bars.

With a jerked movement, my body betrays me and I'm sick on the grass, my shoes, down my front. I retch for what seems a long time, bucking forwards and backwards with the waves of sickness. I hold on, white-knuckled, to the freezing railings like I'm on a ship in a violent storm. I wipe my mouth on the sleeve of my shredded coat and I start to cry – huge, racking sobs of grief and stress that I can't keep hold of.

What am I doing inside this park? Was I looking for Dad? Why didn't you tell me about the letters, Dad? Why didn't you let us go to Mum? How could you lie, Dad? How could you let us believe that she didn't want to say goodbye to us? If I'd known she had tried to contact us, had written, had begged, perhaps I wouldn't have sabotaged the good memories of her. My lasting memories of her could have been looking into those soulful eyes and holding her tightly and not the moment when she closed the door with the yellow bag. The feelings of abandonment and rage that have circled my heart for all these years could have abated.

He was a selfish, proud coward.

Forgive me for what I will do today. I am a coward, but I love you all and never forget it.

Gertie barks and I look at her. She's shaking from cold. I heave myself to standing and I reach into my coat for my phone. It's eight in the evening and I've had nine missed calls from Lissy and five from Bobby, and eleven from Jim, but I swipe them all away and call Euey.

I'm still behind the bars of the park when he comes for me, and I stare out at him like an animal. He gets out of the car and I see that his eyes drop down to take in the state of me.

'Ah,' he says. He's wearing those kind, owlish eyes and his oversized black leather jacket. 'This is why I couldn't find you.'

'Can you help me, Euey?'

He steps up to the low wall next to the railings. 'Give me your hand, love,' he says, and he helps me back over again. He opens the door to the cab and I clamber inside. Gertie follows. 'You have a dog?' he says.

'She doesn't belong to me,' I say. 'I mean, at the moment I suppose she does.'

'Oh,' he replies. 'Are you OK, Eleanor?'

'No.'

We drive in silence and he pulls up at my front door. I bungle out of the cab and fumble with my key, until I feel a hand on my arm.

'Do you want me to call someone?' he asks. He takes the key from me and opens the door.

'Who would I call?' I say wretchedly as I take the key back. I fall into the flat and Gertie skitters in after me. I close the door and whisper, 'Sorry,' though he can't hear me.

'Liss?' I say, though I know the flat is empty and Lissy isn't here because I told her not to be.

I ache to be with her, want to bury my face in her hair, and also, paradoxically, I don't want to see her or Charlie at all ever again because I'm a failure, a disappointment to myself and to them. I start crying and Gertie jumps up at me, licks at my tears.

FORTY

I'm roused from sleep by an incessant buzzing which I realise is my phone in my bag. I take it out, look blearily at the
screen and see that it's a work number. It's ten-twenty in the
morning and I'm not at the office. In a panic, and before I
think not to, I answer.

'Matilda!' Jim barks. 'I've been calling your office phone
and your mobile for fucking forever! Where the hell are you?
Playing away again?'

'I'm . . . I'm not well, Jim,' I say. 'I'm so sorry I didn't call
you yesterday and let you know. I was in bed and I . . .'

Something on the bed moves and I realise that it's Gertie
and that she's been curled up with me all night. I reach out to
her and she comes to me, butts my shoulder.

'Fuck that,' Jim shouts down the phone. 'Tonight is the
awards ceremony so you can be ill tomorrow. Meet me at the
Mayfair Hotel *now*.'

'I . . .'

But he's hung up. I stare at my phone and wonder what I
should do. I never need to see Jim again because the reason
I became his PA has paled into nothingness. My dad ended
his life because of the prank that reminded him of his own
selfishness. Maybe he was always selfish. Maybe he would
never have reached for Christopher Barrows even if he hadn't

been pranked just weeks before? Who was my dad? Who has defined me all these years?

I look at my laptop. I don't need revenge. I'm best off a million miles away from Jim and all the shit I've accumulated because of him. Even if I wanted to hurt him, I have none of those files because, somehow, they've corrupted. I only have Jemima Mataya's phone and what would I do with that footage when I haven't even seen it all yet? How would I explain how I got the phone without incriminating myself in an investigation? Or incriminating Chloe, who would probably lie and back the horse who's already paying her – Jim. Jim is playing games with a lot of people, but they're not my games. It's not my fight any more; I'm not the David to his Goliath.

The room smells funny and I think Gertie must have weed somewhere.

'I'm sorry,' I say to her. 'You must be hungry. And I need to get you back to Jim.'

I also need to get rid of Jemima's phone. I open the bedside cabinet drawer to remove it, feel sick at the thought that it's here pulsating with life even though Jemima is cold in the ground.

The phone isn't inside. My heart jumps. I sit up properly and my head throbs with the movement. It's gone. I didn't move it from this place.

I take my phone and my sister answers immediately.

'El!' she cries. 'I waited for ages for you! I went looking for you and then I locked myself out! I had to stay over with—'

'Did you take the phone?' I say.

'What?' she replies.

'The phone,' I say. 'Jemima's phone?'

'What are you talking about?' she says. 'Jemima who? El, what's going on? What are you doing?'

I hang up and she rings back, but I ignore it.

Someone has been in my flat.

I don't shower. I throw on a dress that needs ironing, tights that need washing and my wig, which knots like my stomach as I run down the road with Gertie. I'm so anxious that I ride the Underground to the hotel because it'll be faster, and I hold Gertie like she's my lifeline. Has Jim worked out what I've been doing? Had me followed by someone who's broken into my home and found the phone? Has Chloe talked to him? Was that her plan all along? He *owns* people. What if he owns her and he's used her to flush me out? What if he's used someone else? Sylvie? Bobby?

I arrive at the Mayfair Hotel at twenty past eleven, flustered and sweating, and I scan the hotel lobby for Jim. I'll know instantly if he knows, won't I? He's not here and I ask at reception and they tell me he's upstairs, that he told them to send me up to his room once I arrived.

I go up in the lift, find his door and knock before walking a few paces back down the corridor. I want to draw him out, I don't want to go in. A few seconds pass before he opens the door and cranes his neck around.

'What are you doing dawdling there?' he says and then he sees Gertie. 'Why have you still got the dog?'

'Lucinda didn't . . . she didn't want her.'

'Fucking story of Gertie's life,' he says. 'Get in here.'

I step cautiously forward, but he lunges towards me, yanks my arm and I gasp at the violence of it. Gertie barks in alarm and Jim shuts the door quickly.

'This is not the day to be testing my patience, Matilda,' he says.

I stay close to the wall with my hands behind my back and watch him as he prowls around, snatching up papers. This part of the suite is the lounge, with two large, moss-green chesterfield sofas and a leather armchair, a huge mahogany writing desk and a sixty-inch television. I can see the bedroom from where I stand; there's a king-size bed with unmade white bedding.

I shouldn't be here.

'What happened to your hair?' he asks. 'You look like you've come through a hedge.'

I raise my hand to the back of my head. 'I'm not well, Jim,' I reply.

'Not my problem today,' he says. 'I need you to be on form. Do you think I pay you to sit on your arse all day? This is *the* night, OK? The night that *Pranksters* gets its new life. *You* chose the star, remember?'

I swallow. 'OK.'

'I need you to buy me a silk tie for tonight. Red,' he says. 'And I need you to buy flowers for Marie Jarski for when she arrives at the office later on. Eric and his new lackey have the montage for the announcement now. I got it from Andrea's house and gave it to Eric. They need to be set up behind that desk by four-forty-five in the afternoon because I'm on at five-fifteen.'

'Is . . . is Andrea OK?'

'She managed to clock the guy so she's proud of that, but her face is swollen and she looks like shit.' He sighs. 'I need you to tell the press downstairs that I'm not talking to them,' he continues. 'They're like leeches. Everything feels like a fuck-up at the moment. I think Bobby Walters is going to walk out on me. And Andrea! And Lucinda! And Miranda Ford cancelled our lunch – did you know that? What the fuck is she thinking?'

'I'll go and buy your tie now,' I say.

Jim rubs Gertie behind the ears.

'Things are going awry, Matilda, aren't they?'

I swallow. 'Are they, Jim?'

He straightens. 'You know, I talked to IT this morning and he told me something very interesting about that article written about *Pranksters*. You know, the one that we found online.'

My body tenses. 'What about it?' I say.

'That though it was written from Gwendolen's computer,' he says, 'it was done remotely. Via a series of very odd VPN connections. IT did some investigating and it turns out some-one hacked into the server. So I'm very doubtful it would have been Gwendolen.'

I swallow. Paul saw me with Gwen's badge. He's been the one I've asked for things I shouldn't have been asking for. Has he revealed me to Jim?

'Who do you think it might be?' I ask.

'Someone who has access to our systems,' Jim says.

'You . . . you think it's someone else in the company?'

He comes close to me, lays a fingertip on my forearm and walks it up towards my shoulder. 'Tinker, Tailor, Soldier, Spy. Is it you?'

I can hear the blood rush in my ears like an ocean. 'Me? A . . . a spy?'

Before I can register what he's doing, his hand has moved from my shoulder and he strokes my cheek with the backs of his fingers. I freeze.

'Lovely, Matilda,' he whispers.

'Please, Jim,' I say.

I move away, but his hand moves down to my chin and turns my face up to his. My hair swings and I'm panicking that my wig is going to fall. What do I do if that happens?

I can hear a phone ring and he smiles, drops his hand and turns to pick up his jacket. It's his mobile and it's saved me. I touch my fingers to my cheek and then claw at it to remove the invisible traces of his contact.

'You might have made a good host for *Pranksters*, you know,' he says.

'I don't think so, Jim,' I say.

'You remind me a bit of her, you know that? Of Jemima Mataya. I see you like I saw her, even when she was thirty-five. The years haven't been kind to you, have they?' he says. 'There's some tragedy in your life and you try to hide it, but I can smell it.'

I'm mute.

'I can always smell tragedy,' he adds. 'What I find hard to smell out is a liar.'

That's it. He knows. His phone still rings, but he doesn't move to answer it. Instead, he watches me with a strange smile on his face.

'Am I . . . Do you think I've lied to you?'

He smiles widely. 'You? Darling, no! You're just a little lost child.'

Lost Child. I stare at him. What will he do to me in this room without any witnesses? My skin prickles with cold fear.

But he turns away from me. 'Things are going awry, but it's nothing we can't handle. Oliver is on it.'

'Oliver?' I say.

He doesn't reply to me. He riffles in his jacket pocket to retrieve his phone but doesn't answer it because he's staring into the mirror at himself.

'All this reeks of an old enemy,' he says quietly. 'I hear that McManus is out and everything starts fucking up. I should have put that fucker inside for longer. Robbery wasn't enough.'

McManus?

Jim answers his phone, spinning away from the mirror. 'Lucy? What the hell is wrong? You'd better be fucking telling me that you're coming tonight? Fuck's sake, I can't hear what you're saying! What are you saying?'

He stalks through to the bedroom. McManus. Robbery. My brain is starting to tick.

'Matilda!' Startled, I look at Jim, who is clinging, white-knuckled, to the door frame. It's been seconds since I saw him, but he looks wilted.

'What's happened?' I ask.

'I have to be at that show,' he says. 'Tell Bobby I'll be late. OK? Please?'

I've never heard him use the word 'please' and I'm shocked by it.

'Are you . . . are you OK, Jim?' I ask.

He picks up his coat. 'It's Ben,' he replies. 'He's not at the school. They've reported him missing.'

He leaves and I'm left alone. Missing? How could Ben be missing?

McManus is out and everything starts fucking up. I should have put that fucker inside for longer. Robbery wasn't enough.

Horsehead went to jail for robbery for five years, set up by a man he committed arson on. Lucinda's words spark in my ears.

Someone threw a firebomb through our kitchen window once, you know that?

A truth settles itself like a hand around my throat. Horsehead isn't in America – he never has been. Horsehead knows Jim. Horsehead is somehow connected to Chloe McManus and her entire story.

All this time I've been playing his game.

FORTY-ONE

Top Step: WHO ARE YOU?

Horsehead: Capital letters?

Top Step: You committed arson on Jim's house. Answer me right now!

Horsehead: Dang, girl.

Top Step: It's true, isn't it! You're connected to Chloe McManus. Maybe you *are* Chloe McManus. Or Tess?

Horsehead: Wow. I shouldn't have told you about the arson, should I? Error on my part. Didn't think you'd piece that together.

Top Step: WHO ARE YOU?

Horsehead: I'm a nobody. Like you, my little Julia Roberts.

Top Step: Don't call me that!

Horsehead: Why not? You liked it before, my little redhead.

Top Step: Things were different then!

Horsehead: Because you thought you knew who I was because I wasn't anybody, right? A faceless therapist? A Dear Diary?

Top Step: Wait. I never told you I had red hair. The photo I sent you for the ID was black and white! WHO THE FUCK ARE YOU?

Horsehead: Your capitals hurt my eyes. Stop it.

Top Step: You've engineered this whole thing? How did you even know who I was at the beginning?

Horsehead: I watched you.

Top Step: HOW?

Horsehead: I've got full access to Jim's private CCTV! That man does love his cars, doesn't he? I monitor comings and goings via the CCTV and a couple of months ago I saw you hanging around Jim's house and I thought your interest looked interesting. The rest I won't explain because you might remember me.

Top Step: Remember you?

Horsehead: You think we've gone all this time without having met?

Top Step: Tell me that you haven't done something to Ben?

Horsehead: He'll be fine. I caught him out of the school grounds and drove him out to the countryside for a bit and left him there, but it's fine. It's like hard-core orienteering, yeah? It'll be the making of him. Man, that kid is trusting, right??

Top Step: Oh my God, no, Horsehead! It's going to get dark soon and he's out there alone?

Horsehead: If I'd left it up to you what would you have done to him? Balled odd socks?

Top Step: I wouldn't have done anything to him!

Horsehead: I did it for you, doll. For *your* justice.

Top Step: Ben's innocent in all this.

Horsehead: 'Lost Child'. Did you like my reference to what happened to your dad??

Top Step: Horsehead, this is wrong! He's just a kid!

Horsehead: Anyone connected with Jim is fair game.

Top Step: Did you break into Andrea's house?

Horsehead: I was looking to buy you some time by giving her a bit of a scare. I also wondered if Jim might have given her any jewellery – the locket – to look after. Didn't mean to punch her, but she came out of nowhere! She's got a good left hook. Jabbed me straight in the ribs!

Top Step: Horsehead!

Horsehead: I know! All in vain because you went and found the USB the very next day. But you don't need to worry, OK? Now I can disappear from your life and you can disappear from mine. It's a shame because I like you, Top Step, a lot. But I'll have to make it so our conversations never happened, can never be traced. It's better that way. You'll understand soon enough.

Top Step: What? What are you going to do?

Horsehead: Jim deserves payback. For Chloe's accident, for putting me away. For so many people's misery. And you've given me the chance to do it by finding that memory stick and the phone!

Top Step: You took the phone?

Horsehead: Told you I could pick a lock. Had to wait for your sister to leave though. Pretty little thing, ain't she?

Top Step: Have you accessed my computer?

Horsehead: Of course!

Top Step: Did you delete those memory-stick videos??

Horsehead: I deleted them from your computer, if that's what you mean, and kept them for myself. Aren't I brilliant??

Top Step: How?? What are you going to do?

Horsehead: I'm going to bring down the fucking house, doll. A montage! Let's fucking do it! Lights, camera, action – the biggest prank of them all!

Top Step: I have to go to the police, Horsehead. Don't you understand? All this is out of control. What you're doing is wrong! Ben could get lost! He could be taken by someone, he could get hurt. Andrea got hurt!

Horsehead: Casualties of war, my friend.

Top Step: But Ben is a child! I have to go to the police, OK?

Horsehead: You still don't know who I am and even if you figure it out, then you're going down with me. This was your idea, remember? And I'll tell you one thing that might stop you going anywhere. You're at home, aren't you? I know you are. So look on your doorstep. Over and out :) :) :)

'Shit, shit.'

I'm typing him messages, but he's gone and all of a sudden the cursor starts to move of its own accord and the screen is scrolling up and up fast and our words are disappearing before my eyes. He's deleting the history.

The screen goes blank. I open a new thread, write his name into the name bar, but I get an error message.

Site cannot find user 'Horseheadinthebed'.

He's deleted himself.

Gertie jumps up beside me and starts pawing at my arm. I took her with me when I left the hotel and flagged the nearest car back to my flat where I could lock myself in. I sit on my bed and I stroke Gertie's ears, but I must be doing it too hard because she whines.

Where's Ben? How could Horsehead leave him in the middle of nowhere and claim it was for *me*? I've become hyper aware of my surroundings, like a deer in a forest is aware that somewhere there's a gun pointed at it. It's three in the afternoon and the sun is still above the horizon, but it will disappear in the next few hours and suddenly I want all the lights on because I want to feel as though they are radiating warmth. I switch them on and draw the curtains in my room and then I sit back on the bed and draw my knees up to my chest. Gertie settles on my feet and stares balefully up at me. My head itches with heat from the wig and I tear it off.

I'm searching every corner of my mind to think of all the men I've met since I created that online thread. Who is Horsehead? Or do I call him McManus? Whoever he is, he knows who I am and yet I have no idea who *he* is. He knows all about my family, my past, my hopes, my desires. Why hadn't I questioned him and his interest in my life and what happened to my dad? Do I call the police and tell them everything? Do I call Jim? What's on the doorstep?

I get up and Gertie follows. I open my door and then creep to the front door and I'm about to open it when I check myself. What if Horsehead is standing there behind it? I go back to my flat and get a bladed knife from the kitchen drawer.

'Get behind me, Gertie,' I say and I open the front door.

On the step is an envelope. Every bone in my body screams at me to leave it there, but I bend and pick it up. In the safety of my bedroom, I put down the knife on the duvet and I rip the envelope open. Inside, there are four A4 photographs. The first is of me in the Covent Garden Hotel at a table with Oliver and Jim clearly in front of me, the second is of Jim and me coming out of the restaurant in Covent Garden, the third is of me at the

Valentes' front door, and the last is of Lissy outside Charlie's house. I stare at this one the longest and my body flushes hot and cold. How did Horsehead get this photo? From an album of mine? From one of her albums? He can't have been at Charlie's house. Please, no.

I pull my phone out from my bag. The ringtone dies and it goes to voicemail.

'Liss?' I whisper.

The sun is withering into its blanket of cloud and staining it blood red. Branches scratch their fingers in the wind against the windows in my bedroom and I hear that it's started raining again. Always raining. Gertie starts whining.

'Go to Pudding Cottage,' I say into the phone. 'Tell Charlie – you need to both go there, OK? Don't tell anyone where you're going. Yes? You understand? Text me, OK?'

I click off and then I dial Euey.

'Euey,' I say when he picks up. 'Can you come to my flat?'

He hesitates. 'Give me twenty minutes? I'm coming back from Gatwick.'

'OK,' I say. 'Please hurry.'

I rush to the bathroom and buckle on to the floor in time to be sick in the toilet. Everything spills out of me until I'm dry-retching and my eyes are streaming. I never meant to reach this point – but where *was* I intending it all to go? I had never written the ending in my head, but I know it wasn't this.

I don't know how long I spend there by the toilet bowl on my haunches like an animal, but presently I'm aware of the buzzer sounding and Gertie barking. I get up, flush the toilet and gulp down mouthwash. I wipe my mouth on my sleeve. My arm is shaking.

'Hold on!' I shout, but Euey can't hear me from where he is at the front door. I go back into my bedroom, drag my suitcase down from the wardrobe and start to cram all that I own inside. It's a haphazard mess of things, but I can call the landlord later, send for the rest of my things.

I open the door and am shocked to see him standing there.

'Your front door was open,' he says.

Didn't I close it? Lock it? I don't have time to ask myself those questions.

'Can you help me a moment?' I ask. 'Can you take the suitcase?'

He grimaces. 'Love, no offence, but you look ill. You all right?'

I turn from him to go into the lounge and pick up my hoodie and coat. 'I am ill. And I have to leave London. Right now,' I say, pulling on the hoodie.

'Are you in trouble?'

I go into my room, scan it and see Lucinda's ring. I shove it on my finger.

'I don't have time to explain,' I reply, returning to him. 'We just need to go, OK?'

Euey sighs and scratches his head. 'I told you about my sister, didn't I? You're reminding me of her. This is how she started. She got really depressed after her accident.'

'No, you didn't tell me about her,' I say. I'm fiddling with my keys, my phone, my purse as Euey hauls the suitcase down the corridor to the front door. 'Let's go, Euey, let's go. Come on, Gertie.'

'My sister was in an accident,' he says with a sigh. 'When she was young. It changed everything.'

I usher him out and go to lock the front door again, but my fingers are like jelly. I have no energy after being sick.

'You are terrible with locks,' Euey says. He takes the key from me and locks the door. 'Where are we going? You said you have a sister?'

'Did I tell you that?' I say. 'I can't remember.'

Family. What did Bobby say? *The upset that I caused to Chloe's mum, her brother. And I can't undo it all.*

Chloe has a brother.

I look at Euey and my body turns rigid. Was it by chance those weeks ago that he happened to be passing in his car when I texted for an Uber to go to the interview or was he waiting for me because he knew where I was going?

'What happened to your sister, Euey?' I ask.

'She had an accident,' he says.

'What accident? Tell me about her accident.'

He shakes his head, but I grab his arm and his body jerks forward.

'Her accident happened on the ice rink, didn't it? Didn't it! You're playing games with me! You picked this lock?'

There's a strangeness in his eyes and, right there, I can see it, an understanding between us. I let go of him. It's him – he is Horsehead. I can't back away; I'm by the front door and he's still holding the key.

'Shall we go back inside and sit down for a moment?' he says.

I panic, start screaming, high and loud, and Euey's eyes widen. He puts his hand over my mouth.

'What are you doing?' he says. 'You want someone to call the police?'

'Get off me!' I begin to kick him in the shins and he holds me tighter, shaking me. Gertie growls, then barks, but cowers against the wall.

'Calm down!' he shouts above my screams.

I bring my knee to his groin and he lets go with a yowl. I scoop up Gertie and run past him down the road. I can hear him shouting, but I criss-cross into small residential streets to lose him, and after I can't run any more, I slow to a jog, trying to catch my breath. I put Gertie down.

I can't go back. He could be sitting there in my flat, waiting for me. My bag is still over my shoulder, but he's got access to all the rest of my things. I feel totally exposed. Where do I go from here?

I look where I've blindly taken myself. To the canal; to Bobby's boat.

He won't be here. It's four-thirty and he'll be at the office with everyone else, getting ready to leave for the awards ceremony. Have I come here because I once felt safe? Perhaps on some subconscious level I still do. Does Euey know where Bobby lives? What if he's followed me here before? Would he think of coming?

I step on to the boat.

'Come on, Gertie,' I say, but she looks reluctant so I pick her up again. 'Just until I can catch my breath, OK? And then we'll get a cab out to Norfolk and we'll forget all of this.'

Although it's moored and stable, I feel dizzy and my feet trip clumsily over themselves as I walk along the wooden deck to the front of the boat. It's wet with rain and I have to be careful with every step, otherwise we'll fall into the canal. I wonder if I did fall what might lurk beneath the water.

I sit at the back of the boat, in front of the locked hatchway, invisible from the towpath. Gertie is heavy and her fur is wet with rain, but her presence is comforting. I put my face into her head and she turns, trying to lick me. She probably comforts Ben the same way. My heart aches. Where is he?

How could Euey have done this? How could *I* have done what I've done?

My phone vibrates in my bag and I pull it out and see that there's a text from Euey.

> I don't know what's going on, Eleanor. Have I done something to upset you? You might want to read this.

He's pasted a link to a browser below the message. Do I click on this? What if it's a trick and it's leading me somewhere where I don't want to go? But what if it's sending me to where Ben is?

I click on it warily. It takes me to a picture of a younger-looking Euey with his arm around a young woman with the headline LONDON DRIVER FUNDRAISES OVER THREE THOUSAND POUNDS FOR ST ANN'S HOSPITAL. I scroll down, learn that the girl in the photograph with him is called Kate Harper, who, at twenty-three, went on a lone skydive with an unregistered company. She fell with her parachute only halfway opened and was in a coma for two months at St Ann's in Tottenham. She suffered brain and physical injuries and is now resident in Ashely Grange care home in Wiltshire. Euey's sister.

I close the browser. He could have put this together, a smokescreen to throw me off the scent – I know how good he is. But I am doubting it. I begin an independent search, look up Kate Harper, Euey Harper and St Ann's hospital and, to my dismay, articles start to line up. There are photographs of him and Kate, of him swimming the English Channel with a boat alongside him and of him presenting a cheque to someone outside St Ann's.

I moan aloud and claw my nails along the edge of the boat. Then I stand up and walk back along the boat. If it's not Euey, then who is he?

He.

Why have I assumed Horsehead is a man all this time? Because he told me he was the first time we made contact? I think about Sylvie, who has access to everything, every single part of Jim. She *told* me to take Jim for all he was worth. Has Sylvie used the McManus case as a shield for her own personal gain, a vendetta against Jim for herself? Or is she related to the McManus family in some way and has faked her ID as much as I have? It was 'Horsehead' who told me to get over to the house the night I found Andrea with Jim. Was that coincidence? Sylvie was there in the house and could have led me there purposely.

I cuddle Gertie to my side and think about the disaster my life has become in the short space of a couple of months. Only before Christmas I was El, a waitress in a restaurant, and now I'm Matilda with a hundred implications to her name.

'We should go,' I say to Gertie. 'I'll take you with me, OK? And then we'll figure it all out.'

My phone bleeps again with a message and I look down, hoping to see my sister's name, but it's Bobby.

What's going on? Where's Jim? He's supposed to be here and onstage in 45 mins.

I never texted Bobby about Jim.

'Shit.'

My battery life is almost zero, but I tap out a reply.

He's going to be late. Or maybe he won't be coming. There's been an incident with Ben. I don't know. Can you go on?

I can see the ellipsis, the three dots as he types.

Who are you?

My phone dies and the screen shuts off, but something in my head clicks on.

I'm going to bring down the fucking house, doll. A montage! Let's fucking do it! Lights, camera, action – the biggest prank of them all!

Is Horsehead going to the awards ceremony? Is he going to set Jim up? Given what he's done to Andrea and to Ben, I have no idea what he's capable of, but whatever he's going to do will implicate me. I stare at my phone. I can't even warn Bobby of anything.

I have to go to The London Palladium.

I jump from the boat and Gertie jumps with me and we run along the towpath to the main road, where I hold my arm out to flag a taxi. The rain has made the pavement bright and I shield my eyes with my other hand as a cab pulls up. All I wish is for it to be Euey, but it's not, of course.

'All right?' the driver says.

'London Palladium,' I say and then I lean my head back on the headrest with Gertie climbing all over me.

I inhale to soothe myself. I can do this, I can do it. I drum my fingers on the cab window. It's loud and irritates the driver because I can feel him staring at me in the mirror. I drum instead on my thighs. I'm still wearing Lucinda's ring. It's so close to Mum's ring. I want it to be her ring so badly.

THE PRANK

I want *her* so badly, want to touch my forehead to her forehead like in Ben's picture of him and Lucinda. I want to hear the sound of Mum's voice, but I'll never hear it again. I wish I'd never done this. I'm a sick, terrible person and Ben is lost and it's all my fault.

FORTY-TWO

Photographers mill outside the grand building talking under umbrellas now that there's no one left to flash with their cameras. They pay me no attention as I sprint up towards the doors with Gertie at my heels. The two security guards, however, block me.

'I'm on the list,' I say breathlessly, and I thrust my company ID at them. 'I'm Jim Valente's PA. Matilda Evans.'

'Think you got a bit wet, love,' says one of the guards, laughing, as the other narrows his eyes at the ID.

'Yeah,' I reply.

The guard nods at the ID. 'You're leaving the dog with someone outside, yeah?' he queries.

I look down at Gertie. 'It's Jim Valente's dog,' I say.

'We don't allow pets,' he says.

'But – it's raining?'

'I know,' he says. 'And?'

'Will you take her?' I ask.

'You think I'm a dog-sitter?' he says.

'Please,' I say. 'Please, you have to let us in. It took me thirty minutes to get here in the rain and I only need to deliver a message and then I'm coming out! Please, I swear!'

He sighs. 'Does it bark?' he asks.

'No,' I say and pray she doesn't.

'Go on then,' he says. 'You'd better be out quick.'

The foyer is empty, save for a few young men and women dressed in black, collecting glasses on silver trays. Everyone else is, apparently, already in the auditorium. I jog up to a woman with an official-looking headset and hold up my ID to her.

'Excuse me,' I say. 'I need to go backstage. I'm Jim Valente's PA and I have to get to the sound and lighting desk.'

She examines me in my wet clothes, scrutinises my pass and scrunches her mouth at Gertie.

'This is very important,' I add.

She shakes her head. 'I can't let you back there, I'm afraid.'

I look her in the eyes. 'There's about to be an industry-wide announcement on national television,' I say. 'And it's going to go very badly wrong unless you let me into that desk right now.' I glance at her name badge. 'And I don't want that on your head as well as mine, Petra.'

She sucks in her lips. 'Follow me,' she says.

She leads me through a labyrinth of corridors towards the stalls entrance and then stops and points.

'Up there is the main booth where our engineers sit,' she explains. 'They're having a quick break whilst your technicians are in there for Mr Valente. I presume you have a key card to get in? It's an electronic system on the door.'

'Yes,' I lie.

She nods, already on her headset to someone else, and turns down a corridor and out of sight.

I wait a moment before I rap at the door. Gertie barks once and I stare her down, pray that no one will hear us over the din of people talking in the auditorium.

'Shhh!' I hiss.

'Hello?' says a voice from inside.

'Paul? It's me!'

There's a pause.

'Let me in, Paul!'

The door opens, and Paul is looking at me, confused. 'What are you doing? What's Gertie doing here? Why are you sodden?'

'I need to come in,' I say, and push past him.

Three monitors and a snag of wires crowd the small set-up. An office lamp is the only light; it creates jagged shadows around the room.

'Everything is fine, Eric, relax,' Paul says into the mouthpiece, and then he clicks a button. He sits in front of one of the monitors and grimaces at me. 'Eric's ill, so it's only me here. I feel a bit nervous, actually. Careful of those wires.'

'Paul,' I say. 'You've got to listen—'

'I've never done this before. I'm actually fairly new still, you know? And I've not got long to sort all this before Bobby goes onstage.' He points to one of the monitors, where Bobby sits in the green room with Marie Jarski. 'Why is Bobby going up there and not Jim?'

'Because – because . . . it doesn't matter,' I say. 'But you can't let Bobby onstage.'

Paul looks at me like I'm mad and gives a small laugh. 'Don't let him onstage? You realise how lowly I am in this gig?'

'Has someone given you a tape for the back screen?'

'A what?'

'There's supposed to be a montage of *Pranksters* clips before the announcement,' I say. 'Have you got it?'

I spin around, not even sure what I'm looking for any more because it could have been converted in a thousand different ways already. Then I see a phone lying next to the mouse for another screen. Jemima's phone. I falter. Horsehead has been here.

'What's this?' I ask, leaning to reach it at the same time he does. He winces, and his hand flies to his ribs.

'Bobby gave it to me,' he says.

Bobby? Jim said that Bobby was the one who suggested this booth. Is Bobby involved in this? Has he been trying to throw me off the scent? Could Bobby have done this for Chloe and for Jemima, for payback on Jim? Is he working with Horsehead remotely and got rid of Jim tonight so that he could control this announcement? A sharp image of those horse brasses in his boat zings into my head. Is *Bobby* Horsehead? Please, not on top of everything else, don't let Bobby be responsible for all this, for Ben being left alone, God only knows where, in the middle of winter.

'Have you . . . have you seen what's on this?' I ask.

Paul's still holding his ribs, looking pale. 'No,' he says. 'Why would I? Mind out, you're dripping water off your elbow on that keyboard. Honestly, look at you! How did they let you in? You look deranged. I'm guessing Lucinda's ring blinded security?'

I look at the ring and then look back at him. 'How could you possibly know that this is Lucinda's ring?'

My skin contorts with an understanding as he closes his eyes and tilts his head to the ceiling.

'Shit,' he says and then he starts laughing. 'Ah, shit.'

'It's you, isn't it.' Nodding to his ribs, I say, 'Andrea did that to you when you went to scare her in her house, didn't she?'

He says nothing for a moment, and then the playful smile is gone, replaced with something calculating.

'Fucking Andrea and her left hook,' he says.

'Are you Chloe's brother, Paul? Are you Horsehead?'

He smiles a slow, victorious smile. 'Very good!' he says in an American accent. 'Hello, Top Step. Welcome to the show.'

FORTY-THREE

Don't worry about the IT nerds. They're part of the game.

Paul. His email address was always from 'IT Helpdesk'. He gave me all the IT permissions I needed. He handed me Tess's email on a piece of paper and I didn't ever question how he got it. He found Tess and Chloe because he already knew where they were, he already knew what had happened to Chloe but needed me to work it out to convince me he was separate from it all. In the office, he rarely left the basement, was always early. He was *new* to the company. He handed me back the lock-picking wallet and Gwen's badge without a word. He gave me all the signs, but I didn't see them. All along it had been Paul.

'Remember that I told you I'd seen you on Jim's private CCTV on the street? I got that by nicking Ben's phone six months ago and installing some spyware for it. I noticed you hanging around there and I followed you home one day, checked out where you lived.'

'But the thread on that website?' I say. My mouth is dry. 'How did you *know* that I was affected by Jim just because you saw me outside his house a few times? I could have been there for any reason?'

'The jolly meter reader who came to your flat – remember him? You locked yourself in the bathroom. Who does that, by the way?'

347

'That wasn't you,' I say.

'It was me. And I installed a little spyware on to *your* laptop too while you hid yourself away,' he adds. 'And then you and I got talking on the website because, guess what? I was watching everything you were clicking on. I had no idea you wanted what *I* wanted, but I lucked out. You were on that website for Jim, which was beyond my wildest dreams.'

I feel light-headed. Gertie nudges my legs.

'Why did you need me if you could skip straight into the company?' I ask. 'Who hired you? Surely Jim doesn't—'

'Obviously Jim doesn't know I'm here,' he replies. 'I'm a freelance IT consultant and security specialist and I put the time in with Eric online. He'd been moaning about being overworked and I became "available for hire" as soon as I knew you got the position as PA so I could help you orchestrate it all. How do you think I could get into the servers and send things on as Gwen? How do you *think* I could do all I did? You think IT is magic? It needs fucking *work*. I risked a lot joining the company, but I could lie low if you were working front of house. And I banked on the fact that Jim wouldn't have enough crumbs to attempt to come down to the IT basement and find his way out again.'

'But all the things you've done, Paul?' I say. 'To Andrea and Ben. It's *wrong*.'

'Is it? It got us here, didn't it? It was all leverage that *you* needed to build up a case against him.'

'Not at their expense.'

'Oh, come on!' he says. 'You threw Gwen under the bus.'

'You did that,' I say.

'No,' he replies. '*You* did. I drove the bus, granted. But you watched her fall under it.'

Jemima's phone is still in Paul's hand.

'You've seen what's on there?'

'Oh yes,' he says. 'You told me that her birthday was the code, remember?'

'What are you going to do with it?' I ask.

Paul looks back to the monitor. 'Jim needs to pay for what he's done to my sister, what he's done to *me*. I tried to avenge my sister by throwing that firebomb and it backfired.' He looks to the monitor in front of him and taps it with a fingernail. 'I've made a little montage of my own. The pranks that Jim thought were deleted, combined with what's on Jemima's phone.'

'But this is national television,' I say. 'You can't broadcast all this out! It's not fair on anyone who was on those episodes!'

'I've thought of that,' he says.

'Bobby will know to stop it,' I add.

'Will he? You told me that no one has seen the montage except for Andrea and Jim. And that's exactly why we couldn't have Jim here because he would know from the start that it's not right. I also couldn't risk him coming here to the desk to check on final arrangements and seeing me. Bobby will be standing there completely oblivious. Serves him right, too.'

'Bobby and your sister are friends, Paul,' I say.

'And you're screwing him, right? So your viewpoint is warped.'

'He's a good guy,' I say, because I know that he is and the realisation is hurting my chest. I need to find him. 'Gertie, come on,' I say and I turn for the door.

'Locked,' Paul says.

I try to turn the handle.

'I control the mechanism,' he explains. 'Soz.'

'Paul . . .'

'We're queued up and waiting,' he continues. 'Live in thirty seconds. Bobby will walk on at minute two of the film and then, boom.'

He flicks a switch, looks at me and then down at Gertie.

'And even when Bobby gets wind of something not being right, he won't be able to stop it either, because now I've taken over control of the main system . . .'

He stops talking.

'Oh my God,' he says. 'Look who's arrived.'

I look to the monitor of the green room and see that Jim has arrived. He's still in the suit I saw him in this morning and his hair is ruffled at the back.

'He's found Ben?' I say.

'Or this is just more important to him than anything else,' Paul counters. He looks angry. 'He can't have driven to Bradbury's and back in this time. No fucking way.'

'What's going to happen?' I ask.

He's still staring at the screen. Jim licks at his fingers, starts to smooth out his hair.

'We have to hope that Jim's ego means he'll not be looking at the stage screen until right at the last moment,' Paul says. 'It shouldn't have the sound on, only the footage, but if he catches wind of it early, we'll have less time to enjoy ourselves.'

I watch the monitor with him and see Jim kiss Marie and then pour himself a glass of champagne from a silver bucket by the sofa. He clinks it to Marie's glass and then settles himself next to her. I can see Bobby talking to him and, at the moment, Jim's not paying any attention to the stage screen.

'This has to work,' Paul growls. 'All this time, all this fucking effort I've put in and he's *still* here. Fuck's sake!'

He takes the headphones from around his neck and picks up a rucksack next to him.

'We leave together,' he says. 'This is the first place they'll come when it starts to go tits up, and I want to have front seats. Put this on.'

Like a magician, he produces an object from his pocket. A black wig.

'I know how you like these things,' he adds. 'Hurry up.'

I shove my hair under it and then he grabs at my arm, opens the door and pushes me out.

'Wait! Gertie!' I yell.

He leans down and yanks Gertie by the collar. I pick her up and, while he locks the door, I look up and down the corridor to see if we could run and get away from him, but he's too fast and digs his fingers into my arm. I go to scream, but he stops me.

'Remember those photos,' he says in warning.

He pulls me along the tight corridor and then opens another door and we're now in the auditorium itself, at the back of the stalls and as yet unseen by the heads all turned to the stage. He knows how to move around the building; I have no time to question how, but this is a man who does his research in advance, that much is now clear. We go all the way to the end and then he stops us abruptly, shrinks back against the curtained exit.

I understand that he means to stay and watch.

'No,' I say, but he pulls me close to his face. His eyes are hard.

'This is what you wanted,' he hisses. 'This is what Jemima was going to do and what my sister should have done but didn't have the guts to. *You* did. You and I did this together.'

The theatre is in darkness, aside from the glow of the exit signs and the flickering of the screen at the back of the stage, and then suddenly the *Pranksters* theme music comes on and a firework of colour explodes into our eyes. Jemima Mataya's face flickers into view. Rosebud lips, bedroom eyes.

'Yeah, baby,' she says. 'It's that fucking time again.'

The entire theatre erupts into applause and Gertie whines into my shoulder.

'This isn't right—' I say, but Paul holds up his hand to silence me.

'This is bigger than we ever thought it would be,' he says. 'You might not like how we've done it, but exposing Jim and this company is *right*.'

FORTY-FOUR

Jemima's face fades into black, but the theme music keeps playing. I can see that the theatre is expectant. People are sitting up and awaiting the set-ups that made *Pranksters* famous over the years, but only Paul and I know that the montage is footage that no one will recall.

The screen opens on a park bench where an old man sits crying and a young woman is blazing straight at the camera.

'Can't you see he's distraught? He comes here to see his *wife!* This is a graveyard, you sick arseholes!'

There's a ripple of laughter from the audience, but it sounds unsure.

The image changes, flipping to a woman who is covered with party streamers. Jemima is dancing over to her in her red jumpsuit with a microphone, but the woman is hysterical.

'Where's my boy? Where's my son?'

The camera lowers; someone runs towards her.

'Jack! He's four! Where is he?'

There is talking now in the theatre; people are leaning into the ears of their neighbours and I can see some apprehensive faces. But now the screen flicks to a woman clutching at her chest.

'She's having a fit! Get a medic!'

Members of the audience are talking with louder voices now as a series of two-second clips explode in front of their eyes: a tiny girl is kicked in the face by a horse and falls backward on to the ground; an old woman wets herself on a pavement; a man holds a cloth to his bleeding face. 'Sorry, man,' someone says off-shot. 'Shit, sorry.'

Gertie makes a whimpering sound and wriggles in my arms and I see what her ears have pricked towards. There's movement onstage. Jim has walked on in the huge red clown shoes, with Marie in her baby-doll pink dress on his arm, and they look up at the screen, smiling, before their mouths fall open in synchrony. He hasn't been watching the stage screen from the green room. He's walked into Paul's trap.

'Yes,' Paul breathes beside me. 'Yes. Stay there.'

Jim looks up to the blackness of the sound booth, his shock replaced by an expression of pure fury.

'Oh, but there's no one there, Jim!' I hear Paul say next to me. 'And by the time they all realise I've gone, it'll be too late. Please God let it be too late!'

The murmur of the audience grows before it's silenced by Jemima's voice, ear-splittingly loud.

'Cheap laughs come at a price,' Jemima's voice booms across the speakers. 'You exploit people, Jim, for the sake of entertainment.'

Jim goes to move forward, forgets himself and trips over the shoes as the screen flicks again to a near empty ice rink where a group of five friends skate together before cutting to an ice roller coming on to the rink.

'It's OK, you can stay on!' a man on the ice roller calls.

The teenagers stay on and start to laugh as the ice roller gives chase to them. One of the girls is separated from the others, but she's fast and gleeful as the driver targets her. Some of the others stop, but she keeps going, turns around to give him the finger. But as she turns, she slips on the ice and the roller skids after her, out of control now because he's pushed it too hard. As she tries to get up, it collides with her, forcing her to the side of the rink, where she folds up against it. Her head bends at a terrible angle and the noise of the roller hisses and someone is screaming. Jemima Mataya launches on to the ice.

'Oh, Paul,' I breathe. 'That's Chloe.'

'You see?' he says beside me, but his eyes don't leave the screen.

And then the screen goes black and the theatre is silent from shock, and unmoving.

'You can't keep me for ever, Jim,' comes Jemima's voice through the speakers.

I watch as Marie backs away from the stage. Jim waves his arms, frantic, at the tech booth that is blind to him.

'He's going to get it stopped,' I say.

'But their tech team are going to have to work out my encryption on the door system first,' Paul replies. 'And that will buy some more time.'

'NO!' Jim shouts, but I can barely hear him. Two people dressed in black appear from backstage and one offers a hand to Jim and speaks words I can't hear, but Jim bats his hand away and gestures wildly to the screen. His shoes flip-flop around the stage as he moves. 'Stop this fucking thing!' he screams again, but he's drowned out as a foghorn blares and the screen changes to a scene I know. Sitting on the white chairs of the Cyclops roof terrace with a bottle of wine on the table are Jemima Mataya and Jim, and she is holding a locket which dangles from a chain around her neck. It's where I saw up to before Lissy came to my door. My heart starts to thud.

'What happens now?' I whisper.

'Everything I fucking wanted and more,' Paul says.

'I have something on you that could trump all of those things,' Jemima says. 'So I think you'll give me what I want.'

Jim smiles. 'Is that right?'

'I have all the evidence.' Jemima fingers the locket around her neck. 'Of all the nasty little surprises you've hurt people with. It's right here in this locket.'

'Nasty surprises?'

'All the *Pranksters* episodes that have gone so catastrophically wrong,' she says.

'They're deleted,' he says immediately.

'No,' she replies. 'I took them all and waited for the right time to use them.'

He smirks. 'Is that so? And the right time to come to me with blackmail was when Hollywood came for you?'

'I should have done it years ago,' she says. 'I'm leaving Cyclops and I'm leaving you and in the morning you're going to take my contract and shred it and then, only then, will I give this USB to you.'

He leans over to her, looking resigned for a moment. Then he draws back his hand and slaps her, hard, around the face. For a moment, her eyes show acute shock, but then she smiles, looks victorious and turns to face straight towards the camera. A mistake.

Jim's eyes follow hers and he springs from the chair, marches towards the camera and her face transitions from triumph to worry.

'Jim . . .'

There's the sound of rummaging before the screen tips and fingers skew the lens.

'Are you filming me?' Jim asks. 'What the fuck is this? You were going to blackmail me with this? Is that it? Your very own *Pranksters* episode?'

He throws the phone and it crashes to the ground, landing sideways. It's still recording. Jemima scrabbles to reach it, but Jim swipes at her arm and pushes her backwards, and she crashes against the chair. He throws his weight on top of her and pins her down with one hand and with the other he reaches for the wine bottle on the table and smashes it on the stone tile next to her head. She screams in shock as broken glass shards scatter across the ground and sparkle in her hair.

'Jim! I'm sorry! I'm sorry! I won't! I won't go anywhere, I won't do anything! Please, let me go!'

He pulls at the locket at her throat and she cries out as the chain digs into her skin before it snaps off. He pockets it in his trousers and she exhales, but he's not finished with her. He picks up a sliver of glass from the ground and beads of red blood drop from his fingertips and on to her face as he looms over her. His eyes are ferocious, animal-like. 'You need to learn some respect for someone who made you what you are, who gave you everything,' he says.

She nods, crying now.

'I decide when you're worth enough to sell to America. But when you do eventually fly the nest and make it there, then this is a reminder that I took my cut of you first.'

He nips the shard of glass into the flesh of her cheek and she shrieks. Bright blood appears at once, waterfalling on to her hair, before he hauls her up by the arm. She stumbles but manages to knee Jim in the groin. As he doubles over, she runs towards the phone and snatches it up. The screen bounces as she runs.

'Jemima!' Jim roars. 'Jemima!'

And the screen goes to static.

The commotion in the theatre is electric. People are standing and shouting, like bees in a hive on fire, chaotic and blind with the drama they were so unprepared for. Others sit silently, staring at the blank screen, shocked beyond comprehension. I see Jim onstage, but he looks like a different man, corpse-white.

'I had to cut a lot of it, but I think that'll have done it, right?'

I wrench my eyes from Jim and look to Paul, see him wrapping a black scarf halfway around his face.

'We need to leave,' he says and he takes my arm and I go with him, because what else can I do?

People are swarming out alongside us and I hold Gertie tightly so she doesn't get knocked. I hear someone ask, 'Is this real?' and I think of my dad, those exact words he used when Christopher Barrows lay under that car.

'This way,' Paul says and we jog down Great Marlborough Street, turning a corner so we're in a side road away from the crowds forming. 'Wasn't that fucking great?' he says through the thin material. 'The night she died and Jim showed himself as the twisted, manipulative fucker that he is. His actions drove her to overdose that night and he tried to cover up even seeing her. Doesn't look good, does it?'

I shake my head, unable to find words, while he glances left and right out of the side road back to the main road again and then holds his hand and waves to a car that pulls up beside us.

'I've arranged a cab for you,' he says. 'To Pudding Cottage.'

I'm horrified. 'You know about the cottage?'

'Of course I do! Full access to your computer, remember? But don't worry, I meant what I said. You'll never see me again.' He nudges me towards the car and opens the door. 'I promise. Leave the dog with me.'

'I can't trust a thing you say,' I cry, and push his hand from me. 'And I'm taking her with me.'

He pauses. 'I know you're mad at me,' he says. 'I left those photographs on your doorstep because I was worried you were getting cold feet, but it *worked*, Eleanor. We did it. Go on, get out of here. No one will be hunting you. I'll make sure of it.'

I get in with Gertie and sit heavily on the seat as he closes the door. The driver pulls away and all I can do is turn and stare at Paul through the back window, watching him sprint away. Gertie mewls cat-like beside me and I stroke her, my head spinning with worry. We go west to Regent Street and then south towards the river to meet the Embankment and the river begins to glint with the reflected lights of the buildings.

'Hope you've got a pillow for your neck if you want a kip, love,' the driver says.

I know that voice.

'Euey?'

He brakes suddenly so I lurch forward, swerves to the curb and cuts the engine. He stares at me in the rear-view mirror. 'Eleanor? You booked me?'

'No,' I say and I pull off the wig. 'No, I didn't. Please, Euey, don't tell me you're involved, too.'

'Involved in what?' he says. 'Some guy just booked me for you.'

'Oh God, Euey.' I've started now and I can't stop. Sobs rack my body. 'I'm sorry! The link you sent me . . .'

'Are you in trouble, love?'

'I'm a mess,' I reply. 'Am I safe, Euey? With you? Here?'

He turns round to look at me and sighs. 'Eleanor, you've always been safe with me.'

I nod, and sink into the seat, realising that my hoodie is still completely drenched. I start to shake with cold and Gertie curls into me as Euey turns on the ignition and begins to drive again. We're soon lost in the sea of cars. No one could find me now. Could they?

FORTY-FIVE

Polo barks at seeing me and again on seeing Gertie.

'Who's this?' Charlie asks, staring at Gertie.

'A friend's dog,' I say.

'You've got some explaining to do,' he says. 'You've scared your sister out of her wits.'

Lissy flies at me, wrapping her arms around my waist. 'Where have you been? Did your phone die?'

I step through into the cottage and Charlie closes the door.

Lissy peels my hoodie from me. 'This is soaking.'

For the first time in our relationship, she's playing mother. Or perhaps I've always been the child. Perhaps I have never grown up past eleven, past what Dad did in that kitchen. I look to the kitchen door. I don't want to be here, but where else could I go?

'Are you going to tell us what this is about?' Charlie asks, as we walk through to the living room. 'Why are we here? And what's with that dog?'

'I needed to—' I stop talking because I've just seen the television.

Lissy follows my eyes.

'It's all over the news,' she says.

'Jim Valente,' Charlie says. 'He's been arrested.'

361

'Really?' I say in a small voice, but I can see it for myself. Flashing photography of Jim Valente being led by a woman in uniform to a police car. Gertie stares at the television and barks and I feel guilty. She doesn't know what he's done; she only knows love for him.

'Apparently at the awards ceremony there was this clip of pranks that were . . . unsavoury,' Charlie explains.

'And then what?' I ask.

'And then whatever happened next was cut to adverts,' he says.

I exhale. Paul's prank was played to the people Jim had spent the years of his life building his career around but no one else. Not Lucinda and not Ben, and for this small mercy I'm grateful. No child should see their parent like that.

'I have to ask you . . .' Uncle Charlie says.

I know what he's going to say, but I can only shake my head in answer because I can't bear to tell them what I've done – how could I?

I keep my eyes on the screen, watch the repeat videography of Jim, gaunt and grey and no longer golden. He's lost his shine, even when the bulbs flash against his skin. What will happen to him? Likely he'll be blacklisted from his own industry, stripped of his seats on the media boards. The company will be dumped by broadcasters. I can almost hear the articles being feverishly typed up, assassinating his character, written no doubt by the same journalists who gave him glowing press releases throughout his career.

There's no doubt that Jim is ruined, and for the girl who set out to achieve it with an awakened fire in her heart, the fallout should be spectacular and I should feel euphoric. But I only feel numb. I exploited innocent people exactly like Jim

THE PRANK

did with *Pranksters* and the weight of that truth smothers anything that could feel like elation. What was it all for? It was for a misplaced truth. My dad had exploited me, too.

I look out of the living-room window. Everything is so quiet here, but inside my head my thoughts are crashing into each other. Paul McManus is still out there somewhere. I don't know if Ben is safe. Am I safe here?

'I can't talk about it, Charlie,' I say.

My uncle and sister glance at one another.

'Not now, Charlie,' Lissy says, and then looks to me. 'I've made up Dad's room for you.'

'I don't want to sleep in there,' I say, because in a short space of time the man I called Dad has become a stranger. 'Can I sleep in with you?'

'I'm so sorry that I had to tell you about Dad,' she says. 'I'm sorry I've made you so sad.'

I *am* sad. I'm sad that Dad lied and that both of our parents have gone with so much unsaid. I'm remorseful that I had anything to do with the games Horsehead played and that I had a part in what happened to Gwen, Andrea and Ben. But there's also a stranger feeling here and it's the disappointment of being exactly back to the person I was before I heard the name Jim Valente. I had come alive with purpose as soon as I had understood – or misunderstood – his part in my dad's death, but now I'm back to a state of locked-in syndrome. Except it's worse than before because I've done all these terrible things that I can't talk to anyone about. All I can do is scream it inside my own head. Is this how it felt for Dad, too? Unable to articulate his guilt so that the voices inside his head consumed all other sound and drove him to what he did?

363

Lissy looks to the kitchen door. 'Have you ... Do you want to go in there with me?'

The kitchen. Where he ended his life because he had been a bad father to us and didn't have the words or the bravery to tell us.

My sister takes my hand and leads me to the door and pushes it open and I'm worried I'm going to faint or scream or both, but I don't because the room is different from that day. The walls have been painted from cream to blue, the floor has been retiled, the cabinets are white. There's a different table, a different clock on the wall, a vase on the windowsill. Here, the room where Dad's ghost should be, he is not.

Uncle Charlie puts his hand to my shoulder. 'Eleanor,' he says, looking worried.

I drag my eyes up to him.

'Is everything OK?' he asks.

'Please,' I say. 'Hide me.'

FORTY-SIX

It's 7 December and the lights are up in the village; big coloured glass bulbs that Dad had loved so much. They hang cheerfully in trees and over door frames, but I'm far from feeling their gaiety. The lanes out of the village are silent and I can hear my trainers scuff along the gravel and Gertie panting alongside me.

Days have bled into weeks and the weeks into ten months of being here in Pudding Cottage. There's a voicemail on my phone and I know it'll be Lissy, trying once again to convince me to come back to Charlie's cottage to spend Christmas with them, but I've told them I want to be alone. They're worried about me because I've become even more of a recluse than I was before, but I refuse to be caught vulnerable outside the village. No one has come for me, but I'm still hiding. Perhaps I'll hide here for ever.

After the night of the awards ceremony, Charlie took the cottage off the market and we all lived here together for a month. Doubtless they had, and still have, their own theories as to the part I played in what happened to Jim, but neither of them asked any questions of me and I'm thankful for it, because how can I answer them? How could they be expected to accept what I've done?

We spent the month walking on the coast with the dogs, went to farmers' markets and played cards. Lissy did her university coursework online for as long as she could without getting struck off and Charlie did nothing but drink tea and watch me like a hawk.

At night, when they went to bed, I stayed up and watched the news and read gossip magazines online, garnering every ounce of information I could about Jim and Cyclops. I read that Lucinda divorced him, that she and Ben kept the house in London and Suffolk and that Sylvie stayed on with them. I was beyond relieved that Ben was safe, though any mention of him being lost never reached the papers. I read that Cyclops was liquidated; read articles from people involved in pranks that had taken advantage of them. I read that the enquiry into Jemima's death had been reopened in light of new 'evidence' disclosed.

The light is fading. It's mostly at night that I venture out. I know which bramble thicket is where, which stinging-nettle patch, which pothole. I find the sounds and the smells of the countryside comforting at whatever time of day, whatever season, whatever the weather. Tonight I inhale woodsmoke, damp bark and mud. The sounds are small, a flitter from an animal in the hedgerow, a gutter gurgling somewhere.

I get back to Pudding Cottage from the village shop, having bought PotNoodle and a sad-looking broccoli, and change into my pyjamas and tatty old slippers. I sit on the sofa and switch on my laptop. It's the same one I had when I communicated with Horsehead, but what would I care now if Horsehead can see me? I log into the suicide survivors' website and immediately feel soothed by those who are on here. All of them use the digital sphere as their place to remember; some openly make jokes about their loved ones, some offer advice and others lament, but I am a wordless observer. Online was once my safe place, hidden behind a screen talking to Horsehead, but not any more. I barely trust the postman these days. On the forum, I go by the name of *Battleships* because Dad and I used to play it together. I feel it's an apt name because, despite this being a forum to help, I feel like I'm drowning. Gertie jumps up next to me and licks my hand.

Richard writes: 'I have learnt that going away at Christmas is the best thing to do. I go to Spain, a yoga retreat in the mountains. I used to think yoga was a load of balls. My wife used to do it. I went because I wanted to be reminded of her in a positive way. I'm a fat, bald sixty-year-old accountant from Suffolk and I can't do a downward dog to save my life, but there you are.'

Zara writes: 'I am trying to cope alone with Elise, 5, and Molly, 2. All because he didn't want to tell me about losing his job. What do we all care about a fucking job? What do the girls care??'

Nicky writes: 'Hello everyone! My family don't like to come around much any more. After the funeral, it was like they didn't know how to mention his name. They all tiptoe around me and I'm all alone with my memories of him and they're suffocating me. I need to speak about him.'

I resonate with all of these people, their hurt and anger and disappointment. Christmas is a lonely time for anyone feeling the coldness of grief. I still love Dad but my feelings for him have twisted with complications. I'm angry at him for not telling us the truth, angry at myself for becoming a shadow. I'm angry that for years I should have been cherishing the memory of Mum instead of tarnishing it. He's fallen from the pedestal

I put him on, but he never should have been on it because he was only human.

I shut my laptop and flick the TV remote, exchanging one screen for another. After twenty minutes of watching a film, I realise I'm not following it and the voices are beginning to sound far away. My limbs feel heavy and I close my eyes to go to sleep, except Gertie's head swivels and she jumps down from the sofa and it brings me sharply round again.

She's at the front door and starts to bark. I follow her there and look at the letter box. There's a card halfway in. Who would flyer me this late at night? I pull it through and see that it's not a flyer but a postcard and on the front is the black silhouette of a horse's head. I drop it immediately, my hand flying to my mouth to stem a scream. Gertie looks down at it. It's fallen face down and I read the writing on the back.

I promised that you wouldn't see me again and it's true you won't, but I'll be looking out for you, doll. It's been nearly a year and you gotta trust that you're safe. No one knows your involvement because I covered you, OK? So do yourself a favour and throw those fucking slippers away, right? And brush your hair because it looks like shit.

Horsehead has found me here. He's been watching me and my heart is racing, even though the words aren't threatening. How *do* I feel about his words?

I touch my hair and then look down at my slippers. Is this who I wanted to be aged twenty-six? I am still the frightened little girl I was all those years ago when I found Dad in the kitchen here. From that moment, I hauled guilt and responsibility on to my shoulders and shied away from getting close to anyone who tried to reach out to me. I am tired of being this girl.

I kick off the slippers angrily. One of them sweeps in a great arc across the coffee table and hits a vase, which falls and crashes to the floor. I look at the glittering green shards of glass and the flowers which lie in the scattered earth and wonder if I can glue it back together. Can I glue myself?

I pick up the postcard from the floor, turn it over and stare at the black horse. Do I dare to believe that Horsehead is right and that no one will ever come looking for me? Do I believe in second chances?

FORTY-SEVEN

Over time, the flame that Horsehead's words ignited caught fire and lit the tunnelling blackness I had found myself in. It's been fifteen months since I fled from London to Norfolk and Pudding Cottage is sold. I've been living with Charlie for four months and it's a quiet life, but I'm glad of it. I'm taking small steps.

Today, however, I'm taking a leap. I didn't think I'd make it back to London again, but here I am with Gertie, both of us side by side on the canal towpath in Little Venice. It's May and the trees are clicking with midday birdsong, their reflections glass-like and lush green in the water below. I'm wearing Uncle Charlie's lightweight mackintosh and a cap with my hair up and Bobby won't recognise me, but that's OK because I don't want him to. I just want to see him.

For a long time, my body ached with a delusional hope that I might see him again, but I knew that he would ask questions that I couldn't ever answer without exposing myself and the extent of the part I played in Jim's downfall. Would he condemn what I did? Condone it? If he ever thought I had anything to do with any of this, he has never gone to the police with it. His last message, *Who are you?*, sits somewhere unanswered in the ether because I changed my number.

I watch him now on top of his boat with a plant pot in one hand and I feel sad. Over and over, I've drawn those hands that once held me when I cried honest tears about who I was. He's talking to the old men we saw the night I spent with him, the ones with the mince pies who played cards on the next boat. I can't hear what they're saying, only know that they're all laughing. I wish that the wind would carry it to me, that lovely timbred laugh that I fell for. I admit it now, I fell for him. I allowed myself to feel and it was good, for a moment.

As if he senses my eyes on him, Bobby looks in my direction and I see recognition register on his face as he blinks into the sunlight. We stand silent but connected and my heart lifts. He raises his hand uncertainly and I mirror with mine in response.

'My name is Eleanor,' I say softly, though he can't hear me.

I turn and walk away with Gertie at my heels and we begin our journey to Belgravia. Because the reason I've come to London today is not so that I can see Bobby; it's so that Gertie can go home.

The door at Wilton Crescent sucks me towards it with the invisible gravitational pull of a black hole, but I fight its beckoning fingers, staying resolutely behind the iron gates of the private gardens. I've timed this visit so it's a weekend and, unless he's gone away for the weekend, he should be here. I pray he's here.

I look at my phone for the time. It's nearing six in the evening. Gertie has been running around the park and is now nestled in my arms. She's been so patient. I stroke her, and gliding my hand across her fur calls attention to the shape of Lucinda's gold and sapphire ring on my finger. I take it off and slip it through Gertie's collar. Sylvie will know that it was me who returned Gertie and the ring, but I have to believe that she'll not hunt for me, because she hasn't so far.

For hours, my eyes haven't left the street, but Gertie spots him first. Ben walks slowly towards the house with a gym bag slung over his shoulder. He's taller now, more filled out, but he looks slumped and I feel a stab of guilt. He'll have grown up fast since that night; has probably built a wall closely against his skin to protect himself from Jim's shame. I did that to him.

'I'm so sorry, Ben,' I whisper.

We're akin, the two of us – both so young when we lost the fathers we thought we had.

Ben takes a key out of his gym shorts and Gertie woofs gently, once, and then she looks at me.

'Go,' I whisper and she hops off the bench.

She darts out from between the railings and bounds down the road, barking joyfully, and I sink down behind the gates and watch as Ben turns around. He is frowning at first, but then his face splits into a wide smile as he realises what he's heard. He pelts towards Gertie as she runs to him and, when she jumps up, he kneels to the ground and they fall into each other and he holds her like she's the only thing left in the world. I can feel the tears on his face because they're also on mine. She licks his cheeks and paws his shoulders as he buries his face into her fur in a tangle of happiness.

'Mum!' I hear him shout. 'Mum! It's Gert! Mum!'

He stands up with Gertie, cradling her like a child and unlocks the door and takes her inside the house. The door closes behind them and I'm left in silence. I stifle a sob because I know she's not mine but I'll miss her. Everyone's confidante.

*

I call my sister.

'Brighton University sent you the brochure,' she says without even a hello. 'I opened it. The art department looks *amazing*.'

For you, Mum, I will try something brave.

'And I got pizza for tonight,' Lissy continues. 'Shall I paint your nails?'

'Sure,' I reply.

'What time will you be back?' she asks.

'About nine,' I say. 'I'm meeting David and Wendy for a drink between their shifts.'

'OK, see you soon,' she says, and the phone clicks off.

I hang up. Lissy and Charlie don't know how close I came not only to destroying Jim Valente's life, but also my own. I'll never tell them, hope that I'll never have to, and I suppose I have Horsehead to thank for that, watching me from wherever he is. Perhaps he's here now, in the fading light of these gardens, making sure that, for me, it *is* all over. I can pick up the shreds of my old life and try to paint myself a new one.

ACKNOWLEDGEMENTS

An enormous thank you to Camilla Bolton at the Darley Anderson Agency. You've been a tenacious champion of both me and *The Prank,* and I'm so lucky to have you. To Jade, Mary D, Kristina, Georgia, Sheila, Rosanna, and all at Darley, thank you.

To everyone at Welbeck, for making my dreams come true. Specific thank yous to Jon Elek for buying *The Prank* and for providing solid advice, to Rosa Schierenberg for your detail and care (and putting up with my emailing), to the amazing Rob Cox, Maddie Dunne-Kirby and the rest of the marketing team, and to Annabel Robinson, Emma Dowson and all at EDPR for being the most wonderful publicists. To James Horobin, Nico Poilblanc, Angie Willocks and all the sales team across physical and digital, I know how hard you all work to secure such amazing slots and deal, so thank you! To Production and Distribution, and everyone else at Welbeck. To Joe Mills at Blacksheep for a stellar jacket design, and lastly, to Celine Kelly, who I've had the pleasure of working with on both sides of the publishing coin, and who is an absolute legend.

To my mum, who never stopped stapling bits of paper together so I could write stories; to my dad for being a tireless publicist on my behalf; and to my brother for buying me Blue the Dolphin, who featured in the stories I wrote when I was five – you started it all, gags!

To all my friends, old and new, who have backed me along the way, thank you. To Tess, Amy and Nic because, well, you know. Special mentions to unfailing advocates: Jen Hawkins for the weekends of writing in pyjamas and teaching me how to chain-drink tea, and Bethan Moore for many c&cs and Writing Club (forever). To Amelia for her endless celebratory messages and helping me put arrows on Instagram pictures.

To my husband, Matt – you have enabled me to chase my dream and for that I am so, so grateful (and so are you because it paid off!) To you and the boys, I love you.

Finally, a heartfelt thank you to all retailers who have stocked *The Prank* and to the readers who have bought it. Thank you to the amazing social network of bloggers, bookstagrammers and Twitter writing community who have encouraged me. It's a huge honour to have people supporting my lil ol' book.

Before becoming a writer, Liv worked for over ten years in
both domestic and international sales for major
publishing houses. She lives in Hampshire
with her husband and sons.

Twitter: @LV_matthews
Instagram: @lv_matthews_author

WELBECK

PUBLISHING GROUP

Love books? Join the club.

Sign-up and choose your preferred genres to receive tailored news, deals, extracts, author interviews and more about your next favourite read.

From heart-racing thrillers to award-winning historical fiction, through to must-read music tomes, beautiful picture books and delightful gift ideas, Welbeck is proud to publish titles that suit every taste.

bit.ly/welbeckpublishing